Necromancer's Lament

Thanks to Athina Paris, Editor for your dedication and tireless effort.

Cover Art by Judas A Iscariot

Published By

RockHill Publishing LLC
PO Box 62523
Virginia Beach, VA 23466-2523
www.rockhillpublishing.com

Necromancer's Lament

By

David F. Balog

To my wife Tammy, my family, and everyone I have had the pleasure of sitting at the table with and playing various role-playing games; there are too many to name you all! You have inspired me, supported me, and allowed me to explore my personal traits and quirks with each character.

This is also for all who have faced the darkness and discovered that is when your inner light shines brightest.

Necromancer's Lament

I understand your squeamishness—
The natural feel of dread,
You may think it is demonish
To animate the dead,
But truly 'tis a sacrifice
That I make for my art.
For greater would you pay the price
Should I not do my part.

The dead I've learned to animate,
In pieces and in whole,
So that my skills may calibrate
The taking of the toll
Of the spells, which draw from planes rife
With strength beyond your ken,
Where shadows live and death survives—
You would not comprehend.

Talking skulls and a walking corpse—
The basics of my art,
Used so that I might find the force
To take them all apart.
I pull strings from the tapestry
To fray apart the Weave
And rend the spell of travesty
Of magicks ill-conceived.
Destroying creatures such as these
Is verily my goal.
So that the dead may rest in peace,
I've lost part of my soul.

--Ial'rafiost of Dureltown

PREFACE

I do not know which irritates me more: the living or the dead. The resting dead, those lying in peace and following the natural course of things, at least, do not bother me. It is the walking dead—the cursed, the animated, the self-willed, whose only aim is the destruction of all life around them—they, I cannot abide.

The living, however, often act in the same manner, causing death and destruction wherever they roam. Armies clash, cities fester, and people lie, cheat, rob, and murder. Even if all the humans were gone, other races, some far more destructive, would only take their place. The world would be idyllic if only the natural plants and animals were left to inhabit it. Mayhap I *should* have trained as a druid.

I am Mithron of the Velvet Shade, a necromancer of the Order of the Ivory Tome, dedicated to life-giving knowledge and power. Most fear necromancy, for its magicks create and sustain the undead abominations I referred to earlier. Necromancy is the power of fear and terror, drawing out the strength and vitality of living creatures. What most do not understand is that necromancy is the magic of life *and* death, creating and sustaining life as well as taking it away. Few necromancers follow the path of life magic, for the arts of death and destruction must be learned first, and their subtle, seductive powers often draw its practitioners into its shadowy embrace. A sacred few rise above the moral morass, but none are untainted by the darkness, myself included.

Why take the risk? Why would any sane person put their soul in jeopardy to learn such dangerous secrets? Some seek the mysterious knowledge hidden in occult lore. Others are so self-assured; they feel strong enough to throw off the taint of evil that necromancy draws its practitioners toward. Some seek power over life and death—the capacity to snuff out a life with but a word and a glance is an ability many would sacrifice much for. Still others consider themselves artisans, working their hands, minds, and hearts to perfect their craft.

I? I am all four.

Table of Contents

Chapter 1 ....
Split Falls...1

Chapter 2 ....
My Training Begins...18

Chapter 3 ....
Blythad 31

Chapter 4 ....
Faldrein 57

Chapter 5 ....
The Tournament..76

Chapter 6 ....
Dual Duel 93

Chapter 7 ....
Escape From Home...107

Chapter 8 ....
Meetings...124

Chapter 9 ....
Ormak's Tower...148

Chapter 10 ....
Within the Jozalk's Lair..175

Chapter 11 ....
Golems & Gold 197

Chapter 12 ....
Alone 212

Chapter 13 ....
Forced Insights..226

Chapter 14 ....
Perspective 248

Chapter 15 ....
Repercussions 280

Chapter 1: Split Falls

My beginnings are humble enough. The son of a village blacksmith, with neither talent nor desire to enter my father's trade, I had an imagination, a skill at sketching, and a mind on an endless quest for knowledge. I studied Father's craft to be sure, for truly I had no other choice, and though I could not even cut a straight nail, I learned the mechanics of *how* a blacksmith works. Fortunately for Father, he had two more sons who were happy to join in his trade; unfortunately for me, I had two brothers, one older, Larshon, and one younger, Verond, who were happy to deride me for being different. At least, until the day Verond grabbed the wrong end of a hot iron.

My younger brother was easily distracted and frightened beyond reason of bees. He had never been stung to my knowledge, and I think his fear stemmed from an association of bees with death. Five years ago, when I was eight years old and Verond only three, we spotted a wolf carcass in the woods while seeking mushrooms to supplement our dinner. Although I have heard that some bees will nest inside a carcass, I believe it is more likely that the hive was nearby on the ground. Either way, the sight of a swarm of bees rising from the wolf's body stayed in his young mind, living in the shadowy recesses only to emerge at the droning of anything resembling a bee.

While Verond was feeding coal into the forge, a hornet buzzed into the workshop, setting him at unease. When it landed on his shoulder, he panicked, dropped the coal shovel, and backed away from the forge, bumping into our father. Trying to keep his balance, Verond spun around, put his hands out for support, and landed palms down on top of the anvil where Father was making a hoe for a neighbor. None of us could react in time to prevent his fall, but thankfully, the remedy was nearby. Though it grows better in the marshes, I had taken Yoffa's advice, the village herbalist, and sown a few mallow seeds at the back of the smithy. She said the gooey sap was a good balm for burns, and I thought it wise to have some nearby. I grabbed a sharp blade, ran to the back of the forge, cut off part of the reedy plant, and rushed back inside to see that Verond had his hand in the water pail used to cool the iron while Father was cursing at him for his clumsiness.

"Give me your hand," I commanded.

He pulled it out, tears streaming down his face.

"Now hold still." I squeezed the reed and globs of sticky white sap dropped onto his open palm. I spread it out as much as I was able, then grabbed a relatively clean rag and tied it loosely around his hand. "Come on," I urged, "let us go find Yoffa."

We crossed through the farmlands of wheat, lettuce, kale, and other vegetables, which was a more direct route to her shack than the road, shortening the trip to about a mile. She lived at the edge of the natural clearing where Split Falls was built, near the river and against the forest, while our home was about a third of a circle sunwise around the clearing, about halfway between the forest and the center of the village.

"Father said that I could burn my hand off," my younger brother whined.

"Unlikely, but possible. You will be fine. The mallow will ease the burn, and Yoffa has better medicines."

Fortune was with us, for she was tending her garden, full of not only foodstuffs, but medicinal herbs as well.

"What has happened here, smith's son?" She always called me 'smith's son'.

I raised Verond's bandaged hand to show her.

"Bring him inside."

I walked my brother in and sat him down on a bench in her small shack. Her home and workshop was not much more than six long paces to a side, though it seemed larger when I visited at Verond's age; at thirteen summers, my stride was much longer. Bundles of herbs hung from the rafters—thyme, rosemary, wormwort, basil, and others drying for storage or future use. A large workbench in the center of the room occupied almost a third of the space, with a pair of stools and a sitting bench placed around the large table. There was scarcely room for her small, straw-stuffed mattress, which lay on the floor without the benefit of a rope bed. Yoffa was clean and organized, not that anyone else would notice, and I had helped her for the past three years while studying herbalism.

She grabbed a stool and sat before my brother and me, her knees creaking audibly as she did so. Yoffa was undoubtedly the eldest in the village by at least ten summers, appearing slightly heavy-set, though in truth much of that was muscle. She seemed not to have aged appreciably over time, perhaps because I saw her as so old to begin with; she had been working on her gardens longer than anyone could remember, and it kept her from getting flabby as many of the older folk tended to. Her face was ruddy and wrinkled, like a pumpkin left out to dry in the sun, and nearly always smiling.

Verond winced as she unwrapped my makeshift bandage, tears welling in his dark blue eyes.

On inspecting the wound, she said to me without taking her eyes off the hand, "Used the mallow, did you?"

"Yes, Mistress Yoffa. Thank you for suggesting planting it nearby."

"You did well. Looks like you got to it right away. And stop calling me 'mistress'; you make me feel old," she said with a wink. If she had not seen more than sixty summers, then I was a pixie!

"Yes, m' lady," I retorted with a smirk.

"'M' lady' is it now? I'll deal with you later," she chuckled. "Now get me the burn salve."

I should have grabbed the jar right away, but I was too busy trying to keep my brother calm. The salve was made from strained fat, mixed with mallow, garlic, and sphagnum moss. I also grabbed some strips of clean cloth for use as bandages and a small pail of water for washing. Yoffa always cleaned her hands thoroughly before treating the injured. "Dirt in the wound always makes things worse," she had told me early on in my training. It made sense, and I still follow her example.

She spread some of the salve on Verond's hand and wrapped it loosely in the cloth strips. "Now, keep this dry, and come see me tomorrow and we will see how you are healing. Would you like a honey drop?"

Verond's eyes lit up. Though bees scared the wits out of him, he had no argument with the product of their labor. A sweet little candy always seems to dull the pain.

"Take him home to your mother and let her know what happened. And come back with him tomorrow. There is someone I want you to meet." With that, she shoved us out the door.

I wondered who this mystery person could be. *A friend of hers, perhaps? Mayhap another herbalist?* I knew better than to pry, for an answer would be forthcoming on the morrow.

As my younger brother and I neared our small mostly wooden home, we espied Mother waiting outside. She was in her thirty-second summer, lean and wiry. Physically, I appear more like her than our bear of a father, much to his chagrin, though my eyes are the same ice blue as his, while my brothers have her darker shade. When she saw us ambling down the dirt road, she rushed out to greet us, her long, light brown hair, the shade of maple wood, flying behind her. "My poor sweet boy!" she cried, grabbing Verond and squeezing him tightly. "How are you? Are you okay? Does it hurt? Come, let me look at it."

"He is fine, Mother," I interrupted. "Yoffa put some salve on his burn and we are to see her again on the morrow."

"Why weren't you watching your brother?" she began to scold me.

"If I were not, the burns would have been much worse. Did Father not tell you what happened?"

"He told me that Verond tripped and fell, and that you took him to that Yoffa woman."

"It was a giant bee," Verond sniffed. "It attacked me."

Mother mewed and kissed his forehead.

"It would have flown away, but you panicked," I chided. "When you got scared, the hornet got scared. Let me see your shoulder." With all the focus on his burns, I had forgotten about the hornet. When he removed his tunic, I saw the large welt from the sting. "I will take care of that. Go inside, I will be right in."

"How could a hornet burn him?" Mother inquired. "Was it magical?" she asked with trepidation.

"Not all problems are caused by magic," I sighed.

Mother always worried that anything unusual was caused by 'evil magic', and she feared that Yoffa was a witch, little understanding how close her guess was. More often than not, she was merely misinformed, and it was no surprise that Father did not give her the whole story. It was years later that I understood the rationale for her worries, for there are many who believe all blacksmiths to be sorcerers, as they combine the iron from the earth with the fire of the forge, the wind in the bellows, and the water for cooling the hot metal. Any who could use all four elements with such ease were to be feared; all this time I thought that the rest of the village avoided us because of my Father's personality.

"The hornet scared him, and he tripped. When he fell, his hand landed on a piece of metal Father was working on. None of us could catch him in time."

"I see," she chewed her bottom lip, as she always does when in contemplation. "Go see to your brother."

"Yes, Mother." I walked to the back of the house to gather the treatment for Verond's sting, which made for interesting conversation when Father and Larshon came back from the smithy.

No sooner had they stepped through the doorway when Larshon exclaimed, "Ye gods! What is that stench?"

"That," I replied, "would be our baby brother; or, more accurately, the poultice on his sting."

"I don't even smell it anymore, "Verond said cheerfully. "It doesn't hurt anymore either."

"Once it completely dries, we can take this off," I told them, prodding the brown and grey mass on Verond's shoulder with my finger. "Before bedtime, I suspect."

"What's in it?" asked my elder brother.

"Garlic and birthwort roots. They are good for stings and poison."

"Poison?!" Verond paled. "That bee killed me!" He began to tear up.

"You are not going to die," I rolled my eyes. "The poison in the sting is what makes it hurt so much, but it would take hundreds of them to kill you. The herbs will draw out the poison; you will be fine by morning. Fair?"

"Fair," Verond sniffed.

"How's his burn?" asked Father, little concern in his voice.

"Healing quickly. We will go back to Yoffa tomorrow so that she can examine it and put on a clean bandage."

He nodded. "Make sure you come by the forge before leaving tomorrow."

"Yes, Father."

"And don't tarry. You spend too much time with that Yoffa woman as it is." He sniffed. "And take your brother outside for a while."

"Yes, Father." I looked over at Verond and jerked my head toward the door.

He grabbed his ball, which was a sphere of wood about the size of Father's large fist covered in leather and headed outside.

I followed closely.

The sun had just set, and the late summer air was warm and inviting. To the west, the sliver of a new crescent moon was resting just above the trees. The evening star had appeared, shining bright and pink. 'The Lover's Star', it was often called, and common lore was that its appearance heralded a season of romance. Perhaps that was good material for the bards, but as families arranged most marriages, romance seemed to be a mere distraction.

Larshon will likely be married soon, I thought. *He's in his sixteenth summer, and well trained by Father. He should be operating his own forge soon. I suppose he will have to move to another village; there is only so much need in a small village like Split Falls for a blacksmith.*

"I wonder who that is," my younger brother queried aloud, dropping his ball and pulling me from my thoughts to see someone ride by on horseback.

"Good question. They already passed the inn, and it is nearly dark. Whoever it is, I hope they are close to their destination; there really is nowhere else to stay for miles."

"Will my hand really be okay?" Tears began to well up in his eyes.

"Absolutely," I smiled. "Yoffa knows her art. Does your hand hurt right now?"

"Some. Yeah. It kinda itches."

"Try not to scratch it, for that would make it worse. You will see tomorrow how well your hand has healed. You will not be working with Father for a while, though, but I am sure Mother will smother you with attention—you are her baby."

"I'm not a baby!" he shouted.

"I know, I only meant that to *her* you are." I chose not to remind him that he was not our youngest sibling—only the youngest to survive. Our little sister nearly killed Mother during the birthing and only saw a few breaths. Since then, our family has not grown.

"Oh."

"Let me see your shoulder again." The poultice had dried some in the night air. "I think it is ready to come off." I tucked my fingers under the edges and lifted the dried mat of crushed herbs. The strong scent of garlic wafted up as I removed it. "The swelling is almost gone. You will not even notice it by morning."

"That's good," he yawned.

"Go get some sleep. This has been a trying day for you."

"Okay." Verond picked up his ball and toddled off into the house.

Suddenly tired, I decided to turn in early myself. I looked up again at the thin crescent moon as it sank beneath the tree line. "New Moon, New Life" was one of the maxims of the priests of Mamoel, who followed the moon goddess and her cycles. Of course, there is no guarantee that the 'new life' will be positive, but that is what they strive for.

I strolled back into our three-room wood, stone, and thatch house to find Verond already asleep on his mat. Father and Larshon were whittling by the fireplace while Mother was knitting a blanket out of thick wool yarn. Years ago, I asked her why she always seemed to be out of season, making warm things in summer and lighter things in winter.

"Knitting and sewing take a lot of time," she said, "if I wait until it's cold to start knitting blankets, it will be warm before I can finish them. It's always best to be ready for what's to come."

I pulled my sleeping mat out of the storage chest, along with a candle, which still sat in its holder, and a book called *Winter Herbs: Useful Growth During the Cold Season* by Therena Willowbark, which Yoffa lent to me for my studies. Apparently, both Yoffa and Mother shared the same philosophy of preparedness. I rolled out my mat, placed the book upon one end of it then went to the fireplace to light the candle, using a longer stick to grab a flame.

"Reading again?" Father asked with resignation as I lit the candle.

"Yes, Father. Yoffa wants to rid me of the misconception that nothing grows in the winter. There seems to be a lot of useful and edible plants available during the snows."

"Son, I understand that she saved your life and is like a hero to you," he sighed with a note of condescension in his voice. "I just wish you would learn somethin' a little manlier."

I simply stared at him. *I help to heal Verond's hand, and this is how you thank me?! In front of my brothers no less. And the teasing shall resume…*

"I'm sure he'll make someone a fine wife someday," chimed in Larshon, right on cue. His remark was quickly followed by a slap to the back of his head by Father. "Oww!"

"Don't even joke like that," Father admonished with steel in his voice. "No man in this family will be… like that." Turning to me, he asked, "You *do* like girls, right?"

"Some of them," I answered. "The ones with a brain in their head, anyway."

"Good thinking, son. You don't have to keep tellin' the smart ones what to do."

I could only shrug in agreement and go back to my book. I glanced over at Mother, who continued her knitting, showing no sign of overhearing our conversation, though there was no way she could not. I set the candle down on the floor, opened the book next to it, and lay face down supporting my head with my hands. When Yoffa lent me the book around the last new moon, I paged through it all the first night, and read it all by the next half moon. I was re-reading it for the fifth time, working to memorize any information I may have missed during earlier readings. A particular challenge is the kuluba root, a potato-like tuber that is said to be tasty, yet toxic. To make the red-veined, yellow tuber edible, it must be grated, rinsed, strained, dried, rinsed again, soaked, strained, and rinsed for a third time. It must have taken a lot of experimentation, and probably a few lives, to deduce this recipe, and it must truly be delectable to go through such pains. When satisfied that I had fully understood the text, I blew out the candle and went to sleep.

The next morning, my brothers and I went to start up the forge with Father, who said that he had to finish up something before we left to see Yoffa. I helped Verond with the bellows, as he could only use one hand, and Larshon shoveled coal until we got the forge up to the needed temperature. Meanwhile, I could hear Father scraping stone on metal, meaning he was honing a sharp edge. A short time later, he presented me with a new sickle.

"Give this to the old witch, as payment for her services," Father said gruffly.

"Yes, Father," I responded without inflection, knowing better than to defend Yoffa to him. Over the years, I have met more than a few witches, and none of them deserved the derision that Father cast upon them. I then turned to my younger brother, "Come along, Verond."

The two of us took the road to Yoffa's house, strolling at a much more leisurely pace than yesterday. When we neared her cabin, we could hear laughter from within. Hesitantly, I knocked on the door. A moment later, Yoffa opened the door, revealing her company. Sitting at the table with a cup in her hand was, I thought at first, a marble statue.

She sat perfectly still, staring at me, through me. Her pure white skin gleamed in the ray of sunlight beaming through the window, her ebon hair flowing past her shoulders. Yet it was her eyes, two circles of obsidian set in alabaster, which held my gaze, and I found that I had no desire to turn away. There was warmth hidden in the depths of her sculpted exterior, which I found unusually comforting.

When she at last took a sip from her cup, smiling quietly to herself, I managed to turn my attention to Yoffa, who was shifting her gaze between her visitor and me.

With a smile, Yoffa turned to my brother and me. "How does your hand feel this morn?" she asked sweetly.

"It itches, but it doesn't hurt too much anymore."

"That's a good sign. Come on in you two. I would like to introduce my friend. Vletraka, these are the smith's sons I was telling you about."

"A pleasure," spoke a voice soft and warm as a summer rose. "Yoffa, take care of your charge while I speak to your student."

I began to step toward Vletraka when I realized the weight in my hands. "Yoffa," I said carefully holding out the sickle, "this is from Father as payment for your healing services."

She took the sickle and looked closely at the blade. "Thank you. This will come in very handy as the harvest grows near."

"And I finished *Winter Herbs*," I said, handing her the book.

"Already? You never cease to astound me, smith's son. Just set it on the table, and I will quiz you later. Not that there's ever any need to," she finished under her breath. It was rare for her to ask me a question relating to her teachings that I could not answer correctly, and her best challenges needed me to connect disparate bits of information into a new form, such as devising a new recipe on the spur of the moment based on its intended use and availability of ingredients dependent on season and climate. I set the book on the table and sat down across from Vletraka.

"How long have you had that book?" she asked.

"For about a moon, my Lady. It took five reads to remember it all."

Her eyes shot up. "You memorized the whole book?" she asked incredulously. "In one moon?"

"Not word for word, but all the pertinent information. Yes, my Lady."

Her smile broadened. "And where did you learn to read so well at such a young age?"

"Mother taught us all, my Lady. 'Everyone should know their letters'," I mimicked in Mother's singsong inflection. "Mostly, I read what Yoffa has available. I am sure you understand that there is a dearth of reading material in our little village."

"Do your siblings read as well as you?"

"They seem more content to follow Father in becoming blacksmiths, my Lady, but they do know how to read."

"You can stop calling me 'my Lady'," she smiled. "Outside of Court, you are perhaps the most polite young man I have ever met."

"If you are on his good side," Yoffa chimed in. "If he doesn't like you, his tongue is sharper than an adder's fang."

"You wound me, Mistress Yoffa," I whined sarcastically, placing my hands over my heart. "Father insists that we do not behave as ruffians. When have I ever acted improperly or hurtful?"

"Remember last spring when that 'potion vendor' came to Split Falls? This one quizzed him in the middle of the village square on ingredients and methods of preparation. He then sniffed a few samples and told everyone that the 'potions' were mostly cheap whiskey with rosemary and clover mixed in. He then gave the poor man a tongue-lashing, as I never heard before! What did you call him? A…"

"A worthless, shiftless swindler, who would not know an herbal remedy from four-day-old porridge. What kind of a fool comes to a village where we rely on natural healing and tries to pass off pigswill as a cure-all? Go back to whatever rock you crawled out from under and rejoin the grubs you sprang from. You are not welcome here."

Everyone laughed, Yoffa nearly falling to the floor. Though I believed as the false potion-maker did that most villagers are an ignorant lot, I realized that it was only due to a lack of time and opportunity for most to gain the kind of education that I had. Even so, villagers know the land, the plants, animals, and crafts that make our small society run smoothly. Any who come here had better know what they are talking about if they are going to fool us, for the simple wisdom of village folk often balances the scales against those who have only studied in tomes and not experienced our lifestyle.

"I shall have to make certain that I stay in your good graces," Vletraka laughed, wiping away a tear. "How long have you been studying with Yoffa?"

"For three winters and summers now, my La... Mistress Vletraka," I answered, "since she saved me from a pair of vulzuu in the forest."

Verond piped up, "Brother has all the fun adventures."

"Yes, it almost got me killed. How are you healing from yesterday's *adventure*?"

"He looks good," nodded Yoffa. "I see no signs of permanent damage, and he should be okay to go back to the forge in a couple of days."

"Yoffa told me that you treated your brother's burn before bringing him here. Do you wish to become an herbalist like her?"

"I do not know where my future lies, Mistress Vletraka. Verond, though five years my younger, already shows greater talent as a smith than I, and Father says that herbalism is... too feminine an occupation for a man."

"Is that what you believe?" Vletraka asked, her face a mask of ivory.

"No, Mistr..."

"Just Vletraka, okay?"

"Vletraka," I repeated uncomfortably. "I have read about male herbalists and druids in Mistress Yoffa's books, so I know that it is not solely a profession for women. I would like to become a full herbalist, but I think that I would have to go elsewhere so as not to embarrass Father."

"A parent should never inhibit the dreams of their children," she replied cryptically. "How did you feel when the vulzuu attacked you?"

*I was searching along the edge of the forest for good wood for the hearth, as it was one of my daily tasks. Father had built a small two-wheeled cart, which I could either push or drag along to make the task easier once he realized, with great verbal disappointment, how little wood I could carry on my own. It was no great difficulty finding twigs for tinder, but Father was quite clear on what constituted a good log for burning.

"Thick and dry," he said. "It's fine for it to be wet on the outside, but it can't be green or rotted inside 'cause it won't burn right."

After gathering about half a cartful, which was at least three times what I could carry, I heard something moving toward me from the forest. It is not uncommon to spot deer, squirrels, and other creatures moving about, but they do not typically approach humans. When I realized that I no longer heard the birds singing, I knew there was trouble afoot. My heart began to race, and my stomach felt like I had eaten a red-striped mushroom. I turned to grab the cart so I could race home when I saw a pair of men walking out of the forest. They were exceptionally thin and wore rags over their taut, yellow-grey flesh. Then, the smell hit me.

The stench of decaying meat filled the air around them, and my stomach turned over, yet retained its contents. They glared at me with malicious yellow eyes and hissed the word "flesh" while baring their long and jagged teeth. I let go of the cart and began to run, screaming for help. Within a few steps, I felt a heavy hand grab my shoulder. Its touch burnt and froze at the same time, and I found that I could no longer flee from those monsters. My feet would not pick themselves up off the ground, my arms would no longer swing to speed up my momentum, and I could no longer shout for help! All I could do was stand helplessly while the two creatures circled me, as if deciding which one was to claim the choicest bits. I knew that I was as good as dead, and I prayed that my family would live well in my absence.

Just as one of the vulzuu reached out for my eyes, the ground erupted; grasses, vines, and tree roots grew rapidly and wrapped themselves around the monsters and me. The abomination's hand stopped just short of my eyes, and my vision filled with dirt-encrusted yellow fingernails, which were curved and sharp like claws.

A woman's voice shouted, "you shall not have that boy!" and the vulzu that was reaching for me was engulfed in flames. It screamed and tried to run, but the overgrown plants held it in place until they and the vulzu burned away together. I felt another wave of heat at my back, and the second one screamed as well. A few moments later, the plants that had held me receded, and the woman stepped into my line of sight.

Of course, I had known Yoffa my whole life. She was the village herbalist and midwife, making potions to cure the sick, and aiding not only the women, but the livestock as well, in childbirth. Until this moment, I did not know that she could use actual magic.

"Are you injured, smith's son?" She paused for a moment for an answer I could not give then slapped herself on the head. "I must be going daft, of course you can't answer. Give it a couple of minutes, and the paralysis will wear off. I'll wait for you."

After what seemed an eternity, I found that feeling was returning to my flesh, and I began to stretch my arms out. She was right, the paralysis did not last long, but it would have been long enough for those monsters to eat me alive! Had she not been there, my story would have had a quick end. "Yoffa? What were those things? What did you do? Thank you for saving me!" I rattled off, finally able to speak.

"Those were vulzuu, I used magic, and you are quite welcome," she answered with a smile. "Are you well? I did not see any injuries."

"They did not hurt me, though, had you not been there…" I began to weep, the fear finally releasing itself.

"It's all right, child. It is fortunate that I happen to be here at the right time—the gods must be watching over you. You are safe now." She wrapped her surprisingly strong arms around me and held me until I regained my composure.

"Can you teach me—the magic, I mean? I do not expect you will be there the next time I am in danger."

"Alas, I am not skilled enough to pass on what little I know. What magic I have is a blessing from Ioddenri for my service to the nature goddess. If you are interested, I can teach you about her and the skills I have learned in her service. Perhaps she will share her blessings with you in time as well."

I sniffed, still recovering from my crying fit, and smiled. "I would like that very much."*

"I fully admit that I was scared for my life. When they touched me, it was as if my body turned to iron—I felt heavy and could not move. I... I was helpless," I stammered. "I wish I could have stopped them myself. For weeks I feared the forest; kept seeing those pale-yellow eyes and smelled the stench of their rot everywhere. I hate them," I finished flatly, suddenly realizing how angry I was. *"Flesh"* I could still hear them hiss harshly as the smell of rotted flesh filled my nostrils again. I was no longer scared; I was furious! "Flesh-eating cadavers," I growled. "If I knew how, I would destroy every last one of them!"

"I could teach you," Vletraka leaned in. "Come train with me."

"My pardon Mis... Vletraka, but you do not appear to be much of a warrior to me, and I am no fighter either. Who are you?"

"I am Vletraka of the Alabaster Moon, Necromancer of Cuyokale and Wizard of the Ivory Tome, and I wish you to be my apprentice."

I heard Verond squeak at this announcement and Yoffa trying to quiet him.

I stared at her for a moment, shock, awe, fear, and hope cascading across my heart. "You are not what I pictured for a necromancer," I said evenly. After years of bullying, I learned to speak calmly even while scared. I knew it was a mask, but I could not show my fear. "The necromancers in the stories are always deformed, malicious, and hideous. You are too beautiful to be evil." *Ye gods! I cannot believe I just said that!*

"Well, thank you," she smiled, causing me to blush deeper. "Not all necromancers are as they appear in the stories, though sadly many are. I am a vitae necromancer, using the tools of the darkness to fight the darkness. I find it is easier to destroy something if you first learn how it's made, and my magicks break apart the force that animates the undead."

Wizardry! I never dreamed that it was even possible for me. "I would very much like to learn from you, but is not wizardry a profession for the privileged? I am the son of a poor blacksmith in a small village. I have no way to pay you."

"That's not important to me. True, many wizards sell themselves to nobility, living comfortably while teaching their charges just enough to be a danger to themselves. It is much harder to seek out those with true potential. You, my boy, have that potential."

"How so?" I asked, stunned at the possibility.

"You are exceptionally intelligent, and have a passion for learning. When I first saw you, I detected your latent talent for magic. You have a good heart, which will help you through the darkness. Let me teach you."

"It's not fair!" Verond wailed. "How come *he* gets to be a wizard? I wanna be a wizard!"

Vletraka smiled at him. "Perhaps when you are older. Magical talent often runs in families. I will check in on you in a few years to see if you are ready."

Verond beamed at the prospect.

Turning to me, she asked, "Do you wish to learn magic?"

Yes! Absolutely! How could I refuse? "I will have to discuss it with my parents," I said swallowing my excitement. Mother would not be pleased, I feared. "Will you come to our house? I am certain you can explain it better than I."

She smiled.

I had never seen anyone so beautiful.

"Of course. Lead on." She grabbed my hand across the table

I almost recoiled from her touch. "Your hand is like ice," I said, feeling the heat draining from my fingers. "You should have sat closer to the fire."

She squeezed my hand once and pulled away. "Sorry, I sometimes forget. I'm always cold; I hardly even notice it anymore."

"Vletraka," I said quietly. "It is an unusual name. What does it mean?"

"It's not my birth name, of course."

I looked puzzled.

"Wizards choose new names when they begin training, for there are spells which can cause great harm if the true name is known. What name would you take, smith's son?"

I paused for a moment. I had gotten used to Yoffa calling me 'smith's son', and just now realized that Vletraka did not know my name. "Mithron," I blurted, the name forcing its way past my lips. My spine tingled. "My name shall be Mithron."

Chapter 2: My Training Begins

"You want my son to do WHAT?" Father shouted, a mixture of incredulousness and rage in his voice.

Mother stood behind him, tears of horror streaming from her eyes. I looked at her, my eyes pleading for her to understand, but the very idea of her son using the magic she so feared caused her to block my silent reassurances.

"I believe that he has the makings of a wizard, and I wish to train him," Vletraka replied calmly, causing Father to redden further.

I think he enjoys a good argument, and always gets angrier if his opponent does not shout back at him.

Getting no reinforcement from Vletraka, he quickly turned on me. "First you go playing in gardens with some old woman and now you think to learn magic from this wisp of a girl? I thought I raised my son to be a man." He crossed his massive arms across the barrel of his chest, demonstrating visibly his definition of manliness, and glared at me.

"Father," I replied with a sigh, "clearly, I am not as strong as you, nor do I think I will ever be. Larshon is quickly growing to equal your size, and I dare not even wrestle with Verond anymore, though he is five years my younger. My body is not strong, but my mind is. Please let me develop what strengths I have."

"You never were any good at the forge," he growled. "You picked up the techniques, but never produced anything from it, so I pushed you all the harder. No, you're not stupid, and you've always worked hard. It's hard to admit that my son can't follow in my footsteps," he said, his rage subsiding only a little. "But you're not going anywhere with *her*. By the gods, boy, if you are going to be a man, you must be taught by a man, whatever your trade." He turned to Vletraka. "You think the boy can learn magic? Fine. One less mouth to feed. But you go have your husband teach him. I'll not have him trailing after your skirts. A woman your age shouldn't be alone with an impressionable young boy anyhow."

"I'm not married. Believe me, there will be no misconduct between Mithron and I," she said flatly. Her expression showed her to be repelled by the idea.

For some reason I could not fathom at the time, I felt insulted.

"Who's Mithron?" Mother asked quickly, before Father could lecture Vletraka on the sins of being an unmarried woman.

Verond mumbled and pointed at me. "Him. Wizards get new names to protect themselves."

"Where did you learn that?" Mother asked.

"They were talking about it a Yoffa's. People aren't supposed to know a wizard's real name, 'cause bad magic can hurt them."

"So, you've changed your name, even," Father spat. "Well, I don't have a son named 'Mithron', so whoever you are, you'd best get out of my house." Everyone stared at him as a grin began to grow on his face, certain that he had finally won this argument.

"F-Father!" I stammered.

"I'm not *your* father. My two sons are smiths. There are no wizards in this family. Get out." He just stared at me, raw fury burning behind his eyes, the faint grin gone now.

Mother tried to speak but he quickly held up the back of his hand. She squeaked and sat down.

He never took his eyes from mine.

"Fine, *sir*. I will take my leave," I said coldly. "Mother, brothers, take care of each other. Goodbye." I turned and strode purposefully out through the door. My heart was breaking, but I was not going to give that hard-hearted man the satisfaction of seeing me cry. I managed to make it all the way to the forge before my anger turned to grief, and the tears overcame my breath. Angrily, I ripped out one of the mallows and threw it at the small building. "You cannot salve this wound," I muttered at the broken reed. It was then that I felt a cold hand on my shoulder.

Vletraka stood silently over me for a few moments, waiting for my tears to stop. Once I regained a semblance of self-composure, she spoke. "I didn't realize that would be so difficult for you. If you wish to stay and reconcile with your family, I will understand. I could…"

"No," I interrupted, turning to face her and wiping the remaining tears from my cheeks. "There is no going back. I have no choice now but to carry on." My grief had once again turned to anger—and determination.

She gave a small smile. "All right then. I was planning to spend tonight with Yoffa while you said your 'goodbyes', but I don't think that she will mind an extra guest for the night. Were there any personal belongings that you wish to retrieve?"

"No, my Lady, there is nothing I want from here. As you heard, I do not live there anymore. To my... to that man, I no longer exist." I sighed. "Actually, I do not really have anything of my own, aside from clothes," I suddenly chuckled.

"What's so funny?"

"I have always been an outcast in the village, and now I have been cast out of my home. I will miss Yoffa, but I never really had any reason to stay here. With my family taken from me, I am free."

She gave me a wan smile. "That's one way to look at it."

"When do I start my training?" I asked, suddenly eager, aware that I had but one path ahead of me. "What do I learn first?"

"Patience, young Mithron," she chided.

"Patience. Okay. How long will that take?"

She stopped in her tracks and stared at me.

I could not suppress a widening grin.

Vletraka followed suit and rolled back her eyes. "What have I gotten myself into?"

"Yoffa, we have an extra guest," announced Vletraka softly as she entered the cabin with me in tow.

"Oh? Who... child, why aren't you at home?" she asked with concern.

I was about to break down again—could feel it. I took a deep breath to steady myself before answering, "I have no home. It appears that I am no longer... my father's... son." I had barely choked out the last when tears began to run hotly down my cheeks once again.

Yoffa frowned and looked at Vletraka.

"His father was rather upset at Mithron's choice of profession, and none too pleased at his son's teacher either. He turned his back on him and cast him out of the family."

"'Tis true he has all the charm and grace of a fresh pile of lamb's droppings," sighed Yoffa, which caused me to sputter with laughter, "but I never thought he would react like that. Most families would be honored to count a wizard among them."

"But I am no smith," I said while wiping the tears from my face, "and I have a new name, and a female teacher. I do not think any of those sit well with him." I sat down on a stool and sighed. *Why should I even care? It was obvious to even him that I would never make a good blacksmith. Of course, I would seek another trade. And I have never done anything right in his eyes; always complaining about my shoddy work in the forge. By the Pits, he scarcely acknowledged how I helped heal Verond's burn yesterday! Why should his opinions matter to me at all? He is just a thoughtless, unfeeling,* "dispassionate, uncaring, self-absorbed bastard!"

The room grew quiet, and I looked up to see Yoffa and Vletraka staring at me.

I quickly realized that I had spoken the last of my thoughts aloud. Embarrassed at my outburst, I turned away and receded back into my thoughts. *I have got to get some control. If I continue to act like a wounded child, Vletraka will think I am not ready to be her pupil. If she turns me away, then I truly have no place left to go. I cannot return home—I cannot even stay in Split Falls. She must teach me. I must become a wizard. I have no other choice.*

Once again, I felt a cold hand upon my shoulder, stealing the warmth from my body. "Are you all right?"

No! I am angry, frustrated, hurt, sad... "I am... tired," I said finally.

"I understand. Would you like your first lesson now? Or would you rather have supper first?"

I stared at her for a moment, losing some of my pain in her jet-black eyes. *She has not given up on me. Yet.* I took a deep breath. "I am your student, Mistress Vletraka. Teach me."

"I want you to take a deep breath, and then release it slowly. Concentrate solely on your breathing. As other thoughts come to you, let them go as you exhale. Continue taking deep breaths until your mind is clear."

"That does not sound much like magic to me."

"Before you can cast spells, you must prepare both your mind and body to handle magical energy. This is but one exercise to ready you."

"Very well, Mistress Vletraka. It sounds simple enough." I took a deep breath, and was glad that Vletraka still wished to teach me. Exhaling, I tried to push the thought away. Inhale. *Concentrate. I do not wish to disappoint her.* Exhale. Inhale. *She is all I have left.* Exhale. Inhale. *'I have no son. Get out,'* I heard in my father's voice. I-inhale. Exhale. *'You're weak—worthless. You're not my son.'* I-inhale. I could feel the tears welling up once again. E-exhale. *'A failure.'* Then, Father's voice changed to Vletraka's. *'A failure.'* I-inhale. Sniffle. E-exhale. *'One simple task, and you could not even accomplish that.'* I-i-inhale. Tears streamed down my face. E-e-exhale. *'You'll never be a wizard. Failure.'*

I began to weep inconsolably, giving up any pretense of continuing the exercise. *They are right. What made me believe that I could be a wizard? I cannot even breathe properly. I am a failure.*

Try again, came a quiet voice.

Why bother? I responded.

Try again, the voice prodded.

I wiped my face with my sleeves and took two short breaths. Inhale. *You* are *a sad, pathetic little creature,* I heard in my own mocking tones.

Exhale. *I have no home, no family,* I answered myself.

Inhale. *Tough. Is mewling like an infant going to make things better?*

Exhale. *No. I just…*

Inhale. *'Just' what?*

Exhale. *I am lost; frightened.*

Inhale. *Deal with it.*

Exhale. *How?*

Inhale. *Vletraka will help.* Exhale. *She is my family now.*
Inhale. *What if I fail her?* Exhale. *I will be lost again.*
Inhale. *Do better. Listen to her.* Exhale. *Do you think* she *gives
up this easily?*
Inhale. *Probably not.* Exhale.
Inhale. Exhale. *I am doing it!* Inhale. *Relax. Do not get
overconfident.* Exhale.
Inhale. Exhale.
Inhale. Exhale.
Inhale.
Exhale. …

I awoke next morning feeling both refreshed and exhausted, the air
smelling strongly of blueberries. Wiping the crusted tears from my
eyes, I opened them to see Yoffa and Vletraka sitting at the
workbench, eating bread and drinking tea.

"Your student awakes," smiled Yoffa, setting down her cup. She
turned to face me with a grandmotherly smile and asked, "Hungry?"

My stomach answered before I could. "Apparently." I got up off
the floor and sat down on the bench next to Yoffa. Upon the table
were most of a loaf of rosemary bread, a small wooden bowl filled
with fresh blueberry compote, and three mugs of tea, which smelled
of sweet summer flowers. "Thank you, Mistresses," I said
gratefully, tearing off a small hunk of bread and dredging it through
the crushed berries. "I believe I missed last night's supper. My
apologies, Mistress Vletraka, I must have fallen asleep during your
exercise."

"I expected you might," she smiled. "In fact, I hoped that you
would."

"So… I did not fail?" I worried.

"Your mind and heart were in turmoil, and you needed time to
process the events of the day. I thought for a time that you would
cry yourself to sleep, but you seemed to quieten and relax before
fading off. Do you want to talk about your experience?"

"Oh, give the boy a little time," Yoffa interrupted.

"It is okay, Mistress Yoffa," I said, taking a deep breath. "The exercise was much more difficult than I imagined. Different thoughts and emotions kept surfacing, and as I tried to push one away, another would take its place."

Vletraka explained, "That is often the way of it, particularly when first learning this concentration exercise. We do not realize just how much we think about things until we pay them heed. That I gave you the exercise while you were under duress only magnified the lesson."

"I do feel calmer now."

"Good. But do not forget that those feelings are still there. In time, it becomes easier to block those extraneous thoughts and focus on the task at hand. It will likely save your life."

My eyes widened in surprise. "How so?"

"When dealing with another mage, or, more importantly, in battle, losing focus on the spell you are casting will cause you to lose the energy of the spell, leaving you vulnerable to attack. You must learn to shut out distractions to be an effective wizard. Besides, as you experienced, it is also a good way to relieve one's self of unnecessary stress."

"I understand. Thank you, Mistress Vletraka." My stomach began to assert itself, protesting my lack of focus on its needs. I tore off another hunk of bread and added more blueberries to it. Hungry though I was, it took little of the hearty bread to sate me. When I finished, Vletraka stated that we must soon be on our way.

"So soon?" I asked, surprised at the speed my life was changing. "Well, I suppose there is no reason to dawdle, is there?" I said looking up at Yoffa, realizing that all ties, save one, had been severed.

She smiled back at me, then reached down under the table and pulled up a small leather satchel. "Here you are, my lad. I made this special for you," she grinned, her eyes beginning to mist over. "I knew you would master my teachings quickly. This herb satchel will serve you well in your studies."

I examined the heavy bag. It had a dozen long pockets on the exterior, each of which had dried herbs and seeds, and a small rod and sickle sat within the main compartment to be used for planting and harvesting respectively, along with copies of *Nature's Eyes*, *Healing Herbs*, and *Earth's Toxins,* and a small jar of lineament. She had given me the means to start my own herb garden!

"This… this is magnificent! Thank you—for everything." I turned on the bench to face her and clasped her ancient, yet strong, hands. "I shall never forget your kindness and generosity."

"You worked hard to earn that. You not only read, but you worked in my garden, traveled into the woods with me to learn first-hand, and helped me clean and keep my house in order—such as it is," she finished, looking around the organized chaos that was both home and workshop. Both she and I knew how to find anything stored within, but an outsider would be hard-pressed to understand her system. "You'll need to work even harder to learn magic."

"I would not expect otherwise." I smiled, let go of her hands, and stood. "It is time." Turning to Vletraka I said flatly, "I am ready."

She nodded in response and walked out of Yoffa's home.

I turned back to Yoffa and bowed. "Thank you again, Mistress. I will put all I have learned to good use."

"Take care, my boy. Come visit if you can escape your new taskmaster," she smiled, her eyes glistening.

"I heard that!" came a voice from outside. Yoffa's grin widened, as did mine.

"Farewell." I stepped outside to see Vletraka standing between two horses, the first a midnight black stallion with a white patch on his head, which resembled an open book. The other was a dark grey mare, like that of old burnt coals, with a similar patch.

"Mount up. We have three days of travel ahead of us."

I eyed the horses suspiciously.

"Have you ever ridden before?" Vletraka asked.

"No, my Lady, I have not. Where have these horses been hidden? I do not remember seeing them before, and Yoffa has no stable."

Vletraka smiled at me. "I conjured them."

"I wish you had waited until I got outside," I pouted. "I would have liked to have seen that."

"You will have plenty of opportunities, apprentice. These will only last until about sunset, and I will have to cast the spell again tomorrow. Let me help you. Put your left foot in the stirrups and grab the pommel," she pointed to the objects as she named them. "Now push off the ground while straightening your other leg, and swing your right leg over the horse's back."

Though her instructions were simple enough, executing them proved more challenging. My attempt to swing my leg over resulted in my kicking the horse in the rump, losing my grip on the pommel, and falling flat on my back with my foot still in the stirrup. For a few moments, I found myself unable to breathe while the grey mare eyed me impassively. I felt a cold touch on my forehead, and my lungs suddenly expanded, the pain subsiding to nothing.

"Better?" Vletraka asked.

I gulped more air and nodded.

"Good, now get up. The pain will return in a few minutes, so you better be on that horse before it does," she warned gently while removing my foot from the stirrup. My second attempt was clumsy, but successful, and I had to spend a minute adjusting myself looking for a comfortable position.

Meanwhile, Vletraka climbed upon her horse with the ease of long practice. "Let's go."

My horse stepped in line with hers, first at a slow walk, then speeding up to a trot and then a slow run. By this time, her magic had worn off and pain shot up my back. I tensed, but held my seat, which became increasingly difficult the longer we rode. In time, I lost all sensation below the waist.

Aside from forays into the woods, I had never left Split Falls before. Our village is mostly self-sufficient, as villages often need to be, with the occasional trader stopping by. An old grommold would visit Father every moon or so with boxes of coal and iron rods, exchanging them with some coin for finished goods—tools and weapons—which I suppose he sold in other villages. We had little coin available in the village as a whole, and mostly worked in trade with the other villagers. Nearly everyone grew their own crops, and non-farmers like Father would provide the services of their crafts in exchange for foodstuffs beyond what Mother could grow in her small garden.

It was not long before trees encased the thin roadway; our path darkening as the arboreal canopy blocked out the sun. The kingdom of Loerendoch is heavily forested, and it is said that a squirrel could run the length and breadth of the kingdom without ever touching the ground. Of course, the squirrel would need to circumvent the larger towns and cities, but the concept has merit. Many villages have hence followed the zylan philosophy of building amongst, or even in, the trees, thinning the forest only enough to make room for construction. Some natural clearings are scattered about, the rich soil beneath the grasses being useful for a wide variety of crops, as in my native Split Falls, but teams of woodsmen had cleared other areas.

Trade roads were established even before King Loeren's time, and each generation has slowly expanded the network to keep the kingdom connected. The road we travelled now is fairly well rutted, forcing the horses to slow, mostly from wagons taking crops to the capital city Arquel or other large towns, and returning with trade goods, such as fine cloth, thread, dyes, glass, lamp oil, and spices. These would in turn be sold or traded for other goods and services in our village. Though we never prospered, we thrived so long as the crops did.

Vletraka had been riding alongside me in silence, eyeing both the path and me in turn. A short time into our journey, she asked, "Is the horse's gait comfortable for you?"

"I cannot tell if I am in excruciating pain or numb," I responded. "I still feel sore from my fall, but I feel nothing in my legs."

"It takes some time to get used to it," she nodded. "With practice, you will find that you could even sleep in the saddle."

"I somehow doubt that. In fact, I feel a little nauseous from rocking back and forth."

"Sit up straight and relax your body. Try to feel the movement of the horse, the shifting of her muscles. Try doing your breathing exercise to relax."

I followed her instructions, straightening my back while letting the tension release from my body. I found that by letting my hips shift in time with the horse's steps, I stopped swaying, which both eased my stomach and my mind. When I inhaled deeply, I suddenly became aware of the scent of the forest; the crackle of the pines met with the pungent odor of the deep soil and the sweetness of ripe blackberries, which grew in thick tangled thatches along the path. I kept my eyes open, for fear of falling asleep again and dropping off the horse, and the world seemed to brighten as I breathed. The trees took on a faint green glow, and I felt a sense of joy as they stretched toward the sun.

While looking around at the green, my eyes fell on Vletraka. She was calm and serene, yet vigilant; though there was nothing in her posture or face that expressed these attitudes, I felt somehow that this was true. Another breath and I followed that thought inward and my spine tingled between my shoulder blades, right behind my heart. *Is this real?* I asked of no one and myself in particular, and the tingle came again. *Interesting.*

I glanced down at Vletraka's horse and it was ethereal, as though not truly there. The horses were solid enough, of that there was no doubt, and yet…. Vletraka did say that she summoned them through magic, so mayhap they are not completely real. As I focused my attention on the conjured steed, I could feel… a presence, like reality was being pushed aside to allow for the horses' existence. It was not an uncomfortable feeling, but certainly palpable. Another breath, and I could sense, for I can think of no better term, a connection between the horses and Vletraka herself. I looked for a visual clue, a glow like the trees had or a line to connect them, but saw nothing, yet I *knew* that what I felt was true. My spine tingled yet again. *That must be my cue.*

"Mistress Vletraka, what does magic feel like?"

"I suppose that depends on the spell. Fire, cold, lightning, all have different effects upon…"

"No. I mean magic itself."

"Oh, you're referring to the Weave."

"'The Weave'?"

"Yes, the Weave is what we call the lines of pure magical energy which permeate everything. It is by manipulating the Weave that spells are cast, and magical effects occur. Much of spellcasting is imagination coupled with knowledge and skill. Any effect that one can conceive of, a spell can be created for—as long as one has the ability to properly alter the Weave through gesticulation, words of power, and a material focus, though not all spells require all three components. Once one has been trained to sense the Weave—each wizard experiences it differently—it becomes easier to manipulate it.

"The Weave is thought to permeate all of the world—the sky, earth, and seas are all connected through it, as are the different dimensions and planes outside of our physical reality. Some believe that the gods created it, while others say that the gods were created by it. The truth may never come to the understanding of mere mortals, but the philosophical debate rages on.

"Manipulating the Weave involves the wizard focusing her personal energy while acting upon the Weave in particular fashions which must be prepared for ahead of time. Though a wizard learns scores of spells over a career, no single mage has the energy to cast them all in a day's time. In fact, unless a wizard takes the time to focus her energy into particular formulae, she will not likely be able to cast spells at all! The focusing process involves the partial casting of the spell, setting up the energy for a quick release with a few words and gestures. Without this preparation, a mage would have to gather the energy on the spot and follow through the entire spellcasting ritual, which would likely get the wizard killed in the midst of battle. Why do you ask?"

"I… felt something while doing the breathing exercise just now. I do not have the words to describe it, but I could 'feel' the magic of the horses, like one feels a breeze or the mist on a foggy morn. It is there, and yet it is not."

Vletraka smiled, and I felt as though she were proud of me. "You should be aware that those who practice magic are often changed by it."

"How so?"

"For instance, you have noticed that my skin is always cold to the touch. It was not like that before I learned the art of spellcasting. Most of these alterations are mixed blessings—I am less affected by heat, but am more sensitive to cold weather, and my friend Nari can read magical scripts as easily as we read mundane writings, but must concentrate to read as we do. I do not know what effect the Weave will have on you; I should have warned you earlier."

"I doubt it would have changed my mind. Have any of these alterations been dangerous?"

"Once they have been mastered, no, not that I know of. Until I learned to steady myself, I often shivered so hard that I could not cast properly, which could have proven fatal in combat. Goldfire actually changed her name again when she developed her aura, which also nearly killed her. She has a protective energy, which grew too strong and was even blocking out the air around her. I hear that she has taken on a new student as well."

"How many wizards do you know? I thought wizardry was rather rare."

"It certainly is. But over time, we were drawn to each other. There are five of us in our little group, plus apprentices. We visit each other from time to time, in between research projects, so you will meet them in time."

Chapter 3: Blythad

Blythad and I met when Vletraka sent me on an errand to Nari's tower. I had been training with her for nearly a year and nine months by this time, reading intently, doing odd chores, learning the art of alchemy, tending the garden, and, in my spare time, actually practicing magic, which one does not learn much of in the first year. At first, it is mostly exercises designed to allow the body and mind to accept magical energy and a fantastic amount of reading; Vletraka was right about the lesson of patience being primary at the start of training, for it was easy to get frustrated at the lack of magic available to me in the beginning.

She worked me hard, and I worked myself harder. When I asked about why I had to do menial labor, which took time away from studying, she commented that keeping the body fit helps it to retain more magical energy. I researched historical wizards to prove her false in the hopes of changing her mind, but it seems that her words have wisdom after all. Even the eldest of mages managed to stay somewhat physically fit, with some suggestion that magic actually fueled their bodies after a point.

I also made a new friend, well, two to be precise. Wizards sometimes summon familiars, a bonded animal linked magically to the wizard, to be both companion and helpmate. Vletraka was bonded to Quesel, a small brown bat, and I soon found myself bonding with Thessylia, a short-eared owl. It is difficult to describe the link between wizard and familiar to those who have not experienced it, and no need to describe it to those who have. Part of the life force is shared between the two, heightening the senses— and in some cases physical skills—of the wizard, while amplifying both intelligence and magical ability of the familiar. I have learned to cast spells through her, using her as conduit for my magic, as well as communicate telepathically and empathically with her.

The summoning ritual is a full day process, often from sunrise to sunrise, though it can be started at any time of the day, wherein the wizard lights rare incense and meditates in a circle of mystic runes. During the meditation, the wizard looks deep into his heart and considers why he wishes to follow the path of wizardry and what he wishes to accomplish as such. At the close of the ceremony, assuming it is done correctly, the familiar best suited to the mage appears at the edge of the circle and speaks its name in a fashion that only the wizard it will bond with can hear. The pair then become life-long companions; their spirits tied to one another so that the familiar lives as long as the wizard does... normally. Should the wizard die from causes other than natural ones, a common occurrence in our profession, the familiar often survives for about a month before passing. Should the familiar be killed, it tears at the mage's spirit, reducing his connection to the Weave until his soul heals. A risky endeavor, true, explaining the rarity of its occurrence, but well worth it, for there can never be a closer companion to a wizard than his familiar.

My Mistress needed some rare components, which her friend had available, and assigned me to fetch them. "Why do you not send a message using magic?" I asked. "Or teleport? Either way would be much faster than having me travel all the way over there."

"There are some things magic cannot accomplish. I could certainly send the message using a magical courier, and my need is not so great as to use the necessary energy to teleport. Besides, I believe it is past time you began socializing with your fellow apprentices," she smiled.

"But I have so much to learn here. Time taken away from my studies is time lost," I countered.

She sighed. "You have much more to learn than what is in these dusty old books, young Mithron. It is better to have friends and allies than to make your way in the world alone." She crossed her arms. "You are by far the most self-sufficient boy I know, and sometimes I feel that you need my library to learn magic more than you need me," she chuckled, "but you know how dangerous the world is. It is always better to have someone nearby in case you get into trouble."

I thought back to my encounter with the vulzuu and shuddered. "Very well. I shall make friends with… what is Nari's apprentice's name?"

"Blythad, I believe. Here is the message, and a map to her tower," she said matter-of-factly as she handed me the proffered items. "I will conjure a horse for you to get you started, but after that, you will need to summon your own. It should take you about three days to get there, so I expect to see you by the next quarter moon. Grab your pack and some provisions for the trip, and I shall meet you outside."

Clearly, there was to be no further argument on the subject. I picked up my spell-book, carried it to my room, and grabbed a thick quilt from a cedar chest. I then went to the kitchen and grabbed my backpack from the hook. After carefully placing my book into the pack, I rummaged through the cupboards for foodstuffs that would travel well—a loaf of bread, some cheese, dried meat, and a bunch of carrots. I also grabbed two water-skins to keep hydrated. I checked over Vletraka's map and saw that there were two creeks to ford along the way where I could refill the hardened bladders, should the need arise. I rolled up the quilt, tucked it under my arm, and stepped outside where Vletraka stood next to a tan and white horse, with the familiar open book marking on its forehead, my Mistress's personal symbol. At some point, I will have to develop my own.

"Are you ready?"

I nodded in response.

"Good. Have a safe journey."

I still did not wish to leave my studies, but there seemed to be no other choice. I tied the quilt to the back of the saddle then mounted the conjured steed, not easily, but I have improved since my first attempts back in Split Falls and rode off towards Nari's tower. Vletraka's conjured horse would last for the rest of the day, so there was no need to prepare additional castings of the spell today, but I calculated that I would need to cast the *hivliuose*[1] spell twice for

---

[1] Magical spells are drawn from the language of dragons, modified somewhat in pronunciation for the tongues of humans and other races capable of using magic.

each day of travel afterwards, reducing the number of spells I could allocate toward combat magic. I did, however, study a few spells while riding, a difficult task while swaying on horseback, in case of trouble and to ease my rest at night. There was no guarantee of an uneventful journey. Though these lands were somewhat settled, any number of creatures could wander into the wooded territory seeking food or conquest. More than likely, I would run into a pack of bandits, but it is not impossible to believe that a passing dragon might take an interest in the land. I checked my map regularly, to make certain that I did not wander off my intended route, and my first day of travel proved uneventful, aside from spotting a mass of one-berry vines, which I took some time out to harvest the berries and leaves, as they are both useful in aiding the body against poisons.

As dusk approached, I sent Thessylia ahead to find a clearing where it would be safe to build a small fire and rest for the night. What she found was a widening in a game trail, where there was slightly more space between trees than my height. I gathered some larger rocks to form a ring, and then piled up some of the numerous available small branches in the center of the circle. Once I was certain I had enough wood to last through the night, and the ring was secure, I cast *uvazsrukak* on the wood enclosed by the stones. *Uvazsrukak* is a myzling, a minor spell with limited effect, which is pretty much only good for starting small fires; in fact, *uvazsrukak* means "little fire" in Draconic, the language of dragons, who taught magic to mortals. It is much faster than using flint, and, though the flame it begets is small, the fire can quickly grow if given the right fuel.

The rugged, outdoor life is not for me. I admit to having been spoiled by Vletraka, sleeping in an actual bed in a room of my own; a far cry from the reed mats my brothers and I slept on in the main room of our little house. Still, I have always had a roof over my head and walls around me. There was little doubt in my mind that Thessylia would spot any trouble and warn me before I could be

---

A short appendix has been placed at the end of this volume to assist the reader in understanding the roots of the spells.

attacked in my sleep, however, there was always the possibility that she would be hunting and miss something hunting me.

"Stay close," I commanded the short-eared owl.

She barked once and disappeared from view.

Occasionally, I get glimpses from her while she is away, a minor vision or sound. I have read that some wizard's familiars bond particularly closely with their masters, and that they can share each other's senses. I cannot say if my bond with her is unusual, but she is the closest companion I have ever had, even more so than Vletraka.

It took me a while to relax enough to sleep, wrapped up in my quilt on the hard ground, using my pack as a pillow, and I did not slumber deeply. I woke a number of times to strange sounds—a branch creaking in the wind, the sounds of footsteps of some small animal, the call of another owl warning Thessylia of her encroachment in his territory—finally waking for good just as dawn broke. I lay still for a few moments, my body stiff from a long day's ride and a fitful sleep on hard cold ground, listening to the sounds of the morning; the chirping of birds, the buzzing of insects, the tapping of a woodpecker, a soft breeze through the late-spring leaves, and the chittering of squirrels. If my body were not so sore, I may have enjoyed it all more. I stretched my arms and legs then rolled out of my quilt. The fire had long grown cold, as had I, so I placed a few more branches into the pit and cast *uvazsrukak* to bring the flames to life once again.

I reached into my pack and pulled out my spell-book, a hunk of bread, the cheese, and a water-skin. The bread was stale, and a bit flattened, either by my book or my head resting upon it, but the cheese escaped harm. I examined them both for mold, then ate unhurriedly. After breaking my fast, I opened my spell-book to prepare the incantations I would need for today. I had to set aside the energy to cast the *hivliuose* spell twice today, as I would need to for the next day, in order to stay on schedule, which left me with little room for other spells. In case I got caught in a combat situation, I opted to fortify myself with offensive magicks, though I dearly hoped that the issue would not arise.

Once I prepared myself, I cast the first of the *hivliuose* spells, conjuring forth a plain, dark-brown steed with no obvious markings. I rolled up my quilt and tied it to the saddle, made certain that everything else was in my pack, hoisted it over my shoulder, and mounted the horse. As the path was still very narrow, I kept at a slow pace until I found a wider trail. Just as my first steed was nearly expired, I came across the first of the two creeks on Vletraka's map. I dismounted at the shore and filled my water-skin. As I did so, I heard my quilt softly drop to the ground as the summoned horse faded away from beneath it. Once I was done refilling, I conjured the second *hivliuose* for the day and rode on, Thessylia sleeping on my shoulder.

"And who might this be, wandering amongst my trees?" I heard a light singsong voice query.

I stopped the horse and searched around for the source, my eyes stopping on a leaf-and-bark clad young woman standing in a tree; embarrassingly little bark and leaves, if truth be told. The sun shining through the trees gave a greenish cast to her hair and skin, and I could just make out the three tiny points of her ears, like that of a zyla, only shorter, poking through her long wavy tresses.

"I am Mithron," I answered politely. *She might be fey,* I thought, *best not to offend her, lest she be dangerous.* "I apologize for my trespass; I did not realize that these trees were yours."

"The trees, nay, the forest, are shared among the poorest. I shall not raise alarm so long as ye cause no harm." As she spoke, she walked forward on the branch, her lithe weight causing it to droop so that she stood at eye level with me still on horseback. As she neared, I could see that it was no trick of the light, and that her hair truly *was* as green as the leaves surrounding us, and her skin the color of young grass.

"I intend only to pass through. Are you the guardian of this forest?" I asked, intrigued by the beautiful creature.

"The forest and I are one. We grow under the daily sun, resting when the day is done." She paused for a moment. "That horse is not a natural one," she accused.

"No, it is not. I conjured this steed to quicken my journey, though it will fade in a short time," I answered calmly, though I was beginning to fret my magical horse would offend this creature of nature.

"Interesting! I see that now. Would you take the time and show me how?" she asked excitedly, releasing me from my worry.

"Effay, are you accosting another traveler?" came another voice from the forest—masculine and stern. Without a sound of disturbed leaves or branches, he appeared from behind another tree. He too was covered in bark, though his appeared more like armor, a sickle hanging from a belt made of vines showed that he was willing to fight if necessary. He stood tall and lean, his arms and legs just a little too long to be human. His face was definitely zylan—long triple-pointed ears, delicate angular features, and pale skin. His eyes, though, were hard, as though he expected trouble from all he met.

"Just having a little fun, Master," Effay pouted, her eyes cast down.

The zyla sighed. "If you wish to learn to guard this forest, you have to control your impulses and stay hidden. A watchful eye…"

"…Is wiser than an open target. Yes, Master Dawnthistle." She turned to me. "Sorry to have bothered you."

"No bother at all," I replied. "You have, at the very least, made my journey more interesting."

"Effay'ost'kao, please get away from that human," Dawnthistle demanded sternly. "I have told you how dangerous they are. Especially the magic-wielders."

"My pardon," I bowed, trying not to fall off my horse, "I intend no harm, and was only passing through. I do not wish to cause strife between you and your charge."

"Go then," he commanded. "Be warned, we will be watching." At that, he faded back into the trees. With a pout, Effay followed his lead, turning quickly to give me a wave before vanishing herself.

They must be the druids of this land. I feel a bit safer, knowing that they are vigilant, but I had best be on my guard anyway. No sense in relying on people who might not be around when needed. Why was Effay green? Does druidic training affect the practitioners the same as wizardly training? I wonder what my gift *will be. Has Nari's student manifested his yet? Considering the odd ways I have learned that it can manifest, do I even want mine to?*

I considered the meeting I had with the two druids—at least, that was the safe assumption as to their profession, based on their appearance, actions, and words—while I continued my journey to Nari's tower. Effay spoke in rhyme while talking to me, then in traditional Umani when her master appeared. Was that part of her game? Dawnthistle kept her under a tight yoke and she bristled under his discipline. I hoped she would do well under his tutelage and gain her freedom from him soon.

Why am I judging him so harshly, I wondered? *I have only shared a few words with the man, and do not know him at all.* Yet, I kept thinking that he enjoyed frightening his charge in order to keep her dependent on him.

The rest of my journey proved uneventful, though now and then I suspected that I was being followed. Even Thessylia's sharp senses could not tell me for certain, and with their connection to the forest, Dawnthistle and Effay could easily use the creatures and plants to watch me even though they themselves were elsewhere. When I got within sight of Nari's tower, the feeling subsided.

'Tower' is perhaps not the best description of her home, though more so than Vletraka's, as Nari's home was two stories tall. But no matter the actual structure, a wizard's home is his 'tower'. The building was round and squat, painted a bright yellow, a shade that was both cheerful and aggravating. Her fence-line consisted of regularly spaced posts with a single arch. I rode up to the arch, dismounted then dismissed the conjured steed. "I am Mithron, apprentice to Vletraka, here to visit the Master of the tower," I called out to the open air.

The first rule of etiquette when visiting another wizard's home is to announce your presence. Wizards are a secretive lot by nature and tend to protect their homes with all sorts of creatures, traps, and magical wards; intruders are dealt with harshly. Vletraka's home is protected by masses of klaatoo—animated hands and claws which scuttle around on their fingertips and attack by scratching and pummeling or strangling if they can reach their target's throat. Individually, they are an annoyance, but they attack in groups, 'skitters' being the proper term, and are as disconcerting in appearance as dangerous in a swarm. Once invited, however, one is typically protected from such obstacles, although the invitation can be rescinded at a whim.

While I waited at the arch, a small whirlwind approached me— Nari's messenger no doubt. It carried a small bracelet in its winds, which it dropped at my feet. In order to secure safe passage, a token from the wizard is often given to the guest. This protects the guest from the guardians of the tower, while ensuring that *only* those given the token are under the wizard's aegis. I placed the bracelet on my wrist, entered through the archway, and followed the winding stone path to the door. As I approached, I could see, even without consciously summoning the sight to detect the Weave, various symbols and wards etched into the house. Upon reaching the door, I knocked lightly.

A pudgy boy, about my age, wearing bright green robes, opened the door. His eyes were of a similar color to his clothing, and he had a mop of dark brown, somewhat greasy, hair. "Welcome. Who may I say is calling?"

"I am Mithron, apprentice to Vletraka of the Alabaster Moon," I told him. "This is my companion, Thessylia," I added, scratching the top of her head under her feathers.

He smiled excitedly. "Welcome. I am Blythad, apprentice to Nari the Gate-Watcher. Follow me." He turned and led me to Nari's den.

The interior of the house was also etched with the same protective symbols, and was as bright and cheery. Though Mistress Vletraka has some decorations, her home is a sparse hovel compared to Nari's. Every color one could imagine was represented in the furniture, walls, floors, ceiling, and general décor. Numerous knick-knacks, trophies, and decorations filled the room, resting on shelves and tables, as well as hanging from the walls and ceiling. Were it not somehow tasteful, it would be gaudy. Still, it far exceeded anything I had ever encountered, and I was caught looking around when Blythad grabbed my attention from the doorway to Nari's study. I quickly moved around the yellow, orange, and green sofa and stepped up to his side.

"Mistress Nari, I present Mithron, apprentice to Vletraka of the Alabaster Moon, and his familiar Thessylia," he announced.

"So, you are Vletraka's boy. Step forward, so I can get a better look at you."

I walked forward a few paces past Blythad and entered the study.

Nari stood in the center of the room, maple staff in hand, and beckoned me forward. I sensed a dome of magical symbols enveloping her, warding her against potential attacks. She was a slight, slender woman, with short iron-grey hair dressed in blue robes with red trim.

She stared at me with hazel eyes and questioned, "What is the meaning and purpose of this symbol?" while pointing to the open air.

I shifted my sight to better see the Weave and focused on the aqua-colored loop at the tip of her finger. "It is a basic rune of abjuration. Its color denotes it to be protective against flames and heat."

"And this one?" she asked, pointing to the one directly over her head.

"Oddly enough, symbols shaped like human eyes tend to involve divination magic. It has an ethereal quality to it, suggesting that it is used in spells to detect the unseen, likely something invisible, as it is linked to those three symbols there," I said pointing to the connected runes.

"Why cannot one travel directly to the Burbling Chaos from the plane of Elemental Air?"

"The Burbling Chaos, where wretched creatures are spewed forth from the land itself, is linked to Nyv, the Great River, while the Elemental planes are surrounded by the Shadow, though also connected to the Material through purified areas, such as a mountaintop for the Plane of Air. One would first need to enter the Shadow, pass to either the River Nyv or any Prime Material Plane, and then open gate to the Burbling Chaos, or the Shadow can be skipped by going directly to the Material Plane. Why one would wish to go to the Burbling Chaos is another matter," I answered with a smile. "Do you have any hard questions for me, Mistress Nari?"

She chuckled. "You are definitely Vletraka's student; there is no doubt about it. Welcome! I am sorry that I needed to check you, but one cannot be too careful about who or what enters one's home. My wards would have revealed you had you been a shape-shifter, but there are a number of forces beyond, and even within this realm which can cause havoc if given free rein. Anyone can claim to be someone else—it is best to verify the truth whenever possible."

"With that being the case then, can you tell me why Mistress Vletraka sent me here?"

She chuckled again. "'Traka needs some henbane, bat guano, raw amethysts, and wild blueberries, all of which can be found just south of here. Blythad can show you the way, but that can wait until morning. You surely need to rest after your journey."

"That would be most appreciated. Thank you."

"Come with me," piped up Blythad. "You can sleep in my room." He led me out of the den, down the hallway, and into a small room with a small bed and footlocker. "I hope there is enough room for us both."

"I can use my quilt on the floor. Until coming under the tutelage of Vletraka, I always slept on the floor; sometimes I still do out of habit."

He smiled widely. "I can't believe that I ever survived without a bed. It's hard to adjust the lumps sometimes, but it is so much more comfortable than a straw mat! I hear that nobles sleep on a bed filled with down feathers. Now *that* has to be soft!" he sighed.

"I imagine it would be warm also. Someday, perhaps we will live in such comfort. For now, I am happy to sleep under a roof again. The outdoor life does not suit me. Which reminds me, what do you know of Dawnthistle and Effay'ost'kao? I assume that they are the druids local to this area."

"Oh, you met *them*, huh? Dawnthistle hates humans, and pretty much anything humanoid for that matter. If you are not a deer or a tree, he considers you an enemy, and even then I would watch my back around him. Effay is just plain daft, in my opinion. I think she is part plant herself; her hair even changes with the seasons to match the leaves! What did they do to you?"

"Nothing, really. Effay appeared out of the trees and spoke to me in rhyme, at least until Dawnthistle came and then she spoke normally. I think it is a game she plays to amuse herself. I imagine she does not have many opportunities to converse with others. She seems very interested in magic and wanted me to teach her how to cast the *hivliuose* spell before Dawnthistle interrupted. Afterwards, I felt as though I was being watched until I got here."

"He didn't threaten you? He told me that if I ever caused any harm to the forest he would feed me to the wolves!"

"Then I suggest that we behave ourselves tomorrow while we search for Mistress Vletraka's ingredients, just to be safe. I do not know how far their reach extends, and I have no wish to create new enemies from neutral parties."

"Good idea. Well, it's time for me to start making dinner. Rest up, and I will get you when it's ready. Feel free to wander about; if you need, the privy is at the end of the hall."

"Thank you. Do you need assistance in the kitchen? I have the same duties, though I have no talent in that area. I do not understand how Vletraka manages to put up with it. One would think that she would either cook herself or hire someone capable to do it. At least, neither of us has gotten ill," I smiled weakly.

Blythad laughed. "I'm not that good either, but I make do with what I have. You are our guest, so no, you are to relax."

"Very well," I responded, not accustomed to letting others work for me. "I shall return the favor when you come to visit us."

"I hope your cooking improves by then," he laughed and left the room.

I sat on the straw mattress and pulled my spell-book out of my pack. Blythad was right about the lumpiness of the mattress, but still more comfortable than a flat mat. My quilt was padded more than a mat, and not as lumpy as the mattress, offering the best combination in my opinion. Perhaps if he placed the straw in the bed with more care, and stuffed it fuller, it would be more comfortable like mine at home. I checked the ropes supporting the mattress and found that they were loose, so I tightened them for him.

Dinner turned out to be a soup of squash, wax beans, and sweet corn, with hearty rolls made from the recent winter wheat harvest. It was rather tasty, and certainly better than what I had been eating while traveling here. "Blythad, I believe you have sold yourself short. You are a much finer cook than I am," I praised around a mouthful of soup.

"Thank you, but my skills have nothing on my mother. Now *she* knows how to cook! You can give her the most mismatched ingredients, and she will find a way to make a delicious meal out of it to feed my whole family and have some for the neighbors as well! I do not have her skill, but I know what tastes good to me— practically everything!" he laughed.

I laughed in spite of myself.

"Cooking is no different than spell creation," Nari opined sagely. "One merely needs to understand the ingredients and formulae. A *srukak* rune should not be used in ice spells, and it creates a very different effect when combined with *alsk* than with *bolmos*. The same can be said for culinary recipes—strawberries and onions do not work well together, but each combines well with the right cheese."[2]

"I had not considered it like that. I shall have to try that philosophy when I return to Vletraka. Certainly, I could not create anything worse than I already have!" I half-joked.

When dinner finished, I retired to Blythad's room to rest, and was sound asleep before he returned, not waking until after dawn.

"You really were exhausted, huh?" asked Blythad, who was lying facedown on his bed, his chin resting on his fists over his spell-book.

"As I said, the outdoor life does not suit me," I yawned. "I suppose that the comfort of walls and a ceiling allowed me to relax

---

[2] For those not familiar with rune lore or the language of dragons, *srukak* is a basic fire rune, *alsk* focuses energy in a tight beam, and *bolmos* creates a wide dispersal of magical energy. Combined, *srukak* and *alsk* create a lancing jet of flame, while *srukak* and *bolmos* manifest as an explosive fireball.

more deeply, as I had no expectation of something waking me up by gnawing on me during the night."

"I was feeling a little peckish, but I controlled myself," he laughed. "We should be leaving soon. It's only a couple of miles to the caves, so a *hivliuose* really isn't necessary."

I massaged my backside. "Now *that* I am glad to hear!"

Blythad laughed harder yet. "The weather looks clear today. I suggest we gather the henbane and blueberries today, and head to the caves tomorrow. The amethysts are difficult to find, and we should allocate more time for them," he suggested.

"That makes sense to me. You know the territory, so I shall follow your lead."

I studied a mix of offensive, defensive, and divination spells to aid our search. In most cases, it is wisest to have a combination of combat and utilitarian magicks available, as situations can change quickly. When just doing research and studying at home, there is little call for offensive spells unless I am practicing combat maneuvers. Defensive spells are always handy, particularly in case of accidents in the alchemy laboratory. Many a mage has been saved by a timely spell to shield one's self from energy or even physical attacks when the wrong reagents were mixed.

Before leaving, we had some gruel topped with grapes and a touch of treacle, hearty and sweet, and took some stale rolls and apricots for later. Blythad talked for nearly the entire journey, about what, I often had no idea. Though he was friendly and jovial, he quickly became irritating, regaling me with stories of his family and friends back at his home village before being discovered by Nari. Fortunately, we reached the clearing where the henbane was likely to be found before I told him to stifle himself. I was his guest after all, and it would not do to alienate myself from my host.

"I see the blueberry bushes over there. I'll start on those while you get the henbane," Blythad suggested.

He will probably eat half the berries he picks, I thought rudely, *while I search for the poisonous henbane.*

I do not know exactly why henbane is named the way it is. I suppose chickens are likely to eat the small, grey seeds out of the purple-veined, yellow flowers and become ill from the toxicity. That is reason enough to keep the plant away from livestock. When prepared properly, by boiling the leaves, roots, and seeds, henbane can be crushed into a poultice, which speeds the healing process and reduces fevers. Inhaling the fumes while it boils, however, can cause mild hallucinations, so it is best to wrap a cloth around the mouth and nose while working with it.

The soft broad leaves at the plant's base prevent other plants from growing too closely, making the yellow and purple flowers easier to spot, though the plant itself has a heavy, pungent odor, and is almost as easy to find with one's nose as with the eyes. I pulled a small sack out of my pack, and began harvesting the henbane, making sure to get as many of the roots as possible. Were I traveling more quickly, I would have dug the dirt up with them for transplanting back home, but even with preservation spells, they would not likely survive the journey.

So caught up in my work was I, that I did not realize I was being surrounded until they were too close to run from. *It is midday, so of course Thessylia is asleep. 'Wake up! I might need you!'* I commanded telepathically. Looking around, I spotted five brezzes stalking me through the tall grass. If I did not take initiative soon, this would be the end for me.

Brezzes are strong, durable humanoids, somewhat porcine in appearance, with wide, round, flat noses, beady eyes, and pointed ears, though their olive-green skin detracts from any comparison to normal pigs. Their brute strength and limited intellect make them excellent soldiers, whether for their tribe or a strong leader of another race. I could not fight them directly—a single blow from one of them with their wide, curved swords, would likely bring me down. I pretended to ignore them and continued my harvesting until they got closer, Thessylia aiding my eyes.

"Five brezzes against a single, unarmed human?" I questioned loudly. "I thought you had more courage than that." I straightened up, looking the closest one in the eye. "And attacking a child no less. Pitiful," I said, shaking my head scornfully.

"You dare insult us?" the lead one growled, spit flying through jagged teeth.

"Look at me." I spread my arms out, displaying my short, thin frame, wrapped in midnight blue robes with leather sandals on my feet. "Do I seriously look like a challenge for five mighty brezzes? I am young, alone, and without weapons, and it takes *five* of you to attack me? I grew up on stories of the mighty brez empires, which raided cities and devastated the countryside. Is this how they did it, by ganging up on *children*?" my words dripping venomously. "Which of you is the strongest one here? I will only confront him."

"I am strongest," spoke two of them quickly.

"I lead this group," spoke a third. They glared at each other and bristled.

"But I am strongest. *I* should be leader!" one of the first two spoke again.

"You would have to defeat me first. Strong you are, but I am better warrior," he nearly shouted in broken Umani, raising his heavy curved sword menacingly.

"Troj is leader, not you, Druk. Listen to Troj," the fourth growled at the second.

"Troj has us fighting children." He pointed at me with his dalbak sword. "Him coward!" he shouted, pointing his blade back at Troj. At that, a general melee ensued amongst the brezzes, Troj and his supporter against the other three, though the first two sparred against each other as well.

I slipped out of the fight, ignored by the angry brutes and watched the carnage until only Druk was standing.

"Druk is mightiest!" he shouted to the world.

"Druk is a fool," I sneered, casting *ajilek*. Two bolts of blue-black energy, vaguely skull-shaped, launched from my fingertips, pelting the injured brez in the chest. He fell like a stone. *I... I just killed a brez.* I had killed chickens for food, but never something humanoid. True, my life was at stake, but I suddenly felt foul. Seconds later, Blythad came up to my side.

"I heard the commotion, and got here as quickly as I could," he wheezed, his hands on his knees. After a couple of breaths, he looked around. "Five brezzes! You killed five brezzes?! By yourself?" He stared at me with a mixture of awe and fear.

"I hate to be disturbed in my work," I growled. "And look, they stomped all over some good henbane." I kicked Troj's head, which bent at an obscene angle from the gash in his neck. "I think we are done here for today," I spat, turning my back on the slaughter, not waiting for Blythad to follow, hiding the fact that I was disgusted with myself.

He ran up quickly. "How did you do it? What spells did you use? How are you not injured? Five brezzes! Amazing!" he prattled on.

I knew that if I did not give him some answers soon, he would continue on the whole trip back. "Brezzes are dull, brutish creatures. They fear magic, and a strong wizard can use that to his advantage. Stay away from their swords and let their stupidity do much of the work for you," I answered cryptically. "Remember, you are a wizard, and you cannot be a wizard unless you are intelligent. When dealing with lesser beings such as these, your intellect is your strongest weapon."

We marched on toward Nari's tower; Blythad digging for details the entire way.

I kept silent as long as I was able, but his relentless barrage finally caused me to shout at him. "Enough! Fine, seeing as you are *so* interested that you cannot stop pestering me for a single moment, I shall give you the details. I told the brezzes that I would only fight the mightiest of them, and they fell upon each other to prove which one that was. I killed the last remaining one with a simple *ajilek*. No grand battle; no powerful castings. As I said earlier, I used their dullness against them. Had you looked more closely at the scene of the battle; you could have deduced this for yourself rather than hound me all this time. Now, let…it…go," I growled.

He was silent after that.

Once I calmed down, I felt decidedly uncivil, and needed peace between us if I was to stay under his roof for another two nights. "Blythad," I sighed.

"Are you going to snap at me again?"

I sighed once more. "I apologize for that. I did not want to talk about it just then, but you kept asking, and I lost my temper. Have you ever killed?"

"You mean, like monsters? No, just bugs and things. I hit a rat with a *klivevalsk* once."[3]

"No humanoids? Brez? Pragun? Raquoli, even?"

He shook his head to the negative.

"Could you?"

"If I had to," he answered quickly, but doubtfully.

"It is not... a pleasant experience. It was my life or his, but I take no pleasure in it." I shuddered, holding back my sudden urge to vomit. I have been growing accustomed to working with corpses, as necromancers are wont to do, but I never did the killing before; it is not something Vletraka ever taught me.

He looked at me strangely, as though looking past me. "Nari tells me that I need to figure more things out for myself than to keep asking her for answers. I guess she's right. I figure that she already knows these things, so why shouldn't she just tell me, but she isn't always here to answer me, and you... are less tolerant of my inquisitions than she." He smiled weakly. "I am sorry that I was such a bother. Alone with Nari, I haven't much opportunity to make friends, and I hate to think that I ruined that already. You are alone with Vletraka, so I know you understand."

I paused before answering. "The difference between you and me is that I do not crave the company of others, quite the opposite in fact. I am... uncomfortable around others, preferring the solace of my studies to social interactions. Also, unlike you, I have few happy memories of my life before Vletraka, thus decreasing my need to be surrounded by my peers."

"You don't like people?" he asked, surprise clear on his face.

"There have been far too few that have been worth the effort to know, and even more that I wish I had never encountered."

He stopped in his tracks. "Me?" His eyes began to water.

---

[3] *Klivevalsk* is another common myzling, which invokes a thin beam of pure cold. It does not cause much damage, but is perfectly capable of killing small creatures.

This is what happens when you feel the need to have people around you. You get emotionally tied and lose your focus. "No, not you. You are an intelligent and pleasant person. Perhaps too talkative for my taste, but you do not inspire me to cause you harm. This has been a trying day, and I am looking forward to some peaceful time to settle my thoughts; do not take it as a dismissal."

"Okay," he responded glumly.

Thankfully, we walked the rest of the way back to Nari's tower in silence.

I wish Vletraka were here. I really need to talk to her. Her combat training served me well and kept me alive, but we never discussed how it would feel to kill.

When we returned home, I set my sack of herbs down in the kitchen and turned back to go outside. Blythad began to ask where I was headed, but stopped himself, remembering my need to be alone. I sat on the grass near the edge of Nari's fence and stared off into the trees beyond, my thoughts drifting to and fro, always returning to the scene of carnage that I instigated. *No, it is not* my *fault! They came for me. I only did what I had to in order to survive. So why do I feel like so much cow dung?*

I jumped when I felt a hand on my shoulder. So lost in my thoughts was I that I never sensed Nari's approach.

"Blythad told me what happened. Do you need to talk about it?"

I turned to tell her that I was fine, but all that came out was tears.

She dropped to her knees and hugged me tightly. "I know. It's hard. It's something we can never really prepare our students for. We teach you combat magic to protect you, but we cannot ready you for the consequences." She squeezed me tighter while I shuddered.

So hard, in fact, that I could not push her away when I vomited all over the both of us. Yet, she would not let go until I fell limp in her arms.

"Come. Let's go back inside." She aided me to my feet and walked me to the kitchen. She placed a mug in front of me and stripped my robes off; I offered no resistance. She disappeared for a few minutes, or hours—the passing of time meant nothing to me at that point—returning with fresh linens. "Drink," she commanded, and I obeyed numbly.

I expected water, but the flavor was much stronger than that. I spit it back out into the mug and looked at her in confusion.

"The taste is strong, but it will help you sleep."

"What is it?"

"Grommoldi copper brandy."

I pushed the mug away. "No. No alcohol. A wizard must keep his senses about him."

"Don't quote Revance's *A Philosophy of Magic* to me. This is not the time for his arrogance."

"Still, I must deal with this, not hide from it." I managed to rise from my chair and drift over to the room I was sharing with Blythad, never noticing that I had not bothered to put on the fresh robe Nari brought for me. Blythad was sitting on his bed, and shortly after I stumbled in, he quietly left. I do not remember falling asleep, but I do remember waking up in a silent scream, having been chased by Troj and his slaughtered crew, his nearly severed head bouncing off his shoulder, holding two crossed curved blades—one vertical and one horizontal. I gasped for breath, and then relaxed when I realized that it was but a dream. "I have to let this go," I told myself in a whisper, "else those brutes may have just as well killed me." I began to do my breathing exercises to calm my emotions, and was surprised when Blythad nudged me.

"It's late morning. Are you up to going to the caves, or do you need more time?" he asked gently.

My stomach decided to answer for me. "I suppose I need to eat something first," I smiled weakly.

He returned my smile and nodded, turning back out the door.

I first went outside to relieve myself before dragging myself into the kitchen, where a plate of thin, crisp breads and an apple awaited me.

"I thought that you might want to eat something light," Nari opined cautiously. "How do you feel this morning?"

"I am… recovering. I believe it will take some time before my heart is settled on the matter, but I feel as though I can function today. We still need to gather the amethysts and guano for Mistress Vletraka, and I need to get the henbane home before it rots."

"Are you certain? An extra day will not hurt…"

"No," I interrupted. "No offense, but I really want to go home. However, I cannot go until I finish my tasks."

She gave me a weak smile. "I understand."

Blythad and I set out for the caves shortly thereafter.

Though I know better, I had very little awareness of my surroundings.

'I am puzzled. If one cannot escape a predator, one should try to kill it. Why are you upset?' asked Thessylia.

'Humans have rules about killing. We are not supposed to kill if there are other options to escape a dangerous situation.'

'Did you break those rules?'

'I convinced the brezzes to kill each other then killed the last one standing. I should have found a better way to resolve the situation.'

'They were going to kill you, yes? Surrounded, you could not flee. Killing the enemy was the best solution.'

'Perhaps, but I did not enjoy killing them. I was angry and frightened, and I lashed out with my magic. I had never killed before.'

'Only the cruel take joy in killing—like cats. Killing is for food and survival. You survived.'

I cannot believe I am being lectured on morality by an owl. *'I suppose you are right. Thank you.'*

Thessylia then punctuated her speech by landing on a field mouse. I felt no joy from her for the kill, only from the eating.

As Blythad and I entered the cave—Thessylia perching outside to sleep—he pulled out a pair of stones, which shone like full moons. "Nari made these a while ago. They are not especially bright but give enough light to see by without the smoke of torches or a lantern."

"Useful. I suppose I should have asked this sooner, but are there any dangers in this cave?"

"Unlikely, though I suppose anything could have wandered in here." His voice dropped to a whisper. "We should keep quiet, so as not to disturb the bats."

"Understood."

Though Vletraka had Quesel, I suppose he does not produce enough guano on his own for her needs. We carefully moved through the cave and soon came upon a large cavern. The stench was overwhelming, and we wrapped cloths around our faces to filter out some of the smell, though it did not prevent our eyes from burning. Blythad placed the softly glowing stone in the palm of his hand and turned it upside-down so that the light shone downward then suggested that I do the same. We set down our small tin boxes and gently, quietly scooped up the bat excretions until we had filled three tins each. Every now and then, a bat or two dropped down and fluttered around us to see if we intended any harm. They must have decided that we were no threat, as they did not swarm us.

When we finished, we moved cautiously to the other side of the cavern to delve deeper into the cave. The tunnel split a few times, and Blythad showed me the markings on the walls denoting the correct path to the amethyst mine.

"They are around here," my guide said, keeping his voice barely above a whisper. "We should spread out to cover more ground."

We used our glowing rocks to look for sparkling in the stone, though not everything that glittered were the crystals we sought. It took hours, I think, as we stopped for lunch at one point, to find and extract enough amethysts to fill the small sack. Taken to a gem-cutter or a jeweler, the stones would have a decent market value, but I am sure she is intending to use them for research purposes. Amethysts are known to heighten and awaken both the intellect and the spirit, and are useful for focusing raw energy; extremely useful for such a common crystal. I believe that it is due to their lack of rarity that so many must be used in conjunction to show a demonstrable effect.

We turned to leave the cave when I noticed a pile of rocks that I did not recall seeing before. As I looked, a pair of wide-set beady eyes became visible as the rock closest to me slowly turned, looking toward first myself, then Blythad. "Blythad?" I queried cautiously, attempting to get his attention. "That is alive, is it not?" I pointed to the slowly shifting rocks.

"Oh, crap…" he said slowly, managing not to raise his voice. "It's a stone lizard. They are faster than you would think, and extremely toxic." As he spoke, the rocks, now clearly lizard-shaped, began to race toward him. "Ahh!" he screamed as it tried to bite him, dancing away from its jaws.

Ajiavulhysayt! I moved to defend myself, calling forth a barrier of force magic to surround my vitals, before taking an offensive stance. It snapped again at Blythad as he tried to call a *bezyamhysa* spell forth to shield himself but lost his concentration as it continued to attack. I cast an *ajilek* spell instinctively, and suddenly felt the same revulsion from it as yesterday, weakening the missiles so that they caused little harm to the lizard. It was enough, however, to draw its attention away from Blythad to me. While I moved to avoid the creature's jaws, a bolt of acid pierced its side, dissolving through the stony flesh and causing it to hiss in pain. The distraction was enough to allow me to summon the energy for a *klivivvad* spell, causing my hand to be surrounded with a pale blue aura, which would steal the heat and strength away from the stone lizard. Though I would rather fight it from a distance, the creature was not giving me that option at the moment.

As I reached down to touch it, it clamped its jaws around my leg, piercing the *ajiavulhysayt* and digging its teeth into my thigh. My leg felt as if on fire, and I remembered Blythad's warning of the stone lizard's poison. I swatted it on the head, draining some of its life force with the *klivivvad* while Blythad's acid continued to burn into the lizard. Suddenly, a second lizard, this one glowing dimly, appeared and attacked the stone lizard, biting its tail. The stone lizard let go of my leg and turned on the new foe, affording me the opportunity to drain it once again before my leg went numb and dropped out from under me, causing me to fall to the hard cave floor.

Our foe easily grabbed the second lizard, which vanished in a puff of smoke as the powerful jaws clamped down on it. As it did, a large dog, again dimly glowing, appeared and pounced upon the stone lizard's back, clamping its jaws around the lizard's rough-scaled neck. It squirmed and circled, attempting to dislodge the new attacker to no avail, while another bolt of acid hit it squarely between the eyes. The lizard slowed, then stopped completely, twitching once as the faintly glowing canine shook its head, the lizard's neck cracking audibly. The dog let go, then faded out of existence.

I squirmed out of my backpack and began to rifle through it when Blythad came to my side.

"Here, let me help you up." He began to tug when I stopped him.

"No, I need to get this first." I pulled out the one-berry leaves I had picked on my way to Nari's tower out of the outer pocket on my pack and wrapped a few of them around the wound. It is not the proper procedure, but I did not have time to crush them down into a poultice. "This will have to hold until we get out of here. Summoning those creatures was a good idea. Well done," I groaned. Though I wanted to stay down on the cool cave floor, I let Blythad pull me to my feet, and steadied myself against the wall. That is when I noticed that the plump boy, I had entered the cave with was thinner than I was. "Pardon me if this sounds rude, but where is the rest of you?"

He smiled weakly at me. "My 'gift'," he sighed. "I grow larger as I gather magical energy, and thinner as I expend it. I used a lot just now."

"Okay," I answered flatly, trying to comprehend through the spreading numbness. "How is that useful?"

"Well, aside from the change in appearance, I can store more energy than the average mage, allowing me to cast more spells. However, it does mean that I need to tuck up my suddenly loose-fitting clothes before I trip over them," he laughed. "Now let's get out of here." He held me as I limped out of the cave, half-dragging my poisoned leg. "We need to be careful not to disturb the bats," he fretted.

"I think I can take care of that." *Thessylia, would you mind flying into the cave and getting the attention of the bats there. Be careful not to let them swarm you. Get out as quickly as you can and lead them out.'*

'I can do that. Maybe I can catch one for a snack.

'Wait until their numbers thin first. I do not want you battered by thousands of bats and getting hurt on my account.'

'Very well.'

As we reached the cavern, some fluttering could be heard, and my head ached from the bats' screams echoing off the walls as they flew en-masse out of the cave. We limped out and as we entered the late-evening air, I felt the satisfaction of Thessylia making good on her plan to find a meal on the wing. We hobbled toward a tree where Blythad helped me slump down against the trunk. I pulled the leaves off my wound and saw that it was oozing a thick yellow fluid.

"Yeck!" Blythad cringed, turning away.

"No, this is good—it means that the poison is being extracted. I need you to crush these leaves and spread them over the wound." While he did so, I fumbled around the pocket where I found the leaves and pulled out three mostly intact berries and popped them into my mouth. I chewed quickly and swallowed the bitter fruit, rinsing with mouthfuls of water from our skins. Five minutes later, I vomited up the berries, which had turned yellow, proving that they had absorbed some of the poison. I bent and stretched my leg and discovered that I had feeling in it once again. "That should do it for now. I think I can walk back."

We stumbled back to Nari's home, with Blythad alternating between worry for me and excitedly retelling the battle we had together. By the time we returned, the sky had gone dark with the sunset and rain, soaking us to the bone.

Nari fretted over us, getting us dry clothes to change into by the fire and checking my wound every few minutes. The leaves had long since fallen off or washed away, but the wound had closed and was no longer seeping, though dark purple bruising was beginning to form around the area. "You two just cannot stay out of trouble, can you? Two battles in as many days—it's no wonder I am grey before my time!" she smiled wanly.

Neither of us wished to speculate on how long she had been grey, but Blythad's look told me she had not changed since he had become her pupil.

We ate quickly, with Blythad retelling our adventure and me correcting him when his story became too grandiose, then retired, falling asleep easily after the day's exertions. I found that it did not bother me to have killed the lizard, though I still felt some remorse over the brez. *Is it because the brez is humanoid? Because it is sentient? Both would have killed me without compunction, yet I only feel bad about the brez. And yet, the brez attacked out of malice, while the lizard from instinct. I should feel* better *about killing something malevolent more so than a base creature, not the other way around. Technically, Blythad killed the lizard, though we both had a hand in it. Revance would say that there is no difference, as both are lesser creatures than a wizard, but his philosophy is more than a bit skewed.*

I awoke refreshed, though my leg was still sore. The bruising nearly encompassed my whole thigh, which would make the ride back home on horseback that much more painful. Blythad prepared a large pot of porridge, which we drizzled with honey and young strawberries, and I ate my fill knowing that it was to be my last hot meal for three days, and that I would have to suffer my own cooking again after this. He and Nari packed my bag with fresh rolls, cheese, nuts, and apricots.

"I planted a few of your henbane in jars, since they still had roots attached," Nari informed me. "With luck, they will survive the journey and you can plant them in 'Traka's garden."

"Thank you! I was trying to figure out a way to keep them alive just for that purpose. I will be exceptionally careful with them. Also, thank you for your hospitality and for… comforting me after the… incident with the brezzes."

"Anytime. You are always welcome in our home. Perhaps we shall visit you next time."

"I look forward to it," I smiled, surprised that I truly meant it. We stepped outside where I conjured the first steed I would need for the day. Mounting the horse was even more painful than I had expected, but I managed to situate myself and rode off.

Chapter 4: Faldrein

It was a scant few months after meeting Nari and Blythad that I met two other wizards of our little circle: Beus and his apprentice Faldrein. The summer had come to a close, yet the heat of the long days continued to hamper my comfort. Through the spring, the building's stonework had kept us cool, but as the stones heated, they stayed hot, radiating their warmth inside our home, causing me to use the occasional freezing spell to create a patch of ice and cool things down again. I had also taken to wrapping a cloth around my forehead to prevent drops of sweat from falling upon my books. Vletraka, with her icy skin, enjoyed the extra warmth, and it seemed that there was no temperature at which we were both comfortable at the same time.

Oftentimes, I appreciated the heat most at night, for it made me uncomfortable enough that I slept lightly, preventing me from dreaming. This also had the side effect of increasing my acerbic nature, however, which combined with the heat of day made me downright unpleasant to be around, causing Vletraka to leave me notes with directions for my studies rather than be in my presence any longer than necessary. At first, I was annoyed that she ignored me, but it only took a stern look from her after one of my tirades for me to understand how I was acting, and I made a conscious effort to tie my tongue before speaking impulsively.

Overall, I found that taking my books outside was far more comfortable than sitting in the oven that was the library. Vletraka had placed a small wooden bench next to the pond, which sat at the southern part of her tree-bordered property. The gentle croaking of the occasional frog and the singing of birds created a musical backdrop to my studies, though I soon learned to return indoors before sunset, as the swarms of mosquitoes found me to be much to their liking! Their bloodthirsty nature did inspire the creation of a new spell however, one in which the target slowly bleeds through a tiny wound that will not heal without magical assistance or at the expiration of the spell; though not usually deadly, it does irritate and weaken a foe, and the annoyance of the bleeding has proven to distract other spell-casters enough to ease my victory.

A wise wizard never claims too much space—just enough to give a buffer between her home and the outer world in general. Too much land is difficult to defend against intruders; too little and one's home can be subjected to attacks from rivals without them stepping upon protected ground. From my vantage point, I could see hidden in the tall grass a few of the numerous skeletal hands which would animate and crawl on their bony fingertips toward intruders. I never asked Nari which protections she used, but judging by her proclivity for conjuration, I would guess that she had numerous portals set up for summoning elementals or denizens from further planes of existence.

Though I abhor undead, these animated claws carried no essence of their original owners, and were more akin to constructs than undead. The undead are the ones who escape the Dark Lady's grasp, either of their own free will or through various magicks, while constructs are mobile solely through magic and without spirit, generally at least. Greater constructs, such as golems, tend to have a rudimentary elemental spirit infused into their being, which is not the same as the soul of a living creature. Whether or not using elemental spirits is just as objectionable as enslaving living souls is still a matter of debate.[4] The claws are animated through manipulations of the Weave, and are no more than puppets, which follow a simple set of commands.

One other benefit of studying by the pond was having the opportunity to wade in and cool myself off. Typically, I would not stay in too long, as I cannot swim, and I did not wish to take too

---

[4] Please read *Animating Principles Differentiating Constructs from Undead* by Dalwren, pages 89-124 to understand his philosophy of the differences in types of spirits. Whether one spirit is "better" or more worthy of attention is still debated by scholars and philosophers, and the side of the debate is often influenced by the philosopher's own ego. The druids compound the argument further by including animal, plant, and mineral spirits, creating a livelier debate.

much time away from my studies; I had set a high bar early on with Vletraka, and she pushed me all the harder to learn because of it. The water was clean and safe to drink from, and I would bring out a large bowl to fill for Thessylia to bathe in and cool herself as well. Owls are extremely well insulated, retaining body heat to the point where she can sit on a branch in winter with a pile of snow collected on her head; no heat escapes through her feathers to melt it and she stays warm and dry. In the summer heat, however, she pants often to cool herself down, and wetting her feathers allows some of that heat to escape through evaporation. She would then sit on the back of the bench to preen while I studied.

I was reading *Quiet Focus*, a book of meditation and techniques to improve concentration by the monk Nara-qi. The first few exercises were the very same ones that Vletraka taught me the night I left my old family. The summer heat made the exercises more challenging, in that it was easy to drift off and nap rather than merely calm the mind. At one point, I found myself dreaming that I was watching a vole slowly inching its way through the tall grass. Suddenly, when I felt that I was certain to catch it unaware, I pounced upon it, my talons holding it in place while I snapped its neck with my beak.

My eyes popped open and I turned to see that Thessylia had done just as I had dreamed myself to be doing! I have often connected with her emotionally, particularly when she was excited or upset, but I have never seen through her eyes before.

'Did you sense me just now?' I asked her mentally, curiosity mixing with anxiety in my thoughts.

'You are right there. I always know where you are,' she returned, scooping up the vole and dropping it into her gullet.

'I mean, did you feel me in your mind, or heart, or however this works?'

She turned her head to look at me nearly upside-down. *'I do not understand.'*

'I was meditating, and I found myself looking through your eyes just now.'

'I did not notice. Can you do it again? I will pay closer attention this time.' She fluttered up to sit on the back of the bench next to me, watching with keen interest.

I returned to the meditation exercise and attempted to focus on her but could not make the connection. *'Perhaps I am concentrating too hard. It was purely happenstance that I did it before, and it may be something we must work on together.'*

She puffed up with excitement. *'Good! You spend too much time in your books. There is more to being a wizard than study.'*

My first reaction was shock and annoyance that she rebuked me so, but I realized that she was feeling neglected. It must be the empathic connection that we share, because I doubt that I would have come to that understanding so rapidly with anyone else. In fact, that has proven to be the case in every other instance. *'You are correct. I have not given you enough attention. Will this work the other way? Can you see through my eyes?'*

'A curious idea. Let me try.' She closed her bright yellow eyes and appeared to fall asleep, though I knew she was awake and alert. After a few minutes she opened her eyes. *'I cannot. As you said, perhaps with practice.'*

'I will ask Vletraka's advice. She might know some techniques to aid us. You should ask Quesel about how he strengthens his connection with her.' Though Thessylia is an owl and Quesel a bat, wizards' familiars are able to communicate with each other regardless of species. I have never understood completely why this should be, but I am certain it has to do with the heightened intelligence of a familiar over a typical animal.

'It's nearly sunset. He should be awake soon.'

Was it so late already? *'In that case, I will head indoors before I become nothing more than a blood bladder for the mosquitoes again!'* I gathered up my books and began to head back to the house when I heard a voice come from my left.

Without even giving a command, Thessylia flew off in that direction to see what the disturbance was. *'It appears to be a pair of wizards, one adult and one fledgling,'* she thought to me. *'Quesel is coming with a pair of amulets.'*

They must be guests then, as the amulets are Vletraka's token of safety through her property. I turned from the house to greet the newcomers as they ambled down the path to our home. "Greetings, my lords, and welcome. Who do we have the honor of hosting this eve?" I called out to our guests with a smile to hide my frustration of their intrusion.

They turned to me, startled by my appearance. One benefit of being built small and unassuming like my Mother is that I am easily overlooked unless I want to be seen. Working with an owl has also taught me how better to be silent and observant, allowing me to assess someone before I am brought to his or her attention. Both men wore yellow-grey robes, akin to the color of sandstone, though the elder of the two had black striping down the sleeves. The older one had short dark hair and was clean-shaven, while his junior sported an unkempt mop of blond hair. As Thessylia landed on my shoulder, they both smiled at me, apparently genuinely pleased.

"Greetings," called the elder to me, "I am Beus of the Final Path. This is my apprentice Faldrein. It is a pleasure to meet you, and we thank you for your hospitality."

"Very good, sirs. Welcome to the home of Vletraka of the Alabaster Moon. I am her apprentice Mithron. If you would please follow me," I requested, following the rote protocol of invitation and led them to and through the door, where Vletraka was awaiting her guests.

She smiled widely and stepped forward to give Beus a long hug as he dropped his pack on the floor. "Beus, it's good to see you again," she chimed, her ebon eyes bright and warm. "I see that you've met Mithron; I take it that this is your apprentice?"

"Vletraka, may I present Faldrein?"

"A pleasure to meet you, my Lady," Faldrein bowed.

"Welcome! Come, sit with me. Mithron, would you bring us some refreshments?"

"Of course, my Lady," I smiled to her and left for the small kitchen.

I put a pot of water in the fireplace and lit a small fire to heat it, letting out a quiet sigh as I did so. *With luck, they will not stay long.*

When it was ready, I steeped mint and rosemary in the pot for a few moments to make a light summer tea. In the meantime, I cut a small wheel of cheese into cubes and, along with some fresh berries and a loaf of crusty bread, piled them on a plate. When the tea had steeped, I cast *klivevalsk* on three mugs to freeze them before pouring the tea, causing the steaming brew to cool rapidly without it actually freezing; Vletraka always drinks hers hot. I first brought out the tray and two mugs for our guests, placing them on the small rectangular wooden table surrounded by the divan and chairs, then went back to the kitchen for the other pair of mugs.

When I returned, Vletraka and Beus were chatting amiably about the joys of teaching; it pleased me to hear that my temper issues of late had not diminished her happiness. I handed her the mug of hot tea and took my place standing behind her chair.

"These are friends, Mithron, please sit with us," she commanded cheerfully.

Unless otherwise told to do so, an apprentice's place is to stand and be ready to serve, either through fetching objects or guarding his Mistress. "Yes, my Lady." I sat on the divan next to Faldrein, as Beus and Vletraka had each taken the soft, padded chairs.

"What were you doing outside?" asked Beus genially. "I would have expected 'Traka to have you chained to a table in the library surrounded by books of magical theory!" he said with a laugh.

"Were it not for the heat, I would gladly place myself in that position," I smiled seriously. "I grew weary of dripping into the tomes, and it is somewhat cooler outside. I was just coming inside when you arrived."

"Then our timing was impeccable," he laughed again. "Tell me, what were you studying when we came by?"

"I was practicing some of the techniques in *Quiet Focus*. My Lady," I turned to Vletraka, "do you ever see through Quesel's eyes? I am not certain how it happened with Thessylia, and I am unsure how to replicate the experience."

"You gazed through her eyes?" both adults yelped at once, turned toward each other, then back to me.

I was taken aback. "Did I do something wrong?"

Vletraka responded with a wide smile while Beus looked at me with curiosity. Faldrein appeared as clueless as I.

"This is a wonderful gift!" my Mistress beamed at me. "Few wizards bond so closely as to be able to use each others' senses; especially not at your age."

And here Thessylia was commenting on how little attention I have been paying her! I could not help but smile. "It only happened just the once. I do not know how to do it again," I shrugged, the smile disappearing. "I take it that you and Quesel do not share this bond." I looked over at Beus, and realized that I had not seen any creatures with our visitors.

Before I could ask, Beus held up his hand, showing his gold-braided ring before my eyes. "Not all wizards bond with an animal. This ring is imbued with part of my essence, as Faldrein has done with his necklace."

Shifting my vision slightly, I could see the Weave tightly woven around the two objects he mentioned.

He continued, "Some more powerful wizards have been known to bond to demons or even dragons. There is a story I heard once about a human wizard and a small dragon each going through the summoning ritual simultaneously and taking each other as a familiar!" he laughed.

"Their bond must have been extraordinary," I said seriously, not understanding the humor.

"It was, and fortunately, for them at least, they were of a similar personality. They were both practical jokers, you see, and no one was safe from their pranks, especially not their friends!" he continued to laugh.

I smiled at his joviality but had no idea why he laughed so hard. Perhaps he was leaving out some details about their bond; what did it matter if their friends were involved? While I contemplated, I realized that all three had begun laughing, and that Beus was telling a ribald tale of the wizard/dragon pair visiting a house of ill repute with a bag of turnips. I laughed along with them, though I was not following the story.

"Mithron," Vletraka turned to me wiping away tears of mirth, "why don't you show Faldrein around? Our guests will be staying for a few nights, and Beus has been here before."

"Of course, My Lady." Faldrein and I stood at the same time. I turned to him, bowed my head slightly, and said, "Come along." We first went to the front door to grab their travelling packs, and then I showed him the guest quarters, where he and Beus would be staying, so we did not have to carry them around. I then took him to the library, including going up the wrought iron spiral staircase, which climbs to the roof, then to our rooms and the laboratory. Faldrein was quiet throughout the tour. "The kitchen is off the study, but you have already seen me come and go there. Please help yourself if you are in need of anything," I told him as we left the alchemical lab.

"You are not as I expected," he finally spoke quietly.

"How so?" I asked with some trepidation. *We have just met; how can he form any judgments about me?* I wondered.

"I had always heard stories of necromancers being cruel and evil beings, yet you seem normal enough. Beus and I both revere the Dark Lady, and she grants us a portion of her power so long as we maintain the separation between the living and the dead; necromancers, so I have been led to believe, blur that line as a matter of course. When Master Beus told me that we were visiting a necromancer friend of his, I began to worry for him."

I could not help but smile. "I told Mistress Vletraka much the same thing when we first met! She was nice to me, and friends with a woman I trusted implicitly, so I accepted her at face value. That, and she rescued me from the life of a blacksmith," I flexed to show how incongruous the idea was, my robes hanging loosely from my skinny arms. "You can see that I would have been a master craftsman!" I smiled wryly, earning a chuckle from my companion. "If it helps, I believe we share the same philosophy: the living should go about living, and the dead should stay dead; they have no business walking about stealing the lives of the living."

"Then let us begin anew." He stuck out his hand and said with formality, "I am Faldrein, apprentice to Beus of the Final Path. It is a pleasure to meet you."

I took him by the wrist, allowing him to grab mine and said with the same grave decorum, "I am Mithron, apprentice to Vletraka of the Alabaster Moon. It is a pleasure to meet you." We shook hands once and bowed our heads slightly, then broke into smiles. "Now that you know that I am not going to drain your essence while you sleep, would you care for more tea?"

"Absolutely! Mint and rosemary, I believe, was it not?"

"Very astute! Beus has you tending garden and cooking as well, I take it," I smiled. Working in the garden always reminded me of my time with Yoffa, and I have used her gift well. Though I am loath to admit it, my time in the smithy taught me how to maintain the blade of the sickle, which was part of her gift, forcing me to appreciate something about my father.

Faldrein gave a sigh. "I was hoping to spend more time aiding others, rather than doing all this drudge work. I get far too dirty in the garden, and I even seem to get dirty in the kitchen! Beus is teaching me magic, both arcane and divine, but I feel that my time is wasted on these mundane pursuits."

"I feel much the same way oft times. I feel that Vletraka would be better off not letting me near the kitchen. I am certain she has lost weight since taking me on, and she was thin already when we met. If I remain her apprentice much longer, I fear that she will be lost with the next strong wind!" I laughed. "Have you met Nari and Blythad yet?"

He shook his head in the negative.

"Nari told me that cooking is like spell creation, and that it is all a matter of combining the right ingredients in the right proportion. If you combine the wrong runes or materials, or incant improperly, the spell will be ruined. Mix the wrong items in a soup, and it becomes inedible."

He nodded sagely. "I suppose that makes sense, though I don't relish experimenting in the kitchen—I have not yet learned how to eliminate poisons yet!" he chuckled.

I thought back to some of my earlier attempts in the kitchen and shuddered. "You said you are learning both arcane *and* divine magicks? That is amazing! How do you handle two separate sources of power, or are you able to combine them somehow? Of course, I have read about the gods, their stories, and how each demands worship, but I do not believe they are interested in my life, and I do not feel especially drawn to theirs; except perhaps the Dark Lady, but as a necromancer I suppose that is a given, though it would be more likely that most necromancers would follow her former consort Coruld, as he rules over the undead."

Faldrein flinched as I spoke the name of the Dread King. "That, exactly, was my concern when Beus spoke of coming here," he said with a shudder. "It's said that the Dark Lady and the Dread King ruled over the lands of the dead side by side, keeping watch over the souls until one of the other gods, or their representatives, came to collect those that belonged to them. While the Dark Lady cared for the souls, particularly those that remained unclaimed, her Consort had greater ambitions, returning some to the land of the living in order to swell the ranks of the dead.

"When the Dark Lady learned of this, she cast him out of her realm, and it is said that he now resides in the deepest parts of the Shadow where it touches the Plane of Negative Energy where all of creation is destroyed; life is drained away, fire turns to ash, earth to dust, and so on. From here, he grants his foul minions with a conduit to the negative energy in order to hasten the death of those they encounter.

"The Dark Lady, however, holds the balance between life and death to be sacred. All that lives will eventually die, though life should be maintained for as long as prudent. It is neither wise to force death upon another, save to survive, nor to put off a natural death if the body cannot be brought back to a healthy state. There are many who fear Her embrace, and cling to life longer than their body can sustain it, while others fear living just as much and hasten their departure from this realm—neither of these paths are acceptable. She commands that we live our lives until we die, helping those who should live to live, and assisting those who are ready to pass on to die comfortably."

"How does one determine who should live and who should not?" I asked, my throat dry as visions of dead brezzes filled my mind.

He paused. "Generally, those who do not seek to take the lives of others should continue to live, while those seeking to end the lives of others should have their own lives taken. I think Beus could give you a better explanation; he keeps telling me to 'follow my heart to determine the correct course of action', which is far from definitive."

I hesitated before asking my next question in fear of his response. "Have you ever... taken a life?"

"No, of course not," he said with disgust, followed quickly by a sigh. "I know there are a number of creatures out there that would happily kill me for a meal, and some that would kill me for the mere joy of doing so, and I am ready to defend myself if necessary. But no, I haven't killed anything, though I still fear my cooking may someday!" he grinned as we walked into the kitchen.

The kettle sat over the glowing coals; steam still seeping from the spout. I again cast *klivevalsk* to chill our mugs and refilled them with the last of the tea. The nice things about minor magicks like *klivevalsk* is that they require little energy to cast, and can be reused time and again, while more powerful spells, even ones as rudimentary as *ajilek*, use enough magical force to clear out the energy needed to cast the spell until prepared again. I then refilled the kettle with water and dropped in some fresh herbs, should anyone want more tea, and placed it back above the coals.

Placing another log in the fireplace, I asked Faldrein over my shoulder, "Would you let our Masters know that there is more tea brewing?" while poking the coals to produce a flame. When I heard the door close, I released a breath I did not realize I was holding. *He did not ask,* I sighed in gratitude. *I do not wish to lie to him, but I have no desire for him to know what I have done either.*

Faldrein reappeared with two mugs, setting down one at a time. "Beus," he said with the first, then "Vel...Val..." he fumbled, his cheeks reddening in embarrassment.

"Vletraka," I answered for him. "Vle-tra-ka," I said again, stretching the syllables out. "It took me some time to get that first syllable correct, so do not feel bad," I smiled. "I suppose that is why

Beus and Nari refer to her as "'Traka'. 'My Lady' or 'Mistress' are not only polite ways to address her, but also avoid that very issue!"

Faldrein sighed in relief. "Bay-oos is so much easier to pronounce!" he chuckled. "I know we took on new names for a reason, but must so many be so difficult to pronounce?"

"If it keeps others from discovering our true names, then I suppose so! Although, 'Mithron' is easy enough; perhaps I will change to something more challenging as I become more powerful, something out of old Draconic, mayhap."

"Then people will think your name is a spell!" he laughed. "Let the dragons use Draconic for their names, while we use their runes for magic. You wouldn't want to insult any dragons by using their names, would you?"

"Good idea! I shall stick to 'Mithron' then." As we laughed, the kettle began to whistle. I froze Beus's mug and poured the tea. We each grabbed our Master's mug and headed back into the next room where our teachers continued to chat.

A sip from her steaming mug later, Vletraka smiled up at me and said, "Excellent as ever. Sit."

Faldrein and I took our places on the divan when Beus spoke to me gravely. "'Traka tells me that you have been having difficulty sleeping at night; that you are having nightmares. Tell me about them."

I turned to look at Vletraka, and I am certain that the hurt I felt was clear on my face. "Why would you tell him about that?" I asked between clenched teeth, my voice scarcely above a whisper. Before I realized what I was doing, my body acted of its own accord. "My pain is my own, and I do not wish to discuss it with strangers, or even at all." I stormed out of the sitting area and went to my room, slamming the door behind me.

She might have called "Wait!" as I stomped out, but I was too lost in my own thoughts to be certain. I fumed as I plopped onto my bed.

How could she? She knows what I have done, what I have had to do. And now she tells some perfect stranger about my crime? It is none of his concern.

Dear gods, now Faldrein will know too. There goes any possibility of a friendship with him! I threw my hands up in the air and let out a groan. *What is the point of trying to make friends anyway? Once they find out what kind of a person I truly am, they will leave me, ridicule me, or attack me. I do not deserve to live after what I have done, and everyone else will see that too. It would be better if I just left. Vletraka could find another apprentice, and if I am lucky, some monstrous creature will eat me and put me out of my misery.*

A light knocking on my door broke my self-indulgent reverie.

"Leave me be," I growled with no attempt to disguise my rage.

Ignoring my command, Beus entered my room, closed the door behind him, and sat down next to me.

Until now, I have never felt the need to have a lock on my door, as Vletraka and I respect each other's privacy. "What in the Nine Pits do you want?" I snarled, venom dripping off every word.

"'Traka asked me to help you," he said calmly, ignoring the rage I had directed toward him, and thereby fueling it.

"I require neither your help, nor the help of anyone else. I can deal with a few bad dreams on my own. What I cannot deal with is rude, inconsiderate louts barging into my room and acting as though they have a right to be there." I stood and pointed at my door. "Get. Out."

Never moving, he looked up at me and said, "I understand how you feel, and have been through the same thing you have. Eventually, wizards must do battle in this dangerous world, and some foes will only stop when slain. Death is a part of life, and sometimes we must kill to survive. The fact that this bothers you so much shows that you have a good heart." He smiled at me then, which made me want to hurt him more. "Tell me about your nightmares."

I smiled beatifically. "Your words have touched me, and you have shown me the error of my rage. I have this recurring dream of some stranger coming into my room, acting like a kindly uncle, not that I ever had one of those, and pushes me to tell him my darkest secrets," the scowl returning to my face. "He tells me that I can trust him, after all, he is a friend of someone I admire, and assumes that a tenuous connection like that is enough for me to open my black, rotting heart. He does not realize that I do not wish to tell him, nor anyone else, about the agony I live through each waking and resting moment, and that it is nothing of his concern." I turned my back to him, staring at the wall through my unbidden tears.

"Perhaps a stranger is just who you need to unburden yourself to. Unless you let go of that pain, it will eventually destroy you."

"Then let it be quick about it then. It is no less than I deserve!"

"That is completely untrue. 'Traka told me about the incident with the brezzes. Few wizards your age would have survived against those murdering brutes, and your actions were in self-defense. You have every right to protect yourself against those that would cause you harm. 'Those who seek to steal the life of others shall have their own lives forfeit in the eyes of the Dark Lady.' You did nothing wrong."

I spun to face him, unaware of the tears streaming down my cheeks. "Then why does it hurt so much? If my actions were correct, why do they haunt me? Why does the rock lizard watch impassively while I flee from Troj and his band?" His look became quizzical at the mention of the lizard, and it became clear that Vletraka had not mentioned it to him. I stepped hard over to my desk and grabbed my sketchpad, flinging the fluttering pages at my intruder. "Here. Here are my nightmares."

Beus spent a long time looking over my drawings while I glared at him, wishing that he would leave. He flipped back and forth through many of the sketches, as if comparing their details, eventually speaking while still examining my work. "First of all, you have a great artistic talent. If you decide to quit studying magic, I know a fellow in Arquel that would be able to tutor you in developing it further."

I sniffed from a runny nose but refused to thank him for his kind words.

"Secondly, I want to remind you that I truly do understand your pain. I felt much as you do now after my first time killing a foe. Three pragun charged at me and my friends, their long, pointed daggers aiming to skewer us. I quickly cast *aatokytsrukak* before the little wide-mouthed monsters could attack, the sheet of flames bursting from my fingertips incinerated them; their charred corpses landed at my feet. Even today, I can still smell them, and it nauseates me. My friends clapped me on the back and told me what a hero I was for stopping them before any of us could get hurt. I knew that I had saved our lives, but I took no pleasure in it.

"I'm not going to tell you to get used to it—by the Pits, I hope you never get used to killing—but the pain does fade in time. So long as you only do it when necessary as a last resort, and when your opponent is willing to kill you, then you absolutely have the right to protect yourself and your friends."

I responded with something between a sigh and a shudder. I could feel a new batch of tears welling up, but I refused to show them to him, determined to stay angry though my rage had passed. Fortunately, he looked back down at my drawings, affording me the opportunity to wipe away some of the tears with my thumbs before they began to flow.

"I've noticed these crossed swords in a number of your drawings," he continued, pointing at one of the images on his lap.

"Troj's curved blades," I answered flatly. "Honestly, I do not know why I always dream of him with a pair of blades, for he only used one when… when…"

"When you killed him?" Beus finished for me.

"No, when he attacked me," I growled, my anger flaring once again. "It was Druk that I killed." Suddenly, I felt nauseous, and I sat down on the bed to keep myself from falling over.

"Yet, most of your drawings are of this one, the one with the severed neck and the crossed blades," he pointed then flipped through a couple of pages to an image of a brez with a pair of holes in his chest. "Is this the one you killed?"

I could only nod dumbly, afraid that if I opened my mouth I might vomit.

"There are only a few images of him. It seems that the one with the swords is more important to you."

"He was the leader, the one I challenged," I managed to eke out before swallowing hard to keep my stomach under control.

Beus turned to another page where I had focused on just the crossed swords. "Dreams are usually more symbolic than directly representational. That you see this pattern over and over again, even though it did not actually happen that way, tells me this is more important for you than the reality of the situation. Meditate on this page, and I think you might gain some insights into your heart." He set the sketchbook on my lap, got up, and left my room.

I nearly slapped the book from my lap, but held my hand, whether because I did not wish to damage my work or for knowing that he was right, I will never know for certain. After a long blink, I stared at the drawing of the crossed swords for a time, burning the image even deeper into my mind, then closed my eyes, determined not to sleep. I took some deep breaths to steady myself and faded into a meditative state.

*I was in a long corridor, where numerous doors lined the white walls. The expected course is to try one of the doors, but I have learned that answers are rarely that easy. This is the Mazeworks, a place somewhere between dreaming and waking, and I have visited often since my tutelage with Vletraka began. The normal rules of the waking world do not apply here, and nothing is as it seems. The doors are all locked if one tries to open them, but once in a while, one opens of its own accord, granting access only when appropriate.

After a short journey, I reached up and pushed open a trapdoor that I could not see yet somehow knew was there. When I pulled myself through, I discovered that I was at the bottom of a lake or pond; no water escaped through the opening. At first, I panicked, as I had not taken a deep breath before becoming submerged. Quickly however, I remembered my state and relaxed, taking a deep breath of the clear water. I swam along the bottom, not knowing where I was headed, but merely followed my intuition. When the time felt right, I turned toward the surface.

Breaking into open air off the coast of a small island, I discovered that night had fallen, or had it already been that way? I gazed up at the crescent moon and stars, which did not seem quite right in their patterns, then swam to the shore. The island had a small beach of sand, which appeared light blue in the moonlight, and was covered in conifers. A small hill rose in the center of the island, which seemed like the best place to head towards. I wound my way through the trees, crunching over old pinecones and dried needles, and took in deep breaths of pine. As I neared the hilltop, the trees began dying off before my eyes; the stench of rotting wood overpowering the fresh scent of a few moments ago. A large patch of henbane covered the top of the hill, and in the center of it stood a brez whose head leaned obscenely to the right.

He said nothing to me as I approached. Intellectually, I thought it was because of the deep gash in his neck, but knowing where I was, such a predicament would not necessarily be an impediment. We stared at each other for a long time, Troj with his hands on his wickedly curved swords still in their straps on his belt.

"What do you want of me?" I asked somewhere between a growl and a plea. He gave no reply, standing in judgment of me. "I did what I had to; you and your band would have killed me, and then probably gone on to kill Blythad. I had no choice." Troj's stance had not changed. "I admit it. I tricked you and your fellows into fighting for me. There were five of you against me, and I could not have prevailed against those odds. The fight was not honorable, but for survival." Still nothing from my companion.

"What do you want from me?" I now screamed, tears forming in my eyes. "I did not want to do it! I just wanted to be left alone and do my duty, but you," I pointed, raising my voice, "you had to threaten me, surround me, put my life at risk. This is your fault, not mine! Druk was right. You led your band in attacking a child and have no honor. You deserved to die!" Troj continued to stand impassively.

"Do you want an apology? I am sorry that I killed you but you gave me no other option. Yet the pain I feel now, knowing what I have done, leads me to believe that it would have been better to have been killed than to have been the killer. Your image haunts me, both waking and dreaming, and I can no longer stand the pain! You win. Come and finish the job. Kill me now and end my suffering!"

Troj lifted his swords to the sky, crossing the horizontal over the vertical. I did not turn away, refusing to allow myself to be afraid of my ultimate judgment. I needed this to end, needed the peace of eternal rest. Rather than attack, however, he instead slowly faded away like a shadow in the twilight. The crescent moon shone in the sky where his horizontal sword had been, and the stars outlined where the other had been, bisected by the moon.*

I pulled myself out of my reverie and quickly sketched the final image in my book, frantically putting it down in charcoal before it left me, though deep down I knew that I would never forget. While I scratched away, a light knock came on my door.

Without stopping my work, I quietly said, "Enter", not thinking about the potential interruption. I heard the door open and was vaguely aware that someone was standing in the doorway, but I paid them no heed, focused as I was on my work. Finally, when the image was perfected, I set down my charcoal and looked up to see Faldrein grinning from ear to ear.

"You seem much more settled. May I sit?" Before I could respond, he made himself comfortable on the bed next to me. He stared at my newest sketch and asked, "What is that?"

"A reminder I believe, to never forget the past. Did the others tell you what is going on?" I asked, choking back my rising bile.

"Somewhat. They told me that you had to kill a brez in self-defense, and that his image haunts you in your dreams. Why didn't *you* tell me?"

"I saw the look on your face when I asked you about killing and thought that you would hate me for it. I would rather that no one knew about this, but it seems that more people learn about it all the time. This," I tapped my sketchbook, my spine tingling as I spoke, "will be my symbol: the magical nature of the moon shall always supersede the blade, and I shall always remember the pain of killing, so that I shall not do it in vain."

"I can't hate you for surviving. From what I understand, you killed only to avoid being slain yourself; there is no shame in that. I only hope that I am never in the same situation as you, though it is entirely likely, given that monsters are still able to roam around freely in spite of the king's forces. I would much rather heal the injured than do the injuring."

"In that, we are in full agreement."

CHAPTER 5: THE TOURNAMENT

Mistress Vletraka and I were both outside on a cool autumn morning, where she was drilling me on improving my aim with targeted spells on thrown wooden plates. "Very good," she smiled, "your aim is improving."

At least with magic, I thought, *just do not ask me to throw a dagger.* "Thank you, My Lady," I nodded as I fired off another *klivevalsk* at the small dish, which barely skimmed the edge, leaving a small patch of ice where the ray touched its target. I wished I could blame my poor aim on fatigue, rather than just a lack of hand-eye coordination!

"I believe you are ready to face some actual wizardly combat."

I stared at her dumbfounded and felt my stomach sink, as I had bad memories of battles already fought.

She chuckled, sensing and misinterpreting my discomfort. "Not to worry, I am not to be your opponent. There is to be a tournament amongst our students, where you can all learn to battle safely. We shall travel to Beus's tower, where he has designed the tournament setting. There you will meet all of your fellow students."

"Who are they? What do you know of them?" I asked, both curious and eager.

"You have met Beus's charge Faldrein, as well as Nari's student Blythad. Tzali has been teaching Uxadul, while Goldfire has taken Glitter as her apprentice. I have not spent a lot of time with any of the apprentices, but I know my fellow teachers. This is your chance to socialize with your peers. They all have different styles and specialties of magic, so be prepared."

"Can you tell me more about the other Masters then? I know that Faldrein has been learning divine magic as well as arcane with Beus, and Blythad is a conjurer. What about Tzali and Goldfire?"

"Tzali is very combat-oriented and is likely teaching Uxadul melee techniques to compliment his magic. Goldfire specializes in enchantments and is a natural charmer without using magic; I expect no less from her student."

"I look forward to meeting them," I said aloud, though inwardly I was nervous. How would I compare to them? I pride myself on my intellect, and the others must be very intelligent as well to master the arcane arts. In Split Falls, my patience with the generally slow-witted folk was tested far more than my intellect. It is easy to be smarter than that lot, but wizards are a rare breed, and it is unlikely that a single village would produce more than one in a generation. If my village upbringing comes through too strongly, the embarrassment would deal a serious blow to my self-image. However, it would be nice to spend time with equals, and Faldrein and Blythad were likeable enough.

We travelled for four days on conjured steeds to Beus's tower. Unlike Vletraka's and Nari's homes, his actually resembled a tower, four stories high and constructed of white stone. The roof was conical, made of overlapping tiles of white marble, with a narrow porch circling the base of the roof. Small glass windows were set at each level, facing north and south on the first and third levels, east and west on the second and fourth levels. Though one cannot truly judge a wizard by his home's appearance, it was obvious that Beus placed a high priority on defense, for he could easily see quite a distance from his upper story windows to spot an approaching enemy. Or, for all I know, he just enjoys gazing over the countryside. After being invited in, we were shown to our rooms to settle in and had not long to wait for the others to arrive.

As we reached the second-floor study, our hosts, Nari and Blythad, who had arrived before us, as well as Tzali and his pupil Uxadul waited. Beus made the introductions as I met the rest of my fellow students and their masters for the first time.

Tzali was tall and lean, with rough, chiseled features and a trio of scars running down his left cheek to his chin. He wore simple grey robes, and carried a staff tipped with rhamic, a coppery metal that is both lighter and stronger than steel, and is naturally tuned to the Weave, on both ends, which glowed of magic. Peering closely,

I could see that the top of his staff was marked with a *klivev* rune, while the opposite end had *srukak* inscribed upon it.[5]

I could not help but notice how Uxadul continued to look about the room, at each of us, as well as gazing at the variety of books and objects in the study. Instinctively, I could tell that he came from a village no larger than my own. In fact, he even smelled of loam, though I was certain that his wizardly studies would not have left him any time to work on a farm. Uxadul himself looked like loamy soil—his hair was dark brown, his skin deeply tanned and rough, his eyes nearly black; his pale grey robes seeming almost white in comparison.

A glow came from the doorway an instant before Goldfire and Glitter entered the study; from Vletraka's descriptions, there was no mistaking their identities. Goldfire was surrounded by a golden aura, her hair a river of orange and gold which cascaded to her lower back. Her eyes shimmered like a pair of emeralds in a face that was perfect in its soft symmetry. She wore a multi-hued robe of fine silk; the fabric must have been expensive, for it seemed too small for her, cut low at her breasts and barely passing her knees.

Glitter's name was also well chosen, for she literally sparkled, motes of magical energy dancing about her reflecting the full spectrum. Her hair was bright purple, contrasting with the deep indigo of her eyes, rolling in tight curls which dropped just past her tanned shoulders, her skin the golden tone of dark heather honey. She smiled as she looked around at her peers, her sparkles flushing to a bright pink before returning to their multi-colored state. Her robes were not as rich as those of her mistress, but again seemed a tad too small for her.

Once we were all together, Tzali got right to business. "Students, here are the rules. In order to keep things simple, you will each pair off twice, for a total of five duels. Each of you will draw a number and a name, and that is the person you will face off against; measures

---

[5] *Klivev* draws energy from the para-elemental plane of ice; *srukak*, as I described earlier in this volume, relates to fire. Placed upon a weapon, these runes add cold and fire damage respectively to the damage the mystical weapon already inflicts.

have been taken to ensure that you cannot draw your own name. We have also set up the dueling area to ensure that the combat will be non-lethal, but that does not mean that you won't get hurt, so healing potions will be at the ready in case of misfortune. The goal is to get your opponent to quit the fight—that is all. How you accomplish this is up to you. You will be judged on your creativity and effort, choices in spells, and use of power, not solely on victory, and you must use at least one of your personal spells in each duel; do not forget to counter-spell when the opportunity presents itself! The tournament will last for three days, ensuring that no one will fight more than once each day. Are you ready?"

"Yes, Master Tzali!" we answered in unison.

"Good. Now then, we have decided that Blythad will choose first."

Blythad stepped forward, reached into first one small cauldron, then the next, pulling out two slips of paper. "I've got number four and Faldrein," he announced looking over to his opponent with a smile.

"Faldrein, Blythad chose you, so you get the next pick," announced Tzali as he dropped an extra slip into the name cauldron.

So, that's how they keep us from choosing ourselves! Once our name is gone, we get to choose. And here I expected them to use magic to accomplish the feat.

Faldrein stepped up and took out two slips. "It looks like Glitter and I will go first!" he grinned.

"Very good. Glitter, you're next."

"I have number three and Mithron," she giggled. "This will be fun!"

Tzali smiled. "Mithron…"

I stepped over to the cauldrons and took out number five and Uxadul. "Uxadul and I will close out the tournament."

"I guess that leaves Blythad and me to duel in the second round," Uxadul drawled.

Tzali spoke up. "You all have your opponents. Prepare your spells wisely. We begin tomorrow morning."

We looked at each other, sizing up our opponents. I had not even met Glitter or Uxadul until today, and I would be facing off against them both.

A row of seats was placed just outside the arena circle where our duels were to take place. Nari and Tzali were already seated with their pupils, while Goldfire and Vletraka were conversing jovially behind their chairs. My fellow students were all seated and looked rather uncomfortable. I too was nervous, though I would not compete until the morrow.

"Is everyone ready?" asked Beus.

We all nodded affirmative.

"Good, then we shall begin. Faldrein and Glitter, it's your turn. One of you stand on that part of the circle," he pointed to the western end of the delineated grassy field, "the other over there," then pointed to the opposite edge. Faldrein moved to the eastern edge while Glitter moved across from him. Once they were both in position, he announced that it was time for the field to take shape.

As we watched, trees sprouted from the ground, filling the fifty-yard-wide circle with forest.

"Begin!" he shouted.

Though the trees interfered with our viewing, they were translucent, owing to their illusory nature. I gathered the forest would appear much more real to those within its confines.

Faldrein stood his ground and cast a spell I had not seen before, surrounding himself with magic.

"*Ubrelbimzilt*," I heard Beus comment. "It improves the target's ability to avoid danger."

Meanwhile, Glitter had begun climbing one the trees nearest to her.

"Why isn't she dueling?" Blythad asked his mistress.

"She is looking for a better position from which to strike, using the forest to her advantage. Notice how she is waiting for Faldrein to come to her?"

Faldrein was indeed cautiously moving amongst the trees, seeking out his foe.

"He better hurry," Beus warned, "his spell is about to wear off."

Shifting my vision, I could see that his spell was beginning to unravel just as he passed the tree Glitter was hiding in. No sooner had Faldrein's aura expired than she shouted his name. As he turned to look up at her, she hit him with a spell of her own. Bright motes of light rained from her fingertips, exploding in multicolored flashes.

"*Juutlek*," smiled Goldfire. "She discovered a way to focus her gift outward, both blinding and damaging her opponents."

Faldrein covered his eyes, blinded by the bursts of light. In response, he cast a minor healing spell to take care of the damage and blinked rapidly in an attempt to regain his sight. Glitter gave him no respite however and pulled a flute out of her pack. As she played, purple mist traveled from the end of the flute to settle over Faldrein. It took me a moment to recognize the music as a *mlarliskukhuuma* spell, the notes matching the tone and intonation of the verbal element of the spell, which placed Faldrein under her thrall.

"Faldrein," Glitter called sweetly. "There is no reason for us to fight."

The violet fog wrapped snugly around its victim. "You're right, friends shouldn't quarrel like this."

"Why don't you go sit with Beus? I'll climb down and meet you there."

"Okay." Faldrein turned away and walked toward us, the trees vanishing as he left the circle. He suddenly shook his head violently and the violet haze dissipated.

"Winner—Glitter!" announced Beus, standing and applauding while walking up to his pupil. "How do you feel?" he asked Faldrein.

"Like a fool. I can't believe I let her charm me like that."

"The common complaint of all men," he chuckled. "What did you learn?"

"My protection spell wore off too quickly... she was watching me, waiting for it to end!" he realized. "And she took an advantageous position in the trees. I never thought to look up!"

"This is exactly why we arrange these duels," interjected Tzali, "to teach you better tactics in a safe environment. In a real combat situation, things could have gone quite differently."

"Precisely," added Beus. "We want you to be able to survive out in the world, and it is best to learn your lessons outside of life-or-death combat."

"Yes, Master."

"Now take your seat, and you can watch the next battle. It is easier to judge what is happening when you are a spectator, rather than in the thick of things."

Faldrein nodded and sat in his chair.

Glitter ran up to him as he sat. "I hope I didn't hurt you too badly," she smiled apologetically.

"Just my pride," he smiled back. "I did not think about using the terrain as well as you did. I thought just to use the trees for cover, but you used them to gain the advantage. I shall always remember to look up from now on!" he laughed. "What was that spell you used to blind me?"

At this point, I tuned out their conversation, as I had already learned about their spells from their masters. I would, however, like to learn their spells for myself; they could prove useful in the future. I shall have to ask them if they wish to trade spells later.

"Next, Uxadul and Blythad," announced Beus. "Step into the circle, please." The two stood and walked into the circle, Blythad moving to the western edge and Uxadul to the east. "Ready?" Both nodded. "Begin!"

The field turned to snow and tundra, with large blocks of ice scattered throughout the tournament circle. A moderate snowfall began, slightly obscuring our vision. Uxadul chanted a few words and pounded his staff upon the tundra. Rocks began to climb up his staff until it was covered in a layer of stone. Blythad made some gestures and uttered three words of power with no apparent effect. Uxadul began to make his way over to Blythad when an image of an armored warrior appeared briefly in the snow and struck the earth-caster across the left side of his ribcage. He turned to see where the blow had come from, but the warrior had vanished.

"Blythad's *mimzelemtzizi* has struck a solid blow, Tzali," crowed Nari. "I wonder if your apprentice can handle an invisible opponent."

Tzali maintained his focus on his pupil, ignoring her jibe.

Uxadul stopped and called upon the Weave to protect him and was answered with a layer of steel covering his skin.

"I wonder if *your* pupil's spell can penetrate Uxadul's *hysavul* spell," Tzali finally retorted.

"If that one doesn't the air elemental he just summoned might," she smiled back.

Uxadul now faced three foes, the thinning wizard, an invisible warrior, and a creature made of swirling air! As the elemental approached, a loud clang informed us that the *mimzelemtzizi* had struck again, but failed to penetrate the metallic armor. Uxadul moved around another chunk of ice and began to charge straight for Blythad.

Blythad quickly cast a *skialosklek* at the earth-caster, who attempted and failed to counter the spell. He screamed in pain and frustration as the acid burned through his armor while the elemental buffeted him with its swirling winds.

I am surprised he is still standing; that is a lot of punishment to sustain.

Uxadul took three steps toward his conjurer foe, slid toward him with his staff outstretched, and knocked Blythad flat on his face as he slid by. Quickly, Uxadul regained his footing and got back over to Blythad just as he was rolling over, pointing his staff at the, now much thinner, prone wizard. "Yield!" he commanded.

"Aah! You win!" Blythad screamed, spreading out his hands in surrender. Uxadul smiled, then dropped to his knees, nearly passing out as the acid continued to burn. Beus and Faldrein rushed into the circle to assist the duelists, the arctic scene vanishing as they did so. The wizard-priests began casting healing spells, and both Blythad and Uxadul quickly recovered. Tzali welcomed his apprentice with a hearty handshake.

Nari gave her charge a slap to the back of his head. "Why did you surrender so easily? You had both your *emtzizi* and an elemental at your side! The *skialosklek* had him finished," she scowled.

"He had me knocked flat and could have taken me out with a single blow. I panicked," he sighed. "He seemed so strong; I didn't think he was ready to fall."

I could not stop myself from interrupting. "That *mimzelemtzizi* spell—I take it you modified the *mimzelhruk* into an offensive force?" A *mimzelhruk* spell calls forth a being of pure energy, capable of minor tasks, such as carrying small loads and moving objects, but has no ability for combat.

Blythad smiled at me with pride. "Yep!" then leaned in closer. "And there are stronger versions with each circle of power I attain. In time, I expect to have swarms of them at my command!" he beamed.

"Interesting. After the tournament, I would like to trade you for those spells."

"Certainly. I'm sure you've come up with some pretty interesting spells yourself. I'm glad I don't have to fight you! I've seen what you can do!" he laughed.

"I have to duel against the only two I have not met yet. Having seen them both in battle today, however, gives me an advantage."

"Ahh, but you have only seen a hint of what I can do," purred Glitter in my ear. "I have other spells to use against you."

I turned to find her grinning at me. "I would expect no less. I hope that I am not nearly as susceptible to your charms as Faldrein."

"You can't blame him, she is a beautiful girl," Uxadul smiled at Glitter, took her hand, and kissed it lightly, causing her sparkles to blush as brightly as her cheeks. "It's an easy matter to fall for her charms."

"It is her wits I should be concerned about. I am not about to battle a pretty girl; I am going to face off against a wizard. One cannot let an opponent's comeliness impede one's judgment."

"You don't think I'm pretty?" she pouted.

"I did not say that. I merely believe that it is a wizard's intellect that is more dangerous. You are no fool; please do not take me for one either."

"Well then, we shall see how you do in the arena tomorrow."

"I look forward to your challenge."

Glitter sauntered off towards Goldfire, and Faldrein turned to me. "How can you act so uninterested in her beauty?" he asked, turning to watch her walk away. "She's very… distracting."

Sensing that she was being watched, she turned and looked Faldrein in the eye, causing him to quickly blush and look away. She smiled and continued walking to Goldfire, her hips swaying in an exaggerated fashion.

"I cannot allow her beauty to distract me. You fell easily for her charms and it cost you the match. Were she of a mind to do so, she could have done a whole lot more harm to you than have you quit the battle. Your cavalier attitude toward your opponent was more dangerous to you than she was. After our match, I can allow myself the luxury of noticing her charms, but not before."

The next morning, we returned to the field of battle to resume the tournament. Glitter and I took to our ends of the field and I watched as the grass died and the field turned to desolation, as if some great cataclysm had taken place, breaking the earth and causing it to jut out at odd angles. I heard the first words of a *srukakbolmos* spell being uttered and quickly spoke the obverse syllables to counter it. At first, I thought I was too late as the fire bead came soaring toward me, but strangely it exploded into a great cloud of sunflowers rather than flame.

Glitter must have run up to me while my vision was obscured by the burst of foliage, for I did not see her coming until she slapped me across the face. I could feel the eldritch energies pouring into my mind, and though I tried to resist, I found myself crying, then laughing, then roaring in anger, my emotions completely beyond my control.

"What's wrong? Are you being distracted by my charms?" she giggled.

"Is this because you could not distract your father while he beat your mother to death?" I cooed. *What am I saying? And why am I talking like this?*

Glitter stood stock still, her fingers and lips beginning to tremble.

"You just stood there and watched," I laughed, "as he hit her again and again," I yelled in fury, "and you did nothing," I said with a sneer.

"How… how could you…" tears began to stream down her face while I stared at her lustfully.

"And then," I shuddered in fear, "he stabbed himself in the heart with a knife!" I screamed in joy.

"You…" She screamed in unfiltered fury and I could see the Weave tearing around her.

I laughed lightly, as I was finally beginning to shake off her spell. Out of the rift came a shadow of intense malevolence, and my fear was as much my own as that of the lingering effects of Glitter's magic. "A wajuvu?" I stammered. "How could you summon such a creature?"

She came to her senses as the frightful presence before her caused her to forget her fury. "I… I don't know. It just happened."

The wajuvu began to drift toward me, and I quickly cast *ajilek* at the umbral creature, as Glitter did the same, each of us launching three missiles; she must have realized that the wajuvu was not under her control. It struck out at me, but I backed away before it could steal my essence. I followed by invoking a *juutaatok*, which I prepared in case of close combat, but the positive energy forming the dagger-shaped force works even better against undead. I slashed at the shadowy form, while Glitter cast her *juutlek* spell, its bright energy partially affecting the incorporeal creature. Between the two of us attacking, the wajuvu vanished without incident.

"Shall we continue?" I asked as Glitter stormed off, not even giving me a glance as she left the field.

I shook my head to clear my thoughts, then followed her, the desolate field turning green again as she left the battlefield. As I walked towards Vletraka, Uxadul intercepted me and punched me in the stomach, causing me to double over.

"How could you be so cruel? That is no way to win a battle!" he growled, preparing to strike me again.

Fortunately, Tzali was there to catch his arm. "Settle it on the field," he warned his charge. Uxadul stomped once and turned away.

As I looked up, I could see everyone else staring at me.

I wheezed a couple of times and looked straight at Glitter. "I had no idea what I was saying. The words just started pouring out of me while I was in the grip of your spell. Was... was all that true?"

Her blank, tear-filled eyes answered for me.

"I am sorry." She turned away and fled toward the woods, Goldfire following after her,

I felt a cold hand land on my shoulder. "Why did you say those things to her?" Vletraka asked, anger and disappointment dripping acidly in her voice.

"I do not know. We had only just met, so how was I even supposed to know something so personal about her? Something about her emotion spell must have backlashed, causing me to speak aloud her deep pain." I turned to face my Mistress. "I could not stop myself." My chest began to hurt, though I had not been damaged there, as though my heart was being crushed.

"I believe a break is in order before we continue," announced Beus, who gave me a dirty look. "We shall resume in one hour."

Everyone walked off, leaving me alone by the field. I sat down on the grass and contemplated the morning's events. I knew next to nothing about Glitter, certainly not anything as personal and traumatic as this, and yet I aired her ordeal to the gathered crowd. It *had* to be her spell. I did not see her cast it, so I did not know what signs she used, nor did I hear the words through the explosion of flowers. *I wonder what went wrong with her spell. Did she misspeak? Make a wrong gesture? Use the wrong materials? Her spell had me in emotional turmoil, and from that I somehow tapped into* her *emotional turmoil.*

"Mithron?" I heard Vletraka call softly. "Can we talk for a moment?"

"Of course, My Lady. I think I figured out what went wrong. Methinks Glitter's spell used her own inner conflict to fuel and exaggerate the conflicting emotions of others. Somehow, it caused me to voice her suffering while I was in the midst of my own turmoil. I will speak to her about it if she will let me."

"We came to much the same conclusion, though it would be wisest to let her be for now. You are not to blame, though I expect you will not be forgiven so easily for your part. Perhaps once everyone understands the situation, but not right away."

"So much for making new friends," I muttered glumly.

When the tournament resumed, it was Blythad's turn to face off against Faldrein; the field became dim with rain. Faldrein cast a protective ward while Blythad conjured five javelins, which floated beside him. Blythad pointed and one of the javelins launched towards Faldrein, stabbing him in the shoulder.

"*Dovlekbokvi*" Nari whispered to Beus.

Faldrein screamed in pain while the ward he had cast fired off in a bolt of lightning back at Blythad, knocking him back three paces.

"*Bulhysakoombatzi,*" Beus returned to Nari—retribution for Blythad's attack.

While Blythad was recovering from the shock, Faldrein cast a *bezyamhysa* spell, which deflected the next javelin to fly at him.

"*Hivlibokwa!*" Blythad next conjured a swarm of spiders, which crawled rapidly toward Faldrein, who countered with *aatokytsrukak*, which dispersed the arachnids, the magical flames unimpeded by the rain. A third javelin flew and barely missed Faldrein, who cast another spell I had not seen before, with no apparent effect.

"Are you feeling alright, Blythad? You look a bit pale," the wizard/priest asked.

"Why do you ask?" responded Blythad nervously.

"You look sweaty and blanched, and your aim is off. Did lunch disagree with you? We can postpone the match if you want."

"No, I'm…" Suddenly, Blythad turned and ran towards the trees, the rain stopping when he left the circle.

As Faldrein returned to the rest of the group, Uxadul asked him "What was that last spell? Did it make him ill?"

"No," he answered with an awkward smile. "I cast nothing at all. My Gift is the ability to see the state of health of others, and I really was concerned about him. I wasn't trying to make him quit."

"It seems that we are not to have fair fights this day," Uxadul grumbled, casting me a dirty look.

I considered pointing out that Glitter had won her match through subterfuge as well, and neither Faldrein nor I intentionally won our matches in the manner in which we did. Instead, I merely commented, "Not all battles are won at the tip of a sword. In a combat situation, Blythad would likely have gotten himself killed just now, while Glitter walked off in the midst of our duel of her own accord."

"Don't even mention her name!" Uxadul roared. "You had no right to act as you did. Never trust a necromancer," he scowled, looking to Faldrein for support and finding silence instead. He pointed a finger at my nose and growled, "Tomorrow," and stormed off.

"I am getting the distinct impression that Uxadul does not care for me," I said to Faldrein sardonically.

"You better be careful against him. He's strong and likes to fight up close, which makes it hard to concentrate on spellcasting."

"So I have seen. I believe I have a good strategy for our duel planned. Why are you speaking to me? I thought I had become a pariah around here."

"I thought about it, and I agree that it was her spell that caused your behavior. I feel bad for her, and I don't think anyone outside of Goldfire knew about her past, so there is no reason to believe that you could have verbally abused her in such a way unless under the influence of magic. I do not know you well, but I don't think you are a cruel person."

"Thank you. I am glad to have an ally in this."

Next morning came too soon, and I had some trepidation about the upcoming duel. Even though I was fully aware of the protections that had been cast upon the battlefield, and that both Beus and

Faldrein would be there to heal any damage done, I also knew that my foe was going to be out for blood. When we stepped into the circle, the field changed to desert, the sands shifting beneath our feet while the heat rose precipitously.

As soon as the signal to begin was given, we both began casting personal spells. I used *yuvjuutubrel* to outline Uxadul in negative energy, which would sap his strength while I prepared my defenses. No sooner had I finished my spell than I was hit with a ball of clay, which stuck to my right leg and slowed my movements. As he was still at a distance, I began casting *bezyamhysa* to block his attacks. He was ready for me and countered it. As the energies subsided, another ball hit me, this one impacting my right shoulder. The heavy clay was interfering with my spellcasting, and when I tried to summon *ajiavulhysayt* to create a magical armor, Uxadul countered me yet again.

"I knew you would try to protect yourself like that," he snarled, throwing yet a third ball, this one sticking to my left shin and dropping me to my knees. He ran up to me then, at least as quickly as one can run on sand, his fist turning to stone as he did so; in his rage, it did not appear that he noticed that I had enchanted my own hand as well. "You hurt her, now I hurt you." He swung back to punch me, and I caught his fist in my own magically glowing hand.

"*Vulzuklavad* is an interesting little spell, is it not?" I causally asked my now paralyzed enemy, not letting on how much it hurt to catch his stony fist in my own. "Your clay may have slowed me, but now you cannot move at all. You let your emotions carry you away. That is why you lost. *Dulaatheedu!*"

Uxadul shuddered from the sonic energy passing through his skeleton, and combined with the draining power of *yuvjuutubrel*, his paralyzed body collapsed to the sandy ground. Immediately, the environment shifted back to the grassy plain it truly was, and Beus and Faldrein rushed out with healing potions in hand. I took one from Faldrein and gulped it down while Beus tilted Uxadul's head back and dribbled the warm, summery liquid down his throat.

I turned to Faldrein, "You added honeysuckle to this? Interesting."

"It heightens the flavor without diluting the potency," spoke Beus. "A vast improvement over the bitter potions my Master used to make, if I do say so myself."

"I cannot disagree," I responded, having never tasted his master's potions, while delighting in the flavor of his. "How is he? The *vulzuklavad* should wear off in a few moments." As I spoke, the clay began to dry and flake off.

"He will be fine. You knew that he would charge you, didn't you?"

"Uxadul is a melee mage, and his rage over the incident during my battle with Glitter led me to believe that he would want to hurt me with his own hands rather than at a distance. I believe his clay was meant to keep me from running away, but I never had any intention of doing so. I was waiting for him."

At that, the paralytic power of the *vulzuklavad* ended, allowing Uxadul to move freely once more. He began to move toward me, but Beus' hands were firm on his shoulders.

"It's over son. Let it go," Tzali chastened Uxadul.

"No! Not until he has been punished," he screamed.

"We discussed this. Mithron was under the influence of Glitter's spell, though we do not yet know why he reacted so differently than I did."

Uxadul turned to him.

"We convinced her to cast the spell again, with me as the target. The effects are… disquieting, to say the least. Perhaps it's because I have had more training, and resisted her spell even though I was trying to allow it to work; or it was due to the stressful situation under which she cast it during the battle. We will determine it in time. I understand why you feel the need to defend her, but it is done. Let it go."

Uxadul lowered his head. "Yes, Master Tzali." He then turned and walked away, giving me a look of disdain as he turned.

"I have a feeling we are not going to be friends," I said flatly to no one in particular. "A pity." For I would not mind trading for that clay spell he used.

For my efforts, not only in winning both matches, but also for creative spell use, I was considered the winner of the tournament, a bittersweet and Pyrrhic victory in my eyes. Vletraka presented me with a magical ring, which creates a minor field of force around the wearer to deflect blows, before the gathering of our peers.

"Thank you," I accepted glumly, standing at my seat, "but I do not feel that I truly deserve this. My match with Glitter was... tainted, and therefore I cannot accept a victory for that match. In fact, Glitter's spells were far more effective and creative in their content, and the prize should be hers."

"No, I don't want anything from you," Glitter pouted quietly. "Keep it." She turned her head away, but I could see the tears welling up in her eyes before she did. I nodded once and sat back down, gently sliding the ring on my finger.

Chapter 6: Dual Duel

It was not long after the tournament, a moon or so, and I buried myself in my studies again, the weight of my new ring a constant reminder of the recent event. I had been tinkering with an improved version of *dulaatheedu* to increase the damage potential of cracking an opponent's bones during battle when a squawking voice filled my ears.

'We have company,' Thessylia interrupted.

'Let me see,' I commanded. Looking at the world through the eyes of an owl can be disorientating at first, and I was still getting used to the sensation. For one, things appear much brighter, especially at night. Second, the way a bird's eyes focus is different from human eyes. The center of vision is crisper, with the ability to discern much greater detail at a distance. Peripheral vision, however, is far narrower, creating an effect similar to cupping your hands at your temples.

Through Thessylia's eyes, I saw two humans on horseback riding toward our home. Both dressed in robes, gave the impression that they were either wizards or monks. One was an older man, heavy-set with dark, thinning hair and a drooping mustache; the younger, about my age, had the beginnings of full facial hair. *They must be wizards,* I thought. *No self-respecting monk would be that fat.*

Peering closer with her amazing eyes, I could see the four wrinkles on the older man's brow, his sweat-matted hair, and the pimples on his bulbous nose. He looked to be in pain from a long ride—something I could empathize with—and breathed heavily through crooked teeth. His companion needed to shave; the fuzz in patches on his cheeks and chin imparted an air of maturity but made him look untidy. His hair was also matted down, though much thicker than the elder's, and had a natural curl to it, which would be the envy of many young ladies. He also seemed more comfortable on horseback, perhaps due to training.

I cast *zelaji* to better see the Weave. Color appeared in the grayscale vision, centered on the horses and various objects on their persons. *So, the horses are conjured. Vletraka feels the same way about having a permanent mount to care for.* The older man's finger glowed a pale green, while a circle of blue wrapped around the top of his balding head; dark green light emanated from a pouch he wore. The younger man's forearms radiated a faint violet and the small brooch pinned to his robe emitted a yellow hue.

Concentrating further, I could see the hidden patterns within the magical auras. The ring on the older man's finger was woven through abjuration magic, giving him some level of protection, but from what, I could not ascertain. The dark green glow was of conjuration magic, but the circlet on his head kept its secrets hidden from me. Both auras on the younger man were also of the abjuration school.

Using Thessylia's eyes, I could see some of the details of the magical implements. The ring was of plain metal with tiny etchings upon it in magical script, of which I could make out the word 'deflection.' The metal circlet had a braided look to it, with small images of foxes woven into the braids. There is a spell to temporarily heighten one's intelligence, useful for learning new spells or gaining insights while researching, which uses a fox's tail fur as a focus; it could be that this circlet might have a continuing effect similar to that—a handy tool for a wizard! The pouch looked like any other I had seen, though perhaps more weathered, and I noticed nothing distinguishing about it. The bracers on the younger man's forearms had images of shields stamped into them, which coincides with the protective nature of abjuration magic—little help there. His brooch was silvery filigree with a dark stone set within. Obsidian is often used to absorb energy, though onyx is better suited to transforming energies; there was no way to tell which stone it was at this distance.

"Vletraka," I called, "we are soon to have guests."

"Thessylia spotted them, I take it."

"Yes, Mistress. Two wizards, by my reckoning. They ride on conjured steeds. The older wears a protective ring, a circlet upon his brow, and carries a magical pouch. The younger one wears protective bracers and a brooch."

"I'm impressed. Few wizards at your age are so tightly linked to their familiars to fully use their senses as your own; and to use divinations through her no less. It sounds like they expect a battle. You had best prepare, just in case."

"Yes, Mistress," I nodded, then ran off to my room to grab my spell-book and travelling gear.

"We will fight to protect our home," Vletraka had told me once, "but I want you ready in case we need to flee. You are a brilliant apprentice, but there are many far more powerful than you, and even I, and this home is not worth your life. Should it come to it, I will not have you die for me."

I had thought her to be merely overprotective then, and not yet appreciated how rare a gift magic is, or how hungry for power some mages are. Twice since then have other wizards come to challenge her—not to duel in a friendly game but with full intention of slaying my mistress and taking her position and possessions, and I have learned the wisdom of her warnings. Any who could challenge Vletraka could also slay her apprentice with ease.

Our visitors would be here soon, so there was little time to study combat spells. I ran into the library, tossed down my backpack, and pulled out my spell-book. I only had time to prepare a few spells when Vletraka called, saying that they would be entering the gate soon. I repacked my spell-book and ran to the kitchen, hung my pack on a hook near the door, and covered it with my travelling cloak.

I then rushed to the door to greet our guests. "Greetings, my lords, and welcome. Who do we have the honor of hosting this eve?" There are certain formalities that must be observed in wizardly society. Social graces are not one of my strong suits, but following rote procedures is a simple task. Seeing them with my own eyes for the first time, I was able to discern new details. They were of similar height, perhaps a shade under six feet tall and a few inches taller than me; I suspect the younger would soon pass his master.

They wore robes of crimson with yellow trim—the elder's being, of course, far more elaborate, emblazoned with streaks of lightning embroidered in gold and a light trimming of yellow lace on the cuffs and hem. Owls have little or no sense of smell, not that I would have picked up their scent at that distance anyway, but the apparently long ride left them with a strong aroma of both their own and the horses' sweat. Tidying up one's appearance can be done with one of the simplest spells, and would be expected of guests; I guessed that they either did not care or did not prepare that spell today, further leading me to believe that this was not a social call. Both wore Vletraka's amulet, which protected them from our crawling guardians.

"I am Larzed the Raging Storm, slayer of the mighty dragon Rimeclaw and scourge of the Kar-Ti Rebellion. This is my apprentice Wosken."

"Very good, sir. Welcome to the home of Vletraka of the Alabaster Moon. I am her apprentice Mithron. If you would please follow me," I led them to the main room where my mistress had settled herself on the divan with a copy of *Quiet Focus*.

"Mistress Vletraka, I present Larzed the Raging Storm, slayer of the mighty dragon Rimeclaw and scourge of the Kar-Ti Rebellion and his apprentice Wosken." I resisted the urge to roll my eyes during the introduction and managed to keep my voice level. Still, I detected the slightest smirk from Vletraka as I recited Larzed's self-importance.

Vletraka set down her book and rose gracefully. "Larzed, Wosken, welcome to my home. Please sit." As the guests settled into the stuffed chairs, she returned to her seat. "Mithron, bring some refreshments for our weary travelers."

"Yes, my Lady."

As I headed to the kitchen, I heard Vletraka ask Larzed about his battle with Rimeclaw. Beaming, he quickly and energetically began his tale, which I was spared by closing the door behind me. There was still a pot on the fire for tea, and I placed some herbs in four cups. I then sliced a few chunks of bread, cheese, and apples and arranged them on a platter. "I will need help to carry all of this," I muttered quietly, and cast *mimzelhruk*.

Mimzelhruk is a useful conjuration for everyday activities, calling forth a being of pure force energy, capable of carrying light loads and doing odd chores. Needless to say, the use of it is banned by most wizard teachers to prevent their students from getting lazy about their duties, which are intended to create discipline, contrary to the popular belief that apprentices are slave servants to their masters. In a case such as this, however, I believe that our loud guest would appreciate the excessive use of magic. "Carry the cups," I commanded the *mimzelhruk*. The four cups appeared to rise of their own accord. I lifted the plate of food. "Follow me."

As I opened the kitchen door, I heard the tale continuing. Vletraka sat with her back to me, but I am certain she was bored out of her mind while giving the appearance of interest. Wosken was present, but it was obvious he had endured his master's ramblings far too often.

"Serve," I whispered. The four cups floated over to the center of the seated group while I followed. Each person took a cup, and the fourth came to me as I set down the platter. I took the proffered cup then dismissed the *mimzelhruk* with a wave of my hand. I took my place behind Vletraka, ready to accept another task.

"An amazing adventure," she exclaimed. "You are truly brave to face such peril." I have learned during my tutelage when she is being sincere and when she is not. There is a slight shift in her voice when she mocks, and I heard that shift just then. "So what brings an adventurous type, such as yourself, to our little household?"

"My apprentice and I," Larzed began around a mouthful of cheese, "Have been hired to find some lost and hidden tomes. Specifically, he tells me that you are in possession of *In Between: On the Transition from Life to Death to Life* and is prepared to pay handsomely for it." He reached into his belt pouch and drew out a leather satchel much larger than the pouch it came out of. He set it on the table with a heavy metallic thud.

"A volume such as that would be worth a heavy sum. Unfortunately, your employer is mistaken. I am not in possession of the prize you seek."

Larzed's expression turned to shock. "My employer was quite certain that *In Between* was here. Are you certain?"

"I know every title in my library, and if I had such a treasure, I would know about it. If you like, Mithron will give you a tour of the library."

"Go with him, Wosken. I wish to speak further to our hostess."

"Yes, sir."

"Come. It is this way." I led Wosken through the ornate wooden door at the back of the main room and into the hallway, which led to Vletraka's room, the library, and the alchemy laboratory, which is in a separate building with reinforced walls to protect our home from any explosive mishaps. A covered walkway, like an aboveground tunnel, connects the two structures. The library door is itself a bookcase, with many oft read titles, such as *Staddi's Book of Potions*, Ormak's treatise on wand crafting *Willow, Ash, and Oak*, *Writing Magick: Proper Ingredients for Inks, Scrolls, and Tomes*, as well as anatomical guides to humans, zylii, dragons, and other creatures. The shelf is set on a pivot, and swings easily when pushed.

I nudged open the bookcase/door and entered the library. Light filled the room from numerous permanent *juut* spells, so that no candle need ever risk setting this store of knowledge ablaze. Shelves lined the walls, filled with tomes, scrolls, and the odd trophy or art piece. Two large tables stood in the center with a pair of lightly padded chairs at each table. While researching formulae for new spells, studying, or merely gathering information, I have often covered both tables with books, moving from chair to chair as each loses comfort. In one corner was a wrought iron spiral staircase leading up to the rooftop, where we made observations of the stars and astronomical phenomena.

"Feel free to look around. Perhaps we will have a tome of interest for you."

Wosken looked around for a minute then asked, "Where do these stairs lead?"

"To the roof. We do not keep any tomes up there."

"May I see anyway? I expect there is a good view of the stars from up there."

"As you wish, and yes, the view is spectacular."

We climbed up the spiral stairs through a trapdoor in the ceiling. This led to a small structure with a door opening to the rooftop. The shack-like structure's purpose is to protect the trapdoor, and the library, from the effects of inclement weather. Should the door leak from heavy rains, the precious volumes housed beneath could be ruined. The structure is tall enough to squat in comfortably, and one practically crawls out onto the roof; were it any taller it would impede observations of the horizon. In a small, tightly sealed cupboard on the outside of the structure is a spyglass, three observation logs, ink, and quills.

After we had clambered atop the roof into the exceptionally warm autumn night, Wosken looked around and said, "Yes, this is very nice. Very peaceful." Just after he spoke, a bolt of lightning flashed out of a window downstairs. "I guess that's my cue," he grinned maliciously.

"I was not ready for a duel," I stated.

"Duel? I'm not here to duel. I'm here to kill you." He launched a bolt of fire, which seared into my right shoulder and caused me to spin around and drop to one knee.

I retorted with *ajilek* while standing back on two feet, but surprisingly all three motes of blue-black energy flew directly toward the brooch pinned to his robe and vanished, leaving him unharmed.

"A handy little item," he sneered. "Too bad you don't have one." He launched a volley of missiles of his own, crackling orange, red, and yellow, like three flaming arrows, which thudded into my chest. I staggered back but kept my footing.

Three missiles—at least he is at my level of training. Still, another attack and I am done for. Although I could not heal myself, I could strengthen my life force for a short time, and cast *mimslookvriiwa.* "A fire mage, eh? I am surprised you did not start with a *srukakbolmos.*"

"At this range? And get caught in the explosion of my own spell? Do you think I'm stupid?" He suddenly screamed as a ball of brown feathers raked the back of his head.

'Thank you.'

'I expect extra scratching tonight.'
'I promise.'

While Wosken searched for his attacker, I took the opportunity to step forward. *Mimslookvriiwa* was good, but I needed more healing than that temporary spell would provide. While he was distracted, I cast *vriiwamrayk*, filling my hand with negative energy.

I reached out to draw away some of his life force and take it for my own, but his arm shot up and held my hand at bay. The leather brace glowed slightly for a moment.

He turned to face me again, forgetting about Thessylia for a moment. "Get away!" he shouted and backed up a couple of steps toward the roof door.

I quickly hid my hand in the sleeves of my robe. "I see, you only fight from a distance. Coward," I spat. "If you wish to kill a man, you should have the courage to look him in the eye."

"Shut up."

"Ooohh, don't touch me," I quailed mockingly. "Let me ask you seriously, are you afraid of me personally, or do you feel that my close proximity threatens your masculinity somehow? At least, what there is of it."

"Shut. Up."

"Maybe you would find it easier to attack me from behind," I turned my back to him and glared over my shoulder. "There is no counter-attack if you stab a man in the back. An even more cowardly way to fight, would you not say?"

"I'll kill you!" He invoked a dagger of flame and lunged at me, searing my abdomen just below the ribcage. I retaliated, spinning to meet his attack and slapping him on the shoulder, activating *vriiwamrayk*. He screamed as his life energy was drawn away, while I felt the elation which comes from the overflow of energy.

"I see your point. Perhaps you should have kept your distance," I sneered, looking him in the eye.

He backed up again and began casting another *srukakalsk*, replicating the first fire spell he attacked me with, when Thessylia swooped in and raked his eyes. While he fought her off, I cast *klivevalsk* at his feet, the small patch of ice causing him to slip, fall backwards, and hit his head on the roof entrance structure.

Careful of my footing, I walked up to the prone and dazed Wosken. "It is always the simple ice spells that seem to undo fire mages," I crowed. With a quick shove, I pushed him through the trapdoor headfirst. I heard him clang three times before the noise stopped.

Thessylia landed on the roof structure and presented her head for scratching. I slipped two fingers under her feathers and began to rub her head.

"Thank you. I do not think I would have beaten him without your distractions. I had better check in with Vletraka." I carefully clambered down the bloodstained staircase to find that Wosken only made it about halfway down before getting caught in the railing, his body folded at an unnatural angle. Holding tightly to the rail, I pushed his body with my foot, dislodging him to roll the rest of the way down. By the time I reached the last stair, I could feel *mimslookvriiwa* fading, lowering my energy and no longer suppressing the pain from Wosken's attacks. I reached down and removed the brooch from his robe. "A handy little item indeed," I told the corpse as I pinned the jewelry to my own robe. "Now I have one. I think I will take these as well."

I unstrapped the bracers. "Abjuration magic; glowed slightly when I attacked—they must act as a kind of armor." I strapped the leather bands to my arms and examined his body again. The contents of his pack had spilled out during his descent, revealing a length of rope, a broken oil flask, which was now staining the rug along with his blood, a smoke-stick, a package wrapped in oilcloth which I suspected to be his own spell-book, and a cloth bag. I grabbed his spell-book and placed it aside.

There are some that would quail at the idea of looting a corpse; whether this stems from the idea that it is theft or because they fear touching a dead body is a matter of debate. I see the matter, however, that the dead no longer need the items they carried in life, and should they prove useful, then they should continue being used. Killing a man *for* his possessions is wrong; killing in self-defense is, as I have painfully learned, at least questionable. I do not like to kill, and still have the occasional nightmare about Troj and his band, but sadly, as in this case, it is sometimes necessary.

Rolling Wosken's body with the edge of the now ruined rug, I revealed the loose slats in the floor, beneath which was the cause of tonight's excitement. The book was, as usual, covered with the bodies of dead insects, a pair of mice, and the bodies of other vermin; its maker enchanted the volume to preserve it from predation. I brushed the desiccated carcasses off and lifted the dark-bound tome from its hiding place. It is a hefty volume, easily weighing ten pounds, standing over a foot-and-a-half tall and nearly as wide, with just over two hundred pages of heavy vellum bound within two planks of hide-covered cedar. I never fully determined the origin of the hide, but my best guess is the leathery material from a black dragon's wing. The full title, *In Between: On the Transition from Life to Death to Life,* is embossed in platinum sealed with diamond dust on the cover.

"There are too many dangerous spells in this tome, and we must keep it hidden," Vletraka told me four years ago, shortly after I began my apprenticeship, after examining it thoroughly. She would not tell me where she had found it, only saying that we are all a bit safer with the book hidden here. "When you have advanced, I will help you understand its mysteries. For now, however, it is all far beyond your ability."

And she was right. Vletraka never expressly forbade me to look at *In Between*, perhaps understanding that it would only serve to drive my curiosity further, and I attempted to comprehend it all the same some weeks later. It *was* far too an advanced work at that point in my studies, and even though I could translate some of the mystical writings, I understood very little of it. Only recently have I returned to the book, gaining insights from the philosophies and spells within its leathery covers. I looked up from the book as I heard the door open.

Larzed stepped in a few feet before adequately assessing the situation. His robes were tattered and scorched. "Wosken?" He looked from his fallen apprentice to me. "You murdered my apprentice!"

"If by 'murder' you mean 'killed my attacker before he killed me', then yes. Had he a better teacher, he might now be alive to say so." He was right though, I had just killed a man—no, a boy my own age. My life was still in danger, however, and I could not give myself time to deal with the moral implications presently.

"If you had a better teacher, she might be alive as well," he sneered.

Shock and anger filled my vision, darkening the world around me. Larzed glowed like an ebon beacon in the twilight, and I could almost see his evil. "What kind of man tortures, sorry, *tortured*, his apprentice with electric shocks for the smallest mistakes? Or even just for fun?"

Fury washed across the old wizard's face. "How could... what makes you think..." he stammered. "Did he tell you that?"

I had no idea what I was saying, only that it was true. *How* did *I know? Good. If he's unfocused, he is vulnerable.*

He began gesturing for a *vezivihalsk*.

"If you finish that spell, the lightning will destroy your precious book," I warned, holding the cause of so much strife to my chest, along with Wosken's spell-book. "I do not believe your employer will be pleased."

Larzed hesitated, losing the spell.

I stomped on the smoke-stick at my feet, causing it to release a cloud of thick, grey smoke, and I then bolted for the door, carrying the two tomes under the cloud's concealment. *The laboratory— there lies my best hope.*

He was not put off for long, and his footfalls were not far behind. *Rather deft for an old man. His anger must be energizing him. Weak as I am, I should still outpace him.*

Larzed began to slow, but it was more to intone more mystic syllables than from fatigue.

This will not be good. He finished chanting just as I rounded the corner in the hallway, bouncing off the far wall as I rushed the turn. As I moved away, I felt the chill as the wall coated in ice. *Brilliant—*

the cold would have frozen me, but not harmed the book like fire, acid, or lightning would. Of course, stupid people do not make good wizards, though they still make mistakes.

I dove into the lab and slammed the heavy door behind me. There was no time to brace the door, and Vletraka never thought that there would be a need to bolt it, so I headed to the cabinet on the far wall.

Suddenly, the door exploded inward, shards of lumber crashing through expensive glass instruments.

Good thing I decided not to hold the door shut. He must have assumed the door would be bolted and threw an explosive spell at it. Good—one less spell in his arsenal to throw at me. I grabbed my salvation from the cabinet and spun to see Larzed stepping through the gaping wound that was the door.

"Nowhere left to run, boy," he spat.

"You could turn and run right back through that hole. A *wise* man always finds a path."

"It will be a pleasure to silence you forever," he sneered and began a new spell.

Though I have no skill at physical combat and have been told that I could not hit a castle wall with a stone from six paces, actually hitting your target is not always necessary. The wonderful thing about using alchemical explosives is the blast radius, especially when thrown by the handful. From the cabinet, I had taken some thunderstones and dazzle-pellets, which I hurled at the old mage. The combination of deafening and blinding explosions not only disrupted his spell, which I have no doubt would have killed me, but left him dazed. I rushed up to him while he was stunned, holding *In Between* high over my head. "Here is the tome you wanted so badly," I growled as I slammed it into his face.

Blood gushed from his nose as he toppled over.

I hit him a few more times for good measure then rushed back to the cabinet, grabbed an iron box from the bottom, and ran to the main room where Vletraka lay prone, surrounded by the remains of numerous hands. I grabbed her wrist and felt the faint flow of blood beneath her ice-cold skin. I opened the box and grabbed one of the four glass vials from the cotton padding, unstoppered it, and carefully dribbled the contents into her mouth. Reaching behind her neck, I tilted her head back so she would swallow the healing potion. A moment later, she coughed and opened her eyes—I had never realized how dark they were.

"M-Mithron? You're still alive," she smiled.

"Not by much," I responded, taking a potion for myself and handing her another one. "Here, you are still grievously wounded."

"Thank you. Even though I expected Larzed's attack, he still nearly killed me. Where is he? Did he… no, I see you have it. It's covered in blood!"

"Larzed's. I flattened his nose for him. 'Knowledge is our weapon'."

That brought a laugh from Vletraka, but she quickly sobered. Slowly, she rose to her feet, and I did the same. "You still need to flee and protect that book. Whoever sent Larzed and his boy will surely send others."

"Would it not be safer to fight together? I would be a more susceptible target alone."

She responded by casting *mimtrezel* on *In Between*. "That should hide the book from scrying eyes for a few days. Your traveling gear is ready?"

"My pack is in the kitchen. I readied it before they came, as you trained me."

"Good. Add this last potion to your gear. You might need it."

From the hallway, I heard the final tones of a *skialosklek* spell being cast. Abruptly, Vletraka shoved me down and I saw acid burning into her shoulder. In the archway stood Larzed, his face a bloody mess. He staggered forward and began casting again.

I should have made certain of his death! I need to save Vletraka; though now, we might both meet the Dark Lady tonight anyway.

"Go!" my mistress shouted. "I'll fend him off, but you need to run!"

I stared at her for a moment. She was living alabaster in black robes, strong and resolute. Though I still wished to fight beside her, I knew better than to question her judgment. I ran to the kitchen, losing my balance momentarily as a bolt of force caught me just above my left kidney, then slipped through the door away from the battle. I grabbed my pack, crammed *In Between* and Wosken's book in with my other supplies, and ran out the back. As I looked over my shoulder, I could see flashes of eldritch energies through the window. Vletraka may not win this fight, but she will certainly make the old man earn her death.

'Where are we going?' asked Thessylia telepathically. *'Someplace quieter, I hope. I cannot hear clearly with all this noise.'*

'I... do not know yet. The village might be endangered if I go there, so we might have to head straight for the city of Dureltown. Maybe we can gather some information there.'

'Cities are even noisier,' she complained.

'True, but they also have plenty of mice and rats. Unless you feel that the cats will be too much competition,' I teased.

Thessylia let out an affronted squawk and flew ahead. It would not surprise me if she ate the first cat she saw to set an example to all others once we got to the city.

Chapter 7: Escape From Home

I am not certain how far I traveled away from Vletraka's tower before wandering off the path into the deeper woods. It must have been over an hour, for the temporary healing effects of *vriiwamrayk* had worn off, causing the burns from Wosken's spells to resurface and bringing back the repressed pain of those wounds.

Thessylia flew nearby, hoping the noise from my footsteps would flush out prey, as well as to protect me in my weakened state. I found a tall patch of undergrowth, huddled within its verdant confines, and allowed myself to cry.

I have never been prone to emotional outbursts, finding that keeping a cool head often results in better outcomes in stressful situations than acting on my feelings, but there are times when the circumstances allow for emotional release. I knew what I had to do, and I had traveled to the nearby villages occasionally in the past and the city only once, but for a time, I found myself unable to move. I had never felt such fear or such a heavy loss in my young life; the pain of losing Vletraka outweighed even the loss of my family. Ashamedly, I even gave myself hope that Vletraka would be along in a few minutes, searching for me to tell me that it was safe to return home. Though she made the book invisible to scrying, I was certain that she would be able to find her own apprentice. Then I realized that Larzed might also find a way to follow me and I shrank deeper into the brush.

'You should rest. I believe your hunters have lost sight and hearing of you,' communicated Thessylia.

'I must find a safer place, further away from home in case Larzed survived and is still seeking me out.'

'I will check to see if anyone is nearby.' She flew off and circled the area for a few minutes before returning to the branch above me. *'There are no other humans about. Rest and get some strength back. You must not become prey.'* Short-eared owls are daylight hunters by nature, but her magical qualities lend her the typical nocturnal

senses of her cousins as well. In essence, she hunts and sleeps whenever she feels like it, regardless of the cycles of her non-magical brethren.

I wiped my nose to clear the excess fluids created by my tears and gave a wry smile. Thessylia's viewpoint was often enlightening and reminded me of how differently she saw the world from me. *'Very well. Be sure to wake me if anyone comes nearby.'* She answered with a quiet trill and took up a guarding position higher up in the large oak tree above me.

I awoke several hours later at the insistence of my own scratching to find myself covered with red ants! I had chosen to rest near their hill, never noticing it in the dark. I jumped up and quickly began brushing them off. Small red welts had already grown on my arms and legs, and I was certain that the rest of me would look much the same. I grabbed my pack and bolted out of the brush. *'Thessylia! Is there a stream or pond nearby?'*

'Go left. There, straight on,' she directed me.

I ran through the trees until I came upon a small creek. "Good enough," I said aloud, quickly stripped in the pre-dawn light, and plunged in. The water was not deep enough for me to completely submerge myself, but I washed as quickly as I could. When I was certain there were no more ants on me, I grabbed my clothes and shook them out over the creek, examining each article, my breeches, midnight blue robe, and sandals, to ensure that all the vermin had vacated them before donning them once more.

I next emptied my pack and checked it and the contents thoroughly. Though there were some ants on my spare clothes and books, the majority was nibbling on the small amount of provisions I had packed for the trip. I do not much care for hard tack or dried rations, I doubt few people do, but it was all I had to last me until I found an inn along the road, or at least a marketplace. I carefully brushed the ants off my food, and took a bite of the dried, hard bread before setting it down on a wide flat rock on the creek bed. I did the same with the desiccated meat, then took a mouthful of water from my water-skin to drink. I then wiped off each book and placed them gently on the rock to avoid re-infestation, and shook out my spare clothes, which consisted only of two extra pairs of breeches and a spare robe, and placed them upon the rock as well.

With everything cleaned off, I took another bite of the tack and washed it down with more water. I carefully put everything except my spell-book in the backpack, sat down on another large rock, and studied my spells. The woods are dangerous, and it is always wise to prepare a number of spells for combat, along with more utilitarian magicks. Though I knew I had to travel on, I could not resist a quick perusal of Wosken's spell-book. As I suspected, there were several fire spells in his book, but also a few others that would be useful later on.

I should have packed some quills and ink. Wait—I don't have time to copy these spells now! Focus! I packed up the two books, glanced at *In Between* longingly, as I wished to delve further into its secrets as well, and began my long journey toward Dureltown, named for Prince Durel, son of founding King Loren.

I decided to walk for a while. As my spellcasting ability has grown, *hivliuose* would last much of the day, but not enough that I would not have to walk more later on or cast it twice. Best I save it until late morning, then ride the summoned mount the rest of the day until nightfall. Dureltown would take nearly half a moon to reach on foot, and though I wished to travel quickly, it occurred to me that some time alone to process yesterday's events would do me well. Thessylia was correct about the noise of the city, though she is unaware of the stench that thousands of bodies living in close proximity exude. Though I am loathe to stop for fear of leading Larzed or another wizard into an area full of innocents, I need to do so at the occasional village to renew my food supplies. Medicinal herbs I can find, but I doubt my ability to find enough food on my own to sustain myself for the journey and I refuse to rely on Thessylia's findings.

My food stocks lasted four days, which was enough for me to skip the nearest villages and put more space between my potential pursuer and me. As time passed, I began to harbor hope that my Mistress had removed Larzed from the equation, but as I had no sign of Vletraka either, I began to suspect that neither had survived.

Whenever these thoughts came into my head, the world became drab and grey until I calmed myself down. I never really thought about the old saying about how one's feelings color their world, but it appears to be true; either that, or my connection to Thessylia is causing me to lose the ability to see in color—a thought that depressed me once again.

While I contemplated how my life was unraveling, a girl appeared out of thin air at my feet.

She shouted, "Mistress, no!"

I jumped back from my visitor to avoid colliding with her, and suddenly realized that there were blue and crimson motes of light streaming from her green, silver, and yellow hair. Her clothes were rumpled and charred, blood welling up from numerous scratches all over her body. "Glitter?" I asked aloud in surprise.

"Who... oh gods, not you," she said with a mixture of surprise and loathing. "Why would she send me to *you*?"

It was plain to me that I was still not welcome in her presence. "I have no idea. What happened? You look like you have been mauled by a dragon."

"A drake, actually, but yes. Another wizard and her apprentice attacked Mistress Goldfire and me in our own home. They came claiming to be seeking some book or another and attacked without warning." She looked around, realizing that we stood in a forest glade. "Where are we, and what are you doing here?" she asked, her eyes on the edge of tears.

"We are on the road to Dureltown, four days out from Vletraka's tower. We too were attacked, and Vletraka sent me away just as Goldfire did you, though without the teleportation head start. I believe our attackers have lost my trail, but I am not yet confident that I... we are safe. If this has happened to you as well..." I suddenly recognized that the others might be endangered as well! *Arrogant fool, to think that you were the only one!* "Do you know the *ikaaskiil* spell?" I asked her quickly.

"I don't even have my spell-book!" she cried. "I'm out here in the middle of nowhere, with you of all people, and I barely have the clothes on my back!"

"Again, I am sorry for what happened before. Here," I took off my pack and pulled out my spare robe. "I understand that it's not the color or style you are accustomed to, but it is all I can offer. Perhaps we can buy you a new one in the next village. You can use my spell-book as well until we can replace yours."

She opened her mouth to shout at me again, that she wanted nothing from me—that look has been indelibly etched into my memory—when she suddenly softened. "You would trust me with your spell-book?" her face a puzzle. "How do you know I won't destroy it to spite you?"

"That you even ask proves that you would not. Here," I handed her Wosken's spell-book. "This belonged to the apprentice who attacked me. Perhaps he has spells more to your liking, though you are welcome to utilize mine as well. I know you are fond of enchantments, and I have neglected that school in my focus on necromancy; he may have something you can use. Contrary to what you think, I never intended to cause you such grief, and I have no call to harm you now. In fact, I need your help as much as you need mine. Until we can learn to be friends, may we call a truce?"

Glitter dropped to her knees on the hard ground and sobbed, various shades of blue, yellow, and green motes dripped from her as she did. I stood my ground until she had calmed herself, not knowing how to respond to her outburst.

When she relaxed, I opened my spell-book to the page where I had inscribed *ikaaskiil* and knelt, placing the book on the ground between us. "We need to warn the others. Blythad, Faldrein, and Uxadul are probably in as much danger as we have been, assuming they have not been attacked already."

She nodded in agreement, and we both bent over to study the runes that would prepare the casting of the spell.

As we had both allotted the energy for spells of similar vitality earlier today, with Glitter expending much of it already, we needed to shift the prepared energy to cast the new spell. It is a complicated procedure, though, one we were both trained to do. The best way to describe it is to think of all the spells we know as being inscribed within us, the mystic runes glowing with energy as we prepare the casting each day. To change spells afterward, the energy for one needs to be transferred to the runes of the other, which takes about ten to fifteen minutes of concentration on the new spell while consciously turning off the energy allotted to the old one. This is the main drawback of needing to prepare spells ahead of time, using our best judgment of what to expect over the course of the day to decide which ones might be needed. Changing spells in the midst of battle is impossible, so proper preparation is essential. In this instance, we had time to make the change, as well as the necessity to do so.

In short order, we sent messages to each of our friends, with Glitter sending hers to Uxadul, as I expected he would ignore one from me.

"Are you ready to travel on?" I asked my reluctant companion.

"I suppose. How far are we from the nearest village?"

I cast *hivliuose* before answering. "We should reach it before nightfall, assuming you will ride with me."

She took a deep breath and closed her eyes, exhaling with a slight moan and nodding. I mounted the conjured horse first, then offered my hand to help her up. She steeled herself before touching my hand, and easily pulled herself on top of the steed behind me. Once she had settled in, we began a slow trot down the rutted road.

"You seem to be comfortable on horseback," I noted. "Did you learn to ride before your apprenticeship or after?"

We rode in silence for some time before she decided to answer. "Before," she said flatly, choosing not to expound any further.

"Until I met Vletraka, I had never ridden a horse," I admitted, attempting to ease some of the discomfort between us. "I fell flat on my back the first time I tried to climb one and had the wind knocked out of me. I find flying to be much more enjoyable than riding, but the spell does not last long enough to cover enough distance for long trips to make it worth casting."

"Yeah," she agreed sullenly, holding lightly to my hips for balance. Neither of us spoke for a while after that, it being obvious even to me that she was not going to engage me in conversation. As we rode, I noticed there was a white mark on the brown mare's forehead, which looked like two crossed crescents, my personal symbol. Yet again, I have been forced to kill in order to survive, this time, a boy of my own age. My breath shuddered as I reigned in my disgust over once again taking a life, albeit one that was bound and determined to take mine. As we rode, I felt Glitter lean down on my back, having passed out from exhaustion.

Shortly before dusk, we rode into the village of Elmvale. I am hardly wealthy—apprentice wizards do not get paid in coin, but Vletraka did grant me a small allowance for duties performed beyond my normal tasks, allowing me to scrape together a handful of copper scales and a few silver talons. I once held a pouch full of golden drakes when shopping for Mistress Vletraka in Dureltown, and was particularly careful about concealing it from thieves, and I have yet to see an actual platinum dragon coin. The scales should afford us food for the journey to Dureltown, and I parted with a trio of talons for a simple robe for Glitter; money I had planned to spend on a room at the inn. Instead, we passed through Elmvale to sleep at the outskirts of the village beneath the large trees that were the village's namesake.

'There are humans trying to hide in the trees nearby.'

I suppose we would not have rest just yet. *'Show me.'* I placed a hand on Glitter's shoulder and closed my eyes, slowing my pace to a crawl.

Indeed, there were five humans that Thessylia had spotted, their perches covered from view from the ground, but clearly visible to a flying owl. They had bows in hand and an arrow ready to nock, and I got the distinct impression they were not hunting deer.

"I think there are bandits up ahead," I whispered gently to Glitter, who was pulling herself away from my touch. "Now would be a good time to prepare defenses."

We both cast *ajiavulhysayt* and *bezyamhysa*, two basic defense spells that would protect us as well as any warrior in full armor and shield. No sooner had we completed the spells than five arrows flew toward us, the two that were on target glancing harmlessly off our spells. We ran to hide behind a large elm, knowing full well that we were not impervious, to find cover until we could strike.

"I can't see them," Glitter shuddered. "How did you know they were there?"

"Thessylia spotted them," I said calmly as the owl flew to my arm. I cast *klivvvad* and her talons crackled with negative energy. Turning to her, I said "Sneak up on one and claw him, while finding me a target."

She blinked once, flew off, and I closed my eyes again to follow her vision. She circled silently for a moment, getting me a fix on where three of them were.

"One there, there, and there," I pointed out to Glitter as a crackle and a scream pierced the twilight gloom.

I chose the first target Thessylia showed me and spotted him through the foliage. Without her eyes, I never would have known he was there. I launched a trio of blue-black motes, courtesy of *ajilek*, at him, the bolts nearly as invisible as my opponent in the late twilight, which unerringly struck him in the chest, knocking him from his perch, stone dead before he hit the ground. At the same time, I heard a flute playing, and knew Glitter was *charming* the archer closest to her; I assumed Wosken had that in his spell-book, though I do not know where she found a flute. Silently, he climbed down from his perch and smiled at her as if meeting a long-lost friend. An arrow landed at her feet while she stood waiting for him.

"Would you be so sweet as to tell the others to stop shooting at us? You know that we don't mean them any harm," she said sweetly to her new paramour.

"Guys, knock it off. These are friends," he shouted up to the trees.

"Then why are they killing us, you idiot?" came a voice from above and to my left.

"Well, we did shoot at them first," he grinned. "We didn't know it was you," he smiled at Glitter.

"That's alright," she smiled back. "So, what are you doing around here, hiding in the trees and waylaying travelers?"

"Well," he blushed, "we were looking for someone wealthy to rob. It's just a job."

One of the other bandits climbed down and walked up to Glitter and his fellow. "We're supposed to be robbing people, not chatting them up! Although…" he looked at Glitter with a strange smile. "You are a pretty one, worth far more alive, I'd wager."

"Marn, I told you she's a friend. Don't look at her that way."

"Trying to keep her all to yerself, lad? We share everything, after the boss gets his, of course. Though maybe we should hold on to this treasure a mite, eh?"

"That is no way to talk to a lady," I said, standing behind the nasty fellow. I put my hand between his shoulders and drained the life from his body with *vriiwamrayk*, his flesh sinking into his bones. An arrow bounced harmlessly off my *bezyamhysa* shield. A moment later, a scream came from where the arrow was fired and the bandit dropped to the ground, his face raked with bloody lines from Thessylia's talons, his right arm broken from the fall. I strode imperiously to the fallen bandit as he tried to raise himself up. He tugged on his rapier with his left hand when I raised my hand, fingers upward as if holding an invisible sphere.

"I would let go of your weapon if I were you. Your comrades are dead, and you can join them just as easily."

He blanched and went limp, staring at me in utter terror.

"What is your name?" I asked with a dark smile.

"K-Korth," he stammered.

Thessylia landed on my shoulder and began to lick the blood off her talons.

Korth quivered. "That demon bird is yours?"

Thessylia screeched. Her ploy would have been more effective had she not been so close to my ear.

I was startled at her vocalization. "Yes, and as you see I can barely restrain her. She believes you to be a very large mouse. Are you a mouse, Korth?"

"No," he answered carefully.

"A rat then. Tell me rat-Korth, why should I not let my friend here eat your eyes out of your head?"

"What are you doing?" Glitter's voice came from behind. "Can't you see that he's frightened to death?"

"She is a merciful angel, is she not," I smiled at the bandit. "You are lucky that she is here. After you and your friends attempted to perforate us with arrows," I said a little more loudly to remind Glitter why we were in this situation, "I would just as soon leave you for the scavengers."

"Look," Korth shuddered, "you can have my coin. Nyv's black waters, I'll even tell you where to find Flinjirt. Just let me go, okay?"

Well, we are short on coin... "Very well. Who and where is this Flinjirt. He is your master, I take it?"

Korth nodded.

"And where might we find this master of bandits?"

"We-we have a small hideout about two miles down this path," he pointed.

"He has a two hundred and fifty gold drake bounty on him," Glitter's new friend offered. "He's a bit of a jerk, and there is another half-dozen or so bandits out looking for targets. If you hurry, you can catch him alone."

"I've had enough 'easy money', as he said." Korth spat. "Easy way to get killed, I say."

"What were you before this?" I asked.

"Just another poor blacksmith. Flinjirt convinced me that my strong arm would be good for fighting, now it's good for nothing."

"Let me see what I can do." I pulled my dagger, making Korth's eyes go wide, and cut off the bottom part of his jerkin. Easily finding two sizable branches, I tied them around his arm in a makeshift splint. "Keep it still for a couple of weeks until it can heal. Now, go... home!" I growled.

Korth shuffled to his feet and scampered off. About this time, Glitter's friend began to shake off the spell.

"What's going on?" he asked, beginning to realize his situation.

"Well," Glitter cooed, "you were about to lead us to Flinjirt and become a big hero."

"No way I'm crossing him!" he held his hands up. "Do you know what he does to traitors?"

"Do you see what we do to bandits?" I asked.

He looked around at the broken bodies of his friends. "Yeah. All right. But afterwards you gotta let me go like you did Korth."

"As long as you promise to give up banditry and take up a legal profession, then yes," Glitter answered.

"Whatever you say. I'm not getting killed for that weasel. Follow me."

He led us through the woods to a small encampment with five small and one large tent around a campfire. Without a word, he slipped off into the darkness of the trees, leaving Glitter and I alone. Well, nearly alone.

'Give us a quick scan of the area. I want to avoid being surprised by a horde of rogues.'

Thessylia flew a trio of circuits around the campsite. *'The only human noise is coming from the larger building. There are plenty of rabbits around here, though,'* she thought hungrily.

'Have at them. Thank you.' "The large tent, as if there was any doubt. No other people nearby."

"Good."

We snuck up to the large tent, tip-toeing to avoid snapping any branches and giving ourselves away. There was an odd grunting noise coming from within.

She whispered, "At least he sounds distracted," a wry smile on her lips.

I did not catch her meaning until she pulled the flap of the tent open, where we saw a large, hairy naked man kneeling behind an, also naked, woman, who did not look nearly as excited as the man did. When she spotted us, she rolled her eyes up and shook her head. Her golden hair cascaded over her bronzed shoulders, draping over her swaying… Glitter dropped the tent flap. Her sparkles were a deep rose, mimicking her cheeks, with occasional flashes of orange. She pointed to me, then the flap, and began chanting a spell. When she nodded her head, I lifted the flap and she pointed at Flinjirt, who ceased moving from her *liskakhuuma* spell.

"Thank the gods, darlings," the woman said, shifting away from Flinjirt and standing up.

I had seen nude bodies before, both in sculpture and on the dissection table, but never alive, breathing heavily, soft, warm, sweaty, and standing with one leg slightly behind her, her knee slightly bent, thrusting her other hip forward, leaving me completely stunned.

"Tie him up," a voice said somewhere in the distance. Then, "Mithron! Stop ogling her and tie this man up!" I shook off the daze and found a length of rope, while the woman smiled at me. I wrapped the rope around his waist and arms, tying them tightly.

"Oh, darling, you are going to have to do better than that," the woman said in a voice that sounded like warm honey. She stepped over and took the rope from me, wrapped it around his wrists and ankles, tying knots far more secure than I could have come up with. She smiled at us and explained that she grew up raising cattle and tying up a man was no different than tying up a calf. Shortly thereafter, Glitter's spell wore off.

"Well, this is interestin'," Flinjirt smiled. "If ye wanted to join in, ye just hadda ask."

Glitter paled slightly, then reddened. I noticed then that Flinjirt's... enthusiasm had not waned while under the effects of her spell.

Turning to her I whispered, "Now, how do we collect the bounty on this man?"

She turned back to me and shrugged.

The other woman laughed. "You kids should be better prepared if you want to become bounty hunters. Tell you what, split the take with me, half for me, half for your two, and I will tell you what to do."

"Perhaps we can make it a little more even," I countered. "Forty percent for you, and thirty percent for each of us. You still come out with a larger share."

"All right, deal." She stuck out her hand, and when I grabbed it to shake it, she pulled me in for a deep kiss, which left me reeling. The world slipped into grey, and I suddenly became aware of the many men this woman had had sex with, rarely for joy and at least one had forced her against her will. Tears began to well up in my eyes as her darkest memories began to flow over me.

"Knock it off, you," Glitter growled.

I pulled back and the images faded. *It happened again! At least I could not say anything this time. I can imagine how she would react.* I looked at Glitter and mouthed, "I am sorry," to her.

She looked at me quizzically then said to our new ally, "Get dressed and help us deliver this man."

"Let me go, and I will pay you more than that pitiful bounty is worth," Flinjirt offered.

This gave the lady pause. "How much, darling?"

"I will give you two hundred gold a piece, much more than the two hundred and fifty drakes you will get from the Captain in Dureltown."

"And you can pay us now?" she cooed in his ear.

"Of course, my dear, the chest is buried right under my cot." He froze, his eyes widening as he realized his mistake.

"Wonderful, we will take that as well," she smiled and kissed him.

I stood guard as Glitter and the woman dragged the cot aside and pulled away the oval woolen rug underneath, which had covered the small wooden chest. Our naked friend then rifled through Flinjirt's piled and discarded clothes until she found a key. With a smile, she strutted over to the chest and unlocked it. It was half-filled with assorted coins and jewelry.

"Well, kids, it looks like we will be on easy street from now on!"

"Should we not return it to its original owners?" I naively asked.

"And how are we to determine who any of this belonged to?" Glitter responded. "The jewelry might be distinctive enough, but anyone can lay claim to coin."

"I'll save ye the worry, lad. A good many of them is dead." Flinjirt laughed.

I reined in the urge to kick him, merely scowling instead.

"Right, take it all. I'll not be in prison long, and I'll remember each o' ye. Ye've made an enemy of Flinjirt this day!"

"Listen to me very carefully, you scale-pinching, backstabbing, good-for-nothing murderous creep," I murmured in his ear. "I have already killed too many tonight, and far more in the past week, than I care to. However, if I ever see you again after this, or you even dare to send your pathetic minions after us, I will hunt you like an owl hunts a mouse—deliberately, silently, and assuredly. I know who you are and what you have done." As I spoke those words, I found that they were true! Is this my gift, to know what evil things people have done? But Glitter's act was not evil, just fearful, and our new friend had evil done to her. I need to think upon this more. "There will be no escape from my talons, and I will make the pain last far beyond your imagining before, eventually, releasing you to the Dark Lady. Am I clear?"

He responded by urinating on my feet.

I stood, shaking the warm liquid from my feet. "Right then, how best to get him to Dureltown? It's a long way still by foot, and longer if we need to drag his carcass around like that."

"We'll tie him to one of the horses, riding is so much faster than walking, darling. We can divvy up the gold here later. We should be gone before his boot-licking bandits return."

"Good idea," answered Glitter. "I shall keep track of the gold until then."

"You don't trust me?" the naked woman scowled. "Smart move!" she followed with a laugh. "I suppose I ought to get dressed now, if only to protect myself from mosquitoes." She gave me an impish grin. "The name is Orla, by the way."

"Mithron, and the Lady Glitter," I introduced.

"And what are you children doing in this part of the woods, anyway?"

"Did you not know?" Glitter responded. "Bounty hunting is what we wizards do in our spare time to hone our skills. Say, you don't have a price on your head, do you?"

"We all have prices, darling, but not on my head." She fluttered her eyelashes and laughed again.

We dragged Flinjirt outside, following Orla to the horses.

"How are we going to get him up there?" asked Glitter, realizing that the three of us were short on raw muscle.

"I have an idea." I began a slow, steady chant, then plunged my hands into the earth at my feet. A moment later, an earth elemental, a four-foot tall creature comprised entirely of living rock, stone, and soil, rose from below. I pointed to Flinjirt then made a lifting motion onto the horse.

The elemental stared at me for a moment, or paused at any rate, as its eyes were made of quartz and it is impossible to determine whether or not it actually stares, as if trying to comprehend my instructions, then lifted Flinjirt and threw him over the horse. Flinjirt landed on his shoulder, and I heard it snap as he landed. I shall not repeat his tirade, which should not have been uttered before two ladies the first time. After further instruction, the earth elemental lifted him once more, not comprehending Flinjirt's protests any more than my earlier instructions and placed him gently on the horse. Orla quickly tied him to the animal face down to keep him from falling and fleeing, while I jammed his shoulder back into its proper place. I thanked the elemental for its service and dismissed it back to its own plane. Years later, I would study the languages of the denizens of the Elemental planes, but at this time, I had other priorities.

We rode out toward Dureltown, picking our way carefully in the dark, predawn light. "How do you know that this is the right direction?" queried Glitter to Orla.

"Dureltown is north of here, and the sun is brightening in the east. So for the morning, we keep the sun to our right."

"Are you from Dureltown?" I asked. "What were you doing out here?"

"Yes, and getting hammered by a brute with no talent for pleasing women," she answered to Flinjirt, who scowled at her over his horse. "Oh, don't look so surprised, darling. Have you ever heard a woman moan in pleasure over your grunting? I was busy planning a shopping trip with the gold you promised me the whole time. Were it not for the constant pounding, I would have been fast asleep!" she laughed, causing Flinjirt to scream against the rag stuffed in his mouth. "A woman likes to be romanced. Treat her kindly and she will do the same for you. Like so many men, you only care about your own needs." She followed with a slap to his exposed backside, causing him to scream further, which in turn caused Orla to laugh harder.

"I have to agree with you there. Men are jerks," Glitter said flatly. I *know* she was looking directly at me when she said it, though I could not see her face.

"So, what's with the sparkles anyway, darling? Is that another wizard thing? I've never encountered the like before. It must make it hard to sneak up on bounties."

"We each have a different gift, this is mine." As she spoke, her sparkles flashed through an array of colors and intensities, from a dark purple which was nearly invisible in the twilight, to bright yellows which made her shine like a beacon.

"I didn't know that you had that much control. I have only seen you change with your moods," I stated in wonderment.

She smiled smugly at me.

"And what about you? Do you have a wizard talent too?" asked Orla.

"I am... still attempting to figure it out. So far, it just seems that I am able to hurt people's feelings without trying." I sighed.

Orla looked at me, then Glitter, figuring out our relationship faster than I ever could.

Having access to real horses, which would not vanish after a few hours, greatly expedited our journey, allowing us to reach Dureltown in a few days. The guards at the gates were amused at our cargo, teasing us about paying an "entertainment tax" before we could explain our cargo, at which point they summoned a page to find Vondelos, the Captain of the Guard, who arrived promptly along with a half-dozen men.

"Well, well, well. Flin*jerk*, we meet at last," Vondelos addressed Flinjirt's mosquito-bitten exposed rump. "You look different than I expected," he followed with a chuckle, then walked around to the other side of the horse. "Ah, yes. This is the face matching the posters. Well done, you three," he smiled at us, "your reward has been well-earned." Vondelos handed me a leather bag with ten twenty-five drake gold trade bars held within, then took the reins of Flinjirt's horse and walked him away.

I dug four of the trade bars out and handed them to Orla. "Forty percent, as promised. It has been a pleasure doing business with you."

"We could have had more pleasure if you wanted, darling," she cooed, smiling wickedly, then rode off with a laugh. It is reasonable to assume that she was referring to physical pleasure, which I suppose might be interesting with a trained professional. Honestly, though, I had no idea how to "romance a lady", to use Orla's words, but her advice on making peace with Glitter would likely prove valuable.

I turned to Glitter so as not to gape at Orla. "Here are your three."

"Thank you." She took the small bars and added them to her share of Flinjirt's treasure, which we had divided before entering the city. With a smile she said, "These belt pouches are getting heavy! I never thought that I would have so much money. What are you going to do next?"

"First, find a place to rest so I may spend a day not on horseback. After that, gather information on who sent Larzed and his boy after us, so I can tell him how I feel about Mistress Vletraka being murdered on his behalf and avenge her."

Glitter stared at me for a moment, then surprised me by asking, "May I join you?"

"I thought you hated me."

"I'm still not happy with you, but we have the same goal right now. If you don't kill the bastard who did this to us, I will! Loathe though I am to admit it, we actually work well as a team, and once I rewrite my spell-book, I will be ready to go."

Unexpectedly, I found myself pleased at having a companion on my journey of vengeance.

Chapter 8: Meetings

Glitter and I found ourselves renting rooms at the Inn of the Weeping Rose, often referred to as merely 'The Rose' by the folk of Dureltown. The accommodations were clean, and Lorgom, the owner and barkeep, brooked no breaching of the peace within his establishment. He was surprised when we asked for two rooms, wondering why we wished to be separated, but was satisfied with an answer of gold for a week's stay for each of us plus stabling. Much of our time was spent in our respective rooms: Glitter re-writing her spell-book from a combination of memory, copying Wosken's book, and purchasing scrolls to fill in the gaps, while I also used Wosken's book to enhance my own while delving into the depths of *In Between: On the Transition from Life to Death to Life*; there was little in my book that she was interested in.

For the first time in my young life, I had enough wealth to do nearly anything I desired, save that gold would not buy my vengeance. Most of my purchasing that first week was on ink and scrolls, both produced by a wizardly scrivener who made his living by disseminating magical spells to the general populace. One of the first things I did was to acquire a scroll with a *juut* spell, which produces magical light similar to a candle without any heat, write it into my book, and cast it upon my dagger so that I would have a steady light source which could not set my books or the inn alight. I should have already had that in my book, but I had relied on Vletraka's previously cast lights, and had not taken the time when I had the opportunity.

While in Dureltown, I also learned of "The Vault", a stone and metal fortress designed and run by a small band of grommoldi and tillalli to protect other people's valuables, for a small fee, of course. Both races are well known for their talent with iron and rock, and to my unpracticed eye, it seemed that the walls were close to impenetrable, at least physically. Grommoldi are renowned for their talent working with earth, whether as farmers, miners, or craftsmen of metal and stone. They are shorter than the average human, coming to about shoulder height with me, but broad from shoulder to hip, with short, stocky legs, appearing somewhat like a scrunched human. Tillalli, tillal in the singular, are shorter still, nearly half the size of a grommold, and tend to be thin and wispy. Proportionally, they look like tiny humans with oversized noses, chins, and fingers, and their skin tones range through a variety of colorful pastels.

There are a number of magicks which could turn the walls to mud or even dust, and when I pointed this out to one of the grommoldi proprietors he laughed heartily, and explained that "That's what the tillalli are for!" which clarified to me both the tillalli's talent with magic and the grommold's disdain for their craftsmanship. Though tillallian magic tends toward the useless school of illusion, many are also talented in working with living stone, much like Uxadul, and have likely reinforced the structure, as well as having the ability to rapidly repair it. When asked, they readily boasted that they could block teleportation and planar travel, which could bypass the walls entirely, as easily as an attack on the physical building. Confident in their abilities, I secured the better part of my gold with them, as I felt uncomfortable carrying around so much wealth, for both safety and the weight of all that coin.

As the proprietor of an establishment for travelers, I assumed Lorgom might be the one to speak to about our quest for vengeance, hoping that he would have overheard some tidbit of information. Sadly, he had not, but he introduced us to Ial'rafiost, rather, the other way around, or 'Raf' as everybody called him. Raf is perhaps the most joyful man I have ever met or will likely meet, and yet I never found his company to be unwelcome. He was proudly half-zylan, having no shame about his poor zylan mother or the human who probably never knew that he sired a son that one night, or about his times growing up and becoming the most talented second-story burglar in Dureltown due to his athleticism and agility. He claimed to have given up the life of thievery as he grew older, finding greater contentment as an entertainer and man of the streets. He kept no secrets, save one, which I would discover later, and made a point of charming everyone he met, myself included.

Raf was a lean, wiry man, with slightly rounded three-pointed ears, a mop of blond hair that remained unruly even after he carefully combed it, and lavender eyes with a touch of darker violet. The Weave wrapped itself loosely around him, showing that he had a minor talent for magic, unlike his clothes, which fit snugly to his thin frame with extra room around his joints to allow for his extreme flexibility. His attire was covered in streamers of various colors, which looked odd when he walked but made a dazzling display when he tumbled and spun about.

Glitter and I sat at one of The Rose's many pinewood tables eating a supper of overly seasoned roasted pork, potatoes, and carrots with too much gravy and cheap beer, which I turned to tea with a simple, apprentice-level spell. I still hold to Revance's rule about avoiding alcohol, as it can impair one's judgment, as well-demonstrated on many nights at The Rose. It is bad enough when men fight while drunk; when that man can command the elements and reshape the Weave to his whims, it can be disastrous. Glitter had a single glass of dark pink wine, assuring me that such a small amount would not be enough to impair her faculties. Though this appeared to be true, I still had no desire to test my own constitution. Ial'rafiost invited himself to our table and sat next to us. We both looked up at the stranger and saw Lorgom nodding his approval to us from behind the bar.

"Hi! Lorgom tells me that you are looking for a powerful wizard."

"That is entirely possible," I answered around a mouthful of underdone potato. "Both Glitter and I have been attacked by powerful wizards, and we are looking for their master."

"Well, if you are looking for someone whom powerful wizards work for, you are going to need some help, I think. I don't know how strong you both are, but I'm guessing you barely survived his minions. You're not planning on going for the head man by yourselves, are you?"

"Actually," spoke Glitter, "we didn't look that far in advance. Right now, we are just seeking information so that we can make a plan of action."

"A beautiful woman such as yourself should not have to worry about such things," he said taking her hand. "You should be living a life of comfort and ease with me," he grinned, then noticed the steel in her eyes. "However, I can see that this is important to you. Meet me back here tomorrow evening, and I'll see what I can find out." He kissed her hand, gave me a wink, and sauntered off.

"I expected there to be a charge for information," Glitter whispered to me.

"I expect the fee will come once he has something to sell," I responded. "Minus the cost of the meat." A large portion of my dinner had somehow vanished during our conversation.

Raf returned the next evening as promised. "Well," he began with a sigh as he joined us at our table.

Today's meal was much like yesterday's but done properly without too many spices. When I mentioned the improvement to Glitter, she smiled and informed me that she had a chat with The Rose's cook. I had ordered an extra plate for Raf, in the hopes that he would leave mine be. My assumption proved to be incorrect, and I was left wondering after having only half of my own meal again how he managed not to look like Blythad after his morning studies.

"I don't have any good information for you yet. However, I found someone who wants to help you on your quest."

Glitter and I looked at each other. She spoke first and said, "We should meet this person before deciding if he is what we are looking for. I assume that you vouch for him."

"Oh, absolutely! He is a man of honor and probably would have been a paladin if he were a more pious man. Being the son of Dureltown's Captain of the Guard doesn't hurt his standing either. Vondro has a lifetime of martial training and would add some physical might to your magic."

Glitter and I eyed each other again and we both nodded to Ial'rafiost, who then waved over a young man wearing a chain shirt and had a longsword buckled to his belt.

His eyes were of a chestnut brown, just a few shades darker than his skin, though not so dark as his hair. He had an aura that commanded attention, though whether it was due to his personal charisma, his fame and prowess, or his lineage was uncertain to me at the time, though I suspected the last.

He strutted up to our table and smiled at the three of us. "I, Vondro 'Brightlance' Serrenthal, will help you track down and handily defeat your enemies," he declared arrogantly and just loudly enough that his boast carried throughout the tavern.

"You conceited, pompous blowhard," I retorted, stunning him and reversing his prideful expression to one of disgust. "You know nothing of the enemies we seek; you do not know their power, their abilities, or their skills. It may be a powerful wizard we face, or merely an aristocrat—both are dangerous in their own way. Yet you stand here and boast to the rafters of your prowess like a young tomcat who has only proven its strength over lost kittens."

"You dare question my ability?" he growled, reaching for his sword.

"I certainly question your wisdom," I said flatly while staring at his sword hand. "Should you draw that weapon here, you will find yourself imprisoned either in a cell or a grave, neither of which will improve your fame or career."

Over his shoulder, I could see Lorgom reaching for the paired battleaxes, "Peace" and "Love", displayed over the bar.

Vondro slowly drew his hand away and eyed me intently. Lorgom relaxed and returned his attentions to other patrons. Against me, Vondro would not win a battle of wills any more than a battle of words, though I must give him credit for the attempt. I am not in the least physically imposing, being much shorter, even if I were standing, and thinner than him. In any physical contest, there is no question that he would win at every turn, but he is attempting at mental games, and is not nearly my equal. At long last, he looked away, though he held his ground far longer than I expected.

Before he could fully turn away, I spoke again. "I do not question your ability, for I have not seen you in action; I have only heard the words of a braggart. I am in need of a strong sword-arm at my side, however, and do not object to you proving your valor on our quest."

"Now who's being arrogant?" he responded. "'Allowing me to join your quest' is it? Why in all the realms should I help you with anything?"

"To turn your back on me is to allow justice to go unanswered. To walk away from aiding us is a loss of honor and the act of a craven. To ignore the plight of this fine lady is unchivalrous. If it helps your decision, any gold found will be split equally among partners."

"I'm not interested in treasure, though I will not refuse my share," he added the last part quickly. "I will assist you and the shining lady, for honor and for justice—not for you," he snarled.

"I am looking for allies, not friends," I said flatly. "We must, however, act as a team, aiding and protecting each other if we are to succeed. Perhaps in time we can at least learn to respect each other's abilities, if not each other."

"Done," he said, shaking my hand then dropping it, he took Glitter's in his and kissed it gently. Pink and green sparkles trailed from his lips to her hand as he pulled away.

"Don't you think you were a bit hard on him?" asked Raf after Vondro left our table. "He really is a nice guy. I hope you will be able to get along."

I took a sip of my beer-turned-tea. "I am certain that there is much we disagree on. If he can steady his temper, I would enjoy debating with him. I have issues with people who act as though they are more important than they truly are—he needed to know that I am not one to back down and fall easily to his command. If he wants to impress me, it will not be because of his father, but his own deeds.

"Glitter and I require the assistance of those with martial training—of that I am certain. In time, we will learn who our enemy is and what their ultimate goal is. Until then all help would be welcome."

"Then mayhap we can aid ye as well," spoke a grommold appearing silently at my side, his shaven head contrasting sharply with his long, thick, black beard. He stood dressed in simple brown robes and wooden sandals. Behind him stood a young human lady in robes of blue and green, her black hair hanging all the way down to her sash. Placing a large fist in an open hand, he bowed slightly and introduced himself and his companion. "I am Brother Ironknuckle, and this is Lady Tsukatta, priestess of Kimitsu of the Gentle Rain."

"Oh! Your hair is gorgeous!" exclaimed Glitter, whose hair was currently tightly curled, split evenly with deep red on the right side and bright silver on the left, jumping out of her seat to examine Tsukatta's locks more closely. Tsukatta's golden brown skin darkened slightly in embarrassment. "How do you keep it so soft and shiny?"

I quickly lost track of the ladies' conversation, though Raf sat rapt eying the pair, as Brother Ironknuckle demanded my attention.

"So what kinda trouble are ye two in?"

"My Mistress and I were attacked in our own home by a pair of wizards. Another pair attacked Glitter and her teacher. We are seeking the one who sent them after us."

"Ah, a mission of vengeance, then. I understand that all too well; at least in yer case, it sounds justified. Do ye think that once ye've vanquished yer foe that someone will try to avenge them?"

"Perhaps. We neither know who our foe is yet nor why they sent the wizards to attack us, aside from the fact that they were looking for old books. Perhaps in time, we will be able to figure out his or her or its plan and we can work from there. Until then, we are merely gathering information."

"I see. Well then, let me know what we can do ta aid ye when the time comes. It seems that the lasses have already become fast friends."

I turned to see that Glitter and Tsukatta were chatting amiably and excitedly, smiling and laughing as though they had known each other since birth. To this day, it amazes me how easily she always did that. It was not just her beauty, but also her spirit which drew them all in, and had I not embarrassed her so badly at the tournament, she would have drawn me in just as easily. Instead, I was the one person she pushed away while attracting all others, and it was at this moment that it truly began to bother me.

I felt a hard tap on my upper arm and heard Brother Ironknuckle repeat, "I said, how long do ye think before ye know what yer next step is?"

"Raf has been asking around, attempting to find us some information to lead us onward, though he seems entranced presently."

Without even glancing in my direction, Raf waved me to silence.

Ignoring him, I continued, "He knows how to accomplish this with subtleties that I lack; my own attempts have met with failure." In truth, I did not ask a great number of people. Lorgom knew nothing, and the scroll merchant told me that business had been slow for him, though I suspect that he knew more than he was willing to share. The few others I asked replied with blank stares or quickly moved away, leaving me wondering if it was the question itself, how the question was asked, or me they were avoiding.

"Well, if ye'd like, Tsukatta and me can ask at the temples and see if they know anything. They have lots of old scrolls and books too, but I don't know how much of it would involve magic. Mayhap they can divine the source of yer troubles."

"That might be worth a try. Let me know which temple might be open to trying that type of divination for me." Though everyone gives respect to the Dark Lady when death is at hand, few temples, or shrines, are built for her worship, as most see death as a necessary evil in the world and cannot understand why someone would venerate her. Further, the assumption is that if one worships the goddess of death, then that person would kill indiscriminately to serve her. The Dark Lady is more concerned with the transition of life and death, and escorting passed souls to their ultimate destination, not about the number of dead. As always, few people actually understand the duties of the gods, their temples, and their priests, and only see what they do not like about any other than their own faith.

Within Dureltown, there were temples to Lephix, the god of the sun and light, Mamoel, the moon goddess, Farvost, the god of travelers and luck, and Acclin, god of craftsmen, plus small shrines to some of the other deities. If there was one to the Dark Lady, it was likely hidden to protect it from the uninformed. If any, it would be Mamoel's temple that would accept my request for a divination, as Mamoel and the Dark Lady are said to be on friendly terms, though who am I to speak for the goddesses?

"Tsukatta and I will begin in tha morning, then." Brother Ironknuckle got up from the table and was immediately bumped by one of The Rose's more inebriated patrons.

"Shorry, little guy," he slurred, "I didn't see you there." As he spoke, beer sloshed out of his mug and spilled upon the monk.

Brother Ironkuckle's fists balled up and his face turned red with rage; I could almost hear the gnashing of his teeth over the tavern noise. Just as the drunkard was beginning to realize the grommold's intentions, Brother Ironknuckle took a deep breath and relaxed, his color returning to his normal ruddiness and his large fists opening. "Never ye mind. It was an honest mistake," he said while attempting to unclench his jaw. As he turned back toward me, the sot made the mistake of speaking again.

"Afraid of me, little guy? You should be. Me and my mates…"

I barely saw Brother Ironknuckle's hand move, so quick was his punch. The inebriated fellow stopped mid-sentence and collapsed to the floor, pouring beer over his chest as his hands instinctively moved to cover the spot of impact. No one else seems to have noticed.

"That was some punch," I said with more than a bit of awe. "When my brother hit me, I could always see the punch coming even if I could not avoid it."

"It's actually more about precision," he smiled. "Speed lets ye hit yer target afore he moves, and strength causes the damage. Hitting the right spot, though, that's where the pain comes in." There was a twinkle in his eye as he gave his lesson on fighting, and I felt glad for the victim of his lesson that the grommold acted after his anger passed and not before; I feared what damage he could have caused otherwise. "We shall talk on the morrow." This time, he managed to leave without incident.

"A story! A story!" I heard the ladies chanting at Ial'Rafiost.

He smiled in assent, lithely rose from his chair, and slipped through the crowd to the Rose's small stage. He stood silently for a moment, staring over the crowd. A hush rolled over the patrons from the stage to the rear of the room as he commanded their attention with little more than a smile.

"Penatecompt lived in northern Uljan, beyond the Sea of Salted Sands, where the ocean reaches inland and tide pools are abundant. He was a dragon of the deepest ebon, and belched forth smoke the thickness of tar, which ate away at armor and flesh alike as quickly as beer washes away a lump of salt. It was oft said that neither knight nor army could defeat this devil, and none had, for his scales were as hard as obsidian, and his teeth and claws just as sharp. All who challenged served only to feed the beast's unending appetite." Raf let loose a roar which caused the crowd to startle, then laugh as he grinned at them. While the patrons recovered, he called upon the Weave to create an image of the beast he had described. In the lamplight, it seemed mostly shadow, the blood-red eyes commanding everyone's attention.

"Knowing that no man could destroy Penatecompt, a fair maid by the name of Cloisette dared challenge the beast. Her skin was as white and smooth as milk, her hair and voice were of honey, and her beauty drew the eye of every man in her village, though she remained pure despite their offers."

The image of the dragon faded away, replaced by the image of the young woman, which had a face matching Glitter's, but the body was more voluptuous, similar to Aubri, one of the Rose's serving girls.

"The dragon, needless to say, was amused at this. 'Child,' spoke the ebon devil, 'wouldst thou be so eager to sacrifice thyself to me?' 'Nay,' she retorted with a soft smile, 'I have come to slay thee.' At this the dragon roared with laughter. 'There are but three things that can slay one of my ilk, mortal. Name them.'"

The image of Cloisette vanished, and all eyes focused on Raf.

"'Love,' she smiled, her eyes filling with joyous tears. At this the black beast stopped, no longer amused. 'Thou knowest one, human, name the others,' he growled, a note of trepidation in its voice. She wrapped her hands around one huge claw of the demonic dragon and said 'Love' a second time. Quickly and calmly, before the great beast could react, she kissed the dragon and spoke 'Love' a third time. At this, Penatecompt began to melt into smoke, flying to the south, over this very spot, in fact, trailing his stench behind him, getting ever smaller, quickly disappearing over the world's edge.

"But as she watched, a shudder came over her, and her feelings of love turned to pity. At this time, Penatecompt, not yet completely gone, appeared from the north, his great foulness having circled the globe, and descended toward Cloisette. When she saw his return, she knew fear, and that was her downfall, for it gave the beast strength enough to land a great paw upon her, crushing her with its last act before bursting into a dark cloud."

Raf stepped quietly off the stage and returned to our table, draining the last of his ale. The crowd murmured, some complaining about the unhappy ending while others drunkenly discussed the moral of the story. Before I could correct him on his obvious mispronunciation of the dragon's name, as half the letters do not exist in the Draconic tongue, Glitter pouted, "That ended sadly. Why couldn't you tell a happy story?"

"Anyone can tell a happy story," Raf retorted, "but no one ever learns from them. If I said that she survived and lived happily ever after, then Cloisette's story would be no different than a thousand others. As it happened, neither she nor the dragon were ever seen again after she announced her intentions and left her village, so my story is more likely truer than most. Besides, the crowd is quieter now, so we can hear each other again," he smiled.

Slowly, copper scales began to fill his mug as the patrons walked by.

It was close to midday when a light rapping on my door drew my attention from *In Between*. "Enter," I said absently while puzzling over a complex magical formula in the tome.

"Brother Ironknuckle said to find you and let you know about which temples might be helpful to you," said Tsukatta with the gentleness of a dove's cooing.

"Mamoel?" I asked without taking my gaze from my studies.

"They do seem to be the most open to performing a divination on your behalf, for a donation, of course."

"Of course. We will have to stop at The Vault on the way so I can withdraw some gold." I slipped the black ribbon attached to the volume's binding over the page, closed the book, and slipped it into my pack. "How much are they asking?"

"As you are not a member of the church, they are asking for 60 gold drakes for a minor divination, or 450 gold for a more direct connection to the goddess."

I stared dumbfounded at Tsukatta. With the reward money, topped with the liberated treasures of Flinjirt, I had considered myself wealthy. The few scrolls, inks, quills, and sheets of blank vellum I had purchased earlier came to a tidy sum, but only a small percentage of my earnings; 450 gold coins would not bankrupt me but would remove nearly half of my remaining assets. Nonetheless, it would be money well spent, and I did not have any other pressing financial needs.

"I was not expecting the price to be so high," I said after my mental calculations. "It must be powerful magic indeed. The scrolls I purchased were not nearly so dear."

"But you can use your scrolls on your own. Not only is it a more powerful divination, it requires a cleric of a high order to cast it, and they are not common, even in a city of this size."

I let a sigh escape from my lips. "That makes sense, and I can understand now why the affluent keep wizards and priests in their employ—it is probably cheaper to pay a regular salary than to pay per spell. Perhaps that is also why wizards generally come from wealthy families, for they have earned it over generations."

"You do not come from such a family? I had thought that true of all wizards."

"As did I, until I became one," I laughed. "I had that same discussion with Vletraka when she…" I trailed off. Suddenly, I could no longer speak; my throat was tight, and tears came unbidden to my eyes. The world turned grey, and I began to sob uncontrollably. I scarcely felt Tsukatta wrap her arms around me as I fell into another vision. I saw Tsukatta standing at the gates to a temple, her back to two older men who shouted at her in a language I could not understand, though it was clear they were berating her for some offense. Tsukatta's face contorted, attempting to control her anger and frustration, and I could make out Kimitsu's name spoken often, leading me to believe that she was praying for guidance.

"Let it go," I heard her voice from afar, calm and serene. "You cannot carry this weight for so long without it breaking you. Let it go."

It felt like hours, though I am certain it was only a matter of minutes before I was able to compose myself. *Who is this woman?* I asked myself. *We met for a few minutes last evening, and I have hardly even had a conversation with her, and I find myself revealing my wounded heart to her. I must be stronger than this if I am going to complete my vengeance. Yet, she makes me feel safe, protected from the pain.* "Why are you so nice?" I croaked out while attempting to steady my breathing.

"Kimitsu of the Gentle Rain teaches us to heal damage to both the body and the spirit. Tears are but one form of cleansing the heart, and we encourage those who need to cry to do so, in order to ease their burden. Do you feel better now?"

"I feel embarrassed, crying like a small child."

"There is no shame in releasing your sorrow, fears, and frustrations. It is in the holding in of one's pain that causes further hurt." Somewhere, she found a small, clean linen square and handed it to me.

After wiping my face and clearing my nostrils, I managed to cast *uvaazrosiit*, a minor spell with a variety of simple effects, including cleaning dirty items, and handed back the untarnished cloth. "Thank you, that was very thoughtful of you. I wish Kimitsu granted that spell; it would be a real time-saver on washing day!"

She giggled. Her laughter was infectious, and I found myself laughing with her, even though I still felt like crying. After composing myself, we left for the Vault.

Before allowing me my funds, I had to stand in front of a large, clear, oval crystal with a pair of tillalli standing opposite me. They smiled, and nodded to the grommold behind the counter, and he walked off to gather my gold. When I asked about the crystal, the tillalli explained that it showed the true form of whoever stood before it, protecting accounts from illusions, disguises, and shapeshifters. The grommold returned during our conversation and handed me a heavy bag filled with trade bars, coins, and a slip of paper informing me of my remaining savings.

Afterwards, we walked across Dureltown to the Ministerial District in search of Mamoel's temple; a simple task, considering its size and prominence. The Temple of Ever-Changing Luminescence, named not only for the shifting of the moon's phases, but for the brightness of the building itself, stood atop a small hillock, even in height with that of Lephix, her Bright Brother, one hill over. Through some trick of architecture or magic, I never received a satisfactory answer to which, the color of the Temple shifts, reflecting the moon above, turning from black marble to white, then back again; currently, only the eastern edge was white.

Upon entering, I discovered that the same held true for the interior, for the inner chambers were also dark except for the eastern walls. While I marveled at this, we were met by Carmia, a young, blonde acolyte with dark grey eyes, which hinted at a profoundly troubled past. I received no visions from meeting her, yet I knew that she suffered deeply. Before I could contemplate this feeling, she forced a smile and asked how she might be of service.

"We have an appointment with High Priestess Varli," answered Tsukatta, who bowed her head with all the due deference of one priestess in the temple belonging to a different goddess.

"Of course. Please wait here, and I shall retrieve her." Carmia then disappeared into the shadows, returning some time later with a short, dark-haired woman in tow. She was dressed in pale yellow and grey robes, soft black slippers, and a knowing smile that brings immediate comfort to all who see it.

"You are Tsukatta and Mithron?" verified Varli with a nod of her head. "Welcome to the Temple of Ever-Changing Luminescence. Tell me how Mamoel's servant can aid you."

"My mistress, as well as that of a friend's, has been murdered. I wish to know who is behind this plot, their reasons for doing so, and where to find them, that justice may be served."

"You are more interested in vengeance than justice," she winked, "but that is not my concern. I am sorry for your loss. Tell me what happened, so that we can focus our questions."

I related to her the events of the past week or so, pausing now and again to maintain my composure, and was never quite certain whether my vision was losing color due to the stark black and white of the chamber, or from the malefaction that had been plaguing my sight since the tournament.

Varli kept her council until I had finished, then spoke. "You have chosen well to seek divination at this time, for Mamoel's balsamic phase is a time for preparations afore beginning a new project or journey. Come tonight at moonrise, and we can begin."

"And when will the moon rise this night?" I asked, knowing that Mamoel's schedule varied with her phases.

"Tonight, she precedes her brother by less than two hours."

She wants me here two hours before sunrise? "Must it be so early? Do the priestesses of Mamoel not sleep?" I said half-joking.

"We sleep when Our Lady sleeps. Moonrise is the most auspicious time for divination. If your comfort is more important to you..."

"Forgive me," I interrupted, "I should have been more aware of the cycles of magic. I will be here at the appointed hour."

With that, Tsukatta and I left The Temple and returned to the Weeping Rose.

"We had best get some rest, if we are to arise again in the middle of the night."

"Perhaps it would be better if Glitter joined you for the divination, seeing as it affects her directly; unless that would be too uncomfortable for you both."

I stopped in my tracks and glared at her in surprise.

She gave a slight smile. "The tension between the two of you is obvious, though she refused to explain the reasoning for it. Although it is not my place to meddle in your affairs, especially as we have just recently met, you share a connection and must resolve your differences if we are to work together."

"I have tried and have apologized to her on multiple occasions. I embarrassed her before our peers, and she has yet to forgive me. Perhaps I do not deserve it." I turned, continuing my journey back to the inn.

Tsukatta fell back into step with me. "When she is ready, she will forgive you. Treat her kindly, so that she can see that you are a good man, and in time her pain will fade. I will ask her to join you at the Temple tonight."

"Thank you. I will have Thessylia wake me an hour before the appointed time, then come across the hall to collect her." One side benefit of having an owl for a familiar, is that she is usually awake while I sleep, and can alert me should I need to arise early.

I ate a light, early dinner—vegetable stew and a hunk of aging bread—and was in my room long before sunset. I was not tired, however, and could not force myself to sleep; excitement and apprehension about tonight's divination exacerbated the problem. I studied Wosken's spell-book for a while to distract myself, then began some meditation exercises in order to relax further.

"A wizard must have complete control over their thoughts," Vletraka reminded me.

I had only spent two nights in her home as her pupil, and she had me under a constant regimen of study, meditation, and menial labor. Normally, I would balk at the extra work, but she had me dusting the library, wiping each volume gently and replacing it carefully on the newly cleaned shelf. I had never been happier in my life! I wished to stop and read each tome, but there was much to be done, and so I did my best to remember where the books with the most intriguing titles were shelved, so that I might find them later.

"When wizards pull on the Weave, we, at least temporarily, have the ability to alter reality, creating effects that would not otherwise occur. If your mind is not clear and focused, you will not get the results you seek, and the magic will surge out of your control. This is a basic lesson of magic, and one of the most difficult. It is easy to get distracted, especially by our emotions, but the mind must rule the heart. Allow yourself to feel, and allow those feelings to pass; suppressing your emotions only makes them stronger. When you act, let your intellect lead."

Memories of my early lessons must have triggered my meditative state, as I relaxed enough to fall asleep, for the next thing I knew Thessylia was tapping on my mind. I pulled myself awake; surprised that Brother Ironknuckle's snoring on the floor did not wake me sooner. Stretching, I got up from the bed, put on my cleanest robe, and cautiously stepped over to the door. I recall his punch to the drunkard the other night and had no desire to test his reflexes if startled awake. The door refused to open quietly, but it was not enough to disturb my roommate; Raf must have found another place to sleep, else he is still telling tales downstairs.

I rapped gently on Glitter's door, hoping she would be already awake, and I would not have to disturb Tsukatta. Just as I was about to knock again, I heard the door's latch turning, and Glitter slipped out into the hallway.

"This better be good," she grumbled through bright blue bleary eyes.

"For the money they asked, I would hope so. I could have easily bought four blank books and enough quills and ink to fill them," I retorted softly so as not to wake any other sleeping patrons. "If this is the cost of finding our quarry, I will happily pay it."

Glitter looked at me as if to say something but kept her silence and continued walking.

We left the Rose in silence, aside from the creaky floorboards, and made our way through the cold fog toward the Ministerial District. As we began the climb up the hill to the temple, a figure stepped out of the thinning mist and deep shadows with a long, thin sword.

"Don't you make a lovely pair? And that satchel looks too heavy for a lad like yourself. How's about you let me carry it for you?"

I glanced at Glitter and sighed, then turned back to the would-be thief before us. "It really is not in your best interest to bother us. Go away."

"Well, that's not very gentlemanly of you." He turned his gaze upon Glitter. "Perhaps you should come with me also. I think I am going to be rich soon and can treat you better than him."

The blue-black missiles that fired from my fingertips were nearly invisible in the darkness, which the lamplights could not entirely dispel, and all three hit him squarely in the abdomen. As he doubled over from the pain, Glitter pulled out her flute and played the notes that I learned made her target friendly toward her.

He looked up at her and sheathed his weapon. "I'm sorry, miss. I didn't realize it was you," he said as if scolded.

"That is no way to treat a friend, or anyone else for that matter," Glitter rasped with sharp iron in her voice. "Head over to the guard station and tell them what you have done."

"Yes, miss. Of course, miss. Sorry, miss." He backed away from us, bowing with each statement, then turned and ran once he entered the shadows.

"I hope he reaches the station before your spell wears off," I said with a smile. "A pity that we cannot be there to see the guards' expressions when he tells them what he has done!"

"Who cares? As long as he's gone. Let's get this over with." The second most important thing I learned this night was to always allow Glitter to get a full night's rest.

We reached The Temple of Ever-Changing Luminescence a few minutes after the failed robbery. Three priests, one man and two women, were chatting outside the temple doors, their conversation coming to a complete halt as we approached.

"We have an appointment with High Priestess Varli," I said with a light bow of my head. "I am Mithron, and this is Glitter."

One of the women stepped up to us, her soft slippers making not a sound across the black marble. "She awaits you within. Follow me." Our guide led us through the dimly lit temple to an inner courtyard.

Varli stood behind a black altar with a sliver of white, placing a pair of silver cups upon it with great care. The air was somewhat cooler in the courtyard than outside the temple, the walls blocking the slight breeze and remaining fog.

I wonder how we are to see the moonrise from in here. The walls block out sight to the horizon.

"Welcome back. Is this the young lady who also seeks vengeance?" she asked without judgment.

"This is Glitter, and we share our predicament."

"Very good. First, do you have the proper donation?"

I handed over the satchel, glad to be rid of its weight.

She opened it, glanced over the contents for a moment, and set it aside on the ground. "Thank you. The Temple of Mamoel thanks you for your contribution. Please, sit, and make yourselves comfortable," she commanded, pointing to the ground before the altar. After we took our proper places, she turned to Glitter. "Mithron tells me that you both had your teachers killed at about the same time, and each of the killers was searching for an ancient tome. Is this correct?"

"Y-yes," Glitter stammered as tears welled up in her now bronze eyes. "A wizard named Forzo, and her apprentice Yurtha, came to our home and asked for *The Dirges of Calnerion*, a book neither Mistress Goldfire nor I had ever heard of. Forzo got frustrated that we would not give her the book and attacked. Before I knew it, I was in a duel with Yurtha, fighting for my life. She shook off my charms with ease, and I was not really prepared for battle. Just before Yurtha could kill me, Mistress Goldfire teleported me away, right in front of him," she pointed her thumb at me. "We came to Dureltown as quickly as we could, so as not to be sitting in the forest awaiting our attackers."

"Thank you. I take it that you also seek the one who sent those people after you?"

"Yes. Mistress Goldfire was like a mother to me." One could almost see the ice in her breath, though the night was not that cold.

I could feel my heart freeze as I realized she has lost two mothers to violence and had an image of Forzo and Yurtha appear in my eyes for but a moment, yet long enough to sear their faces forever into my memory.

"Then let us begin." Varli began chanting, calling upon Mamoel's guidance in her role as the Keeper of Hidden Mysteries.

While she recited her prayers and wove the magic around her, we could see the image of a thin crescent moon appear on the eastern wall of the courtyard, surrounded by the rising stars. I should have deduced that the stone would reflect the heavens as the whole temple mirrors the moon itself. I pulled out a blank sheet of vellum, an inkwell, and a pair of quills, in order to record whatever message, we were to receive.

Varli's hair then began to rise in a nimbus about her head, and I could feel the hairs on my arms rise along. Her voice halted for a moment, then changed to an otherworldly timbre.

"The master has lost his eternal heart.
His servants know the path;
Jaundiced eyes are filled with wrath.
With anger, one shall depart.

"The sleeping shall awake; the sleeper has left
To roam forever more.
A friend shall open the door
Leaving the others bereft.

"Surrounded by shadow, the lost are astray,
Each to their final fate;
The Dark Lady shall await,
For one has a longer delay."

Glitter and I turned toward each other, both awed by the divine presence we had witnessed, and confused by her words. I returned to the page, working to finish the prophecy before the words left my memory. It turned out to be an unnecessary precaution, as the memory of that early morning is as clear now as it was then.

When the magic settled, I turned to Varli, who seemed to be coming out of a trance, gazing upon us with a smile. "Though I appreciate Mamoel gracing us with her wisdom, but… I mean no disrespect, I suppose that you are probably unable to clarify her foresights," I said to our hostess, pleading in my voice.

She blinked a few times, still grounding herself. "I'm sorry, but when Mamoel speaks through me, I am overawed by her presence and scarcely present in my own body. I do not even know what she said."

I handed her the page with Mamoel's prophecy.

Varli read them over a few times. "My understanding of such divinations is that they make themselves clear in due time. Typically, the first few lines happen within a week, so I am guessing you will soon be led to this 'master' and his 'servants'."

I looked over to Glitter, who shrugged her shoulders, suggesting she had nothing else to say on the matter, then turned back to Varli. "Thank you, and thank Mamoel, for your time and energy. We shall puzzle over her words and see where they lead us." We stood, bowed our heads, and left the temple.

While walking back to the Rose, we were both muttering the prophecy just loud enough that we could hear each other and not broadcast it into the early morning.

"It all sounds like nonsense to me," Glitter grumbled. "A proper divination should have answered questions, not raised more of them."

"One cannot compel the gods, and I am certain the information is valid, although cryptic. In time, and after some rest, mayhap it will become clear."

"A waste of good gold."

"There was a lesser divination which was much less expensive, but it required that I ask particular questions which would only be answered in the affirmative or negative. At this point, I do not even know what to ask," I sighed. "Varli said we should understand the beginning of the prophecy within a few days. Let us wait and see where we are led.

"What news?" I asked Raf as he joined us at our usual table in the Weeping Rose's large dining area three nights later.

"The townsfolk here say they have not seen any travelling wizards, though a couple mentioned the tower of Ormak."

My eyebrows shot up.

"Some wizard from centuries ago, from what they say. Rumor is, of course, that it's haunted—ghosts, ruklaa, etc., just like every other old ruin to hear the tale."

Ruklaa, along with kuldaa, are the first undead all necromancers learn how to create. They are both mindless servants, best used as combat fodder, with the main difference being that ruklaa are made from whole corpses, while kuldaa are basically just animated skeletons. Of all the various types of undead, I have the least issue with them, as there is only a faint spark of the original soul left attached, unlike the wholesale corruption that infests most others. "I have not heard that name in a while, aside from his writings," I said. "According to my studies, he was a great alchemist and a talented wand-wielder. Mistress Vletraka said that her master was taught by a student of a student, etc., of Ormak. I guess that makes me his student as well. Did your people tell you how to get to his tower?"

"Wait," interrupted Vondro, slapping his hand on the table, "I thought we were chasing after living murderous wizards, not delving into ancient, abandoned ruins."

I continued, "If the ones who killed Mistress Vletraka and Mistress Goldfire," the sound of Goldfire's name causing Glitter to tear up, "have been in the area, they may have heard of Ormak's tower. They were seeking lost and hidden knowledge, and where better to seek it than in an 'abandoned' tower. Besides, Vondro, if the place is full of undead, are you not interested in vanquishing such abominations?" I asked, already knowing the answer.

"Of course, we should destroy them!" he nearly shouted, drawing the attention of the nearby tables.

Tsukatta nodded at his resoluteness.

"I merely thought your quest had a greater importance to you, but if this coincides…"

"We should get some rest tonight then, and get an early start for the morning," said Raf easing to his feet. "The city can be a dangerous place at night, especially for beautiful young ladies," he glanced between Tsukatta and Glitter, "If you need someone to guard you…" he smirked.

"I think we'll be fine," retorted Glitter, also smirking, "but thank you for your kind and generous offer to stand *in the hallway* and protect our door. You should get some rest too."

Blushing, realizing how easily Glitter turned his wording against him, Raf turned toward the stairs.

"You did not answer my question, Raf. Do you know how to get to his tower?"

"Of course. It's half-a-day's journey on foot northwest of here in the deeper forest. It should be easy enough to find; just look for the area where everyone else avoids."

Smiling, we all stood and went upstairs to our rooms, except Vondro who returned home. Sitting on the bed with my enchanted dagger thrust into the side table, I studied *In Between* more. I think I may have puzzled out a few of the secrets within, including some powerful spells that are far beyond my current ability to cast. If performed as a ceremony, with assistance, perhaps they can be done. I have only recently found the inner strength to power magicks of the fourth tier, and there is still not enough within me to cast most of the spells I have uncovered within this text.

I needed to prepare. If Ormak's tower was haunted, then we could expect to battle numerous undead. Good—the more I destroy the better. *And does Ormak still haunt the tower?* That posed a problem, for a wizard of his magnitude would be beyond our scope even if living; as an undead spell-caster, his power would be even greater. What might he be? I doubted that he could fall victim to a maraika or spectre, but I could not rule those out. All descriptions I had read make him seem to be a good man, so going through the ceremony for becoming a jozalk was unlikely. But if he felt that he left some great task undone, he might be a ghost. I would have to prepare for the strong likelihood of dealing with an incorporeal host on the morrow.

Chapter 9: Ormak's Tower

I woke to the sound of thunder rolling across the sky. This was not to be a good day for travel, but I prepared myself, nonetheless. If Ormak did still haunt his tower, there were many forms he might possess. I would wager that his spirit lived on as a ghost, a considerable challenge, as incorporeal undead may be the most difficult to destroy, for physical objects and energies tend to pass through their forms with little to no effect; that and the fact that one does not so much destroy a ghost, but merely discorporate it for a time, typically for a day or so, unless its mission can be completed.

A haunting spirit lingers because of a great, all-consuming task, which it left unfinished in life. If the ghost feels communicative, we may learn of its goal and help it rest without combat. I doubted that we would be so fortunate and prepared my spells with care. Spells of pure magical force, such as *ajilek* and *ajiavulhysayt*, are capable to affect incorporeal subjects, perhaps by disrupting the dimensional flux, which causes them to be partly in this physical world and partly in another plane. Ghosts and spectres are linked to the Shadow Plane, which connects the physical realm to the planes of energy and the pure elements (air, earth, fire, and water), while other incorporeal undead, like shadows and wajuvuu, draw power from the dimension of negative energy. Fortunately, earlier mages have developed spells to cut these creatures off from their dual existence, forcing them on the Material Plane where they can be more easily affected; unfortunately, ghosts tend to be more dangerous when solid than when incorporeal.

While I poured over my spell-book, studying closely the intricate patterns for the spells I planned to use, I realized that I was not the only one preparing for what might be a difficult day. Raf, who had won the use of the bed last night, was checking over our cloaks, rubbing oil into them to help ward off the rain, while Vondro, who had come to our room to gather the group, was sharpening his sword with a slow, steady rhythm. Brother Ironknuckle was upside-down, balancing on one hand, chanting quietly in Grommoldian.

After finishing my spell preparations, I pulled *In Between* out of my pack. A particular spell had caught my attention and I wished to examine it further. It was far beyond my current ability to cast, but the formula had secrets that might be of use in less powerful spells. I decided that Glitter might find this fascinating as well and went across the hall to her room. I knocked thrice upon the ladies' door. "Glitter, may I enter?"

"Hold on," came her reply, "we're naked."

I stood outside the door for about a minute, pondering why they were not yet ready for travel when Glitter threw open the door.

"The others would have burst right in," she frowned. "You're no fun. Come on in." They *were* both ready, and I think they misjudged our reactions. Well, perhaps not Raf—he likely *would* have come right in. Glitter flounced over to the bed where Tsukatta sat, leaving a trail of silver sparkles in her wake.

"I discovered something interesting in this book that I think you should see." I walked over to the bed and set down the book opened to the page I had been perusing. "Do you see this set of symbols?" I pointed. "They seem to refer to calling or contacting a departed soul. And there are a number of these," I pointed again, "which denote positive energy. I think this is some wizardly version of a resurrection spell."

Both ladies studied the formula closely.

Tsukatta surprised me be speaking first. "I think you might be right."

Glitter and I both turned to her in shock.

"Don't look so surprised," she laughed. "We priests use magical writings too. This positive energy symbol is similar to the one we use in meditation to empower both our healing and disruptive abilities. I have read the rituals for raising the dead, and I think you may have something similar here. I don't see anything about communicating with the soul though."

"I didn't know wizardly magic and divine magic were so close," said Glitter in awe.

"Well, I can only cast what Kimitsu allows. She determines whether or not I have earned the trust to cast, and can physically handle, spells of greater energy. I have studied the *zuklawavriiwa* ritual, which calls the soul back into the body, for example, but I am not yet able to perform it. Wizards, as I understand, draw their magic from personal power, while we clerics draw ours from the gods."

"Actually, we draw our power from the Weave, using our personal energy to fashion the spells we wish to cast," I rebutted. "As far as I can determine, all magic is cast using the Weave; it is the method of casting, the formulae used, the process of gaining the knowledge and ability to cast that differentiates our spells. Using *zuklawavriiwa* as an example, it appears that the knowledge to cast this spell requires access to the divine, as no arcane caster has successfully brought the dead back to life—though many have tried, often with tragic results. This spell, however, seems as though it can resurrect the deceased without divine aid."

"It's extremely complicated, and it looks like it takes a great deal of energy to cast. I know I'm not up to it, and I don't think you're that much stronger than me," Glitter frowned, looking at me as if wondering if I possessed a hidden reserve of power.

"It is far beyond my abilities as well," I answered, relieving her of her musing. "I thought that if perhaps we were to cast it in unison, with a boost of energy from Tsukatta, that we might have enough energy to do it."

"I suppose it's possible," hummed Tsukatta. "Combining arcane and divine magicks can be tricky, but if Kimitsu allows, and the cause is just, perhaps we can. Do you think we will need to use this?"

"If Ormak has succumbed to the curse of undeath, then perhaps we can save him," I said mustering more hope in my voice than I truly possessed. "Should it fail, then we will have to find another means of stopping him, assuming of course that he haunts his tower still. We do not really have enough information to go on at this point, but my best guess is that Ormak might be a ghost, and most of our magic will simply pass through him."

"Well then, my charms won't work. I guess I should concentrate on preparing spells using raw magic rather than elemental energies,"

Glitter mused, reaching for her new spell-book. "Give me half an hour, and I'll be ready."

I stood, nodded, and returned to my room.

Two hours later, our horses were tramping through the dense woods to where the townsfolk claim Ormak's tower still stands. The low-hanging clouds had ceased their deluge but appeared ready to renew their efforts at any given time. They blocked the sun's light so completely that it seemed more the middle of night than day; the track of thick mud that we followed apparently was once a dirt path.

"I hope this place isn't really haunted," Raf complained yet again. "I hope we don't have to get into a fight out here."

"Yes, the footing is rather treacherous," agreed Vondro.

"Maybe we will get inside the tower before the rains begin again," spoke Brother Ironknuckle in an attempt to lift Raf's spirits.

Tsukatta rung out her long tresses and added, "I find it refreshing."

"Yes, but you're a rain priestess," frowned Raf.

"Still," she continued, "it is an act of nature. You can enjoy the experience or complain about it. I would rather accept it for what it is."

"Who would have expected it? Our Priestess of the Gentle Rain is the group's ray of sunshine," I smiled at Raf.

He glared at me for a moment, then chuckled. "I guess you're right. Still, I wouldn't mind a nice warm fire and some clean, dry clothes right about now."

"There it is," interrupted Glitter, pointing up through the trees.

Soon afterwards, the trees parted, opening to a clearing, which gave us a full view of the tower and its environs. The tower stood three stories of smooth stone with a conical roof. No window marred its surface, and only a single door could be seen at its base. A fence of iron pikes surrounded the structure, rusted with neglect, yet sturdy enough to keep intruders at bay. We circled the fence until we came to an arched gate. Above it was, also in iron, a stylized "O" with two thin wands crossed below it.

"That *is* Ormak's symbol. This is his tower," I informed my companions. "If Ormak does still haunt this place, mayhap I should go and speak to him."

"What? Go in there? Alone?" Vondro asked incredulously. "Not on your life!"

"Wizards value their privacy, and certain protocols must be followed," I responded. Glitter nodded in agreement. "A rag-tag group of armed people would never be allowed access without invitation, and I would rather not have a hostile spirit attacking us when we could possibly get more information diplomatically."

"Then Glitter should, at least, go with ye," recommended Brother Ironknuckle.

I turned to Glitter. "I think you should stay here. I am used to dealing with dead things, and, in a fashion, I am his student. I believe that he would be more open to me."

"I don't like this," rumbled Vondro, "but you may have a point. Don't tarry too long—we won't wait forever."

I nodded. Turning to the gate I lifted my head and voice. "I come to speak with the Master." Silently, I watched through the gate.

Nearly a minute went by before Raf spoke up. "Should the gate have opened or something? If there is no response, then maybe we should push our way in."

"Have patience;" I said calmly, "an answer should come soon. Besides, the lock on the gate is enchanted; it would not be easy to bypass."

"I know. It's a greater challenge, but it would not be the first *emajisklid* I had to pick."

We all turned to him.

"What? I grew up on the streets of Dureltown. I had to survive, and my fingers are as nimble as the rest of me." He winked at Glitter, who blushed deeply in response. "I learned my way around a lock before my fifth summer, and mystic locks soon after. I gave up that life a long time ago, but I have not forgotten how to do it."

His explanation was cut short by a raspy croak. "Rrrrawwwk."

We turned to see that a skeletal raven had perched atop the gate. From its beak dangled an amulet on a silver chain, which it then dropped into my hands. The amulet was embellished with the same symbol as the top of the gate. I held it up and the gate opened with a loud creak.

"I shall return anon," I said to my companions, burying the fear, which was welling up from within. The gate clanged shut of its own accord four paces after I stepped through, and I could feel the Weave tie into the lock.

A skeletal raven. Familiars typically die with their masters. I wonder if they reflect the undead state of their masters as well. If so, then Ormak might be a jozalk after all. Seeing the skeletal raven forced me to think about Thessylia's fate upon my demise.

'Be careful out there. And watch over everyone. Let me know if there is trouble.'

She replied with a yawn that was both physical as well as mental. *'I have a bad feeling about this place. There are unnatural things moving about down there.'*

I peered around into the gloom and saw shapes lurking about the courtyard. Ormak, it appears, uses undead guards, and many more than we would be willing to battle all at once, though part of me wished to try. The full-bodied creatures were more intimidating than Vletraka's swarms of, now destroyed, klaatoo, though the psychological effect of seeing a dozen skeletal or mummified hands running on fingertips would likely cause an intruder to take flight rather than try to fight them off. *I wish we never allowed Larzed past the gate.*

I took a deep breath to steady myself. As I told the others, this was to be a diplomatic mission and must not show my revulsion while speaking with Ormak. Whatever kind of unliving abomination he has become, he is still a powerful wizard and must be treated with respect. As I stepped up to the heavy wooden tower door, it opened of its own accord. Crossing the threshold, I spotted a pair of dull yellow eyes by the door and my nostrils filled with the scent of rotting flesh. Once I was inside, the creature slammed the door shut.

It held a candle, which glowed with magical light rather than a flame, and was dressed as a servant. Much of its skin was gone, either stripped away or desiccated into small patches, revealing the musculature beneath. The yellow eyes stared at me hungrily and saliva seeped past its jagged teeth, dripping down its chin and to the floor. Though it was the first one I had seen with my own eyes, I knew this creature to be a yomki. The negative energy that animates these creatures is powered by living souls, and yomkii need to feed regularly or else go dormant. Yomkii attack both body and spirit with their powerful fists, literally pounding the soul from the body with each blow.

We stared at each other for a time, the yomki seeming to be forcing itself not to attack, then it turned away and said, "Come," in a harsh whisper.

I followed cautiously in the dim light. *"His servants know the path; Jaundiced eyes are filled with wrath,"* I remembered, but was too focused on keeping myself calm to interview the creature. The stone floor had bits of rotted corpse in patches and I could see a sitting area for receiving guests, which appeared to be long disused. We ascended a wide spiral staircase, which wound around a central pillar to the second floor, where we entered a maze of bookcases. Books, scrolls, tablets, and trinkets filled the shelves, and I felt as a child given a chest full of toys! As my excitement grew, the wan light began to dim further, and I could feel the greed and hunger emanating from the yomki. I stopped and took another calming breath and the feeling passed. *What is happening to me?* I wondered, but had no time to contemplate the issue as we turned a corner to face Ormak himself. At least, what remained of him.

At first glance, one could misconstrue the thing that was once the man called Ormak as but a desiccated corpse posed in a comfortable position sitting in an overstuffed chair. He sat with legs crossed, his elbows on the arms of the green-grey padded seat, and his ring-studded finger bones bridged in front of his solar plexus, where two ribs poked out through his tattered dark grey robes which were likely black at one time. The taut flesh remaining on the left side of the skull, leaving him one cheek and one eyebrow, gave him an expression of thoughtfulness. A circlet sat on his brow, similar to the one Larzed wore, and a silver necklace with a charm resembling a silver snowflake hung loosely around his neck. One *could* mistake him for only a corpse, but one would be a fool to do so.

While I gazed upon him, orange light, like twin candles, began to glow from empty eye sockets, and the cheek flesh pulled back to a rictus grin. Even without using any spells, I could feel the Weave twisting into arcane knots around and within him; the raw power stored in those bones began to make my head throb.

"Another visitor? So soon after the last?" came a hollow chuckle, which seemed to emanate both from Ormak and from a great distance. His head turned to the yomki. "A friend of yours, Jarlisk?"

The yomki glared at Ormak for a moment then lowered his eyes. "No. Master," he whispered softly, each word articulated with a single harsh breath.

"Ah. Good," the creature that had been Ormak turned back to me, the glow in his eye sockets softening somewhat. "Jarlisk and his young apprentice stole their way into my home about a moon past and sought to remove my library. I do not take kindly to thieves."

So, Ormak has *become a jozalk! I must tread carefully here, for undead wizards such as he are known to be unstable and dangerous.* I gasped, "A moon ago? That is when my Mistress and I were attacked by Larzed and his apprentice."

"Fat. Bastard," hissed Jarlisk.

I turned to look at the yomki, then back to Ormak. "A group of wizards have been travelling about seeking lost and powerful books for an unknown master. Vletraka may have been slain, and I intend to find out for what reason."

"Vletraka? She's old enough to have an apprentice?" The jozalk's lone eyebrow lowered, and the orange glow dimmed momentarily. "Why, I guess it has been a long time." In one smooth motion, Ormak clattered to his feet and stuck out one hand, light flaming from his eye sockets. "Welcome, my boy!"

Stunned by his amiability, I took his hand. Vletraka's skin was always cold, and her touch was shocking every time, but the intense cold of Ormak's touch burned my hand and made my arm grow numb. I tried to pull my hand away, and found that I could not move my arm, and the nether chill began to spread to my chest when he let go.

"You are the first of my students' students to ever visit. Actually, you would be about eight generations removed. I had not realized that I had gotten so old! Come, let me show you around."

The last thing I had expected was for this abomination of nature to treat me like a long-lost grandchild. I am not fully certain as to whether I was paralyzed from confusion or Ormak's freezing touch, and it took a minute to find my feet and follow. Meanwhile, warmth began to return to my arm and hand. Ormak, it seemed, had been surreptitiously keeping watch over his students over the past century-and-a-half or so, noting their exploits and collecting keepsakes. Kindly though he was acting now, Jarlisk's presence was an easy reminder of just how dangerous he could be.

"This bookcase is dedicated to Decru, my first student. I have his original spell-books, research notes, skull, personal effects—this is his first wand, which cast *bezyamhysa*,[6] his wedding ring—would you believe he married a woodreeve? Rybese, her name was. Lovely girl, but far more interested in badgers than magic. Love does turn a man's head..." he trailed off, his voice echoing melancholy. He wandered off, seemingly forgetful of my presence and I followed him to his work desk. The old jozalk reached his bony hand to gently pick up a small golden harp, at the base of which was a small key. He turned the key and the harp began to play a haunting melody, which I later determined to be *The Eternal Heart*, composed by the bard Lixia. He then stared at the small device in his hand in uncomfortable silence long after the last note had played. "Suzelle," he finally intoned in his hollow, echoing voice.

"Your wife?" I queried cautiously, thinking of his apprentice's skull and fearing the consequences of a misspoken word.

He responded with what might have been a sigh. "Have you ever been in love, boy? Been so close to another that you felt as though your very souls were as one?"

"No, my Lord, I have not."

---

[6] A spell that creates a small barrier in front of the wizard, typically about the same size as a warrior's shield, to deflect attacks.

"You will. It happens even to the best of us. You will meet someone who finds their way into your heart, and soon their presence becomes so comfortable that you cannot imagine that person *not* being there. Then, sometimes far too soon, they will be stripped away from you, and you cannot imagine that pain ever receding. I would recommend against it, but it is as inevitable as the sunrise.

"But enough of this maudlin talk. You did not come all this way to listen to the ramblings of an old man. Tell me about yourself— your studies, your history. Have you crafted your first wand yet? Any new spells you would care to trade? Any questions my years of experience might help you with?"

"I have been studying magic with Vletraka for four summers, focusing on necromancy..." I began.

"Why do you kids always have this need to specialize in one school of magic or another?" he interrupted, sighing heavily. "I blame Dalen. He was so interested in the Negative Energy Plane that he neglected some of his other studies. Since him, all of my students have been necromancers."

"By concentrating on one school, like necromancy, I find that I have an easier time drawing together the energies for those spells. In gathering those energies, my necromantic spells become more potent."

"But surely you had to sacrifice studies in other areas in order to excel in necromancy."

"True, but there are only so many spells I have the energy to cast in a given day. Even if I knew that many more spells, I could not cast them all. Even with my focus, I have learned a wide variety of magicks—Vletraka made certain of that. She knew that too tight a concentration could leave me vulnerable to the other magicks."

"And why choose necromancy?"

I certainly was not going to tell the jozalk, genial though he was, that I wanted to learn how best to destroy every undead creature I came across, so I simply said, "Vletraka is... was my Mistress. I learned what she taught. I *would* like to swap spells with you," I said, trying to change the subject. "Granted, yours are far more powerful than mine, but if you are still interested…"

"Invention and innovation are what keeps our profession alive, my boy. It is heartening to know that students are still encouraged to create their own spells."

"Not so much 'encouraged' as 'required'. Mistress Vletraka and the other teachers would not allow us to leave their tutelage unless we designed at least two spells of our own."

"Other teachers? Are you gathered together now?" He asked, though out of curiosity or disdain I could not tell.

"They are friends, forming a loose-knit group. We each learn from our individual teacher, and meet on occasion to share stories and information. No, we are not together, though most are within a few days travel to each other."

"Are they specialists as well?" he asked with a touch of venom.

"Some are, my Lord. It seems that each student learns according to his or her personality. Perhaps the student and teacher are drawn together somehow. The Weave connects us all; it could be that it knows more than it lets on."

"Are you suggesting that the Weave is *sentient*? That is the most preposterous thing I ever heard!"

"No more so than leaving things up to fate or the machinations of the gods," I answered calmly. "It was merely speculation, nothing more. Though now that I think on it, does the Weave choose who becomes a mage, or is the ability to cast spells inherent in the caster?"

"Inherent, of course," he responded without hesitation. "Many families have magical talent which runs for generations, and entire races, such as tillalli and ulzyl, all have at least a minimal ability to cast spells, while other creatures are magical in nature and have been as long as we have known about them."

"Then, I wonder, where my talent arises from. As far as I know, no one in my family has ever been a wizard. If it is inherent within me, then where does it stem from?"

"Perhaps it is merely a quirk of nature. Poets and artists appear in families without a history of those talents, and wizardry is an art. Does your family have craftsmen?"

"I come from a long line of blacksmiths. I suppose I shape the Weave just as they do iron."

His cheek flesh pulled upward, and I got the impression that he was smiling, though the bare teeth and bone gave that impression at all times. "The power, the talent, the ability is within you, my apprentice. Whether crafting iron or crafting spells, your heart is that of an artist."

I found myself smiling; it was as if a shadow had lifted from my soul. Would Father understand or accept that my crafting medium, though less tangible than his, was just as valid? More than likely, no; had I learned to craft gold or another metal, maybe. If I had learned instead to chisel stone or carve wood, he would likely treat me with the same disdain as he does now; though he does whittle in his spare time, I do not believe he would accept it as a profession for me. I find, however, that I no longer feel the need for his approval, having gained this bit of wisdom from a senior wizard—a *very* senior wizard. "Thank you, Master Ormak. I appreciate your insights."

"Not at all, my boy. It is my job to enlighten my students. Now, what kind of spells are you interested in learning from me?"

"Contrary to Dalen, I am interested in the Positive Energy Plane. Do you have anything on that subject?"

He paused for a moment, his eyes dimming then returning to their normal glow. "Actually, I do not have much dealing with positive energy. No spells, at least, though I do have a copy of *The Light of Life: Positive Energy and Magickal Healing* by Cerinaj. Will that help?"

"I believe it will, thank you, Master. I have a second-tier spell called *juutaatok*, which draws on positive energy if you are interested; it creates a dagger made of light. I have also developed *dulaatheedu*, which uses sonic energy to damage foes; *uvazuzul* and *yuvjuutubrel* are also useful in combat." I paused for a moment, then continued, "It appears that I have focused too heavily on offensive spells."

"Not surprising. The world is a dangerous place. One must be prepared for…"

"Intruders!" the skeletal raven suddenly croaked in the same hollow voice of its master.

"So, your friends have made their move at last," Ormak snarled.

'Thessylia, what is going on out there?'

'Vondro saw too many ruklaa shuffle past the fence and attacked.'

"More allies than friends," I countered. "They were supposed to wait…"

"To wait until you lured me into a false sense of security? Until you had robbed me as that sack of sinew over there tried to?" he accused, pointing at Jarlisk, then commanded him. "Take care of my apprentice while I dispose of his 'allies'. There have been far too many interruptions as of late." He turned and rattled toward the outer wall, which parted before him like stone curtains. As he stepped out into the open air with the raven in tow, the wall closed behind him, leaving me alone with Jarlisk.

Jarlisk's eyes narrowed and saliva oozed past his jagged yellow teeth, just as when we first met, but this time there was nothing to prevent him from attacking. He struck out at me quickly, narrowly missing my chest; my robe pulled slightly by his backswing. Fighting alone, especially against such a dangerous creature, my first thought was defense. Necromancers, through our understanding of undead creatures, typically develop the ability to keep them at bay through force of will. I attempted to cower Jarlisk, but Ormak's command was too strong to overcome, and I narrowly dodged another attack for my efforts. I invoked *bezyamhysa* just in the nick of time as another powerful blow came toward my head. The mystic shield blocked his attack, crackling with blue energy as his fist impacted upon it.

I had to be careful about my choice in spells, surrounded as I was with rare books and historical artifacts which could easily be damaged by many of the more effective offensive spells, though a bolt of lightning should easily destroy him, but I also had to strike quickly and destroy this abomination before he could feed off me. I considered using *juutubrel* to surround myself with light and defend against his negative energy, but I hoped to survive this conflict and have the spell available against Ormak. I stepped backwards to get out of his striking range and loosed a volley of *ajilek* at the yomki. Four motes of blue-black energy streaked toward him, striking his shoulder and chest. It was not enough to deter him, however, and Jarlisk lunged past my *bezyamhysa* and punched me square in the solar plexus.

Reading about the soul-draining ability of creatures such as the yomki is far different from the actual experience; a distinction I hope you, dear reader, never have the opportunity to make for yourself. Not only did the physical blow force the breath from my body, it also stole the light and joy from the world. Everything took on an ashen hue in the already dim light within the tower, and I felt despair creep over my heart. I remembered vividly my father turning his back on me, all the hurt and anguish of having my life up to that point being stripped away, leaving my heart and soul bare and raw. I remembered the dread I felt as a bloodied Larzed stood in the doorway of Vletraka's den, still bent on our destruction. It was my fault that he still lived, my fault that Vletraka had to trade her life for my own.

Somewhere in the midst of the darkness, which washed over me, I also felt rage. At first I thought it was merely my own anger at myself for Vletraka's untimely demise, but that was soon overpowered by the hatred I felt emanating from my enemy. I gasped for breath as *bezyamhysa* deflected another blow from Jarlisk.

"It's your own fault, you know. You were too weak to stand against Ormak," I growled. My vision began to return from the daze caused by his body blow, though, there was no color, only images. "You can hate me, Ormak, and every living being all you desire," I sneered at the yomki, "but had you been a better wizard, you would not have ended up this way."

Jarlisk roared, clenched his hands together, and swung a double-fisted blow against the *bezyamhysa*.

If it were not for that, I surely would have been crushed by now. I invoked *juutaatok*, which had worked so successfully against the wajuvu during the tournament with Glitter, and managed to slice the yomki's side. As the blade is made of positive energy, it is very effective against undead and is not at all hampered by the thick muscles.

Jarlisk howled in pain and swung wildly, missing me completely.

I stabbed out with the *juutaatok* again but could not get close enough while avoiding his attacks. Another powerful swing, and the *bezyamhysa* shattered and dissipated. I realized that I had but one chance left, and lunged, stabbing him in the chest with the mystic blade. "Give me my soul back, you worthless fiend!" I shouted while Jarlisk screamed.

His body froze and dropped to the floor. As he did, color returned to the world and I took a gasping breath.

Now, to stop Ormak. If my plan was to work, I needed a personal item, and my eyes fell upon the clockwork harp on the desk. "Perfect," I muttered aloud and grabbed the trinket.

Fire shot through my body; lightning raced through my veins; acid dripped along every nerve—at least, that is how it felt. The magical ward inscribed on the harp glowed momentarily when I grabbed the keepsake then shattered, bathing me in eldritch energy. I screamed in agony as the magic coursed through every muscle, organ, and tissue of my body. I tried to hold perfectly still, and the pain increased. I set the harp down, the pain still increased. I found myself taking short rapid breaths and tried to force myself to calm down.

What was her name? "Suzelle," I forced through clenched teeth. The pain began to subside, but my entire body ached from the experience. *It belonged to his wife; of course he protected it! I should know better than to act in haste, especially in a jozalk's lair. Yet I must still hurry and see if I can save my friends.*

I grabbed one of the enchanted candles and dragged myself to the staircase, forcing myself to move against the desire to lie down and rest. When I reached the stairs, I closed my eyes and took a deep breath before beginning my descent. With each step, the pain began to ease, as though I were working the spell's effect out of my system. As I reached the door, I also reached out to Thessylia. *'How goes it outside?'*

'It is raining. Hard. The battle does not go well.'

'Give me a quick synopsis. I need to know what I am walking into.'

'Glitter is entangled in a magical spider web, Tsukatta in encased in the darkness of a looskim *spell carried by Brildon, the raven, Ial'rafiost has been paralyzed, Brother Ironknuckle is wrestling with the tentacles of a* looskjejleemyt *spell, and Vondro is entombed in ice.'*

'No one has been killed? I am surprised and impressed. Perhaps I have taken my friends far too lightly.'

I set down the candle and slipped out the door of the tower into the downpour. Ormak appeared to be floating a few feet off the ground about a dozen yards to my right, dark indigo light emanating from his body. I needed both Glitter and Tsukatta for my plan to work, if it would work, and stealth seemed a better option than dealing directly with the jozalk. Of the few spells contained in *In Between* that I was able to cast, I made certain to prepare *zuklayuvzel*, though I expected to use it during an escape attempt in case our plans went awry. *Zuklayuvzel* shuts down and blocks all the senses of an undead creature temporarily; not only does it blind and deafen, it nearly neutralizes any spellcaster when they cannot see a target or hear the words of power they are attempting to intone. Once cast, I would have to act quickly to free the ladies. I cast it upon Ormak and ran.

While I rushed to free Glitter from the magical web, I saw the globe of darkness which had surrounded Tsukatta dissipate. The skeletal raven hovered above her and scanned the area; Ormak could see through Brildon's eyes the way I could use Thessylia's! I had not expected to need *zuklayuvzel* twice and had not prepared it for a second use. I had to keep it distracted.

Using notes from *In Between* I developed a spell I call *ivriiemtzizidovlek*. It invokes a thin plane of positive energy, roughly shaped like a lance used by knights on horseback. The spell is designed to harry its target, attacking repeatedly and following the target should it attempt to flee. Being created out of positive energy makes it more effective against undead as well. I cast it and pointed out my target. The *ivriiemtzizidovlek* flew through the rain, impacted on Brildon, and exploded.

I stared at the site of the explosion in stunned disbelief. Granted, I had not tested the spell during battle, but it had not done that before in practice. While I stood dumbstruck, something hard hit my leg. I looked down to see a bird's skull on the ground between my feet. *I... have made a* big *mistake.*

"Brildon!" screamed a hollow voice, full of shock and fury. I could barely see the old jozalk through the rain, but the red glowing bead flying in my general direction was unmistakable.

It was too late to counter the *srukakbolmos* spell, so I dove to the wet ground hoping the blind mage misjudged the distance. The ball of fire exploded high, heating my back but causing no serious damage. Glitter, however, trapped in the web, which now burned away, could not dodge the blast. With the silken strands no longer keeping her upright, she collapsed in a smoking heap.

I rushed to her side, though there was nothing I could do. Her skin was red and black, charred, and blistered. Thankfully, Tsukatta was not far behind. She said a short prayer to Kimitsu and laid her hands upon Glitter's seared body. Blackened skin turned red, then pink, while her blisters shrank and vanished. The few healing spells I have merely shift or bolster the life force already within the body. Tsukatta's, on the other hand, appear to replenish the life force from without. Perhaps *that* is why divine magic is capable of healing to such a greater degree than arcane magic.

"Glitter?" I asked. "How do you feel?" I made a point to not notice how much of her robes had burned away.

She smiled up at me, "Like a roasted leg of lamb. Are you actually concerned about my well-being?" she teased, wincing as she sat up.

"Of course," I responded, genuinely shocked that she would even ask and completely missed the teasing tone in her voice. "You are the closest thing I have to a friend. Also, I need your help to cast *umslyktvriiwa*, and we need to act quickly. I wish we had some shelter from this rain, though."

"Allow me," said Tsukatta with a smile, her eyes darting between Glitter and me. With another short prayer, we three found ourselves separated from the rain, as though under a dome of glass, protected by *roziitubrel*. A horizontal bolt of lightning hit the fence about twenty paces away, reminding us of the danger we faced.

"I have blocked his senses, but I do not believe the spell will last much longer." I pulled *In Between* out of my pack and opened it to a page, which I had marked earlier with the attached ribbon, and set the golden harp down next to it. "Quickly, as we discussed. But first..." I cast *juutubrel* on myself, which should help me attune to Tsukatta's ability to produce bursts of positive energy.

The rain began to subside, and we could see Ormak clearly through the light drizzle. He looked right at us and pulled out a pair of wands.

I had never cast a spell in tandem with another wizard before, let alone with a cleric, though in theory the spell should work. Tsukatta's positive energy burst should boost the spell, and if Glitter could draw additional energy from the Weave while I created the foundation, we might yet save us all. Elsewise, I feared the strain might make us defenseless against Ormak's fury.

In unison, Glitter and I chanted *umslyktvriiwa*, while Tsukatta focused her disruptive energy on Ormak, causing some of his withered flesh to powder and flake off of his petrified bones and to drop his wands. I could hear him beginning to cast a spell I did not recognize, but one that I instinctively knew would kill us all. As we completed ours, I felt a surge of power surround Glitter. We looked at Tsukatta, who sent another wave of energy at Ormak. Upon uttering the final syllable, the spell's energy braided with Tsukatta's burst, forming a lance of energy, which pierced the jozalk's desiccated heart.

The world turned white for a moment as an explosion of light filled our eyes. As the dazzling effect subsided, I could see Ormak's heart begin to beat, turning bright red, pumping blood once again. His lungs inflated then let out a scream that still sounded inhuman. Organs grew to normal size while muscle and flesh crawled over bare bones. The pinpoints of orange fire in his empty eye sockets burned white, and then vanished as eyeballs returned to their rightful place. In moments, the man called Ormak stood before us in tattered robes, barely concealing the pink flesh beneath.

He appeared to be in his middle years, his bright orange hair lightly frosted with grey. Dropping to his knees, he stared at his hands, his arms, and his body. "What… what have you done to me? WHAT HAVE YOU DONE?!" He leapt to his feet, rage and terror mixing on his returned features, and hastily teleported away via a *bezyamlial* spell.

"It worked?" asked Glitter. "That was way beyond anything *I* was taught."

"With our combined efforts," I responded. "Yet I must admit to being a mite surprised myself. I was not certain that we could do it." Realizing that Vondro was still trapped beneath the dome of ice, which had gained in thickness from the rain freezing upon its surface, I brought forth a *srukakarih* to roll against the frozen hemisphere and weaken it. The flames were not powerful enough to counter the spell, but it could make Vondro's escape easier. To my surprise, I saw his sword pierce through the ice just as my sphere neared the dome.

Impressive, I did not believe he had the strength or stamina to break through. The srukakarih *will aid him, nonetheless.*

As the sphere contacted the ice, it immediately began to diminish from the intense cold. Still, it managed to melt through a two-foot-diameter hole. A final chop by Vondro cracked the opening wider so that he could finally make his escape.

"Vondro missed the entire battle; he is going to be furious," quipped Glitter.

When he stepped free, it was apparent how close that dome of ice nearly became his tomb. His skin was pale and cracked, and frost covered his armor. A few steps after leaving his imprisonment, he collapsed on the worn grass. Tsukatta bolted to his side to administer her healing arts, while I gathered up the tome and golden clockwork harp then strode over to Brother Ironknuckle. Fortunately, his impressive constitution kept him alive, though he had been squeezed into unconsciousness by the magical tentacles. The combination of magic and the jozalk's unnatural strength made Ormak a dangerous foe, especially when fighting solo; the *looskjejleemyt* finishing the job that Ormak started.

Though I am certainly out of Tsukatta's league, I have a few healing tricks of my own, and cast *umakraazt* to bind his wounds. Necromancy is, in part, about controlling the life force. By drawing it away or redirecting it, a necromancer can cause a great deal of harm, even outright kill. By moving another's life force to injured areas, I can help a body to heal itself, though I doubt that I could ever duplicate the power that Tsukatta gets from her goddess.

"Eh? I'm alive?" Brother Ironknuckle queried as he sat up. "Good, I'd hate to go out by a mass of tentacles." He looked up at me. "Did we get the blighter?"

"Yes," I smiled, helping him to his feet. "Yes, we did."

"What was that thing? I never saw a spellcasting rukla before."

"That was once a good man. The creature was a jozalk. How or why he changed I have yet to determine."

"Huh. How are the others? Tsuk…"

"They are fine, I think. Tsukatta is tending to Vondro, and I believe that Ial'rafiost is merely paralyzed. I should check on him next." We walked over to where Raf stood, rapier out in a stabbing position and a look of horror on his face. "Wrong weapon," I said to my frozen comrade, "jozalka need to be smashed, not poked. I hope this works." I cast *iulvaktwa*.

Raf shimmered for a moment but did not change his stance.

"I was afraid of that. Ormak's touch is too powerful."

"What did you cast?" asked Glitter as she and the others joined us around Raf. It seems that she had taken time to repair her robes.

Pity, for seeing her nearly naked might have made Raf move or driven him mad from his current impotence.

"*Iulvaktwa*. It helps to prevent paralysis, and I was hoping the spell would break it as well. He moved some, but Ormak's touch still holds him."

Tsukatta spoke up. "Let me try." Her prayer and spell had similarities to mine, but hers was designed to end paralysis where mine was intended to prevent it. Thankfully, her spell was more effective in this case.

"Thank you!" Raf exclaimed in relief. "I was afraid pigeons were going to start roosting on me! There's no greater torture for an acrobat than being immobile," he joked, though we could all see the truth in his words.

"I shall have to remember that for future reference," I smiled evilly.

I received first a look of horror then a laugh from him. "Mithron, my friend, I believe you frighten me more than even that jozalk."

Breaking the mood, Vondro said, "We should probably get out of this rain." A moment later, a lightning bolt shot across the sky and the rain began to fall heavier, as if to punctuate his words.

"I find it refreshing," smiled Tsukatta, stretching like a cat before a fireplace.

"You can stay here then. I'm still freezing from those spells."

"Of course, how thoughtless of me," Tsukatta pouted. "Is the tower safe?" she asked me.

"Probably not, but it is our best option. I would not mind perusing Ormak's library before we travel on, but I am certain danger still lurks within. If nothing else, we should check for magical wards before touching anything."

As we scampered to the tower, Tsukatta cast healing spells upon each of us in turn, caring for any wounds sustained during our battles.

"Faldrein does the same thing," Glitter called to me over the sound of the downpour. "He always knows how injured or ill everyone is. It's unnerving."

"True," I answered, "but he is excessive about it. Remember how he convinced Blythad that he was sick during our tournament? I always wondered if he was bluffing or not."

"After he ran out of his duel, he vomited outside." I looked at her quizzically. "Goldfire told me," she finished quietly.

"So, either he was truly ill, or Faldrein convinced him that he was. An effective ploy either way."

The oak door was still ajar, and we entered the dark, gloomy tower. Thessylia landed gently on my shoulder, shaking off the rain as we went in; her keen eyes and ears would help us stay alert. I picked up the glowing candle, which at least provided some light and turned to my comrades. "There is a sitting area over there, and the library is upstairs. That is all I have seen. Jarlisk, one of the wizards sent out to attack us," I said looking directly at Glitter, her sparkles turning a bright red, "was turned into a yomki by Ormak. Unfortunately, I had to destroy him before I could get any information. I do not know what happened to his apprentice or what other surprises the tower holds. We need to be cautious."

"The first thing we need to do is dry off," opined Brother Ironknuckle.

"I'll take care of the fire," offered Glitter, and walked up to the sitting area, her sparkles giving her just enough light to see by. She let out a yelp, and the fireplace blossomed with flame.

"Are you okay?" asked everyone as we rushed to her side.

"Yes," she sighed, laughing to herself. "I moved a log and a rat jumped out and startled me. The fire's lit," she shrugged.

"And we have dinner cooking," quipped Raf, which earned him many dirty looks.

'I was going to eat that!'

I could now get a better look at the seating area. A long couch, four chairs, a short rectangular table, and a small sofa, which looked like two chairs facing opposite directions, were placed with care in the room, the seats circling the table and the chairs closest to the fireplace. All the fabric on the seats was faded and torn, and any padding had either rotted or been removed, leaving the seats hard and uncomfortable. A large book of sketches by Y'liam'fi, a zylan artist of some note who focused on close details of flowers, sat in the center of the table, along with a brass goblet that smelled of long-dried wine. Crystal figurines of ravens in various poses sat on the mantle above the fireplace.

"All right everyone, get dried off but don't get too comfortable," said Vondro taking command. "Let's treat this like camp. Don't go off alone. I'll keep first watch."

"Nay, lad," Brother Ironknuckle interrupted. "You were nearly frozen to death by that jozalk, first with the blast of cold then the ice dome. You go sit by the fire." Vondro began to protest but knew the grommoldian monk was right. "I'll take watch."

"Glitter and I are going to change into something dry," said Tsukatta pointing at a door. "Raf, you stay here," she commanded the bard before he could move.

"All right," he pouted teasingly. "If you find any more rats, bring some for the rest of us. There's hardly enough meat to share on that one."

The ladies rolled their eyes and turned away. Tsukatta grabbed the candle and they walked to the door.

"Be careful," warned Vondro, "and don't stray too far."

"If there's trouble, we'll let you know," Glitter responded. The door creaked closed behind them.

After they went through the door, I quietly cast a cleaning myzling on myself, drying my clothes and removing the dirt and dust. I could have cast it on the others, but I like to promote a certain level of mysteriousness. Perhaps I would have helped them, had they asked. Thessylia stood atop a statue of a woman in repose, her talons wrapped around the statue's waist and neck, preening herself.

'Do you see or hear anything unusual?'

'Glitter and Tsukatta are giggling. I think they are preparing a prank. There is a rat behind that cabinet; I am waiting for it to sneak out.' She stopped preening and began bobbing her head, as she does when listening intently. *'Someone is moving upstairs.'*

That news was not entirely unexpected, yet it still disturbed me. "There is someone moving upstairs," I informed my comrades. They all stopped and stared at me.

"How do you know that?" asked Vondro, his eyes wide, then suddenly narrowing. "And how come you're already dry?"

"I am a man of many talents," I answered cryptically. "Someone should warn the ladies."

"I'll go!" Raf nearly shouted, springing to his feet and bolting to the door. As he reached for the doorknob, he suddenly slowed, his movements becoming more careful. He turned the knob gently and carefully opened the door. It made not a sound. For someone so boisterous and energetic, Ial'rafiost can be very stealthy when he wishes. He crept through the door, and it slammed behind him!

From behind the door, we could hear Raf's panicked cry, followed by a woman's voice, which said scornfully, "Are you looking for something?"

"Should we rescue him?" whispered Brother Ironknuckle with a grin, wringing out his clothes again and getting dressed.

"Nah. I'm sure he will charm his way out of it," answered Vondro.

"Besides," I added, "the danger *is* real."

The others returned, and Glitter asked, "Is it true? Is someone else here?"

"Yes, and the slamming door told them exactly where we are," I sighed, causing her to blush. "Do not fret. Whoever it is probably already knew we are here. Let me check if they are close." As necromancers train with the life force, we tend to develop a sense for it. With some small degree of concentration, we can detect the presence, or lack of, life energy nearby, allowing us to determine how many living and undead creatures are in the area. Unfortunately, golems and other constructs are overlooked by this sense due to the elemental force which animates them, as explained in Dalwren's work *Animating Principles: Differentiating Constructs from Undead.*[7]

---

[7] From the introduction of this seminal work: "Whereas undead creatures are animated by negative energy, which tethers the soul to the body in intelligent corporeal undead, golems and other constructs are animated by an elemental spirit, drawn from the Inner Planes or the River Nyv, which has no prior connection to the body it is induced to inhabit. This spirit is separate and

I narrowed my eyes and felt for the signs of life energy around me. Thessylia and my companions emitted strong signals. I also detected the rat that Thessylia was waiting for. It had crept to the edge of the cabinet to see what the noise was about, and I informed her of its current location. Behind a freestanding bookcase was a 'hole' in the field. "There!" I shouted, pointing at the bookcase.

"But that's just a..." Raf began while Brother Ironknuckle charged into the bookcase, knocking it over onto the intruder, the head and left arm managing to escape from the attacking furniture. Brother Ironknuckle sat on the bookcase while Vondro put his sword up to its throat. Yellow eyes glared out of a skinless face, and it hissed at the warrior.

"Another yomki," I said, scowling at the creature. "You would not happen to be Jarlisk's apprentice, would you?"

The beast hissed again. "No. Longer. Grustan. Free."

"Free? Ah, with Ormak no longer a jozalk, we must have broken his control," I postulated.

"Ormak. Is. Dead!" Grustan spat gleefully. If an undead creature is happy, there is bound to be trouble.

"Dead? No, we made him alive, I thought," wondered Tsukatta.

"Was. Alive. Was. Weak. Grustan. Killed. Former. Master."

Glitter, Tsukatta, and I all took a step backward in shock.

That was not *how it was supposed to happen! He was supposed to come to his senses, help us, and live out a normal life. There was so much I needed to learn from him.* A deep ache welled up in my heart, and I grew angry and... hungry? I was doing it again! I think I understand it now. When my emotions get too strong, I become aware of the darker passions and memories of others. Is this my magical gift? It seems more of a curse.

Vondro snapped me out of my thoughts when he asked aloud, "Why shouldn't I just slay this monster?"

"Wait," I said, calming myself and trying not to look at anyone. *His servants know the path.* "Grustan, where can we find your previous master? The one who sent you and Jarlisk here?"

_____

different from the life force, and is only connected to the construct by a magickal tether, and flees back to its place of origin when that tether is broken."

"Why. Should. Grustan. Tell. You?"

I finally snapped. All my pent-up rage and grief broke loose as I pulled a dagger out of Vondro's scabbard and stabbed it through Grustan's bloody, grasping palm, pinning his arm to the floor. "Why will you tell me?" I growled. "Because your former master is responsible for the death of my teacher. And hers as well," I said pointing at Glitter. "Because he sent you here and now Ormak is dead. Because *everyone* I hold dear is either dead or in grave peril because of him. Because," I lowered my voice, "if you do not tell me, I will remove your limbs and sew shut your eyes and mouth and leave you here with your insatiable hunger for the rest of eternity."

Everyone was quiet but I could feel them staring at me.

Grustan's eyes were wide as he answered. "Ehrghex. Cratillus. Is. In. Ehrghex," he finished with a whimper.

"What does he want? Why has he been sending out lackeys for old tomes? What is he planning?" I asked, my anger beginning to subside.

"Cratillus. Wishes. To. Raise. An. Army."

"In Ehrghex?" Raf laughed. "What kind of... wait. Is 'Cratillus' a necromancer?"

I turned to him for a moment, then back to Grustan as he answered.

"Yes."

"Oh, Pits. This is not good." Raf turned around and put his hand to his head.

"What is it?" Glitter asked before the rest of us could speak.

"Centuries ago, long before even King Loeren, Loerendoch was a group of small kingdoms. Two of these, ruled by the brothers Inester and Roltri, were bitter rivals. Their father's land was split evenly upon his demise, which rumors claim was instigated, if not caused, by Inester's wife in her desire to be queen. Each brother claimed Ehrghex as part of their kingdom and fought over it for years until Roltri finally slew his brother on the battlefield and reunited the kingdom. It's believed that tens of thousands of men died around that beleaguered city, most of which were left for the scavengers or buried on the spot. There were just too many dead and too few living to carry them all home."

"So, by 'raise an army'," Brother Ironknuckle began.

"He means to bring back the dead soldiers," I finished, then turned to Vondro. "End that poor creature's misery. We have a kingdom to save."

Chapter 10: Within the Jozalk's Lair

We chose to rest in the sitting area, once we relocated Grustan's remains to the kitchen, where Glitter and Tsukatta had changed into dry clothes. Though I was driven to explore the tower and rummage through Ormak's extensive library, I acquiesced to Brother Ironknuckle's wisdom, who reminded us of how spent our energies and resources were after a long day of wet travel and dangerous battles. Each of us took a turn at watch, ready to wake the others should further danger seek us out again within the tower. Aside from Thessylia's successful hunting, we managed to remain undisturbed through the night.

Perhaps, whatever guardians Ormak had, were ordered to secure certain rooms or were part of the battle outside; regardless, we should be ready to face guardians that do not require care or feeding, such as golems and undead, though I would not be surprised to encounter something extra-planar, such as a demon or elemental, as well.

Glitter, as usual, handled the care and feeding of our small band. I awoke to the smell of warm bread and cheese and looked to see six rolls of bread hovering over the open flames of the fireplace. Typically, on the rare occasions I traveled, I took basic provisions: bread, cheese, fruit, vegetables, dried meat, and water. These would be eaten in turn as needed, preferably before getting moldy or rotten, and were not designed to please the palate so much as to fill an empty stomach.

Glitter's talent with food may outstrip her talent for magic. To break this morning's fast, she sliced the fist-sized bread rolls in half and stuffed them with a tangy yellow cheese and slices of tart, green apples, which she had picked up at the market in Talloak. She then used *aatokemaji*, which allows for telekinetic movement of light objects, to float the rolls above the flames and prevent them from catching fire, thus warming the bread and melting the cheese.

Her knowledge of herbs is comparable to mine, but where I studied the medicinal qualities she concentrated on their culinary effects. For instance, I see garlic as an antiseptic—the cloves to be crushed over open wounds to prevent infection. I have seen Glitter fry garlic in olive oil and drizzle it on trenchers of bread or even roast whole heads of it over an open fire, turning the bulb into a creamy, pungent paste which combines well with many other herbs and meats.

"Glitter, my dear lady, these are wondrous!" beamed Vondro around a mouthful of her latest concoction. "Certainly, far better than the porridge I am used to eating in the morning. Where did you get the idea to melt it all together like this?"

"From my mother, I suppose," she shrugged. "She was the best cook in Springmorn's Run. Her pies won contests at every faire, and she used the prize money to open a tavern where she made meals for travelers from all over Loerendoch. We even served Queen Mara and Princess Isaquel a few years ago, when the Princess celebrated her coming of age and toured the kingdom. Shortly after that, I worked for a zylan couple in their kitchen."

"I have yet to visit Springmorn's Run," spoke Raf excitedly. "We should all go for the Spring Festival! It's said that on the first day of spring, the sun rises directly through a pass between two mountains, making it the brightest morning of the year."

"Yes. Everyone gathers together just outside of town to watch for the first rays of sun, then there is a parade leading back to the center of town for a full day's celebrations—games, food, performers..."

"It sounds like fun," chimed in Tsukatta.

"Town celebrations have the best crowds," smiled Raf, turning to a handstand. "We should all go next spring. And if your mother's cooking is as good as you say it is..."

"She's dead," Glitter said flatly, shooting me an angry glance. Obviously, she was still upset about what happened during our duel. I should talk to her about that.

Ial'rafiost dropped into a roll and sat at Glitter's feet. "I'm sorry. I didn't know."

Glitter gave him a wan smile. "It's okay. How were you to know?"

Everyone got quiet and avoided looking at her, except for me. I knew her pain; I had shared it, in a fashion. This sullen mood would last all day if someone did not break it. "We all share in your grief," I said genuinely. "However, we still have work to do, and other lives to save."

"Yes. Umm, we need to explore this tower and, uh, find a way to stop this Cratillus person," Vondro stammered.

"The library first," I offered. "Ormak may have spells and information we can use."

"Agreed," Brother Ironknuckle got to his feet. "We should see if we can learn more about our enemy. Mithron, you are a necromancer as well. How would you fight against us?"

I stopped and stared at him. The grommold had an interesting insight; I had not thought about what tactics I would use. "First, if Cratillus is powerful enough to raise an army, then he has access to the most powerful spells we know of, many of which can kill us all outright. Second, he appears to let others do his dirty work for him, sending out lackeys to gather the things he needs, one of which is this tome." I pulled *In Between: On the Transition from Life to Death to Life* out of my backpack for all to see. "There is a spell in here called *avrimemzuklayt*, which animates every corpse in the vicinity, turning them into either ruklaa or kuldaa, depending on the level of decay, under the control of whoever casts the spell. This, I believe, is the key to Cratillus's plan—we must keep this tome out of his hands."

"Why don't we just destroy it, then?" asked Vondro.

I stared at him in horror. "One does not destroy knowledge!" I nearly shouted, appalled by the suggestion. "One gathers it; nurtures it; builds upon it. Knowledge is the lifeblood of civilization itself. It must be preserved, utilized, expanded, and passed onto the next generation of scholars. 'Destroy it' he says." I threw up my arms in exasperation.

"But if it is used for evil…" Vondro began.

"Knowledge is not evil—men are. How many have you killed with that sword of yours?"

"Several, but I use the sword to defend myself and others, not to commit murder."

"But others do. Is the sword evil, or the wielder?"

"Okay, I see where you're going with this. But this knowledge, the ability to animate an army of undead, tell me how this can be a good thing."

"Simple enough. If you can learn how to create something, then it becomes easier to take it apart. 'Knowledge is our weapon', as Mistress Vletraka used to say. Besides, Cratillus was seeking numerous lost tomes, so it could be that this information has been copied into one of the others. In which case, he may already have what he needs."

"Well, don't you just know how to brighten a room," sniped Raf.

"If you rely on me for that, half of you will commit suicide by next morning," I retorted. "Best we leave morale in your hands," I smiled, as did he.

"Thank you," he bowed graciously with the usual gleam in his eye. "I didn't fancy an air walk from the rafters anyway."

"Now we need to do some research. Ormak has... had an extensive library. We should find out everything we can before moving on," I said.

"I'm liking the idea of hanging myself again," Raf frowned.

"Ah, but think of the stories you could learn," I countered. "Ormak kept a close eye on the progress of his students, and their students, and on until now. He was as good a historian and biographer as a wizard. No one else knows these stories like he did. You could tell tales that no one else knows, and have the facts to prove it!"

Ial'rafiost's eyes lit up. "Research... I *love* research!"

"Let me remind you all again," I warned, "be careful. Ormak has likely trapped his most valuable possessions, so check for magical wards before touching anything."

We all went upstairs to the library. If only we were not in such a hurry to stop a madman from... whatever his ultimate goal might be. With an undead horde at his command, he could devastate the entire countryside; perhaps even conquer Loerendoch itself. I do not think, however, that he would be satisfied as a king ruling over a mortal realm. No, a man of his power is trying to become a god; I can see no other outcome of this path.

"Eep!" Glitter's sudden cry reminded me of Jarlisk's body still lying on the floor. Now that his spirit was no longer animating the corpse, the natural process of rot had begun.

"That was Jarlisk," I informed my comrades, "Grustan's master."

"Auff! He stinks!" Glitter shrieked as she covered her mouth and nose with her hands. The others followed her example. Over the years, I had gotten used to the smell of death and decay, though by no means do I find it pleasant, and barely noticed the odor.

"Without his spirit, the body is decaying quickly," I thought aloud. "Interesting. I suppose we should get him out of the way. Vondro, would you and Brother Ironknuckle remove him to the kitchen with the other one?"

Vondro looked at the body with disgust. "Why us?"

"Because you two are the strongest ones here. Between the two of you, the task should be easy. Meanwhile, the rest of us can begin looking for clues and ideas. If it is the smell which bothers you..." I cast *uvaazaji*, the spell I had used to dry myself off. Though its effects are minor, the spell literally has hundreds of uses for the creative caster. I made Jarlisk's body smell like freshly picked lavender. "Better?"

Vondro lowered his hands from his face and took a tentative sniff. "Yes. Alright, fine," he sighed in resignation. "We'll be right back."

They lifted Jarlisk's body, Vondro taking the arms and Brother Ironknuckle the legs, and carried it off.

I turned to examine the bookcases nearest to me and discovered that Cratillus was wise to seek old tomes here, though he should have planned his attempted theft better. I found copies of *Making Space: The Art of Expanding Volumes Through Use of Extra-Dimensional Pockets* and *Magivore: Nourishing the Body With*

Magic, both proving to be exceptional reading material, as well as *The Light of Life* and *Absolute Darkness*, both of which Ormak alluded to yesterday. I also found the cursed tome *The Indistinct Shadow*, which is rumored to drain the life of its possessor, and the original *Willow, Ash, and Oak*, which Ormak penned with his own hand. A priceless treasure indeed!

Turning a corner, I discovered the true cost. Ormak lay on the floor atop a toppled chair, his throat torn open. It appears he was sitting at this desk when Grustan found him. Examining the corpse closely, I could see the throat was not torn out, but pierced and crushed. Grustan must have grabbed the neck from behind, his powerful fingers crushing and penetrating the soft new flesh, causing the man who had not needed to breathe in more than a century to suffocate.

On the desk sat a blood-spattered book, open to the page of Ormak's last entry. It read, in small, meticulous handwriting, "Suzelle, I am so sorry! All this time and I still could not find you. I sacrificed everything—my humanity, even my very soul—and yet I failed you. I have been forced to live again without you, but I must keep searching. The demons cannot", the missive ended with a scratch of ink, the quill etching a permanent groove into the page.

Suzelle—his wife—it was all for her. He loved her more than life itself and accepted the immortal curse of jozalkivi to find her. Perhaps his diary holds more.

I reached out for the book then quickly pulled back my hand, remembering the agony of the golden harp, and shifted my gaze to better see the Weave. As I suspected, the journal was protected with another magical symbol, this one of revulsion. *Clever. Anyone affected by this spell will avoid the object it was cast upon, so no one will wish to even touch the diary, let alone read it. I doubt that invoking Suzelle's name will work against this ward, and it will be difficult to dispel.* I cast *yuviiaji* so I might unravel the symbol's magic.

In most circumstances, *yuviiaji* has an immediate effect, tearing apart the Weave where the spell is manifest—inartistic, but generally effective. With practice, wizards learn more intricate methods of crafting spells, making them stronger and much more complicated to unravel, thereby requiring greater effort to dispel. When there is time, a wizard can study the patterns, slowly pulling apart the threads that make up the spell until it comes apart the rest of the way on its own. The *bulumslyitlial*, as the symbol of revulsion is rightly called, took a great deal of concentration and time to unravel, and it nearly released its effects upon me when I worried at the wrong thread.

This journal appeared to be just one of many, not surprising considering Ormak had roughly one hundred and fifty years to write down his thoughts. It was bound in brown, unadorned leather with pages of fine paper, and there were numerous descriptions of failed experiments, many of which included methods of divination, which apparently failed in their intent. One passage in particular caught my eye:

> *My dearest Suzelle,*
> *I am still haunted by your loss. I know that we did the right thing in closing that Abyssal portal, but I cannot forget the look of terror on your face as that demon pulled you through as the gate closed. I have tried every method of divination I can think of, consulted experts, and even visited the Burbling Chaos itself in search of you. I can accept that you have died, but I cannot even find your soul to be resurrected. Where in the realms are you?*

A tear came to my eye as the crushing despair written into the page began to overwhelm me. I set down the book, took a step back, and began my breathing exercises to bring myself under control. The bards sing about the joys and power of love, but if Ormak is an example of the consequences of love lost, then it may be best not to fall in love at all; especially given the chaos that comes with strong emotions since my "gift" manifested. If I were to lose my heart, I would likely lose my head as well!

I picked up the journal, carefully marked the page, and walked over to Glitter, who was leafing through a copy of *Diagrams, Runes, and Symbols* by Tahje. "Read this, then read the last entry," I requested softly. While she did, I noticed that Ormak had etched his own symbols into Tahje's book, probably improving on his work.

"By the gods!" Glitter exclaimed after reading the two passages. "That poor man! Everything he did was for the love of his life. Now he's dead because of us!" Her sparkles turned a pale blue-green as tears welled up in her deep violet eyes.

"Ormak was killed by his own creation, though we did help create the circumstance which led to his death," I corrected her. "I wanted him to be alive. There was so much to learn from him—about magic, my history, and his experiments—now, he is gone, and all that knowledge is lost, except for what he put in writing. We must continue to search for any reference to Cratillus or how to stop a horde of undead."

Glitter's sparkles shifted to crimson and back, causing kaleidoscopic patterns in her aura.

She is angry again. What did I say this *time?*

"You're a cold, heartless bastard," she seethed. "You don't care at all about what Ormak went through. You were willing to torture Grustan to get what you wanted. You're mean to everyone and think you know it all. I don't think you even care about any of us! Leave me alone!" Her voice rose to a scream.

I could feel the Weave tear apart then restructure itself and with her final word, I felt a wave of nausea and had to spend a moment to clear my head. *What brought* that *on?*

"Is everything all right?" Brother Ironknuckle asked, peering around the bookcase behind me.

Glitter let out a long sigh. "I'm fine. Mithron was just being his usual unfeeling pain in the neck; he's gone now."

I stared at her quizzically.

"Don't be too hard on the lad; he's suffered a great loss."

"So have I!" she barked. "Goldfire is dead as surely as Vletraka, yet no one seems to care about *my* loss." She began to cry.

"Of course we care. Ye both simply handle it differently. Ye express and release your emotions, while Mithron keeps his sewn up tighter than a miser's purse. Soon, this will cause him to crack."

"Why can't he just let himself feel?" Glitter continued.

"Mayhap he's not comfortable with his emotions; maybe he's afraid of them."

Glitter sighed and shook her head. "Boys."

I marveled again at the grommold's insights. I *am* afraid of my emotions, for I have seen the ill effect they have on those around me.

"Well, if ye see him, tell him to take his head out of his book and grab some food. I've seen how ye wizards are, and he's likely to starve before setting down a good read," he smiled.

"I see. You are all trying to ignore me. Fine then, I'll do this on my own." I reached over to snatch up Ormak's journal and my hand passed right through it! "Oh, what fresh new damnation is this?" I grumbled in exasperation. I reached for the book again, and again my hand passed through it, then through the table.

I began massaging my temples with my left hand, closed my eyes, and let out a low sigh. "She knocked me out of phase. Wonderful. *Now,* how am I to get any research done?" My stomach began to grumble. "I guess Brother Ironknuckle is right about that too," I muttered. "Of course, now I cannot even *touch* food." I sighed again.

I decided to explore the tower, since I could neither be seen nor touched; though, I reminded myself that care must still be taken, as I had no inkling as to when the spell might wear off. Out of habit, I began to wind my way around the bookcase maze toward the stairs when I realized that I could take the direct route and cautiously stepped through a bookcase.

Rather useful, even enjoyable. I need to learn how to do this at will. As I phased through a second bookcase, another thought occurred to me. *Is this what a ghost is like? To be in the world and yet separated from it? I can see how this could become maddening over time.*

"Actually, ghosts *do* manifest on the Material Plane," I said aloud. "'The standard method of attack by ghosts and other incorporeal entities is to fly through a nearby physical barrier, such as a wall or ceiling, and disrupt living organisms with their distorting touch'"[8] *Fly?* I thought excitedly.

I concentrated on lifting my body off the ground, as when using *aaslska*, and soon found my point of view rapidly changing as though I were shrinking and realized that I had sunk halfway through the floor! Instinctively, I put my hands out to push myself up and they passed through the floor as well. *Relax,* I told myself, realizing I was starting to panic. *Focus.* I continued to sink until I was hovering in the room below.

I expected complete darkness, as I had no source of light with me, but everything in the room had a strange glow of its own. It appeared to be a long disused bedroom. I passed easily through the cobwebs and looked around the chamber. The bed frame still stood, though it was devoid of any bedding, having long rotted away or stolen by rats, and two chests of drawers stood against the far wall. In the center of the bed frame sat a small coffer, which glowed more brightly than anything else in the room. As I stared at it, I found myself getting closer to it, as if it were drawing me in.

Pity I cannot see what rests within. I reached out for the coffer, and as expected, my hand passed through, only to touch something inside! Quickly, I pulled my hand back in surprise. *What might be inside that I could touch in this state? Is the ethereal effect wearing off? Should I try to grab whatever it is, or should I get out of this chamber before I get trapped in here?*

In a bout of impracticality, I chose to try for the object in the coffer. I reached through the wooden box and my hand once again bumped against an object. Cautiously, I felt along the object. It was long, thin, and smooth, like a wand. *That would make sense, given Ormak's talent for crafting them.* I grabbed the object and pulled my hand back, only to have it stop when it contacted the inside of the coffer's lid. *Solid enough to stay in the box, but ghostly enough that I can touch it. I shall come back for it later once I am part of the Material Plane again and will get Ial'rafiost to open the lock.*

---

[8] *In Between: On the Transition from Life to Death to Life*, page 133.

I need to get back to the library, I thought, and instantly began to rise to the ceiling. *Interesting. Is that how one moves through the Shadow, by thinking about where to go, rather than the direction?* I decided to experiment. *The sitting area.* My ascent ended and I floated through the wall next to the bedroom door and into a short hallway. I then passed through a bookcase at the end of the hall and through another on the other side of the wall where I could see the stairs leading up to the library and sitting area. As I neared the stairs, another wave of nausea came over me, and I thumped solidly on the floor.

"Ow." *At least I can touch things again.* I climbed up the stairs to return to the library when Brother Ironknuckle came around a corner and began to come down.

"Ah, there ye are, lad. What are ye doing down here?"

"An experiment," I answered with a sigh. The sight of him reminded my stomach of his earlier words. "What do we have for rations?"

He smiled broadly and chuckled. "And here I thought wizards never left their books to eat. Here ye go." He handed me some strips of dried beef and a hunk of stale bread. "I'm not the cook Glitter is, so this will have to do."

"At this point, anything will do. Thank you." I took the proffered rations and tore off a bite of the jerky. It was tough to chew, and bland of flavor, but it was food, and my stomach grumbled again in anticipation.

"Ye've got to eat more often. Maybe keep some food beside you while reading."

I held up my fingers. "That is not a good idea. My fingers are greasy from the meat, and that can damage a book, as would crumbs from bread, for they attract pests and promote the growth of mold. Better to keep the food away from the library." I hesitated for a moment, and then fretfully asked, "Do you think I am a 'cold, heartless bastard'?"

He gave a wan smile. "Glitter is upset. She nearly died yesterday, she lost Goldfire, we are in a tower with dead yomkii littering the place; we have not exactly been chanting around the forge."

"This is all true; however, that does not answer my question."

Brother Ironknuckle let out a sigh. "Ye are not the most diplomatic of speakers. Ye say what is on yer mind with little or no regard to how others may react. No, ye are not heartless nor cold, but ye do lack a certain amount of social grace. Mayhap if you take a moment to consider how others might feel about yer statements before speaking, ye can find a better phrasing that will not set others against ye."

"I am merely being honest. I, usually, do not seek to harm others with my words."

"Ye've got a sharp mind, and an even sharper tongue. Mind that ye don't cut yer own throat with it."

I chuckled. "That sounds just like what Yoffa would say."

"Who is Yoffa?"

"She was the village herbalist back in Split Falls. She taught me herbalism and introduced me to Vletraka. Thanks to her, I escaped my father's forge."

"Didn't like the forge, did ye? I miss mine."

"As you can see, I'm not built for working iron. And it was not so much the forge I needed to escape, but my father. *He* was a cold, heartless bastard. Why did you leave your forge?"

"I—I used to have a bit of a temper. I suppose I still do, but I've learned how to control it, channel it. *Crozzung* is the term we have for it; it means 'blood-rager' or 'someone who lives in fury'. There are elite troops who learn to channel this rage and are some of the most fearsome opponents one can imagine facing. The drop in morale from the other side often wins the battle before the first axe is swung.

"Unfortunately, not all who have the inner fire learn to use it properly, and I was one who failed. Raging against an enemy is honored, raging against your fellow grommoldi, particularly a non-warrior, is a crime, and my fury stole the life from an innocent man." He let out a long sigh and sat down on the top step.

A grey vision of his crime flashed though my vision as he spoke.

While I tried to suppress the images, he continued, "I fled my home, knowing that my punishment would be to trade my life for the one I took, and released my rage against myself and anyone I thought would be able to give me an, undeserved, honorable death in battle." He smiled up at me. "As you can see, I have yet to earn that honor.

"I eventually came across a monastery hidden in a shadowed valley, where I learned to channel my rage through discipline and exercise. I not only became a stronger warrior, but also rediscovered a warrior's spirit, which I thought I had lost. When my Master thought I was ready, he released me back into the world, where I work to save lives in the hopes of redeeming myself for the one I so foolishly took. I hear that same rage oft times when ye speak. I was born with the fire in my belly; where did yer's come from?"

I opened my mouth to deny his charge, then realized his words were true. I sat down beside him and answered, "My father, who was a controlling man, with limited insights, and limited vision. He was a fine blacksmith but knew little else. My frame is more akin to my Mother's than his, and he often ridiculed me for my inability to do the heavy chores necessary to work the forge. My older brother is a slightly smaller version of him, and I fear for the family he will one day have, as I fear for my younger brother, who will likely become just like them now that I am no longer there to protect him. Mother obeys him out of fear, and I wish I could have brought her along with me when he decided I was no longer welcome in his home.

"To make matters more challenging, I have come to understand my 'wizard's gift'. I am able to know the pain and suffering in the souls of others, but only when my emotions are heightened. It first manifested during a duel with Glitter, when she used a spell which caused my emotions to run rampant, and I told her story to everyone." I turned to face him. "I tried to stop myself, but her spell had me in its grip, and wizard's gifts typically take practice to control anyway. She has not forgiven nor forgotten how I embarrassed her, and I cannot seem to make her understand that I was not in control."

"Have you explained your gift to her?"

"I have come to understand it only yesterday. When we last spoke, she pushed me right out of the physical realm. That is why I was downstairs when you found me. Which reminds me, have you seen Ial'rafiost? I need his skills for something."

"He should still be in the library. He found a book detailing another wizard's life and has been reading it intently. I have ne'er seen him sit still for so long!" he laughed.

"Thank you," I said standing up, "both for talking and for listening. I... do not have many friends."

He also stood, smiled, and clapped a heavy hand on my shoulder. "Ye have us. Talk to her, lad. Ye make a good team. Dangerous, both, but a good team!" he laughed.

I smiled back, then turned to go find Raf. It felt good to be able to talk to Brother Ironknuckle, as if a chunk of iron had been removed from atop my chest. There is something about him that puts one at ease. Perhaps it is the wisdom of his years and experience, or that he has reversed his inner rage to create an aura of peace. Whatever the reason, I have always been proud to count him among my friends.

As I sought Raf out amongst the stacks of books, I nearly bumped into Glitter, who was piling tomes on a shelf. It appeared she had come across a run of Ormak's journals and was preparing to read a large portion of his history. Now was as good a time as any to talk to her. I took a deep breath and stammered, "I, uh, I need..."

"No," she interrupted with a glare, her sparkles flaring red and yellow. At least her gift is easy to read.

I began to anger, then my heart turned to ice. "Fine. Stay angry. It will do wonders for your concentration," I snapped at her sarcastically. I stepped past her to continue my search for Ial'rafiost. Three steps later I realized what I had done. I closed my eyes, took a deep breath, and kept walking away.

After turning two corners, I spotted the half-zyla, his attention buried in a book. "Is that what I look like while studying?" I asked, drawing him slowly away from the text.

"Hmm? Oh, hi. You should read this. Ormak really did keep track of his students. These are his notes on Ru'uz, another one, fifth removed. This book details his training, his companions, their adventures together, and his love for the sea. They would often sail to exotic lands solely for the enjoyment of doing so, and fight monsters wherever they encountered them. We should go! I want to see these places!" he rattled off quickly, then paused, "I just need to find out where they are. Have you seen any maps around here?"

"I have. If you will do a quick favor for me, I will show them to you."

"What do you need?" he asked with some hesitation.

"I discovered a box downstairs that I cannot open. You have skills in that regard. Open the box, and I will show you the maps."

"Sounds easy enough. Lead on!" He followed me downstairs toward the unused bedroom, past a still fuming Glitter. She shot me a glance as we walked by, but I did my best to ignore her, as her sparkles were still shades of crimson.

After we reached the ground level of the tower, Raf whispered conspiratorially, "She likes you, you know."

"It appears quite the opposite to me. She is full of rage, bile, and hatred, and, though I can understand her reasons, as she clearly pointed them out to me, I do not comprehend her vehemence in those feelings," I sighed.

"It's because she likes you," he smiled. When I turned a confused look upon him, he continued, "If she didn't like you, she would not feel so angry. See, most people do not show their true feelings, because they are afraid of those feelings getting hurt. She does not think you like her, and she would rather drive you away than find out for sure, because that would hurt her more than not knowing. I've been with a lot of women. Trust me, I know these things," he grinned.

"Why is everyone suddenly interested in my relationships or lack thereof today?" I growled. "First, Brother Ironknuckle, and now, you, both commenting on how I should behave with Glitter. Why is everyone so interested in my personal life? Besides, you have been trying to get close to her since we all met, why are you pushing her toward me?"

"Glitter and I kid each other, but there's no spark there—if you'll pardon the pun. We are a team, and we need to keep working together. You started us on this mission, and are the leader of this little band, whether you like it or not. Unless you resolve this, we lose cohesion, and in a fight, it can get one of us killed."

I stared blankly at him for a moment. "I would have expected battlefield advice from Vondro, not you. I do not want to lead…"

"But you sure do like to give commands," he interrupted. "You tell everyone what to do, and act like you know what you're doing all the time. Look, you're really smart, we all get that, but you really need to learn to understand people, not just books. I can help you with that. I learned early on how to please a crowd, and to entertain individuals. You just have to tell them what they want to hear, not what you think they need to know."

"That sounds… dishonest to me."

"Not if you believe what you are telling them. You do not have to lie to make someone feel better, in fact, that usually fails, though it doesn't hurt to stretch the truth now and again. You are a bit too honest with your thoughts, painfully so at times, but I don't think you are honest with your feelings. Do you like Glitter?"

"Yes. She is an intelligent and skilled mage. Her knowledge of herbs and her innate understanding of the nature of the Weave are peerless. I enjoy her culinary expertise…"

"Do you think she's pretty?" he interrupted.

"Yes, but what does that…"

"Does thinking of her make you happy?" he interrupted again.

I thought back to our duel, and how I revealed her darkest secret to our peers. I thought about our battle with Ormak, and how she was nearly killed when I angered him. I considered her words to me in the library just before she shunted me to the Shadow. "No," I finally responded, "thinking of her frightens me. I seem to cause no end of grief for her, and I fear for what might come next."

"So, you're concerned for her feelings. You feel that you're hurting her, putting her in danger, and worry about her safety. You'd rather she left so you don't have to worry about making her mad at you or her getting hurt."

"Yes."

He grinned from ear to ear. "Then you like her too. Your fears about her are the same as her anger towards you. If you didn't like her, then you'd not care so much to be frightened for her."

"Of course, I like her. As I said, she is a colleague, who has some good qualities." I paused for a minute, while he waited for me to figure it out. "I see. You mean 'like her' in a deeper, more emotional sense."

"See, I told you you're smart!" he laughed. "You just need to tell her how you feel."

"The trick is getting her to listen. You saw her sparkles as we passed her upstairs—she is in no mood to listen to me."

"Then you shall have to choose your time. Now, where is this lock?"

"This way." We walked to the bedroom door, which opened easily enough. Rats skittered away as we stepped in, causing me to begin uttering *aatokytsrukak* in case they came at us, but two syllables later, they were gone and I clamped down on the energies of the spell; no sense in channeling fire unnecessarily. The small coffer sat in the middle of the bed frame, still undisturbed.

Raf walked up to it and examined it thoroughly; he even wisely cast *trezelaji* before touching it. "Nothing magical on the outside, but there is something magical in there."

"I think it may be a wand," I volunteered.

He turned to look at me and asked in amazement. "How do you know that?"

"I have my ways," I said mysteriously.

"Yeah, you've used that line before. It's kind of annoying, you know."

"'A mage must keep a proper air of mystery about him'," I said quoting *A Philosophy of Magic* by Revance.[9] Wisely, I stopped before finishing the line, which continues, "so that lesser creatures will be both intimidated and honored by his presumed greatness. The mage must not be worshipped, but must be treated with

---

[9] Page 17.

reverence due to him, for even an apprentice is beyond the scope of most men." Revance must have had a big ego, but his general point is valid. There are few who can understand, and work magic the way a wizard can, and if it leads to someone fearing my potential power rather than confronting me directly about it, then the battle is won before it starts.

"Fine, be that way." He pulled a small leather case out of his pack, unbuttoning and rolling it out to reveal a set of fine tools. He picked up one in each hand and set to work on the inside of the lock. "All right, I think I got it." There was a grating 'click' and he opened the small chest.

True enough, a wand sat on top of a pile of coins.

He turned to me again. "Okay. So, you were right."

I smiled back at him and reached for the wand.

He slammed the lid and said, "Not until you tell me how you knew."

"It was an educated guess. Ormak was known for his ability to craft wands, and I suspected that he would keep a special one hidden beneath his bed." Not the whole truth, but enough to satisfy his curiosity. I did not feel like explaining, at that moment, my ethereal jaunt or how I came to be in that predicament.

His eyes narrowed. "So, you do know how to stretch the truth without lying. But I want the whole story at some point. I don't know what you're hiding, or why, but it's your business. You will have to trust us more fully at some point." He sighed, opened the small chest back up, and handed me the wand.

It felt light, lighter than it should have done.

He closed the coffer and picked it up.

I sighed. "I wandered in here after Glitter threw a tantrum, found this, but it was locked. Something rattled inside that sounded like wood, and I surmised that it might be a wand, so I asked for your expertise. I truly had no way of knowing for certain." That was still not the whole truth, but I hoped it would keep him from pushing further on the issue.

"Fair enough. I hope you two can settle your differences soon. It's getting hard to work around you two."

"I am willing when she is." I examined the wand, casting first *trezelaji* to look for clues to its power, then *embulaji* in the hopes of finding the keyword to activate it. The *trezelaji* revealed conjuration magic within the wand, but I could elicit no other clues, while *embulaji* showed no signs of runes, which would tell me how to effectively activate it. With practice, those who have learned the secrets of such tools can activate a wand blindly, but there is always a chance of misfire, or worse, backlash, unless the proper command word is used to activate the power.

The wand itself appeared to be made from willow, nearly white in color with a small dark stain near the tip, but even so it should have been heavier than it was. Were it made from balsa or cork, it still should have been weightier. The fact that I could touch it while ethereal led me to believe that the wand itself was in a trans-dimensional state, and its magic might be too.

A wand that issues spells that affect both material and ethereal targets? Ormak was truly a genius! Further examination of the stain showed it to appear like a dragon's head, mouth open as though ready to bite its foes. *Or breathe upon them! A spell that mimics a dragon's breath would be a powerful offensive tool. If this is the case, then the dark stain would suggest the acidic bile of the black dragon, though it could be another type as well. I will have to seek out more of Ormak's notes.*

I turned to tell Raf the prize I had discovered, only to find that he was already gone, as was the coffer of coins. I tucked my prize into my robe and climbed the sweeping stairs once more, returning to the library. Everyone save Vondro was pouring through one volume or another, while our swordsman appeared bored, sharpening his blade without enthusiasm.

"A blade honed to too fine an edge might snap," I warned.

"If I sit here any longer, I'll snap," he retorted with a sigh.

"I realize that this is dull for you, but personally, I am glad to be out of danger for the time being. There is something I would like us all to do. We should bury Ormak."

"After he tried to kill us all? Let him rot."

I sighed. "I understand that, but he was not a bad man, just in a lot of emotional pain, and did things that I do not believe he would do under normal circumstances. He deserves better than to putrefy away on the floor."

"I'm more than just physical labor, you know," he snarled.

"I know," I assented, "but you are the strongest of us. This, I think, is something we should all do together. After all, as Glitter so rightly pointed out to me, we are responsible for his death."

"We didn't bring any shovels. I don't suppose you have a hole-digging spell."

"No, I do not," I confessed. *I would wager that Uxadul would know of one.* "Perhaps we should cremate him then. Glitter and I both know more than a few fire spells." After I removed the numerous valuable and magickal items from Ormak's body, Vondro heaved up and carried it down the stairs and outside to the wet grass.

The rest of us followed.

"I wish we had more time to talk," I began. "You carried generations of knowledge and had much to teach us. Though I did not know you, I believe that becoming a jozalk was never in your plans. You began to speak to me about love, and I read how Suzelle was so cruelly taken from you. We never meant to harm you, only sought your advice and wisdom. I can only hope that now you are finally reunited with the one you love." Before I could let myself cry, lose control, and begin ranting about what a fool he was to allow himself to transform into an undead abomination, I motioned everyone to stand back and cast *srukakarih*.

The sphere of flames landed on Ormak's abdomen, igniting his tattered robes. Soon, his flesh charred, and the spell burnt him down to the bone before expiring. Glitter then cast the same spell, rolling the sphere over the scorched skeleton until it too was consumed by flame.

As we re-entered the tower, I heard Vondro mutter, "I guess I'll go back to sharpening my sword," as he pulled a whetstone out of a side pouch on his backpack.

"It might be safe to explore if you take Raf and Brother Ironknuckle along," I offered as we began climbing the stairs. "The rest of us will continue our research while you wander. Remember, be careful, as Ormak may have any number of guardians or protections about the place."

"As I am more likely to die of boredom than by a blade, I am willing to take the risk," he half-smiled. When I gave him a pleading look, he continued, "Fine, we'll be careful." He carefully rewrapped the whetstone in a cloth, placed it into his pack, and called to Brother Ironknuckle and Ial'rafiost to follow him.

After they left, I sat down across from Glitter, glad I had only eaten little food earlier. "I wish to apologize to you." I blurted, fear causing my chest to flutter and the world to grey. I stopped to take a calming breath and continued. "I know I have hurt your feelings time and again, but I believe I have come to understand the reasons for my behavior." I awaited a response, expecting her to tell me to leave or that she did not care. Instead, she continued to stare into one of Ormak's journals, showing no signs she heard me at all. "When my emotions are heightened, I can see the darkness within the soul of another, whether it was evil they caused or harm that was done to them. When you cast your spell at the tournament, it caused my Gift to manifest for the first time. Grustan's undying hatred overwhelmed me, causing me to return his emotion in kind.

"My Gift is to know the worst in people." I sighed and turned away. "To make things worse, I feel compelled to relate what I see. I will learn to control my Gift in time, now that I understand how it works, but I am certain that I will blurt out things from time to time, especially when tensions are high. I never intended to cause you grief. I would actually like us to become friends, if that is still a possibility." Still receiving no input from her, I stood with a sigh and began to walk away.

Before I had taken my third step, she decided to speak. "You really hurt and embarrassed me that day. I know you didn't mean it and could not have possibly known any of what you said beforehand, but I always wondered how anyone could be so cruel. You even blamed me for causing it, though I suppose that's partly true after all. You must promise me that, when we are done with this, you will tell the others from the tournament the truth. They deserve to know what happened."

I turned back to look at her, tears streaming down her face, though her voice gave no indications that she was crying, her sparkles dim and pale blue.

"I promise. Whatever it takes to make amends, you tell me, and I will comply, until you feel I have atoned for the harm I caused." As I spoke, I could feel the tears welling up in my eyes and the colors faded from the library. The sound of Glitter's father hitting her mother over and over again filled my ears, but I managed to force myself into silence. It suddenly occurred to me that I was going to have to face Uxadul again, and that thought came with the certainty that my troubles were far from over.

A loud cursing in Grommoldian broke my reverie, and I was oddly thankful that the others seemed to have found trouble.

Chapter 11: Golems and Gold

Before I could move, a blue and green blur passed by me; only the sound of Tsukatta's sandals scuffing along the wooden floor gave her presence away, which was soon overwhelmed by the sound of Glitter's chair sliding back and falling to the floor. I fell in behind her, red and yellow sparkles drifting over me as they cascaded off her shoulders and multi-hued hair, and we ran to the source of the cursing.

One of the bookcases was turned perpendicular from the wall, revealing a staircase ascending through a small recess in the wall. A flash of light and the smell of ozone emanated from above, along with a continuous stream of Grommoldian curses, which I believe would be best not to translate.

"How was *I* supposed to know that a pile of twigs was going to come to life?" I heard Raf say as a wave of heat pushed its way down the stairs.

Reaching the top, I was surprised by the scene before me. Raf was flipping, rolling, and arcing his way through the air as jets of flame shot past him; the streamers attached to his outfit made him appear like a bounding pinwheel. Vondro crouched behind his rapidly dissolving shield as acid poured on it, and Brother Ironknuckle tumbled and dodged in an attempt to avoid a trio of glowing darts which turned in midair in pursuit of their target. The source of these magical attacks seemed to be a man-shaped stack of wood standing atop a chest surrounded by all manner of coins and miscellaneous items.

"What happened?" asked Glitter as a thin lance of ice fired above Vondro's head.

"Raf found one of the guardians Mithron warned us about," he shouted, abandoning his shield's remains and dropping prone as a bolt of lightning lashed past his head, his metal armor attracting tendrils of electricity as the main part of the bolt whizzed by. No sooner had the lightning passed when Tsukatta appeared at his side, her hands glowing brightly as she poured her healing energy into him.

"Well, that is different," I spoke, amazed at the scene before me. "Golems usually are not that adept at spellcasting."

"I just read about this in Ormak's journals," Glitter remarked as she ducked behind the wall. "He called it a 'wand golem'. It's constructed out of fresh and spent wands and held together with platinum wire. Like most golems, it's resistant to physical blows and magic, though it seems that it is vulnerable to spells that disrupt magic. Force magic actually repairs it, so don't use *ajilek* or the like."

"Of course, he would develop a golem made of wands; he was a master at crafting them. Fascinating!" I smiled at the handiwork, forgetting for a moment that the lives of my friends were in peril. While I commented, Glitter cast *yuviiaji* to disrupt the golem, causing its movements to slow and decreasing the speed of its casting. Guessing her spell would not last long and knowing that any other I had studied would be useless against this creature, I prepared to cast the same one to give our warriors a better chance at destroying it.

When the golem's movement slowed, Vondro and Brother Ironknuckle took the opportunity to charge the construct from opposite sides. The wand golem let loose with a cloud of noxious green gas, causing its living foes to choke and gasp, though, it did not stop them from attacking near the creature's center. Brother Ironknuckle's quick fists struck first, cracking the wooden frame, though not as much as expected, knowing his strength and skill. Vondro's sword did little better, chipping the creature slightly where he should have cut it in twain, and Raf's thrown daggers merely bounced off it. Glitter was certainly right about its durability.

The golem's arm crackled with electricity and it swatted Vondro, his armor again drawing the energy, causing him to spasm in pain. Tsukatta soon appeared behind him to administer more healing while the others continued their assault. The wand golem shook off Glitter's disruption and I cast *yuviiaji,* which I had ready to slow it down again. I had prepared it to break Ormak's protections in his library and would be able to cast it once more if necessary. "Did Ormak's journal say the golem was resistant to fire or other energies, or just magic?"

Glitter was silent for a moment. "He made no mention. Why?"

I shouted to Raf by way of an answer. "Try alchemist's fire or acid! It might work better than your daggers!"

Ial'rafiost reached into a pouch, pulled out a small flask of yellowish liquid, and hurled it at the golem. It impacted squarely in its head, or at least the part of it where a head would be on a man, and shattered, spraying acid all around, burning Vondro and Brother Ironknuckle as well. The creature showed no signs of pain, though the physical damage from the acid was evident. It responded by glowing dimly and touching itself with one arm. I sighed as the damage reversed itself, repairing not only the dissolving section but also the chips and cracks created by the others as well.

"One of the wands must cast *umakraazt*. It can repair its own wounds." I smiled in spite of myself, proud of Ormak's creation. At least that meant it was not causing more damage to my allies if it had to take time to repair itself. The hard part was going to be causing damage faster than it could repair it. "Glitter, do you have any alchemical items to use? I think we must do more than disrupt the golem if we are to defeat it."

"I have fire and frost, but it will damage everyone next to it as well."

"Do what ye have to do," Brother Ironknuckle shouted back. "Better a little fire from ye than another blast from this stack of cordwood!"

I shrugged, cast *yuviiaji* for the last time to slow the golem's spellcasting speed and ran in with a flask of alchemical fire in my hand. I knew I had to get in close, else I might hit one of the others or, more likely, miss altogether. I threw the flask at its feet, and green-blue flames spread out in a circle around the golem and up its legs.

Brother Ironknuckle jumped straight up in the air and kicked the golem with both feet, shoving it toward Vondro while pushing himself outside the circle of flame. Vondro responded by sweeping out the legs of the golem with his sword, causing it to crash to the floor.

While the construct tried to rise, both Glitter and Raf dropped flasks of alchemical fire upon it, increasing the surrounding pool of flames. Brother Ironknuckle kicked it repeatedly, forcing it to crash back on the floor, cracks reappearing in its wooden structure. It began to glow with the same energy that repaired it earlier, when Tsukatta cast *yuviiaji*, disrupting the golem's spell and giving us more time to cause as much damage as possible before it could attempt it again. Moments later, movements ceased, and it began to glow.

Oh gods! "Everyone get away!" I screamed and dove behind the wall by the staircase.

The golem exploded in a blast of eldritch energy.

Pieces of wands and metal flew past me and bounced down the stairs, while the sounds of moaning came from within the chamber. I peeked around the corner to find Vondro lying atop both Tsukatta and Glitter, his armor ripped off his back, and Brother Ironknuckle and Ial'rafiost flat on the floor behind and under piles of coins and debris. Before I could speak, everyone began to stand up, slowly and deliberately. As Vondro attempted to stand, he started to wobble and dropped down to one knee between the two ladies.

Tsukatta immediately began her healing ministrations on the injured warrior.

"Well, that was a bit of fun!" beamed Brother Ironknuckle.

"I thought you were angry," Raf responded, appearing confused.

"Only because it surprised me. Once I knew what it was about, I found it a good exercise partner," he chuckled.

Raf shook his head and laughed. "This will make a fine tale, at least. Now let's see what stick-thing was guarding." He went straight to the chest the golem originally stood upon, which was now charred and blackened. "Great," he sighed, "the lock melted. Now we'll have to break the chest open. How about one of those golem-stomping kicks right about here?" he called to the grommoldian monk.

Brother Ironknuckle put his stone-hard foot right between the hinges on the back of the chest, causing the lid to rip halfway off.

"Perfect!"

Meanwhile, Tsukatta finished tending to Vondro's burns and examined Glitter for damage. Assured she was generally unharmed, she moved softly about the room to see to the rest of us. Fortunately, I managed to escape the golem's final strike completely, and Raf and Brother Ironknuckle were far too interested in the scattered piles of treasure to notice their wounds.

I shifted my vision to see the Weave more clearly, and noticed that some items within the treasure-hoard glowed brightly, items which Ormak undoubtedly collected over the years, as layers of dust were evident where the golem's final strike did not burn it away. Mostly, the items were utilitarian for travelers and those seeking treasure and glory by defeating creatures such as Ormak, including weapons, armor, bags, packs, jewelry, and clothing; no wands, staves, or the like, which led me to believe that anything useful to him was kept elsewhere, and better guarded.

Those of us who could see the Weave, meaning all but Vondro and Brother Ironknuckle, who instead counted the piles of coins, began examining the items to determine their use, a process which took well over an hour due to the number of objects to analyze. Much of it was mundane, with basic enchantments to increase the potency or resilience of the item, particularly the weapons and armor.

The item that first drew my eye, however, was a black leather shoulder bag which showed indications that it would be resistant to damage, and thus a great place to carry my valuable tomes. Upon further study, I learned that it contained an extra-dimensional space within, so that it not only held my spell-books and *In Between* but had room for a number of additional volumes as well with no added weight! To me, this was a treasure even greater than the ring that brought forth a shield of magical force or the bracelet that granted resistance to fire.

Once the inventory was completed, we divided the spoils and found ourselves wealthy in both monies and valuable magic. Were we not on an important mission, I felt as though I could adequately retire to a quiet life of study, requiring no further funds for the rest of my days!

In truth, the difficulty with large piles of metal coins is the weight. Even if I were to fill my shoulder bag with coins rather than tomes, it could only stow so much, and there were more coins than even it could hold. "We must devise a way of guarding what we cannot carry until we can return for it. Now that the golem has been destroyed, anyone could walk in here and help themselves," I announced.

"We can close off the hidden passage, for a start," smiled Raf as he stuffed gold coins into his pockets. Luckily, he had found a belt among the treasures, which helped to keep his pants from falling down from the weight of the coins. Still, gold spilled out of his pockets, and he would find himself poor after his next cartwheel.

"I can seal off the passage entirely," smiled Tsukatta, placing a magical tiara upon her brow, "then re-open it when we return."

"I can ward it," Glitter and I spoke simultaneously and smiled at each other; we quickly turned away. I felt a small flush of joy. *She smiled at me!* Though elated, I quickly tamped the emotion down before my vision changed. "I have a ward that will enhance yours, but we will have to cast them together," I offered.

"A double-punch. I like that idea!" she smiled again; her sparkles golden. "Tomorrow, before we leave, so that I can study."

"Agreed. Hopefully, we will find some information we can use against Cratillus by then. Either way, we should not delay any longer."

The group retired back to the library to rest after our exercise with the wand golem and to further our research. Would that we could take the whole library with us to peruse along the way to Ehrghex! Of course, I could spend a large portion of my lifetime here, studying magic, history, and lore, both arcane and mundane, but I feared that we had already wasted far too much time, and were going to spend yet another night in the vain hope of finding the right tidbit of information which would stop Cratillus's plans.

I had finished leafing through *Transconducing Magickal Energies* by the tillallin wizard Copprin Flauginbood, which detailed different ways to repel, channel, and alter spells evoking flames, intense cold, electricity, and the like, and had switched to another volume when I was interrupted by an odd voice.

"What'cha weadin'?" asked Raf over my shoulder in an imitation of a curious four-year-old.

"Making Space: The Art of Expanding Volumes Through Use of Extra-Dimensional Pockets by Forderoff Theralis. It discusses the nature of sectioning off areas of the Shadow Plane and binding them to material objects, like this shoulder bag and that pouch you picked up from Ormak's hoard," I stated, never taking my eyes from the page.

"You know about this?" he asked fearfully. "Are you going to tell the others?"

"If I were, I already would have. We all found objects of great value from the tower; you do not have to hide your prize. However," I warned, reading directly from the page, "'…two extra-dimensional pockets should never be allowed to interact, for this bends the tether connecting the pockets to the material realm too far, causing the tether to snap. Should this occur, the pockets will tear asunder, causing their contents, their material bond, and all things nearby in material space to be flung into the Shadow Plane, scattered and lost for all eternity.'"[10]

"Well, that sounds ominous. So, what does that mean? Don't put one inside the other or they will explode?"

"Basically, yes. Should you find another pouch similarly enchanted, do not place one within the other for safe keeping."

"Good to know, thanks! Anything else I should know?"

"Actually, there is a spell in here that you might find useful, if you have the training to comprehend its complexities, called *uvazajidmalvyt*, which creates a number of small temporary pockets

---

[10] Pages 27-28.

wherein you could hide valuables or other items to protect against theft."

"Let me look at it," he demanded excitedly. "I don't have your formal studies, but I've picked up a bit of arcane knowledge in my time." After a few minutes of study, he recited the mystic runes from the page, and I could see the Weave knot up in various places in his jerkin.

He grabbed a quill from the desk and slipped it into his clothes through an opening that only he could see, but I could get a hint of. The quill and half of his hand disappeared in a manner suggesting that he should have stabbed himself through his liver were it not for the magic.

"This is great! Now I can go back upstairs and get more gold!" he said spinning like a top.

"For a while at least. It appears the spell will only last for about an hour or so. It should still prove useful, especially when walking through large crowds; no one can pick your pocket if the pocket does not really exist," I smiled.

"And no one can accuse me of picking their pocket if they cannot find the pocket their coins went into," he smiled back, laughing when my smile turned to a glare. "Don't worry, I gave that up when I learned how to get coins through performing. It's so much better when the crowds *give* you their money, and you never have to worry about the town guard hauling you away afterwards!"

"Has anyone ever told you that you are incorrigible?"

"Only the ones who know what the word means. Most just call me troublesome," he laughed again.

I shook my head, got up, and ambled back over to one of the overloaded bookcases. I still could hardly get over the sheer volume of tomes, scrolls, and manuscripts littering the shelves; it was difficult to focus on finding a way to cut the strings animating an army of kuldaa with so many other choices to peruse. *Knowledge is our weapon, knowledge is our weapon,* I repeated in my mind as I gazed over the titles, hoping the mantra helped me focus. On a high shelf, my eyes were drawn to a bronze-colored book, dulled with age, entitled *Accentuating the Positive: A Study of Divine Channeling and Its Arcane Equivalent* by Falleoraeli Zolthliam.

Realizing the tome was out of my reach, I memorized its location, then proceeded to search for a stool. Tsukatta, also trying to get a book off a high shelf, was using the only one I came across. She had one foot on a shelf and was balancing on her toes on the stool while stretching for her target, a tome bound in blue leather with a lightning bolt emblazoned on the spine. I watched silently as she struggled, afraid I might startle her and cause her to fall. As it turned out, she did not require my assistance in that department.

I jumped to her side to catch her, cushioning her fall as she knocked both of us over onto the hard-wooden floor. "Vondro probably would have caught you in his arms and remained standing. I apologize for not doing as well," I said with a smile to hide the pain in my backside.

"Thank you for trying just the same," she smiled back. "I'm sorry to have fallen on you. Are you injured?"

"No, you are much lighter than my brothers, and there is a difference between falling on someone and tackling them. If you were one of them, I might be unconscious right now," I laughed lightly, putting out of my mind the pummeling I took from Larshon over the years to 'toughen me up'. The only lesson I ever learned from him was how to run quickly after provoking him; I knew I should not ridicule him when he was within earshot, but he so often inspired my disdain with his incessant boasting, causing me to, as father put it, 'poke the bear'. Unfortunately, though I was faster than my elder brother, he could run for longer periods, eventually wearing me down and catching me. I could sometimes gain sanctuary if Mother was nearby, but eventually Larshon's wrath would find me.

"Yes, family can be cruel sometimes, though in my case, my brothers were overly protective." Her smile faded, almost imperceptive, but returned after a moment while she got to her feet. "I never suffered physical harm from them, but I had little freedom. After a few beatings from them, the rest of the children in the village avoided me. I had no enemies, but also had no friends. Fortunately,

I heard Kimitsu's call while still young, and my brothers could not prevent me from visiting the priestesses, for they feared Kimitsu's wrath."

"I would have thought that the Lady of the Gentle Rain would not act in rage," I mused while standing back up.

"She does not. Rather, she withholds her blessings, parching the village and the land until absolution is made. Should the offender not take responsibility for his actions, the people of the village take matters into their own hands."

"They execute him?" I asked, my voice rising with incredulousness.

"No, nothing so extreme, unless the crime is unforgivable. The offender is removed from the village and invited to never return until they make restitution for their crime, often through donations to the priestesses and village or through servitude. We have found that social isolation is more effective than physical punishment. When a man is treated as though he does not exist, he quickly learns how much he needs his friends, family, and loved ones. Even those who left with no intention of returning often come back once this realization sets in."

"I suppose that is effective, assuming they were integral parts of society in the first place. Personally, I neither miss my family nor the people of my village, save the one who made my life bearable: Yoffa. I would like to see her again."

"You should not say such things. Family and community are important, for they define us. We are born as blank slates, and it is their teachings that guide us to adulthood. Our parents, and theirs, and all of our ancestors are part of us, and we must honor and cherish their wisdom."

"If their teachings are positive, I agree with you," I sighed, my vision graying slightly, "but were I to follow my father's example, I would berate you for your clumsiness and chide you for not preparing a hot meal for me after a hard day's work. Likely, I also would have struck you by now for some unfathomable reason. From my Mother, I learned to pretend that all is right with the world and to ignore every slight, no matter how blatant and hurtful.

"Yoffa was my only positive influence during my childhood, until Vletraka came along and rescued me from my family. She taught me herbalism, respect for nature, and that following my own dreams, rather than my father's, was a possibility. Part of me still wishes to rescue her from village life, but I understand that if she had wished to leave, she would have done so at a time of her choosing. She is a grown woman, and capable of making her own decisions. I honor her teachings and wisdom, and rail against the rest."

"And yet, you learned much from your parents, even if only to discover which path *not* to follow. You do not like the way either behaves, so you try not to act in the same way. Don't believe they have not influenced you, however. Like it or not, we all carry aspects of those closest to us. My father was cold and strict with my brothers, but doted on me. I never knew if my brothers guarded me so closely because father commanded them to do so, or if they were driving any potential friends away to make me miserable. Though I was easily accepted by the priestesses, it took a long time to learn how to be friends with them."

"Well, you have friends here," Glitter's voice wafted from the other side of the bookcase, "and perhaps we can become a better family together than the ones we grew up with." She came around to where Tsukatta and I stood, a light smile on her face and turquoise sparkles floating around her shoulders. She took Tsukatta's hand in hers, then after a moment's hesitation, took mine in her other. "We work together, protect each other, travel together, and learn from each other. Though we have only journeyed together for a short time, I feel we have bonded well, and considering the danger we are preparing to face, we *must* trust one another." Her eyes narrowed a bit at me at the last part. "Anyone found anything useful?"

"I was trying to get that book down when I fell on Mithron," Tsukatta answered, pointing to the blue leather-bound tome.

"Easily managed," Glitter smiled, holding up her hand, spoke the word *aatokemaji* as a command, and the book lifted itself off the shelf and gracefully flew to her hand, trailing a queue of dust. She handed the volume to Tsukatta with a flourish. "Here you are, my friend." More dust puffed off the tome as Tsukatta grabbed it.

I smiled and shook my head. "I should have prepared that spell myself. It would have saved me the trouble of searching for a stool, and made things less dangerous for us. Another spell to dust things off would have also been appropriate."

"I shall retrieve it for you then, so Tsukatta doesn't have to heal you after you pull a loaded bookshelf down on top of yourself." Her smile broadened, while her sparkles glimmered a bright yellow.

"That would be most appreciated, my lady," I responded with a bow, "although it would not be the first time, I was accused of being buried in my work."

Glitter sputtered with surprise and both women laughed. "I didn't know that you were capable of making jokes!" Glitter accused between laughs.

"Well, times have been rather tense," I sighed, my smile fading somewhat. "There has been precious little to joke about."

Glitter and Tsukatta both sobered as they considered our purpose here.

"We should get back to work."

With a nod, Tsukatta took her volume to a table while Glitter followed me to where *Accentuating the Positive* sat high on its shelf. Glitter recast *aatokemaji* and called the tome to her hands. The book struggled off the shelf, and plummeted into her waiting hands, along with the webs that held it in place. "You are doing some heavy reading, I see," she jested, lightening the mood that I had broken. "Were this tome any heavier, the spell would not have worked, and you would have had to climb up after it anyway."

"It is a good thing, then, that Falleoraeli Zolthliam did not have more to say on the subject," I responded with a smile.

When she plopped the book into my hands with a thump, I nearly dropped it from the weight. A small yellow spider scrabbled across the front of the volume and gently rappelled down off the edge to my shoe, where it dropped off and disappeared between the planks in the floor.

"Next time, I will have Vondro follow me around to carry these. Or at least, I should join him in his morning exercises so that I can become strong enough to carry my own books." I feigned struggling with the tome, waddling over toward the table, though in truth, the book really *was* quite weighty. "With volumes such as these, I do not understand how wizards have a reputation for being physically weak. I am certain this must weigh more than Vondro's sword." *Knowledge is our weapon,* I heard Vletraka's voice clearly in my head as a tingle went up my spine.

As it happened, *Accentuating the Positive* was exactly the book I had been searching for. Falleoraeli wrote at length delineating the various techniques to command, repel, and destroy undead by channeling positive energy. The trick, it seemed, was to gather the energy in the first place. Clerics, like Tsukatta, are trained in this skill from early on, and their gods provide the energy they channel. But in order for someone to gain this skill without divine assistance requires tapping into one's personal life force to open a pathway to the Plane of Positive Energy, then focus the energy outward. The first exercises demonstrated various ways to enhance and strengthen one's personal energy, in order that one does not die in an explosion of life force, then to only use the excess energy, and avoid tapping into the power that sustains one's life.

I gathered up the heavy tome, and took it over to Glitter, who was in deep study of *The Immobile Caster: Directing Magic without Gesticulation* by Geimoll Ovicht. "That looks interesting. It could be useful to be able to cast spells without waving my hands about," I mused aloud, gaining her attention.

"Of course, there is a cost," Glitter responded, her eyes not leaving the page. "To do so, additional energy needs to be expended during preparation, causing the spell to act as though it were of a higher tier. If stealth is in order, it's one way to avoid attracting attention. Casting without gesturing could also be handy if one is tied up."

Perhaps the best way to stop even the most powerful wizards is to tie their hands and gag them. There are precious few spells that require neither movement nor verbalization, and a bound wizard is, generally, a helpless wizard.

"Careful thought must be put into that spell, it seems. It should be one that can either free the mage from bindings, or harm a foe without seeming to be the aggressor." I set my tome down on the table next to hers. "This one teaches how to channel positive energy in the manner that Tsukatta does." I could not help but smile, knowing that bursts of positive energy are just the thing to destroy an undead horde.

"I thought only those blessed by their deity could do that!" she jumped, pulling the volume to her and opening it to a random page.

"Of course, there is a cost," I mimicked. "In order to do so, one must draw on one's personal life energy and expel it. This tome teaches some techniques to enhance the life force so as to prevent harming one's self, but it looks like it will take more time to master than we have at present. I will work at it while we travel, in the hope that it can be of some use."

"That must be why only priests normally do it then; with their gods giving them the extra energy, they don't have to worry about draining themselves." She looked pensive, staring out at nothing for a few moments. She then looked at me directly and asked, "Are you sure it's safe for you to do this? It sounds like this can be very dangerous."

I did my best to tamp down my elation that she was concerned for my wellbeing, and instead gave her a weak smile. "If nothing else, if it kills me, I can at least take a few undead creatures back to the grave with me. Until I learn to do it properly, it will be a weapon of last resort."

"It better be. We have a good number of spells to use, and I don't want any of us throwing their life away, especially not to test a theory. I know you are anxious to destroy Cratillus. I am too, but we can't let ourselves act out of vengeance."

"I know, and I am certain that it is as difficult for you as for me to not charge blindly after him. Personally, I would rather it be over with quickly, so I can return here and read for the rest of my life. There is more knowledge stored here than I have ever dreamed possible, and I wish I could absorb it all! To do so, however, I would likely need to stay here as long as Ormak." I sighed, in part because I knew that in the morning we would have to leave this trove of information, and also from the full awareness of how this came to be in our possession. *Grustan, I hope that your soul is rotting somewhere horrible.*

When I glanced back at Glitter, she was downcast, a single tear slipping from her bright orange eyes, and I could not help but smile thinking of the different colors her hair and eyes have taken during the short time I have known her. Every gift has its downside, and I suppose her constant color shifting could be hers. It does, however, suit her personality, which, wizard's gifts often do, and I am glad that I do not have hers; her sparkles and wild colorations draw far too much attention for my tastes.

I dove back into *Accentuating the Positive*, devouring every word, every line, learning the tome's secrets as quickly as possible, so I might practice Zolthliam's techniques to prepare my body and life force for the damage I was expecting to cause them.

Focused as I was, I did not realize how much time had passed until Brother Ironknuckle tapped me on the shoulder. "Get some sleep, lad. It's long after middle night, and we were hoping to leave shortly after dawn."

"Already? I feel as though I have just started reading." I often had the same difficulty in Vletraka's library. When one is surrounded by magical light, which does not burn out as candles do, in a windowless room, one cannot as easily detect the passage of time, for there are no signs that it has passed. Now that my attention was drawn away from my reading, my stomach grumbled loudly.

My grommoldian friend smiled, pointed to a plate of cold meat and bread, which likely had been there for hours, and went off, presumably to sleep, though for all I know went to tell Glitter to go to sleep as well.

I took a few bites, and promptly fell to sleep in my chair.

Chapter 12: Alone

"Flesh," rasped the yellowed walking corpse.

"Drink its marrow," hissed a second vulzu.

Four others circled around me, poking at me from all sides, measuring my worth as a meal. I could not run, or even move, as the supernatural force that animates them stole my ability to even twitch. I stared unblinking as one crooked a finger at my right eye before another pulled the creature's hand away.

"Eye is mine. You had last," it said in a harsh whisper through long, sharp teeth.

"Fine. Kidney then," capitulated the vulzu that almost took my eye. It shuffled behind me, and I could feel its fetid breath as it sniffed through my shirt.

The others closed in, raising their claws and stretching their jaws, preparing to devour me.

'Swing your right wing now!'

The vulzuu vanished as my right arm shot straight out to my side, impacting something soft. I heard a gasp of pain and something wooden clacking as my head shot up from its nestled position in Falleoraeli Zolthliam's thick tome.

I heard a gasp and laughter from behind me, a moan to my right, and a pair of groans from my left. I looked around to see Raf doubled over next to me, a wooden cup on the floor at his feet; the floor was wet around the cup.

"What happened?" I asked, my eyes still bleary.

The laughter behind me grew, and I recognized both Tsukatta's and Glitter's voices in the sounds of mirth.

"For a sleeping wizard, you have amazing reflexes," smiled Vondro, standing on my left with Brother Ironknuckle. "Is that part of your magic?"

"Not exactly," answered the grommold before I could comprehend the question, pointing over me. I followed the path of his finger to Thessylia, perched atop a bookcase. "I'll wager his bird warned him."

The girls' laughter grew to fits.

"I promise," wheezed Raf, "to never try that again."

I heard a light thud, and turned to see Glitter on her knees, laughing hysterically. A moment later, she fell to the floor, clutching her stomach.

"Again, what happened? Glitter, are you all right?"

She was smiling, struggling for breath, sparkles flying off her in a rainbow of hues. She began kicking her feet as her laughter rose to new heights.

"It seems that our young bard sought to wake ye by pouring cold water down yer neck. Ye swung out and punched the lad in the tenders." Vondro looked visibly pained as Brother Ironknuckle described the recent events but maintained a smile.

'Thank you for protecting me again.'

'Scratchings?' Thessylia responded, her thoughts somewhere between hopeful and demanding.

'And well earned.' Although owls cannot smile, I could sense her joy.

She floated down to the table, landed next to the tome, and presented her head, the feathers on top lifting to allow easier access for my fingers.

"Raf, are you okay?"

"'m fine," he said through clenched teeth then looked over at Tsukatta and pleaded, "Heal me."

"I'm not touching you there," she blushed, and Glitter's laughter grew to a pitch that made Thessylia's sensitive ears twitch.

"He'll be fine," said Vondro. "I'll bet he's been hit there before. Probably by someone's wife." He began to chuckle.

Raf glared at the warrior, and something in the way he looked at him begged for silence.

"You should break your fast and prepare to travel. Ehrghex is a long way off." Vondro pointed to a small wooden plate, which I had not noticed until now, with three pieces of toasted bread covered in warm mashed apple, spiced with cinnamon and nutmeg.

I carried the plate out of the library and over to the stairway; I had not realized how hungry I was until I started to eat and devoured my meal in short order.

Meanwhile, Glitter finally regained her composure and began preparing her spells, occasionally sputtering with laughter. "Don't forget to prepare that ward to protect the treasure," she reminded me when I returned.

"Thank you. It had slipped my mind after this morning's events," I responded, which sent her into fits once again.

Glitter's mirth was contagious, and I began to laugh myself, but when her sparkles turned grey, I forced myself to calm down before any more visions could appear. While studying my spell-book to gather the energy needed for today, I first focused on *looskimbul*, a rune that draws life energy from those who read it and uses that energy to empower another magical rune.

When we finished our preparations, we walked over to the hidden stairway to see Tsukatta grabbing the wall at the entrance and pull it across, stretching the stone like clay until it fully melded with the other side, completely sealing off the passage. Glitter then drew *bezyaamyuvbulyt*, a tight group of symbols which explode when read, damaging both the surface it is drawn on as well as anything nearby, upon the new stone. While etching, she spoke all our names, tying us into the spell and preventing us from setting off the unstable magic. Nonetheless, I still had to be cautious while inscribing *looskimbul* over her *bezyaamyuvbulyt*, lest I either ruin her ward, or worse, set it off regardless of her measures to protect us.

When all our magicks were finished, Raf gently swung the bookcase closed until we heard the clicking noise, which indicated that it was back in position to conceal the passage. He then produced a purple velvet pillow, grayed with age, and slapped it three times, causing it to erupt into a cloud of dust. We all broke into spasms of coughing, each of us giving the bard dirty looks, as we could not express our ire with words.

Vondro was the first to recover, and choked out, "Why?" before succumbing once again to the cloud.

Raf could only point to the floor where the bookcase had left a dust-free patch along the arc of its swing then finally choked out. "There. That should protect our gold nicely from anyone else stumbling upon it."

I still had difficulty thinking of the treasure upstairs as ours and not Ormak's, and I had to suppress a tear when I thought of his tragic life and death. *We should have done more to save him.*

Once we regained the ability to breathe again, Vondro asked, "Everyone ready for travel?" while adjusting his pack. When no one dissented, he commanded, "Let's move."

We fell in line to descend the spiral staircase and out the tower's sole door to the outside, through the open grounds, littered with fallen corpses, past the gate, and over to our horses, which were tied to trees and saddled.

"I was so focused on searching through the library that I forgot about the horses," I muttered under my breath, surprised they were still here and alive.

"It's a good thing we didn't," smiled Brother Ironknuckle. "Vondro and I also cleared out the last of the wandering ruklaa and such over the past few days as well while ye were buried in yer books. They made excellent exercise partners; the ruklaa could really take a hit, while the kuldaa were fast and hard to dodge."

I looked at him with astonishment.

He shrugged, "We got bored watching the lot of ye reading. A man has to get his blood up every now and again."

"You should have said something. I would have been pleased to join you in their destruction."

"Aye, but ye had other things to concern ye. I'm sure ye'll get more opportunities soon, if things are as Grustan said. With luck, maybe we can stop much of it afore it starts."

"I suppose you are right. Still, I would not have minded the interruption."

We rode on through the dreary day until it got too dark to travel safely. Vondro found a small clearing off the road where we set up camp for the night. Brother Ironknuckle dug a small pit for a fire, Raf, Glitter, and I gathered wood, and Tsukatta and Vondro searched for stones to ring the pit. Once everything was ready, Glitter cast *uvaazsrukak* to ignite a few of the twigs and start the fire. During the gathering of campfire materials, both Raf and Vondro managed to kill a pair of rabbits each, their fresh meat thankfully replacing the dried salted jerky I expected as part of our meal. I do not know where Glitter procured the herbs she used to season the rabbits, whether found fresh during her gathering or if she had a store of them in her pack, but we were all once again grateful for her cooking talents.

Once I finished eating, I cleaned my hands, and the travels of the day, with an *uvaazrosiit* spell, grabbed a candle out of my pack, and lit it from a small branch from the fire.

Vondro asked, "What is the candle for?"

"So I have light to read by," I responded with the air of the obvious.

"What is wrong with the campfire?" As he asked, a spark popped out of the fire and scorched a nearby leaf on the ground.

I merely pointed to the leaf, turned, and walked a few feet away where my books would not be endangered. "I am used to reading by candlelight, whether natural or magical, though I prefer natural," I finally answered after getting comfortable on my bedroll and opening *In Between* at the beginning once again. "It makes me feel at ease."

"Why didn't you just flick your fingers at the candle and light it the way Glitter lit the fire? It seems weird to see you do something without magic."

"It is not a spell I had planned on using today, so I had not allotted the energy for it. I could redistribute that energy, which would take more time and effort than lighting a candle with a tinder."

"There are spells to do just about anything," Glitter added, "but no wizard, no matter how many spells they have learned, can cast them all. It just takes too much power, so we are selective about what spells we expect to need. If I only knew a couple of spells, it wouldn't be an issue, but there is a reason we write everything down in these big books," she grinned.

"Most spells are combat-oriented, probably due to the dangerous world we live in, as I was discussing with Ormak before you trespassed on his land," I continued with a quick glare, "and there are a great number of ways to disable an opponent. Fire, freezing, negative energy, electricity…"

"Charming, illusions, sonic…"

"Curses, acid, forced transformations; you get the idea. It is important to know a variety, because although the results can be similar, the effects are quite different, which is especially important if your foe is resistant to one attack or another."

"A lot of spells are utilitarian too, useful for enhancing skills, gaining insight, or making changes in objects or the environment to better suit the wizard's needs. I could have waited for you to strike your flint until you got a good spark to light the fire, but I did it with one of the simplest magicks.

"On the other hand, once we've used up our store of power, we are pretty defenseless. You can swing your sword until you're exhausted, and I'm pretty sure Brother Ironknuckle never gets tired!" Glitter laughed. "It takes a lot of focus to cast a spell properly as well, so if you can keep your enemy distracted, he won't be able to use his magic to full effect."

"As we are pretty sure Cratillus is a necromancer, it is important that you understand the weaknesses inherent in spellcasting. Loathe as I am to admit it, we are not all-powerful," I said with a wan smile.

"Don't let Revance hear you say that," Glitter chided with a grin then turned back to Vondro, "Revance was a wizard/philosopher who believed that wizards are the epitome of what one can achieve in life. Some of his arguments have merit, but he was an arrogant sod. He doesn't seem to understand that no matter the chosen profession, it takes hard work and skill to master one's craft. As difficult as magic is to learn, I'm sure I would have a harder time learning swordcraft."

"As a child," I added, "I studied in my father's forge. I have neither the strength nor the skill to hammer iron, and if magic had not discovered me, I might be an herbalist right now."

"What do you mean 'magic discovered you'?" asked Vondro. "Shouldn't that be the other way around?"

"I never considered that magic might be an option for me, as it is typically the province of the wealthy. Yoffa, my herbalism teacher was friends with Vletraka, who discovered I had a talent for wizardry."

"Goldfire found me the same way; said I could be much more than a scullery maid, and though I was concerned that it might be a trick, I really had nothing to lose by following her." Glitter stood and stretched, sparkles flying in all directions. "Best decision of my life."

"Sounds to me like someone can't be a wizard until they have lost all other options," Vondro opined. "My father taught me how to use a sword from the time I could walk."

"Most wizards are brought up in households with other mages," I corrected, "just as you were raised by a warrior, and often by families who have gained wealth by being employed by generations of nobles. Neither Glitter nor I had the fortune to be born and raised in such an environment, and we cannot all follow in our parents' footsteps. Some of us would rather not." With that, I turned my attention back to my studies and lost track of the conversation.

Fortunately, it did not rain during the night, though the skies were threatening when I finally fell asleep. I never did become comfortable sleeping outdoors but having Thessylia and a group of friends around helped me rest with a bit more ease. As the day passed, the clouds eventually parted, bathing us in sunlight that refused to warm us. Three more days of cold sun passed before we met some travelers on the road moving in the opposite direction. As it turned out, they were fleeing Ehrghex, and the madman who was killing everyone in town and turning them into ruklaa.

"What can you tell us about this man?" we asked.

"'e's a cruel an' vicious sort. Smilin' and actin' though 'e's doin' us a favor by killin' us. Says we should be 'appy to serve 'im an' 'is cause," replied one older woman before spitting on the ground. "Menfolk tried ta fight 'im off, but he just waved 'is arms about an' they all dropped down dead as stumps. Some o' us ran, some di'n't get away." Tears filled her eyes, and she was quickly wrapped up in Tsukatta's arms.

"We have heard of this man," spoke Vondro with resonance in his voice, "and are on our way to stop him and his evil. Please, rest a while with us and share a meal."

"We've little ta share," the woman began before Vondro waved her off.

"We will share our provisions. You have had enough to deal with, dear lady. We only need to know more about this man and your city and figure out the best way to handle him."

"Yer too kind," she smiled, crying once more into Tsukatta's robes.

Glitter passed around some hard bread, carrots, celery, and a clay jar of nuts that had been crushed into a paste. I never saw her conjure the food, nor did I see from where she had procured it. She must have bought a lot of provisions in Dureltown, yet it seemed more than she should be able to carry. That the vegetables were cold definitely implied that there was magic involved. Nonetheless, we enjoyed our repast while gaining much needed information about Ehrghex.

Like most towns, it has strong stone walls, harkening back to the siege so many generations ago. It boasted a population of over eight thousand souls, though now, merely bodies, the souls having departed to the domain of the Dark Lady. *"The sleeping shall awake; the sleeper has left to roam forever more."* Assuming Cratillus is reanimating the populace as ruklaa, the town alone would prove a formidable force. Should he raise all the fallen bones of the past armies, I do not foresee a way to put a stop to his forces without an army of our own. The trouble is any soldiers that fall in battle would only add to the ranks of the enemy. We need to stop this before it goes any further.

Vondro listened attentively to the refugees, taking in all that they said, and after spending a few minutes considering, implored them to seek out his father to tell him everything they told us. Vondelos would be able to raise a force against a potential horde of undead soldiers and protect Dureltown should Cratillus head in that direction.

When I brought up my point about fallen soldiers, he asked what other options I could offer. Abandon the town, and all others that could be attacked? Simply give up and allow everyone to be slaughtered? Yes, men would fall in battle, but with luck and skill, they would destroy more creatures than they could replace.

I had no argument against his logic, which rankled me to no end. I should have foreseen his line of reasoning and considered the other options. "There must be another way that we have not yet considered. None of these choices seem adequate to stop Cratillus's forces. It still appears that we must remove him from the equation first; without his control... wait, how is it that he can control so many undead at once?"

"What do you mean?" asked Vondro.

"Even a high order necromancer can only control so many undead at once. This is why things like this do not happen. He must be getting extra power from some other source."

"Maybe he's delegating," Vondro quipped. I gave him a confused look, to which he responded, "Every army has generals. Could he control them, and let them handle the troops?"

Again, he has bested me in this argument! I could feel the bile bubbling up through my innards as this meager-intellect over-muscled cretin continued to make me look like a fool. The world turned grey, and it took every bit of my will to tamp down my anger before I said anything about what a small and pathetic lamb he is. Once I relaxed, I responded, "That is possible. He has proven to send out other wizards working for him, and they would be able to handle some of the burden. The rest would have to be controlled by more powerful undead, of which there is a long potential list of candidates. Should he lose control, they would likely turn on him to maintain their freedom. If we manage to defeat Cratillus, then we will have his generals to contend with as well."

"If we take out the generals first," recommended Vondro, "then he will lose control of his army."

"If we take out the generals first," I returned, "he will make new ones and we will lose any element of surprise. In addition, we will have a large number of uncontrolled undead roaming about."

"In that case, we cut off the head first, and deal with his generals after. I am guessing they will either fight each other for control, or go their separate ways without Cratillus, which means smaller armies to contend with."

"Which," I added, "will again leave numerous free-roaming kuldaa and ruklaa meandering about. Those will also need to be dealt with."

"Perhaps then we will need an army to deal with the organized troops, and small bands like us to deal with the wanderers, though they really don't represent much of a challenge."

"Not to us maybe, but a group of ruklaa wandering into an unprotected village would be devastating. We need to contain this as much as possible or a lot of innocent people are going to get killed."

"Agreed. Let's go."

We broke camp, said farewell to the refugees, and prepared to continue our ride to Ehrghex. I found that I was still on edge from earlier, and every small annoyance began to bring up my ire. I tried to meditate and do breathing exercises, but to no avail. An inexplicable rage was building up in me, and it took all my will to clamp down on it. I thought it might be anger at Cratillus for what he had done to Ehrghex, not to mention Glitter, myself, and probably others, but I would not learn the truth until later. My skin burned cold, the back of my neck itched, and my jaw hurt from clenching my teeth.

"What are you muttering about now?" asked Glitter with exasperation, who was riding on my left, sparkles of crimson and bruised purple dripping off her. I knew that meant she was furious about something, but presently, I chose not to care.

"Just thinking about all the suffering Cratillus has caused, and how I wish to return the favor," I growled. "We are finally getting to the source, and I intend to exact my vengeance for Mistress Vletraka's death."

"And Mistress Goldfire," she added, her sparkles darkening further. "You never think about her, and what she meant to me. It's always about you and your pain, never anybody else's!"

Before I could respond, Raf's loud, exaggerated sigh came from behind us. "Again, with you two! All you do is argue like an old, married couple, and neither of you will admit that you're in love. Either kiss or kill each other already. This drama has gone on long enough!"

I was too shocked and embarrassed by his words and attitude to speak, but Glitter recovered quickly. "What business is it of yours anyway? Who I like or hate is my choice, mister 'romantic poet', and *I* decide if and when I will act! If you want to write a love story based on us, go ahead, but it comes more out of your deluded imagination than any reality. We," she wagged her finger between me and herself, "are not a couple."

"I have tried to tell you this before," I added. "She hates me. She always has. Glitter is only putting up with me because our goals are the same. Once we are finished, I fully expect her to turn her back and walk away forever. The last time she yelled at me, she pushed me out of this plane of existence. Her feelings about me are quite clear, and one would have to be a blind idiot not to see it."

"You both are blind," Raf countered with a snarl, "but you are both too afraid to admit the truth. You're both miserable because you won't admit your feelings to yourselves or each other, and this constant bickering is getting on our nerves!"

"Enough!" shouted Vondro from the front then turned his horse around and rode back to us.

At some point, our horses had stopped moving, but I was not paying any attention to them.

"I don't know what you are all fighting about, and I don't care. There are more important things to worry about right now than any personal squabbles. So, either apologize, let it go, or fume about it quietly. We have all worked too hard and sacrificed too much for us to lose focus now!"

I had finally had enough. The world turned to a dark grey, deeper than at any other time. I take no pride in what happened next, and though I would prefer to be the shining hero of my own story, the rest would be incoherent if I were not honest here. "And what do you know of hard work and sacrifice, you who have hid so long behind your father's armored skirt? Not once have you ever considered creating a life for yourself, and instead followed blindly in Vondelos' footsteps, doing everything that he wanted; just a boy covered by daddy's armor and prestige who has no will or goals of his own.

"Although you could have been a lowborn thief, taking whatever could fit in your pockets," I ranted, turning on Ial'rafiost. "At least you did not rob a man on the streets, stealing the ransom money that would have saved his daughter."

Raf paled at my accusation as the others, save Brother Ironknuckle, turned toward him. I was beginning to catch myself from saying anything else until the grommold spoke. "That's enough now, lad."

"Why? Are you going to silence me like you did Devvor? I will not be as easy a target for a raging murderer like you! You think yourself a *crozzung*, but you are as bad as Glitter's father. Although, he at least had the decency to kill himself after beating her mother to death.

"Tsukatta is the only truly innocent one here. Her only crime is running away from an arranged marriage to the temple of a deity she did not even begin to worship until after she lived in the temple for three years. She fled from a man she did not love to a deity she did not love, and the only thing her selfishness cost her was her family.

"Do what you will. I will seek out Cratillus myself and save you all the trouble. I knew it was a mistake to have involved all of you. This is my fight, and I will battle it alone!" At this, I wheeled my horse around and stormed off into the night, continuing along the path Vondro was leading us before I completely lost my temper, and all the friendships I had forged over the past week.

It was inevitable. I knew better than to bother making friends, especially non-wizards. The only one who understood what this is about is Glitter, and she never wanted anything to do with me in the first place. She is better off without me always reminding her of her sorrows, and I am better off without worrying about her feelings. All I seem to do is cause pain. I should not be with anyone; I cannot hurt anyone else if I am alone.

I was so deep into my self-pity, that I did not hear Thessylia calling to me. She was never a target of my vindictiveness, but then, there was no darkness emanating from her, no malice, no regrets, and no sorrow. Had I been able to see it at the time, I would have seen only myself reflected in her aura and come face to face with my own troubles.

Somehow, I managed to ride through the night safely, though I am certain that my horse slowed down and chose his own path once I lost myself in thought. I was exhausted, yet the rage refused to pass. Whenever I would steer my thoughts away and begin to calm myself, the anger would well up again and the visions of my once-friends' misdeeds and sorrows would dance before my eyes. I turned my horse off of the road, which had reduced to a beaten track at this point, and found some tall grasses to sleep in.

There was, unfortunately, little rest for me that night, or even the next two. Aside from sleeping on the hard, rocky, uncomfortable earth, my dreams were plagued with nightmares, wherein I was the one responsible for the misfortunes of my former comrades: scolding and berating Vondro for wanting to be anything other than a warrior, riling up Brother Ironknuckle and goading him into attacking his friend, convincing Ial'rafiost to rob that merchant at knifepoint, giving Tsukatta's father a pouch of gold in exchange for her hand in marriage, and, worst of all, repeatedly punching and kicking Glitter's mother and gasping awake as I plunged a knife into my own heart. I could find neither rest nor solace; even the horse had left me that first night, as I forgot to tether him. Distracted as I was, I never saw the pack of vulzuu I wandered into until they had surrounded me.

I felt a mixture of terror and joy at that moment. The vulzuu have been haunting me since childhood, but I was a trained necromancer now, and I wanted revenge, redemption, and release. As the first one neared me, I released a bolt of lightning from my fingertips, which burned through not only the one closest to me, but another behind it as well. I am pretty sure I was laughing, and if so, cannot be certain if it was from excitement or madness. As the next one approached, I decided to try out a spell I discovered in Falleoraeli Zolthliam's *Accentuating the Positive: A Study of Divine Channeling and Its Arcane Equivalent* called *bezyaamvroktjuutwa*, which invokes a bolt of positive energy and infuses it into an undead creature, affecting it in the same way the negative equivalent, *zumulalsk*, drains life away from a living being, causing it to be weakened, or even incapacitated, until it wears off.

When the bolt of light hit the vulzu, it froze in its tracks, bright yellow light spilling out of its eyes and mouth. It dropped to the ground, shaking and convulsing, hissing in agony and unable to speak. Were it a living creature, I might have felt pity for the pain I had caused, but there was no remorse within me for this monstrosity. Rather, I laughed at it, berated it, and even kicked it at one point, but not until after dispatching the last two attackers. In retrospect, however, I regret having felt gleeful at the time; my years of anxiety are no excuse for my behavior. Just because the vulzu would have enjoyed my suffering does not give me the right to torture it in return.

It was while I was enjoying the torment of my victim that an overwhelming, nauseating stench overtook me, causing me to vomit on the writhing corpse at my feet. I thought that all my years of training and study had inured me to the reek of death, but this was far beyond anything I had experienced until then. By the time I realized the source of the odor, the vulzaam, a more powerful version of a vulzu, punched me squarely between the shoulder blades, causing me to topple over the fallen vulzu. I could feel the paralysis spreading through my body and fought it off to the best of my ability, but the creature grabbed my face with both hands, insuring my immobility, and smiled.

"Wizard. The master seeks your kind. Kelthid will be rewarded." Rather than eat me, the vulzaam picked me up, slung me over its desiccated shoulder, and carried me off to its master.

Chapter 13: Forced Insights

It took more than a day to reach wherever the vulzaam was carrying me. He licked me a number of times but refrained from biting with obvious effort; I realized that I was hungry as well, now that I had gotten used to his stench. At least I appeared to be more valuable to him as a captive than as a meal, which only made me wonder what kind of trouble I would be in next. Our constant contact prevented me from shaking off his paralyzing touch, leaving me completely helpless.

Near evening the next day, we reached the outskirts of a walled city; Ehrghex, I surmised, both by its appearance and by the large number of ambling corpses milling about. Kelthid found a pack of vulzuu and commanded them to find the 'master', whom I guessed would be Cratillus, then dropped me down at the base of a large maple tree. Perhaps an hour passed, perhaps more, before the vulzuu returned, followed by a middle-aged man in black robes, his dark brown hair tinged with spots of silver.

He called Kelthid over, who jumped like a puppy awaiting his master and carried my satchel to him. After a short discussion, the man handed Kelthid a wide red leather belt. When Kelthid put in on, he visibly grew in stature and musculature, standing taller by a few inches and his skin tightening over the growing muscles throughout his body. He tested his newfound strength by grabbing one of the vulzuu by the head and crushing its skull with a single hand, gore oozing through his clawed fingers. With a smile to his benefactor, he stomped off back the way we came to seek out new victims.

Two of the remaining vulzuu stood me up against the tree and bound me to it with thick ropes. They then stretched my arms back, wrapping them around the trunk and tied my hands to keep my arms pulled back. I heard my left shoulder pop as they did but do not know whether it was the constantly swelling anger or the paralysis that kept me from feeling the pain. One of them sniffed my breath and turned toward the human who was directing them. "This one is diseased. Useless. May we eat it?"

"No," replied the man. "He is not useless, not yet anyway. Should he prove to be, then, if it pleases me, I will give him to you."

The vulzuu cackled with glee, sniffing and licking me as if to whet their eternal appetites. When they finished, the man waved them away and strode up to me.

"Greetings. I am Cratillus. And you are?" He chuckled to himself, holding out his hand, knowing that I could neither answer nor shake his hand. "I see you caught the raging fever. Let me guess, you encountered some refugees from Ehrghex."

I glared at him with all my pent-up, paralyzed fury.

"Oh, don't blame them. They have no idea that I infected them before their 'escape'. I made certain they wouldn't be affected by it. After all, it's of no use spreading a contagion if those infected kill each other before proliferating it."

The old woman was accurate in her description of Cratillus's smile, for there was certainly madness mixed in with his joy.

"Now that I have you, and your present," he said with glee, holding aloft *In Between*, "it would be for the best if we got rid of that pesky rage. You are of no use to me as a babbling, frothing idiot." He pushed my head back and poured a thick, purple syrup down my throat. "There. Wasn't that easy? You should be back to normal by the time the paralysis wears off."

Fever or not, quelling my rage would prove to be a monumental task. Knowing what he did to the townsfolk, and what he had planned for the long dead soldiers of this region, would have angered me enough, but to be brutally honest, what infuriated me the most was being helpless. Again. By the touch of the same creatures who nearly took my life when I was a child.

For all my training, all my accumulated power, I was still weak and vulnerable. In addition, there was no mistaking I was outclassed by Cratillus's level of magic. He already controlled a horde of ruklaa and appeared to be capable of casting the most potent of spells contained within the tome I was supposed to keep safe from his hands. Not only am I weak, but also an utter failure.

I could feel the rage subsiding, being replaced by depression. Unless I somehow managed to escape soon, I realized, everything would be lost. With the power of the magic contained within the covers of *In Between*, Cratillus could wreak absolute devastation.

"You seem to be calming down. Good. Now we may talk," said Cratillus calmly.

Why would he not be calm? Clearly, I am no threat. "You have your treasure," I sighed, "what use do you have of me? I will not help you awaken the fields of the dead."

"So, you *do* understand why I wanted this book so badly. When Larzed and his boy failed to return, I thought that perhaps he wished to keep this beauty for himself," he mused while stroking the cover of the heavy tome with affection. "Did you kill him?"

"Just his apprentice," I sneered. "I believe my Mistress used *her* last breath to take Larzed's from him."

Before I could speak another word, Cratillus pointed at me and a nearby rukla stepped forward and slammed a mighty fist into my chest, forcing out what I thought might be my last breath.

"You have no mistress. I am your Master now. You will follow my orders." Though his voice remained calm, there was a rage behind it that rivaled my own.

"I may no longer have a mistress, but I shall never call you 'master'." My defiance was answered with another blow from the rukla, and for a moment, I thought my jaw had been taken off. Something hard sat on my tongue, which, I realized after spitting it out, was a tooth.

"This punishment is unnecessary. I am your superior, and there is much I can teach you. In time, you will accept me anyway, so why put yourself through all this agony?"

I believe he was trying to sound reassuring, but all I heard, through the ringing in my ears, was arrogance. Before I could speak again, the rukla struck again and again, bludgeoning me nearly into unconsciousness. It was more than a few moments before I regained my senses enough to continue our conversation. "I will not let you succeed. You are mad if you think this is a path to godhood," I spat, blood trickling out of the corner of my mouth. My breathing was ragged, and at least two of my ribs were broken. I wanted desperately to cast a spell to mend my wounds, but could not make the necessary gestures, and my uneven breathing and blood-drenched lips would likely cause me to mispronounce the spell, which would allow the energy to fizzle away.

"Godhood? Is that what you think this is about? I am but a servant, doing the will of Coruld, and through my good works, I seek a place at his side. No one in history has brought about so many undead! As my army swells, Coruld grows stronger. Soon, he will be able to take his rightful place upon the Throne of the Dead, where he will rule over both the dead and the undead, in full control of every soul in this realm. I will open the path for him, and he will reward me with eternal existence and power! I will be the general of his dark armies, and we shall wipe out every living thing in this world!" Throughout his speech, his grin continued to widen.

His earnest joy filled me with dread, and the world plunged into darkness. Image after image streaked through my vision: a young, well-dressed boy breaking a cat's legs, then poking it with a sharp stick until it finally died; a teenage version of the same child molesting a servant girl in a stable, beating her with a horseshoe while he fulfilled his lust; the same boy a few years older chopping up a henbane plant and adding it to a large pot of soup, watching with undisguised glee over a second story railing as his family and household died from the plant's toxins; the young man studying necromancy from a frail old wizard, and later shoving him off the tower roof; and further acts of depravity, torture, and murder as he aged into the Cratillus of now. As my vision began to clear, I realized he had been speaking to me.

"Well, what shall be your choice? I will have all of eternity, but I have more important things to do with it."

"Choice?" I asked, clearly confused.

"What form would you like to spend your eternity in? As you were so kind to bring me *In Between*, I shall give you the choice of undead forms when I recreate you. Spectre, ghost, maraika… jozalk. You probably want to be a jozalk. I think that would serve me best."

"What would lead you to believe that I would ever serve you or your terrible Master? You represent everything I have ever striven against."

He stared at me for a moment, his eyes expressionless. "I do not understand why you don't already. You are not just any wizard, but a necromancer. One does not follow that path without understanding the misery of life, and the power that comes from controlling lost souls, especially ones you removed from their physical form yourself. Your bearing is not noble, implying that you come from common stock, and therefore have led a hard life. You have killed, plenty of times, and whether or not you admit it, the power over the lives of others thrills you. You are isolated and alone, no family, no friends. There is no reason for you to do anything *but* stand with me."

"Is that your gift, to see into the souls of others?" I asked, trying desperately to keep my voice from shaking. His words hit far too close to the mark.

"No, my gift is a superior sense of direction, so I never get lost," he said with a wave of his hand to demonstrate the irrelevancy of my statement. "I am merely observant, and I can see that you know my words to be true."

"What does it matter to you whether I believe you or not?" I wheezed. "You wish to kill me, and have already taken the book from me, so why keep me alive?"

"Oh, you will be dead soon, but under my terms. You see, it is better for both of us that you *want* to die. It makes the transition less painful for you and guarantees that you will not try to thwart me. I only need to hear the words 'Cratillus, my life is yours', and I will end your suffering." His smile was kindly, yet there was no disguising the malice behind it.

"You may break my body but will never break my spirit. You are a cruel, viscous, sadistic, petty little man, who can only cause harm because you are afraid of being hurt by others. You are the one who is truly alone. I have known friendship, and I have a family of my own choosing. Any who have ever shown you affection, you have murdered. Why are you so afraid of being loved?" I had barely finished when I broke out into a coughing fit, the pain from my broken ribs searing through my body, so much so that I never felt the slap across my face.

"Don't you *dare* to presume to know me! I have the right to defend myself against my oppressors, and no one shall stand in my way of ridding this hate-filled world of the infection of life! It is the only way." Cratillus turned his back to me, pointed at a rukla, then pointed his thumb at me over his shoulder.

After a few hits, I thankfully lost consciousness.

When I next awoke, I was greeted by the night sky, the faint glow on the horizon telling me that it was shortly before dawn. I was cold, yet my skin burnt where the corded ropes bound me, and pain raked through my body with every breath. My throat was dry, and I my lips began to chap from dehydration and dried blood. I parted them to lick them, and almost screamed from the pain in my jaw. I probed the inside of my mouth gently with my tongue, confirming that my cheeks were swollen, and that I had lost at least one more tooth. A chilly fog had settled in, and the cold and dampness made me that much more miserable.

No rescue was forthcoming, my argument with my allies saw to that, and I was at a loss of how to free myself. I had neither dagger to cut the rope, nor any spell that I could use without moving my hands. I began to slowly rub my arms against the tree, hoping the bark was rough enough to begin breaking the fibers of the rope. With my hands behind me, there was no way to tell if my efforts were in vain unless and until the rope snapped. The bark was strong enough to tear my flesh, and I could feel the pain of my arms being rubbed raw just as my wrists were by the rope. I was still woozy from the beating I had taken, and threatened to pass out on several occasions, but I found that the searing agony of taking a deep breath would force me back into full consciousness for a time.

"Shhh…"

I turned my head to see Ial'rafiost holding a finger to his lips while pulling a dagger out with his other hand. I nearly screamed for joy but heeded his warning to remain silent. He slowly crept behind me and grabbed my wrist to hold it still, but rather than cut my bonds, he stabbed me though the wrist, pinning my arm to the tree! "You bastard!" I screamed in pain from this betrayal.

He responded with a low giggle, "That is what we criminals do: we rob and betray one another. What else did you expect from a 'lowborn thief'?" I heard him run off through the grass.

Growling in pain, I tried in vain to reach the dagger with my other hand. I knew that he was angry with me, but I never suspected that he would act out in such a manner.

"You have no need for us, remember?" Vondro was coming straight toward me, sword drawn. "Why would you need a 'boy who hides behind daddy's armor and prestige and who has no will or goals of his own'?"

"I should not have said such things," I pleaded. "I apologize. Please, help me."

He responded by tracing his sword down the center of my chest, splitting open the tatters of my robe and leaving a trail of blood. He followed with a series of shallow, deft strokes, cutting my chest further, laughing the entire time, then spat on the ground at my feet. Turning his back to me, he strode off and disappeared into the fog.

"Come back!" I cried, but to no avail.

While I shouted for Vondro, pain seared my other wrist, as I felt it being stabbed and pinned to the tree just as the other one was.

"I may be a 'raging murderer', but I've never tortured anyone. Until now, that is," came Brother Ironknuckle's voice from behind me. "I have to thank ye, ye've taught me cruelty. How am I doin', oh great necromancer?" The blade twisted, tearing at the tendons and scraping the bones.

I am certain that my screams could be heard for leagues, and they eventually gave way to panting, my breaths coming shallower as I tried to stifle my agony.

"Shh, it will be alright," said Tsukatta appearing out of the fog. She wiped my brow with a cool, damp cloth, allowing me to relax somewhat.

"What are you going to do?" I asked, fearful of her role in my torture.

She responded by dabbing me with herb-infused oils, paying close attention to the scratches made by Vondro's sword.

I recognized the strong scent of clove and almonds, but there were other odors as well, disguised by the blood in my nose. At first, the oil felt soothing, but then it began to burn. I gritted my teeth to stifle my screams as best as I could, the pain of my battered jaw competing with the acid heat on my chest. She then kissed my forehead and glided away.

"You really shouldn't have said such things to us, airing all our painful sins."

I closed my eyes, for I did not want to see *her*. Still, I could not help but notice the flashes of her sparkles through my eyelids.

"And this was the second time for me. Just when I was starting to trust you, that you were learning to control your gift, you had to go ahead and use it on all of us. We were your friends!" she suddenly shouted.

I could not stop the tears from slipping out of my shuttered eyes.

"I can't tell you how much pain you've caused each of us, but we are here to repay it." I flinched as I felt her brush my cheek, and then whisper in my ear, "I cannot, will not, ever love you. No one ever will. Your heart is too cold."

"That is not true," I wanted to shout, my voice hoarse from both dryness and pain, but I barely managed a harsh whisper. "I have made mistakes, and my anger sometimes gets the best of me, but I do my best to be a good man. Please do not forsake me," I begged, tears streaming over my bruised cheeks. My entreaties went unanswered, and after a time, I dared to open my eyes, my vision filled with the thick morning fog. I wept openly, the emotional trauma competing with my physical pain for supremacy.

I cannot be certain how much time passed after Glitter left, but the fog had brightened by the rising sun when another figure stepped out of the fog.

"Did you sleep well?" asked Cratillus with a wry grin. "Oh, look, you cut yourself. That must have been difficult with your hands tied."

I glared at him as he circled the tree.

"Hmm, I was sure I disarmed you, but you have two daggers I must have missed. Let me relieve you of those." He pulled the blades out quickly, dropping them dully to the ground.

The pain scarcely subsided, but at least it released the pressure on my wrists and shoulders, though I could feel the blood pooling in my palms.

"Here, drink this." He held a small vial to my lips, tilted my head back, and poured the bittersweet liquid into my mouth.

It tasted of rotted fruit and valerian. I let it sit on my tongue for a moment to soothe my dry mouth and spit it back out at him.

"Well, that wasn't very polite, now was it? Then again, you only reserve your manners for teachers, don't you? I am to be your teacher now, so you had better start treating me with respect," he leaned in, practically purring in my ear.

"You... you did this," I accused, my throat cracking, part of me wishing I had swallowed whatever was in that vial. "You enchanted my friends; had them attack me."

He shook his head gently and smiled. "I have enchanted no one. And you have no friends. If someone came during the night to harm you, it was of their own volition."

"That cannot be true. No matter what might have transpired between us, they would not behave in such a fashion unless coerced. I will not play into your twisted game."

"I see you have much to think about. I shall return later when you are more rational." He turned his back and strode off into the fog.

Over time, the sun burnt away the morning mists, and I was treated to what would otherwise be a beautiful day, nearly cloudless, the sun shining brightly, the breeze slightly cool against the sun's warmth. The rukla that had beaten me yesterday stood guard.

"Still here?" I asked my rotting companion. "Are you here to make certain I do not escape? Tell your master that I cannot, so that he might find a better use for you." I received no response from the creature, nor did I expect one. Aside from battering others with their untiring fists, ruklaa are mostly useless. However, I must admit that the one thing they are capable of, they do rather well.

As the day grew warmer, the sun's heat began to outmatch the breeze, and I could feel my skin begin to redden under its harsh glare. My bonds were tight, preventing me from shifting my way around the tree, and my thirst grew steadily. I could feel myself weakening from the past tortures, plus the realization that I had not eaten in the last two days, and I knew that I had to keep my mind sharp if I was going to survive this. I began reciting spell formulae to my undead guard, focusing on correct pronunciation and rhythm through my swollen jaw, though without my books and proper rest, I could not gather the energy to cast spells, even were I to be freed.

I believe I may have nodded off to sleep for small moments out of exhaustion, but I cannot be certain. When my body did relax, the pulling of the ropes on my dislocated shoulder snapped me back into full consciousness. Evening came faster than I expected, though the day seemed too long by half, and I was surprised to feel the chill as the sun slid past the horizon. As the darkness waxed, it was my blood that grew colder, for I feared a repeat of the previous night's performance. First, however, I would have another visit from my captor.

"I see you got some sun today. That should bring color to your pallid skin. You really should get outside more and stop hiding indoors; a little tanning is healthy." Cratillus placed a hand on my bare shoulder and it burned like fire. He laughed after pulling his hand away and said, "Look, my hand leaves a print on your skin!" He then began playing with my sunburn, watching with glee as his handprints and fingerprints made my skin pale before returning to redness.

It took all of my will to not scream out in pain and tell him what part of a sow's anatomy he reminded me of at that moment.

Finally, he tired of the game. "No agonizing screams? No witty comments? You're beginning to lose my interest. Oh!" he popped, one finger over his pursed lips, "you're probably dehydrated. Here, drink some of this." He poured a vial of the same liquid as this morning, or yesterday—I was already losing track of the time—into my mouth, and I wanted to swallow it, but feared what effect it might have, so I began to let it dribble out of the corner of my mouth before he pushed up my chin and tilted my head back. I fought, but it did not take long for the potion to run down my throat. "There, we can't have you wasting another of these, now can we? This will make you feel better too."

He pulled a small, white clay jar out of a pouch, broke the wax seal, and discarded the lid. Dipping two fingers into the pot, he pulled out a glob of clear, orange goo, which he proceeded to rub into my burnt flesh. The smell was sweet, but I could detect a bitter flavor from it as well.

"Is that... there is hemlock in that poultice, correct?"

"My, you certainly know your herbs, especially the poisonous ones, if I am not mistaken," he smiled. "Yes, but there is not enough to kill you, just enough to preserve your skin tone. After all, you don't want to rot too quickly after you die," he giggled.

I knew that any struggle would be useless, and it would likely please him if I showed any fear of dying by his hand, so I stayed as stiff as possible while he coated my body with the goopy mixture.

"There, doesn't that feel better?"

It did, but I remained impassive.

He sighed at my silence. "I understand how difficult this is, and I really am looking out for your best interests here. No one else has come to slake your thirst or salve your flesh. The people you thought were your friends are nowhere to be seen, and no one can help you reach your true potential but me. You just have to learn to accept that, and everything else will be much easier."

"If you really wish to show me kindness," I rasped, "then let me go. You have what you want, so there is no need to keep me prisoner."

"You misunderstand. I do have what I want, but you have yet to accept what you want. It would be unkind of me to let you wander through the rest of your living days knowing that I could have saved you so much time and trouble. I am here to give you the power all necromancers seek. Just say the words, tell me 'Cratillus, my life is yours', and you will have all that you ever desired. Stop denying yourself."

"I want nothing that you can give me," I coughed, the taste of iron filling my dry throat.

"You want freedom. I can grant you that. You want power, respect, and knowledge. I can give you those as well. You want the shiny girl to love you. I can make that happen. Just say the words."

I glared in response.

"I can see you need more time to consider your options. We will discuss it in the morning." Cratillus spun on his heel, and strode purposefully away, leaving me nearly naked and exposed to the night.

I stayed awake as long as I was able, for fear of the effects my tortures might have on my dreams. As it turned out, my fears were well founded. While I counted stars in an attempt to keep my mind active, I heard the ringing of iron and the whooshing of bellows. I turned my head slowly to see my father and brothers working at the forge, the heat from the flames washing over me even though I was outside of the shop.

"So," my father grunted, "you wanted to leave our small, backward village to become a great wizard, to chase that hussy around like her pet. A boy has no business following anybody's dreams except his father's."

"Exactly," spoke Vondro, stepping out of the shadows, picking up the still glowing sword from the forge's anvil. "What kind of man turns his back on his father? A man should be proud to follow in his father's footsteps, to take up his craft and trade. I did, and there is no shame in that. Why do you think that should make me less of an individual?" The sword shone more brightly as he spoke, his anger heating the blade past red to white.

"I only spoke what I saw in you," I rasped back to Vondro, the heat growing as he neared me. "There is nothing wrong with staying in the family business if that is your desire, but you want to do so much more. Your father's title and celebrity, forced to become a warrior just like him because that is what your family and friends expected of you, have confined you. I take nothing from your skill and strength at arms, but until you left the city with me, your life was already mapped out. You had no sense of individuality. Now, for the first time, your path is open, and it frightens you." As I spoke, the sword lost its heat.

Vondro lifted the blade to strike but vanished in a cloud of coal smoke during his swing.

"That is what your magic does, boy," father yelled, pointing his hammer at me, "it makes people disappear. You left us for your magic, and now you are a boy without a family, without friends. You turned your back on your past, and now you have no future."

"Sometimes, *father*," I snarled, "the only way to become who you are meant to be, is to leave the past behind."

"In that case, why must you always bring up other people's pasts?" whispered Glitter in my ear. "Bad things happen to all of us, and we all do things we are not proud of. Yet this is all that you see in us: our failings and troubles."

"That is not true!" I rasped in response. "My Gift shows me the pain and sorrows of others, but, like my father's forge, it is the heat and pounding upon the anvil that tempers, creating a more resilient steel. Yes, I see your past pain, but I also see your present self, and I am proud of how you have managed to grow into the woman you have become despite your past. I cannot fathom how you manage to be so light-hearted and joyful after your experiences, and I envy you for that. I have been made to feel that I do not deserve to have joy in my life, so I push it away. Perhaps I even feel I deserve the tortures that Cratillus is putting me through, allowing me to pay a penance for the pain I have caused you and the others. But you are not even here, are you? This is either an illusion of Cratillus's doing, or a hallucination brought about by dehydration and starvation, so this conversation does not even matter."

"But it does, lad" said Brother Ironknuckle, his voice as gravelly as mine. He sat upon the grass in front of me, looking up into my eyes, his hands covered in blood. "Ye see the sins of others, but ye have not looked at yerself with those eyes. Aye, I have caused great harm, which I can never wash away, but I have dedicated my life to making up for that mistake. What have ye done for your soul?"

I was taken aback by his words, for there was the heart of it all. Could I use these eyes to look within, to gain a greater understanding of my own pain?

"You already have," walked a figure out of the shadows, a great gash not quite separating his head from the rest of his body.

"Troj! At least I can be positive this is a dream now. Tell me, what is it about me that I cannot stop causing others pain and sorrow?"

He stared at me a long while, his eyes burning with rage. "You, sad, pathetic little child! You expect me to escape from the Dark Lady's grasp and give you answers every time you get into another fit of whining? 'Nobody likes me'," he bleated, his voice rising while his lips pouted. He lifted his hand to wipe away fake tears, knocking his head ridiculously to the side so that he could stare at me upside-down. "Maybe there is nothing likable about you. You gripe about all the bad things that happen to you, with no regard for other peoples' issues. Anyone who disagrees with you is wrong, whether they are or not. You are physically weak, so you bully others with your intellect rather than with your size. You are a cruel, spiteful, vindictive little piece of garbage, just like your father!"

His last words stopped me cold. My anger had been rising along with his until that point. *Am I like him?* "You… you are at least partially right," I stammered. "I admit, I am too self-absorbed, and do not pay enough attention to others or give them credit when it is due. I have my father's temper, though I lash out verbally rather than physically. What you missed is the fact that I am already aware of these issues. What I want to understand is why I continue to repeat the same mistakes; why do I attack those I care about and push them away? Why do I project my pain… that is the answer, correct? I see the pain in others because I have yet to deal with my own.

"Do I hate my father? I hate that he was a cruel, petty, small-minded man who treated me worse than a broken hammer. I hate that I received more backhands from him than smiles. I hate that rather than accept my choice of craft, he shunned me from his household; though, to be honest, I never expected to return to Split Falls anyway. I admire his craftsmanship and dedication to his work.

I admire that he managed to keep us settled in a home large enough for the five of us, and that, though not wealthy, we never starved either. Like all men, he had both good and bad aspects. Do I hate him? No, but I do not love him either.

"Am I like my father? We seem to share the same inner rage, and I have no notion of what I am angry at, generally speaking. Right now, I am upset at being tied to a tree and tortured with images of my friends attacking me. Am I angry that I am responsible for your death, Troj? Yes, although I have come to terms with the circumstances. But my anger has roots far deeper than that. Perhaps I learned to deal with the world by mimicking father, or I have carried my hate for him so long that it influences all else. I do not know, but I do know that I can no longer live with my heart filled with rage. I must be better than that."

"It's not just your anger that pushes us away," accused Ial'rafiost, his arms around the shoulders of Glitter and Tsukatta. "You need us, and that rankles you to no end. You want to be left alone, to deal with whatever comes your way, but you know you can't do it without us." As he spoke, his flesh turned pale, his long tongue snaked out of his fang-filled maw, and his eyes turned a bright yellow. He turned to each of the women at his side, his sharp claws digging into their arms, causing rivulets of blood to stream down their sides, and bit a chunk out of each of their necks. Rather than screaming in pain, or even collapsing from the mortal wounds, they instead changed to resemble Raf. "You're weak, and can't survive without our help," he hissed, while a susurrus of "flesh" emanated from the ladies at his side.

I found myself paralyzed with fear, forgetting that I was already immobilized. Had Yoffa not saved me from those vulzuu so long ago, I would not be here now. Or, more likely, I would be terrorizing Split Falls as one of them.

"You couldn't even scream for help," continued Raf. "The only reason you are alive is pure, dumb luck. *That* is something you can never control," he grinned wickedly, saliva dripping over his needle-like teeth. "You're powerless. Helpless."

He was right. I could neither move, nor cast spells. Should Raf and the others attack, there was not a single thing I could do to stop them. I took a deep, painful breath, closed my eyes, and exhaled slowly.

"Is that a surrender?" hissed Raf; I could hear the smile in his voice. "Shall we come over there and tear off your tasty flesh? Remember, girls, take the skin and muscle first, so that he stays alive longer."

When they got close enough so that I could smell their fetid breath on my skin, I opened my eyes and released the energy I had been gathering. I am not, nor ever will be, as powerful as Tsukatta in this regard, but I had studied Falleoraeli Zolthliam's work *Accentuating the Positive: A Study of Divine Channeling and Its Arcane Equivalent* since finding it at Ormak's tower, though I had yet to test his theorems. I gathered as much energy as I could and released it in a burst around me, causing the undead flesh of the surrounding vulzuu to burn and peel away.

It was not enough to destroy them outright, but it did give them pause. "Surrender? No, I will not surrender to you; you are nothing but a ghoulish figment, an illusion called forth to deepen my fear in order for Cratillus to cow me into capitulating to his schemes." I was no longer afraid. I was furious! "Cratillus!" I shouted, wincing immediately afterwards. "Enough with your games! Every image you send only strengthens my resolve. I will not bow to you; I will not become your slave. Either kill me or release me, for you cannot break me!"

In response, I heard a scratching behind me, then small pricks on my wrists and hands.

"Now, what are you doing?" I growled.

'We finally found you. Hold still. The ropes are tougher to break than a rat's neck.'

"This one will fail like the others. I may have pushed the others away, but Thessylia is part of my soul. You cannot use her image against me."

'I do not know how he blocked us, but he did. The barrier is down. Be silent.'

'Is…is that really you?' I asked telepathically with caution. As I did so, I began to tear up as I felt her misery at our separation. *'It is not safe for you here. Fly away and find the others. Tell them it is too late. Cratillus has the book and is too strong for them to fight.'*

'They are already coming. I cannot leave you to die. Together or apart, I die with you.'

Was our bond truly that strong, that she could not survive if I should die? Typically, a wizard's familiar merely becomes a conventional member of its species over the course of a month or so after its master's passing. In a way, I suppose that is a kind of death as well, as the personality and magical enhancements slowly fade away. Thessylia's meaning was definitely more literal; she would actually die without me.

'In that case, I shall have to live a long and full life,' I smiled inwardly. A few seconds later, I felt a sudden release of tension on my arms and shoulders as the rope fell away from my wrists. I pulled my arms forward slowly and with caution, though in truth I had been bound so long that I could not have moved with haste anyway. I shook my hands to speed blood flow back into them, and saw the various wounds from the ropes, bark, daggers, and Thessylia's beak. My hands were crusted with blood, much of it from the dagger wounds, which, until now, I was not completely sure had really happened. Loathe as I am to admit it, Cratillus's tortures did have an effect on me, and I was still questioning the reality of the events since my capture; in fact, part of me believed that Thessylia freeing me was yet another stratagem in Cratillus's plans.

Thessylia nipped through the rope around my waist, breaking the last bond. No sooner was I free from my arboreal prison, I fell to the ground. It was not a graceful drop. I did not fall to my knees and then stretch out onto the dewy grass. Rather, I plunged straight down, my knees crumpling beneath me, like a marionette released from the support of its strings. I would say the fall hurt, but I had suffered so much in the past few days that I hardly felt the impact. At this point, I considered letting myself fall asleep as stars and darkness vied for attention at the back of my eyes. Were it not for an owl pecking at my ear, I may have yielded to my body's desire for rest.

'No respite. We must flee.'

It took all my willpower to gather myself together, push off the soft earth, and pull myself up the tree that had held me for what seemed weeks, though only a couple days had passed. I think. Thessylia fluttered away in short bursts, making sure I followed her at every move. I could barely walk, and I shambled after her like the rukla that nearly broke my jaw, falling to the ground on more than one occasion. After a few dozen yards, or miles, for it all felt the same to my wrecked body, I stumbled into Tsukatta's arms, her hands aglow with healing light. According to her, I apologized before passing out.

When I awoke, I again found myself unable to move. I panicked and urgently looked around for a means of escape, the sounds of metal scraping on stone grated behind me.

"Sharpening your blade, Cratillus? What plans do you have for me today?" I coughed, failing to keep the quavering out of my voice.

"Bastard did a number on you, didn't he?" Vondro responded. "Granted, I have not seen as many battles as my father, but I've seen corpses in better shape than you. I'll give you credit; I didn't think you had it in you to survive something like this."

"Cratillus continued to stoke the flames of my rage. I suppose there is a positive benefit to my anger after all." I again tried to sit up and found myself immobile. "Why can I not move?"

"Tsukatta bound your wounds tightly and swaddled you in a blanket like a newborn to keep you still. She was afraid you'd thrash around in your sleep and undo her work." Something in his tone made me think that he thought Tsukatta was being far too kind.

I agreed. "Why are you here? I gave every one of you reason to leave me to die; it would be no less than I deserve. I cannot apologize enough, nor take back my words, but I am truly sorry for the pain I have caused you and the rest." Tears rolled from my eyes and into my ears.

"The problem is, and I am loathed to admit it, everything you said was true. After you stormed off, and we all fumed about it, we started talking about the things you told us. Fortunately, Tsukatta recognized that Raf and Glitter had caught a disease that made them lose control and was able to cure them. We assumed that you had the same problem."

I nodded my assent.

"I make no apologies for following in my father's footsteps, but my dreams were always superseded by his. I joined in this quest because I wanted a life of adventure; to battle the forces of evil, save the maiden in distress, and come home dripping with the wealth of a great dragon, just like in the stories. This is hardly like those tales," he chuckled without humor.

"Not at all. The maidens do the rescuing, the forces of evil are winning, and we have not a copper scale to show for our efforts."

Vondro's laugh became more sincere after my statement.

"Are the others nearby? I would like to speak to everyone."

"They are, but Tsukatta says that you need rest and shouldn't be bothered. Her and Glitter are talking magic stuff, Ironknuckle is getting firewood, and Raf is watching our flank."

I flexed my arms and kicked at the blankets to no avail. "I need to get up, for there is much going on here." I began to roll over in my attempts to escape my wrappings.

Vondro put a heavy boot on my chest. "Hold still. Our priestess said that you were barely alive when we found you, and I am ordered to make sure you stay that way until she is ready to do more healing work."

"Let me go!" I shouted, terror and rage vying for dominance in my voice. "I will not bow to you! You will never be my master!" When he pressed down harder, I felt the fear overwhelm my anger, which brought my mind back to the present. "I am sorry. At least undo these bonds and let me sit up, seeing as I am already awake," I begged, my vision beginning to blur with unformed tears. "I have been bound for the past few days, and I wish to move about."

Vondro sighed, then called out to our healer. "'Katta, your baby's fussing about. Can you come see to him? He probably needs his milk and his nappy changed." He smiled down at me while I glared back up at him.

A few moments later, I heard soft footsteps come my way.

"Welcome back to the land of the living," said Tsukatta softly. "Let me check your wounds." She gently unwrapped the blanket, slowly peeling it away where it stuck to the blood-soaked bandages wrapped around my chest and hands. The cool night air felt good on my skin, and I was just realizing that I was only wearing breeches while Tsukatta and Glitter peered down on me. I also realized that Vondro was nearly correct about my state, in that I was suddenly famished and in need of relieving myself. When I attempted to sit up, she eased me back down.

"I need to get up," I pleaded.

"You will stay here until I can at least determine the extent of your injuries. It took all I had earlier to make you stable."

"You do not understand. I really need to go, at least as far as those bushes."

She blushed and nodded to Vondro, who guided me to my feet and kept me steady. I had not realized how weak I had become and could barely walk even with his assistance. We shuffled a few paces from the ladies, and he leaned me up against a tree so that I could empty myself. I considered escape, but realized I was in no state to flee. My only choice was to hope there would be no further tortures tonight. He then led me back to where Glitter and Tsukatta were sitting and sat me down between them.

They carefully unwrapped my hands, and I saw Glitter's jaw clench when the bandages were removed. Tsukatta sighed and shook her head. I could smell the rank odor of sepsis wafting from my wrists, dark yellow pus oozing from the wounds.

"I will try again to draw the infection from you. It has proven to be rather stubborn." Tsukatta placed her hands over my wrists and began to softly utter her spell. Warmth spread through my hands and up my arms as her magic combated the disease festering in my blood. A few minutes later, she pulled back, and I felt the heat drain back out through my wounds.

"Did you cure him?" asked Glitter, worry emanated unbidden through her voice.

"Not entirely, but I have reduced the infection to manageable levels. I will keep an eye on it."

"Do you have any henbane or adder's wort? We could use those as a poultice," I recommended while she unwrapped the bandages around my chest.

"Would that we did," she responded with a sigh. "I have some ointments that will help, but fresh herbs work best. What happened here?" she asked, gently tapping my chest.

"Vondro, or at least a duplicate of him, cut me with his sword. The wounds did not feel deep but were likely intended to be merely painful. Afterwards, you, or your image, came by to rub ointment on them, which burned as though it were made from lemons and salt."

All three stopped and stared at me.

"You thought *we* did this to you?" Vondro asked, shock and insult clear in his query.

"None of you acted normally, so I thought either you were compelled to act, or it was all an elaborate illusion. After our last conversation, I felt that whatever actions you took on me were justified. As you were not there, and the wounds are real, there must be another explanation."

"What happened to you?" I could see a tear well up in Glitter's eye.

"I… I would rather not discuss it right now." How could I tell her that Cratillus's torture included her rebuffing my feelings for her? What if it were true? I have certainly done everything possible to make her hate me, and yet I am inexorably drawn to her. *Can Cratillus and Ial'rafiost both be correct in their assertions?* I could tell she was worried about me, but that does not mean that she shares my affection. Were I to confess my feelings, especially with the others present, and she denied me, I do not know if I would be able to climb out of the darkness that would cloud my vision. Better I should keep my feelings buried. "Can I have some water?" I asked to change the subject.

"Of course. Just a few sips though for now. We don't want your stomach to cramp." Glitter handed me her water-skin.

I took two short swallows. I wanted to guzzle the rest of it but held myself back. I had not realized how dehydrated I was until those sips and smiled my thanks to her as I handed the skin back.

"I hate to push you, but did you learn anything about Cratillus's plans," asked Vondro without the compassion he expressed.

"He was rather talkative when he came by to harass me. He plans to kill and reanimate every living thing on this world to honor Coruld, so that he may command all the dread god's forces and unseat the Dark Lady. Cratillus was cruel and malicious from childhood, and I believe that, aside from his intelligence, there are no redeeming qualities to him. We have to put a stop to his madness," I finished with a series of coughs. It appeared that Tsukatta mended my broken ribs, but the pain had yet to fade.

Chapter 14: Perspective

After rewrapping my wounds, Tsukatta and Vondro tightly tucked the blanket around me again. I closed my eyes and worked to steady my breathing, repeating over and again that these were my friends, and that this was not the prelude to more tortures.

When Vondro picked me up, however, my control broke. "No! Let me go! I refuse to be part of your plans!" I growled in pain and fear.

Tsukatta put her hands on my face and asked me to calm down. Her hands were warm and gentle, and I felt no reason not to comply.

My body relaxed, as did my breathing. "My apologies. I lost control for a moment."

"You have been through a harrowing experience," Tsukatta said with the placid calm of a still pond. "We understand."

Vondro placed me down gently against a large round stone, ample in size to prop me up in a sitting position, near the campfire. He and the others took positions around the flames so that we could all see each other. I looked into each of their eyes in turn and saw the pain I had brought to the surface in every one of the people I wanted to call 'friend'. I tried to speak, but instead lowered my own eyes and took a deep breath. Before I could try again, Tsukatta interrupted me.

"First off, Mithron, you have reopened many emotional wounds in each of us, wounds we had long thought healed, though never forgotten. We each know what we have suffered, and do not appreciate that you blurted out our deepest anguish for all to hear. The circumstances: the raging fever combined with your wizardly gift, as Glitter has explained it, makes sense that this should have occurred. However, we are all not ready to forgive you just yet."

I felt hot tears running down my cheeks as she spoke, while I stared at the fire, willing the flames to remain orange and yellow, rather than the shades of grey that they threatened to turn. I continued to breathe as deeply as I dared, as the physical pain of the previous days matched the emotional pain I was working to overcome. I spoke to the fire, afraid to look at any of my comrades directly. "I understand, and deserve little else. I have hurt you all, and cannot apologize enough for my harsh words. Although the disease burned away my self-control, it is no excuse. I should have understood my gift sooner, and better learned to control it. Perhaps if Mistress Vletraka were here, she could have helped me. But she is not, and I cannot hide behind her murder as an excuse either."

The disease! *'Thessylia, come quick!'* "Raf, I need you to write a quick note, warning Dureltown against the refugees that we sent there," I nearly shouted with sudden urgency. "They are the carriers of the raging fever. Should they infect the city, there will be chaos in the streets, and Cratillus will be able to walk in through the main gates and take the town even without his undead horde."

Everyone stared at each other as Thessylia landed on top of the boulder I was leaning against.

"Please. I am not rambling. Cratillus boasted of this himself in order to add to my feelings of helplessness."

After another moment's consideration, he pulled out a quill, ink, and paper, and began to write.

While he wrote, I continued, "When you are finished, tie the note to Thessylia's leg. She will fly to Vondelos and bring him the warning. I only hope that she can arrive in time."

"You're still being bossy," I heard him mutter as he wrote.

"I know, but this is imperative. Please."

He finished with a sigh, carefully rolled the paper into a tight spool, and attached it to my one true companion.

As Thessylia prepared to fly off, Glitter gently petted her head, arcane energies sparking from her fingertips. "This will speed your journey, at least for a time." Her voice was melancholic, torn between her desire to help the townsfolk and her disdain for me, I suspected.

The short-eared owl flew off as if launched from a bow, and I could only hope that her speed would allow her to get to Dureltown first.

"Thank you. Now, I wish there were some way to remove the pain, but I do not know how that would be done. All I can think to do is share in your pain by telling you what I have learned about myself." I stopped to take a deep breath, then related my first encounter with the vulzuu, and how my father expelled me from my family. I spoke of my inner conflict; feeling that I should be able to survive on my own versus the actuality of needing friends. "I have seen the darkness within each of you, now you know the darkness within my heart. I can only hope that it is enough to regain your trust, if not your friendship."

For some time, the only sound was the cracking of wood in the fire and the hiss of fat dripping off what might have been a trio of rabbits. Try as I may, I could hardly look at my fellows, for fear of their rejection.

Brother Ironknuckle was the first to speak. "Thank ye, lad. It took a lot of courage for ye ta share all that, and we appreciate it. When I got ta the monastery, it took years before I could confess me sins, and even longer ta forgive meself. None of the monks treated me any different afterwards, for everyone carries something they're ashamed of. If they can forgive me, then I can do no less for you."

I wept openly at his kindness, taking care not to let myself feel it too deeply.

"The priestesses treated me in the same fashion," Tsukatta added. "There was no mistaking the fact that I did not belong in the temple, though they hoped that in time I would understand Kimitsu's teachings. When I did finally accept her and took my vows, there was a celebration, but no one ever reviled me for hiding within their walls. Thank you for coming out from behind *your* walls."

"We were at odds from the moment we met, and I had no intention of liking or respecting you in any fashion. You are bossy, arrogant, and rude." Vondro glared at me for a moment, then his gaze softened. "Over the past weeks, you have proven to be intelligent, resourceful, and strategic, all necessary qualities in a good leader. When you called me out at the Rose, my only thought was to remove your head, but when I had time to reflect on my actions later that night, I realized you were right to chide me so. You reminded me much of both my father and my training commander; I just wasn't ready to accept such words from a small, weak man I had just met. I meant what I said earlier—you have more courage than I would have given you credit for. You have proven it again just now."

"I remember that night," Ial'rafiost chimed in. "Thought you were going to kill him too! I've always prided myself on my ability to get along with everybody, regardless of any differences, but you, Mithron, pushed that to the limit. I'm still mad, but I understand how and why it happened, and I wouldn't be much of a friend if I couldn't put something like this past us."

Glitter was the last to speak, and her response was the one I most feared. "I hated you from nearly the beginning. You have caused me no end of suffering and strife, and have been a general pain in my backside. Your pride, sense of superiority, and cruelty toward me and others made me wonder how anyone could even want to speak to you. Yet, you have also shown me your gentle side, trying time and again to apologize for the tournament, and for consoling me when Mistress Goldfire sent me to you. Every time you get me to like you, you say or do something stupid and push me away again, and I don't really know how much more I can put up with. I'm with you until we stop Cratillus, but I make no promises for after."

I did not know how to feel. Part of me was shocked that she said such things, especially in light of what the others had said, but in truth, it is what I expected. I caused her more pain than any other, and she is the one I want more than any other to not hurt at all. I took a moment to quiet my breaking heart before speaking. "Thank you, all, for your forgiveness, or, at least, acceptance. I still feel it is much more than I deserve. Glitter is correct, Cratillus must be dealt with, and the sooner the better. Afterwards, if you want nothing else to do with me, I understand completely. He will try to use our differences against us, as he tried to convince me that you had all become my enemies. He is powerful, with a horde of undead at his command and other wizards and magical tools at his disposal. We must attack quickly."

"You are not attacking anyone," Tsukatta said with a gentle smile. "You can barely move, and even with my magic you are still sorely wounded. We shall rest and plan until you are ready."

I wanted to argue, but there was no denying the truth. "Now that that is settled, I think my appetite has returned."

There was a general chorus of agreement, and the meat was passed around. Brother Ironknuckle unwrapped me enough so that I might feed myself, which proved to be more challenging than I expected. Not only was my body still stiff, I had not realized how much my shoulder hurt until I tried to lift my arm. My pride would not allow me to be treated like an invalid, and I fought through the pain. I did not eat much; however, though I had not eaten for days, my appetite was reduced due to the physical and emotional stress, not to mention the ache in my jaw. In addition, I was exhausted, and soon asked to be able to lie down and sleep.

As the sun's light was just beginning to glow on the horizon, after a fitful night of bad dreams, mostly involving Glitter finding different ways to attack me, with both spell and weapon, I awoke to find that my bonds had loosened somewhat. With as much care as my battered body could muster, I slithered out of my wrappings and slipped into the thicker woods away from the small clearing where I was being held. The cool air felt good on my mostly naked skin, at least where it was not covered in bandages. I stepped with care, attempting to be as stealthy as possible so that the ruklaa and vulzuu would not hear my escape.

Would that I had my spell-book, but Cratillus took that along with everything else. I hate to give up on it, but I cannot see a way to steal it back from him. It will cost a fortune to replace, but my only hope is to flee and hope that I can find Glitter and the others.

Wait a moment. Did I not just see them? They... they convinced me to confess my fears! All this time fighting off his tortures, and Cratillus still tricked me! Certainly, he will use that against me during his next round of torments. I should have realized it was all going too well. What do I do now? If I stay with these duplicates of my comrades, they will surely make me suffer.

Or are they real, and I am letting my fear rule me? Did Cratillus break my will that easily, that I cannot even accept my escape? Or did he allow me to escape so that I might endure greater agony? I dropped to my knees and sobbed. *What do I do?*

"Mithron?"

I jumped at the sound of my name. I never heard Ial'rafiost come up beside me and found myself trying to scuttle away from him.

"Mithron, are you okay?"

I wanted to run, to shout for him to leave, to cast a spell that would drain the life from him, but I could neither move nor speak. I just stared at his regrets, watching him visiting the grave of the merchant's daughter with a bottle of zylan brandy. He stepped closer and I fell back on my haunches.

"It's me, Raf, your friend," he cajoled, holding out his hand.

"No," I burbled out, "you are another figment here to torture me. Go away!"

"I'm real, see?" he said, tapping his chest. "You are among friends. We want to help you. Please, come back to the campsite with me where you'll be safe."

"No. You are not my friend. You hate me; all of you do. There is no reason you would have tried to rescue me, so this is merely another trick."

"This is not a trick. I'm still upset about what you did, but I don't hate you. Please, let us help you."

"So, you can stab me again? Or turn back into a vulzu?" I paused. "Wait, one does not just change into a vulzu and back. That does not make any sense." I stared at Raf for a few long moments, where he stood with hand still outstretched, looking into my eyes, waiting for me to figure out the incongruities of my situation. "That was not you, but Cratillus."

He nodded.

"You visited her grave nightly, drinking yourself into a stupor. Cratillus would not carry such memories."

He grimaced. "At least you can use this power to tell friend from foe. It would be prudent, however, if you could at least stop announcing it," he said through his teeth.

That is why he stabbed me. No, wait, that was not him. Was it? While I wandered aimlessly amid my thoughts, Raf had approached closer.

He grabbed my forearms and gently pulled me to my feet. With his hand on the small of my back, he directed me back to the small fire where the rest of our group lay sleeping.

"They are all real, correct?" I asked my companion, who nodded in assent. "I am very confused. Why can I not coalesce my thoughts?"

"I don't know. What did he do to you? Maybe you can find the answers there."

"I was caught by a vulzaam, carried for about a day, still infected with the raging fever. Cratillus had some vulzuu tie me to a tree and used a rukla to batter me. He forced me to drink a potion, but I did not eat or sleep, though the visions might have been dreams. It could have been any of those factors, or maybe all of them." Without warning, I felt my body beginning to collapse. "So tired," I heard myself say as I dropped to the ground.

When I next awoke, I found the others eating small bowls of gruel around the renewed campfire. Their quiet conversation ended as I approached, and everyone stared at me.

"I think I am feeling better. Though it is still painful, I can walk on my own now. Thank you," I said directly to Tsukatta.

"Did you sleep well?" she asked. Something in the tone of her voice was off.

"I did have some strange dreams, and I am still a bit worn out, but otherwise, I think so. My blankets were loose this morning. Did I move around a lot?"

"You might say that," said Raf. "I spotted you wandering about in the woods last night and had to bring you back."

I stared at him dumbfounded. "I... I dreamt that."

He shook his head.

"I did not? You are sure?"

He nodded.

"How could that be?" I dropped to the ground, staring at the fire.

"I think Cratillus' machinations have affected you more than you think," said Glitter, a slight quaver in her voice. "The things he did to you. He probably used magic in conjunction with depriving you of sleep and nourishment. He damaged your mind as well as your body."

"No," I denied, though I could already see it to be true. "I told him that my will would not break. I cannot allow him to make a liar of me."

"It appears that he already has, lad," Brother Ironknuckle said with a sadness that I could almost taste. "If ye have a mind to, the monks taught me ways ta work through this kinda thing."

"I will manage, thank you," I said curtly, not wanting to hear any more of the subject.

"No, you won't," Glitter's voice rose, nearly to a shout. "Let him, let *us*, help you. You have been through a terrible ordeal, and it's not something you just 'manage'. You told us last night that you had come to terms with 'needing friends' and not just doing everything on your own. Prove it. Let us help."

"But," *you hate me*. I could not pull my eyes from hers, shining platinum in the morning sun, the determination within them would not be denied. *This is a trick! You cannot trust them. They want you to let down your guard so they can torture you more.* I fought the impulse to flee, and even as my body began to turn, I was still caught in Glitter's eyes. With a sigh of resignation, I dropped to the ground, sitting uncomfortably on the hard earth. "What must I do?"

"Firstly, ye need ta relax. Take a few deep breaths, and calm yer mind. Now, what is the first thought to spring?"

"You stabbed me through my wrist with a dagger," I mumbled under my breath. I looked up to see him stare at me.

"I couldn'a heard ye right. Did ye just say that I stabbed ye?"

I nodded. "Both you and Raf, through my wrists, pinning me even more tightly to the tree to which I was tied." I then held up my hands, both of which were heavily bandaged to protect the wounds on both sides. "I know it was not you, and yet it was. Some part of the illusion was real, and right now I cannot tell the difference. You all say you were not there, but the wounds that each of you caused are. I do not wish to believe you are responsible for my injuries, but they exist. Cratillus is ultimately responsible, but who did this to me?" I pulled open my blanket to show the large bandage on my chest. "I know this was not Vondro's doing, yet the wounds are there by his hand."

"Alright then, focus on... on me stabbin' ye. How did I look? Were me actions otherwise normal? Can ye describe th' dagger?"

I closed my eyes and took a deep breath. "You were laughing, thanking me for teaching you how to be cruel while you twisted the blade. You came up from behind and disappeared afterward, so I never saw you nor the knife."

Brother Ironknuckle continued to stare at me in surprise. "Truly, ye canna believe I would act in such a manner, no matter how angry I might have been."

Again, I held up my bandaged wrists. "It was all very convincing. I had not eaten in at least two days by this time, and the only sleep I got was after the rukla knocked me unconscious. Honestly, there is little I would not give to be in my own bed right now," I smiled.

"Tell us," interrupted Vondro, "all that happened, from the point where you were captured."

I related as many details as I could, fumbling over the part where Glitter's image said she could never love me.

After a minute or so, Vondro spoke again. "So, the images of us came to you one at a time? You never saw two of us together?"

I was silent for a moment. "Not during that instance, no. Later on, I did, but I am fairly certain that I might have been unconscious, since I also spoke to my father and Troj."

"Who's Troj?" asked Raf.

"The leader of a small band of brezzes I encountered some time back. He shows up in my dreams once in a while, reminding me of the price of killing, even in self-defense."

"There is a lot going on inside of your head," quipped Raf. "Once this is done, you *must* tell me all of your stories."

"If we survive, I promise," I smiled back, thankful that things seemed to be returning to normal.

"Back to the matter at hand," Vondro stated, clearing his throat. "Since you only saw one of us at a time, could it be that there was only one person torturing you? Someone who could change the way they looked?"

"It could be," I answered. "But it would have to be someone able to change appearances quickly and able to know my words and thoughts."

"Ryelt!" Glitter and I shouted together.

The others looked at us confused.

Glitter explained. "A ryelt is a shapeshifter that can read the thoughts and emotions of those nearby. Usually, they act as spies and assassins, taking on the likeness of a person, killing them, and taking their place. They are very difficult to detect and can cause a lot of havoc before moving on. Having one read Mithron's mind and torturing him with his guilt, that's just diabolical," she finished, looking at me with new pity.

"It all makes more sense now. For all I know, the ryelt was the rukla guarding me as well. I do not remember seeing it while being tortured by you…it…the ryelt. Then again, I was rather distracted, and it was dark. The rukla might have just blended into the night. When we attack Cratillus, we need to keep careful tabs on each other, lest the ryelt sneak in and copy one of us."

"Great, something new to worry about," remarked Raf with a hint of jesting. "How do we plan for something like that? If it can read thoughts, then code words are useless, and it can appear to have anything that might be identifying."

"We will just have to be careful," sighed Glitter with an air of resignation. "Ryelt have been around for a very long time, and are quite good at their craft. If anybody acts out of character, then they might be the shape-changer. Most likely, it will be one of the three of you," she pointed to Vondro, Raf, and Brother Ironknuckle, "as none of you cast spells."

"I know a few spells," mewed Raf. "I just don't use them unless I need to."

"At least that narrows the choices down by half," said Vondro with a shrug. "How are you feeling, Mithron? Do we need more time for you to heal, or should we prepare to move on Cratillus?"

I looked to Tsukatta, who nodded gently, though without conviction. "If Tsukatta believes me to be healed enough, then I am ready. Unfortunately, Cratillus has my spell-book, as well as all my other possessions, so I will need to borrow Glitter's for study. Without it, there is little I can do to assist."

"It's the least I can do," Glitter responded. "You have done the same for me."

We then settled down to formulate a strategy for assaulting Cratillus and his forces. Stealth was determined to be the best option, attacking outlying groups when they could be destroyed swiftly and quietly, while trying to get to Cratillus as quickly as possible before he realized that we were coming after him.

Glitter and I had very different foci in spell selection; her being as much an enchantress as I a necromancer, though her occasional and, often random, surges of power, have proven to create a wide variety of effects, most of which seem to be beyond her control. Enchantments are one of the two areas of magic I neglected in my studies while focusing on necromancy, illusions, the other, and she had little in her book with my specialty, though what she did have, she more than likely copied out of my book when she was rewriting her lost one. Fortunately, she made good use of Wosken's spell-book, and I was familiar enough with many of his spells that I could learn them without spending too much extra time.

Seeing Wosken's spells reminded me of our battle atop Vletraka's tower, just a few weeks prior. "Do not bother with casting *ajilek* against Cratillus," I warned Glitter and Raf, in case he knew the spell. "I had a small pin, which I took from Wosken, that absorbs that spell, and I suspect Cratillus might now wear it. If he does not, then it is likely still a viable option, although there are other defenses against it, such as *bezyamhysa*."

"Good to know," smiled Ial'rafiost, who was doing a handstand on a low branch. "It's not a spell I know, but it's good information. Anything else of interest that he took from you?"

"The satchel had an extra-dimensional space, which allowed me to carry a number of books from Ormak's library, and the wand we found, which I never took the time to fully examine. My best guess is that it squirts out a jet of acid, which can affect creatures out of phase with this plane, but I cannot say for certain."

"That's pretty detailed for a guess," he smiled, still upside-down. "So, I'm guessing there is still more to the story than you told me before."

I explained how Glitter had pushed me into the Shadow and my discovery of the wand. "In truth, I did not know for sure it was a wand until you opened the coffer, nor did I know what else was in there. But since I could touch it while in that condition, and yet it would not pull free from the box, led me to believe that it existed in both states. There is an image of a dragon's head near the tip, and since it is black, it suggests acid. However, it could very well be any energy type, and the image could be black for any reason.

"I also had a pair of arm braces which helped me fend off physical attacks, though it would not surprise me if Cratillus has something similar with greater enchantments." Wizards, indeed, most arcane spell-casters, eschew the wearing of armor, mostly due to its bulk, which interferes with the precise gestures needed to cast most spells. To compensate, smaller devices, such as arm braces, rings, and cloaks, are often constructed to defend an unarmored mage, which are rarely as good as a full suit of metal plating, but sufficient in their limitations. Besides, were I to try to wear something that heavy, I would probably collapse under its weight before even fully donning it!

Divine casters, such as Tsukatta, do not seem to suffer the same constraints overall. Though she only wears a fine mesh of chain-mail beneath her robes, she would be able to cast her spells in the heaviest armors, though, I suspect she chooses something lighter because she cannot carry such weight either. Much of divine magic is channeled through a symbol or emblem of the priest's deity, reducing the need for as many gestures; often, simply grasping the holy symbol is all that is required.

Once I finished with Glitter's spell-book, I returned it to her for safekeeping. Her book reflects her personality, as I am sure mine does, now that I think on it. Glitter's book is covered in bright red leather, which cascades through the rainbow in iridescent hues as one changes its angle to the light. Small gemstones adorn the cover, shining and dazzling in the sunlight. My book, in contrast, is bound in leather of the deepest blue, nearly black, with no adornment aside from my personal symbol of a curved dagger crossing against a crescent moon etched into the leather, barely visible unless tilted against the light.

With our preparations complete, we carefully traveled on to Ehrghex. Ruklaa were scattered about the land but paid us no heed as we kept our distance. The vulzuu, led by Kelthid, the vulzaam that captured me a short time ago, and still wore the bright crimson accessory that enhanced his undead strength, smelled our warm flesh on the wind and raced to the attack.

"Beware of the one with the red belt," I warned as the pack neared. "His stench is overpowering, and that belt makes him incredibly strong."

As the undead closed to attack, I heard everyone take a deep breath to ward off the vulzaam's rotting odor, though it was of little use, as the smell permeates through the soft flesh of the nose, even if one does not inhale. Glitter and Raf reeled back into near-faints when the smell hit them, whereas I had grown accustomed to it during the long day in which he carried me. The others must have extraordinary constitutions to withstand such a sensory assault. While Vondro and Brother Ironknuckle cut down vulzuu as quickly as they neared them, Tsukatta called upon her goddess' power to annihilate them. Within moments, only Kelthid was left standing against us, and he seemed to be intent on me.

"Wizard escaped from master. Kelthid shall return you to his kindness," he grinned, his long tongue rasping against sharpened teeth. "A second reward for a second capture!"

As he lunged for me, Brother Ironknuckle kicked him in the side of his head, neck bones cracking under the strain. Kelthid responded with a backhand blow, which knocked the grommold to the ground, paralyzed from the vulzaam's touch.

"Your master is *not* mine!" I growled, invoking a pale grey beam, which burned into his pale-yellow belly. *Yuvamimzuklii* is but a minor spell, which affects only undead, but I needed to save my more powerful spells for later.

"Cratillus will be master of us all!" Kelthid responded, wrapping his large, meaty hand around my throat. No sooner had he grabbed me, the paralytic nature of his touch froze my body stiff, leaving me once again helpless and at his non-existent mercy. Fortunately, I was not alone this time, and my friends were there to save me.

Raf recovered enough to throw a dagger into Kelthid's back, before losing the last of his lunch, followed by Vondro's sword, which sliced off the arm holding me at the shoulder. As he began to scream in agony, Vondro silenced him with a reverse thrust through the ribcage.

It took a few minutes for Kelthid's horrid touch to wane, leaving both Brother Ironknuckle and I as active as stone. His stench, however, would not fade so quickly, and we left his corpse as soon as we were able, though it was late afternoon before Glitter and Raf fully recovered. We were unable to avoid two other groups of ruklaa, which were easily dispatched, before we found our quarry.

When we finally came upon Cratillus, he stood in the middle of a farm outside the walls of Ehrghex, along with three others, the full moon illuminating them all enough to distinguish them even from that distance.

It will be difficult to creep up close to them, I thought, *with the bright moon and no trees. If only the grass was taller.* I crawled on my elbows and belly, my shoulder aching every time I pulled forward, careful not to draw attention to myself or the others. As I approached, the four figures separated out, each walking directly away from all the others, sprinkling something that glimmered in the moonlight as it floated to the earth.

I realized then that we were out of time. *They are casting the mass animation spell!*

I did not fully understand the mechanics behind it, nor could even pronounce the spell's name, for I had not been able to decipher all the runes, but I knew what its purpose was. There was no longer time to plan, no time for reconnaissance; action had to be taken immediately before there was a field of kuldaa dragging themselves from the earth to follow the commands of this madman. One of the figures was heading in my general direction, and I shifted my crawling to intercept her. As we neared each other, I cast, as quietly as I could while still shaping the needed energy, a sphere of silence, which I planned to use against Cratillus to prevent him from casting spells, at least while he was contained within its confines. When the woman suddenly lost her voice, I jumped up to grab her and pull her down.

When I saw her face, I realized the trouble into which I had gotten myself. Her skin was pale and cold, her eyes a deep crimson, and her teeth sharp enough to tear flesh with ease. I had hoped that by wrestling this figure down and interrupting her journey across the field, I could disrupt the spell that they were casting in unison, but instead I had just offered myself as a meal for a maraika! Once her initial shock of being tripped wore off, she smiled and mouthed the words "thank you" before lunging for my throat. In retrospect, I should have checked beforehand whether or not she was alive with my necromancer's sight, but I panicked at the time.

It was all I could do to hold her head and keep it away from me, though her claws tore into my sides and I could feel not only my blood, but my life draining away with every scratch. She rolled us over, so that she sat atop my abdomen, pushing the breath from my body as well. I managed to get my thumb into one of her eyes, which distracted her for a moment. She swiped my hands away and pinned my arms down, licked at the ichor oozing from her damaged eye, and pulled her head back to lunge for my throat. As she did, Vondro's blade sliced through her neck, dropping her severed head on my chest before it and her body melted into a green mist, which flowed across the field toward the city proper like a toxic haze.

Vondro dropped to the ground next to me and looked at me as if I had lost my senses again. I took a moment to dispel the silence so

I could explain my actions. As I did, I could hear Cratillus's voice call over the field.

"Damn it, Verria! Where in the Pits are you?" He and the others began to make their way toward us.

I hoped the others were ready; meanwhile, I took a moment to drink a potion to restore my vitality. My answer came in the form of a bright blue-white beam of light, which tore through one of the other figures, causing it to shudder for a moment before bursting into a cloud of dust. Cratillus's third ally became the target of what started out as a bolt of lightning, which coalesced into the form of a unicorn, impaled its victim, tossed it into the air, and trampled upon it after it landed; arcs of electricity danced along the victim's body from the moment of first impact. Glitter shrugged as if that were what she intended all along.

Cratillus was left standing alone against the six of us. "Well done, Mithron," he clapped, venom dripping with every word. "You actually managed to get your allies to forgive you, and you haven't yet abandoned them. It won't last, you know. You will turn on each other soon, just as everyone does. I've gone over your spell-book and see that you have only reached the fourth tier of spells, whereas I have mastered all nine. You cannot hope to stop me, so why don't you make it easier on everyone and join me instead; my offer still stands to kill you quickly if you accept. It seems that I have an opening for a general or three."

"It seems that your army will soon be without its high commander as well," I retorted, anger and bile rising unabated within me. "I will tear out your soul and grind it into powder, which I will sprinkle a pinch of on my morning porridge each day, so that I might savor your terror and despair of knowing that you will sink a little deeper into the depths of the Pits as I crap you out." I assume that my vision had shifted at this point, for I could not tell in the moonlight. "There will be no armies, no grand plans to take over the Land of Souls, no forgiveness for your multitude of crimes, no more murder, and no raising of bones. I do not know whether your mother realized what you were to become when she rejected you as an infant, or if her callousness triggered your evil, but this ends *now*!"

As I finished, I released the *zumulalsk* spell I had prepared while he was taunting me. The bolt of negative energy I had been gathering in my palm caught the man who just recently made me a victim of his tortures in the belly, tearing through his center while arcs of energy chased each other over his flesh. It would not kill him, or truly even damage him much, but it would weaken him temporarily.

"You will need much more than that to make your words true, but unfortunately, you will not have the time." Cratillus chanted a few magical syllables and slapped his hand to the ground, just as our warriors were rushing toward him. A wave of energy washed over all of us, which sucked some of the life force out of each of us, leaving Glitter and I reeling from the sudden loss of strength. How the others managed to fight off the full effect of the spell I attribute to great physical training, luck, or both. While I tried to regain my footing, Vondro, Brother Ironknuckle, and Ial'rafiost circled around the mage, punching, and stabbing at him, keeping him distracted from casting another spell that might devastate us completely, and Tsukatta called upon the healing powers of her goddess to restore some of the life that Cratillus had so easily stripped away.

I missed what happened next while trying to regain my focus, but could see that Vondro was paralyzed, likely from *vulzuklavad*, and Cratillus was attempting to touch Brother Ironknuckle with the same spell. The grommoldian monk proved to be far too agile for the middle-aged wizard, his training and intuitions always placing him a few moves ahead of the necromancer.

"Fine, try and dodge this!" Cratillus shouted in frustration, throwing his hands in the air and bringing them down with force. As he did so, a gust of arctic air blasted Brother Ironknuckle from above, blowing him down to one knee and leaving him covered in ice crystals. When he tried to get up, he found his leg had frozen to the ground.

I had regained my wits enough by this point to launch a pair of bolts of purple fire, one at Cratillus, which only grazed him, and the other at the ground near Brother Ironknuckle, in the hope that it might thaw him without hurting him more. Meanwhile, I heard Glitter cast *liskakhuuma*, the same paralytic spell that she cast on

Flinjirt just a few weeks before, but Cratillus's incredible willpower shook off her spell. Tsukatta joined us on the offensive by invoking a dagger of magical force to harry the necromancer while she prepared to bolster the health of our warriors.

Defending himself, Cratillus evaded Raf's blade long enough to transform his body into a giant kulda, nearly three times my height, his robes and other items growing with him. The spell made Raf's and Vondro's blades nearly useless, as they passed through the gaps between or bounced off the petrified bones, and which are designed to cut or pierce flesh. In addition, kuldaa are unharmed by the cold, protecting him from any magic that uses ice, and any negative energy would heal him instead of harming him, negating the largest part of my offense, as I had expected to face more living foes than undead today.

Tsukatta, however, has magic and abilities tailored for fighting undead creatures, and she released a blast of pure white light, which seared through Cratillus's sternum, burning through to his spine.

Once he regained his balance, he shouted, "That will be enough from you!" his voice roaring in a strange, hollow echo. He pointed a large bony finger at her and chanted the words to complete a *zukliihilsk* spell; one I was familiar with, though it was still beyond my ability to cast. I could only stare in mute horror as a red-black line of energy lanced out from his fingertip and hit Tsukatta squarely in the chest. Though she opened her mouth to scream, no sound came, and I could almost feel her soul tear away from her body as the energy of his spell drilled into her heart. Moments later, she dropped to the ground, dead as stone.

Not again! "Monster!" I screamed, releasing *vezivihilsk* fueled more by rage than proper study and technique.

The bolt of lightning arced through his ribcage, traveled up his spine, and dissipated through his rictus grin, scorching his bones along the way. As he staggered back from my spell, Glitter launched *srukakbolmos* over his head, burning the top half of his skeletal form and causing him to stumble further backwards into Brother Ironknuckle's path. The grommold had freed himself from the frozen earth, allowing him to grab Cratillus's tibia and yank him to the ground where a waiting Vondro hacked at the large skeleton with all his might, chipping away at the fossilized figure.

The undead form of our foe swept his skeletal arm across, knocking the warriors away from him. He then stood up and raised his arms in preparation to cast another spell. As he did so, I spied Raf clinging to Cratillus' leather belt, a small pouch in his hand. Just as I realized what he was doing, he crammed his magical pouch with an extra-dimensional space into Cratillus' similar one. Energy of complete non-color danced over the large pouch on Cratillus' belt and exploded into a vortex of nothingness. Before Cratillus ever realized what was happening, and while Ial'rafiost was blowing Glitter a kiss, the void spiraled around the pair for a few moments, and then the tear was gone, along with my friend, my enemy, and a circle of earth that was the bottom part of the spherical rip in reality.

I stood in mute silence, staring at the location where the world had torn apart. Glitter would later jest that it was the first time she ever knew me to be speechless.

"A friend shall open the door, leaving the others bereft." Raf, you noble fool! We could have beaten him! We could have found another way! Why?

I felt two thin arms circle me from behind and heard Glitter sobbing into my shoulder. A roar of anguish came from behind me from Vondro, who was cradling Tsukatta's lifeless form. Brother Ironknuckle muttered a prayer in Grommoldian, which loosely translates to "Traveller, may you find your path back to your warren" at the spot of the dimensional rift, then turned to shuffle over to Vondro and Tsukatta, softly uttering a similar prayer over our fallen priestess.

I turned around, still wrapped in Glitter's arms. "It is all my fault," I croaked into her red, purple, and orange hair. "They died because I brought them here. It should have been me."

"You're wrong," Glitter cried, backing up a step and gripping the front of my robes in both hands. "We all knew the dangers. We all knew the reasons why we came. We all were willing to give our lives to stop Cratillus and his madness." She shook me once so that

I would look her straight in her softly glowing pink eyes. "We succeeded. How many more would have died?"

"Too many," I sighed through tears. "Too many have already died. The line outside the Dark Lady's gates must be staggering." I looked over to see Vondro still wailing over Tsukatta's body; Brother Ironknuckle had a hand on his shoulder. "He is taking her death exceptionally hard."

Glitter stared at me in shock. "They were in love."

I returned Glitter's stare. "They were?"

She shook her head in exasperation. "You couldn't see? They rode next to each other, slept side-by-side, and he was always the first one she healed. For the last week, they have been inseparable."

I continued to gaze into Glitter's eyes, trying to put the pieces together as she laid them out. Before I could complete the picture, she shook her head with a chuckle.

"You really can't see it, can you? You so easily see the pain and suffering of others, but cannot see love and joy?"

I stood mute at her revelation.

"Why is this so hard for you?"

I stood silent, seeking an answer, while she waited patiently during my contemplations. "I suppose I do not understand people and their social interactions. Until now, I have always been someone's student, whether learning at father's forge, Yoffa's cabin, or Vletraka's library, and my pursuits have been mainly solitary. You have a natural gift for making people feel at ease around you, while I am uneasy around others. As Raf..." I choked a bit on his name, "pointed out to me, I need to learn to lead, and not just command. But I have no idea how to do that."

Glitter smiled. "You finally admitted that you don't know something. That's a start!"

I was angry for a moment, before realizing she was right, and had chided me about it in the past.

"You are good at strategy and understanding situations, which makes you a good commander. If you want to be a leader, you have to learn about the *individuals* you are commanding. Now let's go over there and comfort Vondro."

I nodded and she led me over to our kneeling warrior with the dead priestess in his arms. Sniffling tears, I knelt across from him. "Tsukatta was dear to us all. Would that my sister had lived, I would hope that she would have had the same loving, gentle presence. I know that she was special to you, and if I can help in any way…"

"Bring her back," he interrupted through clenched teeth.

"I… wish that I could, but that is far beyond my ability…"

"Bring her back," Vondro uttered again with more vehemence.

"That would have been her purview," I said as calmly as I could, though I was on the verge of tears myself, "and even she was not capable of returning the…"

"Don't say that word! I had only just found her, and I can't lose her so soon!"

Glitter wrapped her arms around the broken-hearted warrior while I stood mute, searching for both the right words and a way to fulfill his desire. "I know a spell that will protect her, until I find a way to do more," I said, making a vague promise, knowing that there was nothing that I could do about her death. "First, I have to find my spell-book, *In Between*, and the other objects Cratillus took from me. Stay with her until we get back. There are still dangerous creatures wandering about, so remain alert."

He laid her down gently upon the grass, stood up, and drew his blade from its scabbard. "Return quickly. With luck, I will have a wall of bodies stacked up around us by the time you get back," he practically growled.

I nodded, then Glitter, Brother Ironknuckle, and I ran toward Ehrghex proper, which I assumed Cratillus was still using as his base of operations while he tried to raise his army from their long rest.

Although I wished to retrieve my spell-book as quickly as possible, part of me also wished to run into a group of ruklaa or such to release some of my pent-up fury, in spite of the fact that I had nearly exhausted all of the magical energy I had stored. Cratillus had managed to kill an entire town, and a large portion of them had already been animated into ruklaa. This would be far too large a problem for the six… no, four, of us to handle alone. Once I had my books back, we needed to speed to Dureltown and hope that

Vondelos would be able to gather enough warriors to attack the necropolis that was once Ehrghex. With Cratillus gone, there would certainly be others who would attempt to take command of the ready-made horde, one of which was certainly the maraika that Vondro beheaded earlier, unless we happened to stumble across her grave and put her permanently to rest.

I focused my sight on the Weave, searching for signs of where my missing tomes might be hidden, but there was no indication of them being nearby. We moved cautiously toward the town's wall, careful to avoid attracting the attention of any meandering ruklaa or anything else that Cratillus created during his stay. We made it to the edge of town without detection, and I shifted my sight to scan for other living and unliving creatures within our proximity. "I detect seven undead on the other side of the wall," I whispered to my colleagues.

Brother Ironknuckle gave me an odd look before remembering my specialty. "Ormak's sitting room," he mouthed with a nod.

I only replied with a smile and pointed toward the town's main gate. We edged along the wall, taking every step with care as I remember Raf doing whenever he needed to move with stealth. I fought back tears as I thought of his incongruous nature of needing to be both the center of attention and invisible. As we neared the gate, more creatures came into my sight, and I tapped Brother Ironknuckle on the shoulder while holding up my other hand for Glitter to halt my comrades' advance. "There are seventeen undead at the gate," I murmured, "one is much emptier than the others."

"Emptier?" asked Glitter in a barely audible whisper.

"Living things glow, undead appear as holes in my vision. I have never observed a mixed group, but I would wager a darker hole means a more powerful creature."

"Do we fight or seek another path?" the grommoldian monk asked.

I turned my face to the moon, as if seeking guidance. "How much magic do you have left?" I glanced at Glitter.

"Not much. You?"

"Nearly exhausted. We could use one of your power surges about now."

She smiled. "If only I could do that on command."

I turned to Brother Ironknuckle. "Are you healthy enough to fight?"

He responded by clenching his fist, every knuckle cracking as he tightened it.

"All right then, quick and silent." Before I could take another step, the grommold leapt to the top of the twenty-foot high wall, quiet as a cat, and crouched as if ready to pounce. Though he insists that his abilities are purely physical, Brother Ironknuckle almost seems to work his own brand of magic at times. Glitter and I inched to the edge of the gate to see a large group of ruklaa milling about while a yomki looked around, apparently bored with her guard duty.

Glitter sidled around the corner while muttering the words for *aatokytsrukak*, which I felt was going to cause trouble for us at first, as the spell typically emits a bright orange fan of flames. Just before she completed the spell, however, I noticed that she rotated her right foot outwards, which is not a normal movement in casting, and the flames came out a dark violet, which were barely noticeable from a distance in the moonlight. Four of the ruklaa caught on fire and burned away in seconds.

I marveled at her technique, but did not have the time to ask her about it at the time, as I stepped next to her and released a burst of positive energy, which tore through the mass of creatures, destroying the rest of the ruklaa and damaging the yomki. Before it could react, Brother Ironknuckle landed on the creature's head, driving both his feet deep into the skull, nearly pushing it into its chest.

"You learned that skill already?" Glitter asked as I staggered back against the wall.

"Learned, but have not yet mastered," I breathed, trying to maintain my footing and clear my foggy vision. "Last resort, remember?"

"Okay, but don't do that again. If you die before we reach your spell-book, then we have wasted our time," she smiled, though not fully in jest. "This may not be as large as Dureltown, but it is big enough. Where should we start looking?"

"My first guess would be the manor of the lord mayor. As a ruler, Cratillus would likely appropriate the seat of governing. Otherwise, any other opulent manor house would probably the next choice, as he grew up in comfortable surroundings."

"Work's fer me. Ta the center of town, then?"

I nodded and we picked our way through the streets and alleyways, careful to avoid any wandering undead. After evading five patrols, we managed to get to the trade district, Ehrghex's center of wealth. There were four families of wealth in town, and each manor house rivaled the others in excess of land, gardening, and style. New construction could be seen on all four, as they expanded to greater size than their neighbor.

"Which one?"

"I have no idea," I answered the grommold. "I expected one to outshine the others. Either the families are equal in wealth, or they are going into debt to keep up. Let us start with that one," I pointed, choosing the closest one to us. After checking for wandering undead, we crept up to the gate of the first house. "I am not detecting any undead or magic so far," I whispered.

"Glad ta hear it," returned Brother Ironknuckle. The iron gate creaked as we opened it enough to pass through, causing us all to stop and double-check our surroundings before proceeding forward. We slipped through and hurried across the open yard to the manor's porch.

"Someone is alive inside!" I nearly said in normal speaking tones from excitement.

"Let's hope they're friendly. I wasn't expecting to charm anybody today," smiled Glitter.

"You're always charming," I could almost hear Raf say, as though he were still among us. I considered saying it in his place, but I felt that Glitter would not appreciate the statement coming from me.

"Door's locked," grumbled Brother Ironknuckle, who then pounded on the door. It opened almost immediately.

Inside stood a small, thin man in his later years, a fringe of grey hair circling his head like a tiara. "How may I serve Lord Cratillus?" he said hurriedly, his reedy voice quavering.

"*Lord* Cratillus is dead," I responded, ready to kill this traitor to the living.

"Oh, thank the gods!" He nearly leapt with joy and grabbed each of our hands in turn. "How may I serve our saviors?"

I was taken aback by this abrupt change. "Why do you still live while Cratillus murdered the rest of Ehrghex?" still not trusting this man.

"I possess a wealth of information about Ehrghex's history, which I shared in exchange for my life. He... promised to spare my family as well but took them one by one until I was left alone, saying that I was too frail to be good fodder." He broke down in tears at this point, turned away, and walked back into his home.

Glitter was up to him immediately. She turned him around and hugged him, letting him cry on her shoulder until he had calmed down. "I can't imagine how terrible this has been for you. We are doing all we can to remedy the situation, dire though it is. Are there any others still alive?"

"I don't know," he rasped, tears still falling from his rheumy eyes. "I've kept myself locked in here, hoping that monster would forget about me."

"Do you know where he quartered himself? We are seeking information on his plans to stop his army."

"Yes, he took over the Byrrel estate. It's the last manor house on the street. I—I can still hear the screams of the children when I try to sleep at night," he began to sob.

Glitter let him cry himself out again before speaking. "Stay here. We shall return shortly and get you out of here."

He nodded and sat down in a large brown padded chair.

We moved with care down the street to the home of the Byrrel family. Outside the gate stood what appeared to be giant knights, standing nearly ten feet tall and covered head to toe in wicked spiked armor. "Well, that makes sense," I said without surprise. "We should have just looked for the best guarded estate in the first place."

"Ye two save yer magic and slip inside. I'll handle these brutes."
With that, the grommoldian monk made a running jump and kicked
the first of the giants in the hip with a hollow thud, causing it to
stagger into the other. Glowing yellow points of light appeared
inside the helmets where eyes should be, and the two creatures
turned toward Brother Ironknuckle, raising great morningstars in
their gauntleted fists. Brother Ironknuckle deftly dodged the first
clumsy attacks, while leading them away from the gates.

A few moments later, Glitter and I entered the estate's grounds.

As we neared the house, a pack of ruklaa came around the corner.
Upon spotting us, they burst into a run, moving at a speed no regular
rukla could match. Without a word, we bolted to the porch, skipping
the odd step, and burst our way through the, thankfully, unlocked
door, slamming it shut behind us and securing the lock just as a
multitude of pounding fists impacted upon the door.

"What are those?" asked Glitter, taking in deep breaths.

"Fast ruklaa," I replied, intentionally not noticing the way her
chest rose and fell with each breath. "They are less resilient than the
standard rukla but can quickly swarm a target and kill it before it can
escape." I shifted my sight to seek out living and non-living beings,
while noticing that Glitter was inspecting the Weave. "There are
four undead and one living creature directly above us."

"I'm picking up tight twists in the Weave in the same place."

We nodded to each other and cautiously picked our way up the
wide carpeted staircase. Were we not in such a predicament, it would
be a beautiful house to explore, with fine furniture, paintings lining
the dark blue walls, and the whole house kept warm by a grand
fireplace in the main room, the flames nearly burnt down to embers.
At the top of the stairs, we turned down the hallway to the right and
stopped in front of a closed door. I half-closed my eyes to gather the
energy I would need for a positive energy burst, and when I felt
ready, I looked to Glitter, who had cast *ajiavulhysayt*, covering her
vitals in softly glowing mystic armor.

I threw open the door, ready to release the energy burst, when I
saw Raf stabbing at shadows flowing across the carpeting and
furniture! I discharged the energy, causing one of the shadows to

evaporate while the other three hissed and released a portion of their essence. Glitter cast *ajilek*, the four projectiles resembling multihued spiked balls, each striking a different target, save one shadow which discorporated after being hit with a second sphere. Raf tumbled backwards over a large desk, landing on his feet upon the large, lavender, velvet cushioned chair behind it and stabbed uselessly at one of the remaining shadows, which began to flow up his rapier.

As he let go of his weapon, Glitter and I both cast *yuvamimzuklii*, piercing the shadow with beams of light, Glitter's ray being orange in contrast to my grey one, causing it to wither away. As the remaining shadow turned away from Raf toward us, we repeated the spell with the same results. With the danger passed, Glitter ran up to our lost friend, nearly tackling him in her enthusiastic embrace.

"How are you here?" I asked, glad to see our bard still alive. "The rift you created should have sent you spiraling away into the void."

"I have no idea," he laughed, kissing Glitter on the cheek, spinning them both off the chair, the acrobat landing on his feet with the lady in his arms. "As soon as we got sucked in, I kicked away from Cratillus and woke up here just a minute ago. I felt dizzy, and it took me a moment to realize that the shadows actually *were* moving of their own accord. I'm so glad you got here when you did, because my weapons did nothing to them at all!"

"That's because they only partially exist on this plane. Without magic, they can hardly be harmed by anything," I answered, still smiling broadly.

"Where are the others?" he asked, still holding Glitter and grinning from ear-to-ear.

"Tsukatta is dead," I sobered. "Vondro is guarding her from predation, and Brother Ironknuckle is outside fighting a pair of empty suits of armor."

"Those were empty?" asked Glitter, sliding out of Raf's arms.

"I am fairly certain. It sounded hollow when Brother Ironknuckle kicked it, and their eyes glowed sickly. If, as I suspect, they are merely hyaklas, then he should have no trouble with them and be here shortly."

"Then I haven't much time," leered Ial'rafiost, slipping a dagger out of his wrist sheath and stabbing Glitter in the shoulder, her magic armor only partially deflecting the blow.

As she screamed in both pain and surprise, one word sprang to mind.

"Ryelt!" I yelled, angry at the creature and myself for not suspecting it in the first place. I had no magic left, save for the most minor of spells, and focused on the Weave, to determine if there was anything useful of a magical nature nearby. Inside the desk drawer, there were four items that drew my attention, plus other objects scattered throughout the room, and I began to work my way over to the desk. "Why would you work for a madman like Cratillus? He would have killed you just like any other living thing once he was done with you."

"It never would have come to that. As he gathered power, I was slowly siphoning off items and allies," he sneered, grabbing Glitter and pulling her close, the dagger pointing at her heart. "Even if I were not able to usurp him, I would have easily disappeared from his attention."

While he gloated, Glitter fished out a small vial from her pouch and smashed it into his face. Ice formed over his features, crawling over the shards of glass imbedded in his chin. She pulled herself out of his grasp and kicked him between the legs while he held his freezing face. Unfortunately, as ryelts are shapeshifters, their vital anatomy is not the same as most other humanoids, and her kick was not as painful as it would be on any other man.

But her attack gave me the opportunity to open the desk drawer to see a pair of wands and a pair of potions. Grabbing a wand at random, I felt the Weave's patterns, hoping to determine its method of activation and function. The ryelt recovered from Glitter's assault and came at her again, dagger held ready to slice her abdomen.

Still not certain what spell the wand contained; the arrangement of threads showed that the target needed to be touched by the wand to activate it. "Leave her alone!" I shouted, poking the creature pretending to be our friend with the wand.

Instantly, color drained from his face, and his features melted into something flat, grey, and indistinct. At the same time, I felt reinvigorated as the ryelt's life force poured into me. A wand of *vriiwamrayk*, just what every necromancer needs!

"Are you alright?" I asked my companion, who was trying to staunch the bleeding from the dagger wound.

"I'll manage," she winced.

Looking again at the contents of the desk, I recognized the function of the two potions, as they were certainly common enough, and passed them both to her.

"Healing potions, just what I need!" she exclaimed as she drank one down, her wound stitching itself closed.

With more time to examine the room, I soon discovered my spell-book, and the other volumes I had been carrying, in a thick iron box, which mostly blocked my view of the Weave, so that I hardly noticed them at first. In another drawer, we found Cratillus' journal, which outlined his plans of attack on Dureltown and the surrounding communities. While paging through the diary, Brother Ironknuckle strode into the room. "Those hollow shells were not nearly as much fun as real giants. They barely scratched me!" he grinned. "The ruklaa in the courtyard fell ta pieces too easily too."

"We found a healing potion, if you need it," Glitter offered.

"Nah, lass. Thanks, fer asking." He looked down at the grey-skinned, nearly featureless body on the floor. "I see ye found some excitement of yer own."

"That," I said while paging through my spell-book to make certain that it was not damaged, "is a ryelt in its natural form. It led us to believe that Raf had survived the void." I exhaled loudly, something between anger and sorrow in that breath, which nearly turned my world colorless.

"Tricky bastard," Brother Ironknuckle spat, kicking it once in the head. "Ye find yer books?"

I held up my spell-book and patted the stack of books that had been in my satchel, plus a couple of other interesting volumes, marveling at just how much fit within its extra-dimensional space. After putting them back inside, I remembered the other wand in the desk drawer, discovering that it was the one from Ormak's tower with the dragon's head burned into it. "I think we have everything we came for. We should leave for now and head back to Dureltown so we can bury Tsuk…" I choked, unable to finish her name. My struggle to maintain any semblance of composure must have been noticeable.

"Are ye alright, lad? Ye look as though about to burst."

It took a few moments before I could answer. "I shall manage. It is difficult to not be overwhelmed by the loss of our friends, and I do not wish to have any more visions."

"Ah," he responded. "With practice, mayhap it won't be such a struggle."

"I hope you are correct." We walked over to the first manor house to collect Ehrghex's sole survivor, then carefully picked our way back out of Ehrghex to avoid the rukla patrols and any other undead that might be roaming about. Once through the gate, we found our way back to Vondro and Tsukatta. He stood tall over his beloved's corpse, and true to his desire, had a small pile of bodies stacked up in front of him.

"Are you injured?" asked Glitter as we neared our grim friend.

"Nothing that won't take care of itself," he muttered, his eyes red from crying and rage, his knuckles white from tightly gripping his sword.

"I have the spell that will protect her," I pointed, afraid to say her name. "I shall require about fifteen minutes to complete the ritual, then she will be safe from further harm."

Vondro gave the slightest of nods, then resumed his vigilant stance.

Though there are various oils and unguents that improve the effectiveness of *drasevla*, it can be done with a handful of salt and a pair of copper coins, which are placed over the eyes during the casting of the spell. The salt preserves the corpse, preventing further rot and protecting it from the curse of undeath; the other ingredients make the body more pleasant to be around, as well as extending the duration of the protections. Regardless, the spell did last long enough to get back to Dureltown, as the few ruklaa and other creatures we encountered along the way did little to inhibit our travel.

In fact, we were all glad of the distractions, which allowed us to relieve some of our frustrations through combat. We all rode in silence, mourning the loss of our friends, and most conversations lasted but a few moments. Outside the city, a group of large tents had been erected, which contained the refugees from Ehrghex. Perched atop the central one was Thessylia, who flew to me straight as an arrow, barking with joy!

'You have been gone too long! I did not know where you were, so I waited here. There are a lot of mice around the tents! Scratchings?'

I could not help but smile as she landed on my shoulder and presented her head so that I could scratch under her feathers. *'I have missed you as well! I apologize for being away so long, and I will relate the details later. Were you able to arrive before the refugees?'*

'Only just. Fortunately, they are slow walkers. Vondelos met them at the gate with his soldiers and kept them outside the walls. Healers come from inside the city, and some got the disease. I think they have it nearly cured.'

"We should avoid the tents and head straight into the city," I recommended. "The raging fever has not been eradicated yet."

Vondro grunted and the others merely nodded in response.

Upon sighting Vondro, the guards opened the gates, one of them running off, presumably to tell his father that we had arrived. We rode straight for the temple of Mamoel, since they had proven helpful before, and there was only a small shrine for Kimitsu. The priestesses removed Tsukatta's body gently from her horse and took her to a rear chamber to prepare her for burial. Though Vondro insisted on following, the priestesses were more adamant that he not interfere, promising to contact him when the preparations were finished. While we waited, Vondelos arrived at the temple.

"Welcome home, my boy!" he shouted, taking his son in a bear hug. "Why are you here? Are you injured?" Vondelos looked over his son's beaten and damaged armor.

"Tsukatta's dead," was all he managed to squeak out before stepping back into his father's embrace, sobbing uncontrollably. They held each other for a few minutes before Vondelos looked at us for answers.

Chapter 15: Repercussions

"What has happened to my boy?" Vondelos asked Glitter, Brother Ironknuckle, and I in the atrium of Mamoel's temple. Vondro sat forlornly on one of the many benches along the wall of the main chamber, so that worshippers sit in a circle as represented by the full moon.

"His heart is broken," responded Glitter through wet, bright green eyes. "Though we have only known each other for a short time, he and Tsukatta grew quite close. She died," Glitter choked, "stopping Cratillus from causing any more death. Our friend Raf was also lost, but Vondro cannot see past Tsukatta to mourn him yet."

"I need to hear this from the beginning. You two," Vondelos pointed at Glitter and I, "I remember from bringing in Flinjirt. Who is Cratillus, what happened, and why?"

We, that is, mostly Glitter and I, as we were the first to deal with his minions, summarized the deeds of the past month, leading up to our return to Dureltown.

Is it really only such a short time? So much has happened! "To conclude," I finished, "there is still a town's-worth of ruklaa and other undead creatures roaming about what used to be Ehrghex, more than the few of us can handle safely on our own. I think it would be wise to send a large group of soldiers and clerics to remove the threat and put those poor souls to rest."

"That makes sense and I will start gathering a force in the morning. You should all find an inn and get some well-deserved rest. I will stay here with Vondro until he's ready to come home."

"Yes sir," yawned Glitter. "I hope the Rose has a couple of rooms available. I liked it there."

"Agreed," Brother Ironknuckle and I responded simultaneously.

As always, Logrom stood at the bar of the Inn of the Weeping Rose, filling mugs with practiced haste for the crowd filling the common room. We grabbed three stools, sat at the bar, and waited for him to notice us.

"Welcome back!" he grinned. "Where's Raf? The atmosphere hasn't been the same without his stories. Never thought I'd miss that little cad."

Brother Ironknuckle spoke first, as neither Glitter nor I could at that moment. "The lad has gone from this world, I'm afraid," he said with a quaver. "He sacrificed 'imself to save us and the world. The boy's a hero, and I'll honor his memory with a round for all," he nearly cried, slamming ten gold coins down on the counter.

Logrom stared in stunned silence at the grommold, his eyes becoming wet. "Would you be so kind as to tell his story?" he pointed at the stage where a pair of tillalli played fiddles for the crowd's enjoyment.

"Aye, after a drink or three. And we'll be needing rooms fer the night."

Logrom scooped up the coins and filled five mugs for us, three of which he placed in front of Brother Ironknuckle, along with two keys.

"One to wash the road," Brother Ironknuckle saluted us, drinking the frothy beverage down. He never seemed to swallow, but rather poured it down his throat as if down a drain. "One to wash the soul." A second mug vanished. "And one to wash the mind." The third vanished.

Amazing! I get heady merely smelling my ale, and he drinks them like water from a spring!

With steady purpose, he left his stool and strode up to the stage, while I subtly turned my ale into a blackberry tea with a hint of jasmine. When the tillalli finished their tune, to great applause from the gathered crowd, they looked to Brother Ironknuckle, to Logrom, and back to the grommold. Bowing to our companion, they vacated the stage.

"This is the tale of Ial'rafiost, roustabout, entertainer, and hero of the realm," he began. The bar quieted to hear his tale. Brother Ironknuckle brought them to tears, both from laughter and sorrow, the tillalli picking out appropriate music to backdrop his tale. Glitter sobbed uncontrollably, as did I, my vision grey through his entire speech.

Looking over the crowd, I could see every mote of darkness that had stained the souls of the patrons. Some were victims and/or perpetrators of violence, some had cheated friends and lovers, some had gambled away their earned wages that were needed to feed their families, and a variety of other sins, misdeeds, and victimizations. Yet, unlike in the past, I felt no need to express what I saw.

We all carry some darkness within, whether created by our own devices, inflicted upon us, or, more often, both. It is not for me to force people to face those blots on their souls, except where it impacts me directly, or when I feel in my judgment that it would serve to an individual's benefit at the time. *I cannot heal the world, but I can prevent the darkness from spreading.* At this thought, I felt some of the darkness of my own soul transform and evaporate.

No sooner had Brother Ironknuckle finished eulogizing our good friend, that Glitter stood up, cried "I have to go," and ran upstairs, tears flying off her as she ran, her sparkles still a dull grey to my eyes. I scarcely noticed when Brother Ironknuckle reclaimed his stool beside me.

"Where'd the lass run off ta?"

"Probably to her room," I answered, still wiping tears from my cheeks. "Your tale hit all the right notes; Raf would have been proud." I began chuckling in spite of myself, "He never got her to run upstairs as quickly as you did!"

He joined in the laughter, with odd stares from some nearby patrons. "This is how I think he'd like ta be remembered, with joy in our 'earts, not mewling over his loss."

"He certainly brought plenty of that. I... had stories that I promised to finish telling him. Now I never will," I sighed. "He was a good man, full of wit and odd wisdom, who understood the nature of people and how to interact with them. I had hoped to study his example further, for I feel that he had much to teach me."

"Best ye can do is remember him as best ye can, and follow his example ta the best of yer ability when ye think appropriate."

I nodded and held up my mug of tea. "To Ial'rafiost, hero of the realm."

"To Ial'rafiost!" he shouted raising his fourth mug, and the rest of the bar echoed his salute.

After an hour or so of drinking and relating tales with other patrons, who knew him far longer than I, but perhaps not as well, I went up to Glitter's room and knocked quietly on her door. At first, I thought I had been too gentle, or perhaps she slept, as it took her over a minute to answer the door.

Her eyes and face were red, her sparkles pale blue. "Yes?" she asked, her voice cracking, dry and full of sorrow.

"I wanted to check on you, to see if you needed anything, to talk, or…" I never finished my sentence as she grabbed my robe, pulled me into her room, and hugged me tight. She was much stronger than she appeared. Not knowing what else to do, I hugged her back, but without squeezing her.

"Thank you," she sobbed into my shoulder, softening her grip on my spine, which was actually starting to hurt by this point.

Still unsure of what to say, I kept silent and waited for her to continue.

"You really do care, don't you?" she asked after a few moments.

"Of course, I do. I always have," I answered, not completely sure of what she was asking.

She responded by maintaining the hug.

"What happens next?"

She broke away, stepped backwards, and sat on her bed. "I have to go home. I need to deal with Mistress Goldfire's…" she choked.

"Body," I finished for her.

She merely nodded.

"Do you want me to come with you? I am more accustomed to this kind of thing, and it is not something one should handle alone."

"Don't you need to go home too?"

"I do, but we can travel to your tower first. Then, if you wish, you can accompany me to mine." It was at this time that I realized that they were *our* wizard's towers now, and no longer those of our

Mistresses. "Afterwards, we should secure Ormak's stronghold, lest his wealth of knowledge be plundered by the unworthy."

"Ormak's is not far from here. We can place a few spells on it as a deterrent until we return. It will only take us another day."

"Very well. Rest easy tonight, and we shall prepare our wards in the morning." I bowed my head, turned, and went across the hall to my room, closing her door behind me. When I entered, Brother Ironknuckle was already asleep on the bed, so I unpacked my bedroll and slept on the floor.

I awoke, still bound to that cursed tree, my whole body aching from being locked in the same position for the past two days.

The giant, skeletal figure of Cratillus stepped up to me, a vial of vile purple liquid in his ossified hands. "Drink," he rasped, "it will take away all your pain. Then, you can be like me!" he chortled through his rictus grin.

"I will never follow you," I growled, "never be like you. You have cost me much, but I still have those who care about me." As I spoke, Glitter, Brother Ironknuckle, and Vondro stepped out from behind the tree to stand beside me.

Vondro turned to me. "You led her to her doom." He then turned away and vanished into the night.

"Ye could've saved him," accused Brother Ironknuckle before doing the same.

"You've served your purpose. I don't need you anymore," sneered Glitter as she followed suit.

"Still alone, always alone. Poor, sad, little necromancer," Cratillus, now back in human shape, mewled. "Just accept it, and all the pain will go away. After all, you are already mine!" He tore open my robe, revealing my bare ribcage, runes glowing deep-bruise black etched into the bone.

I awoke with a scream, causing Brother Ironknuckle to sober in an instant and pick me up off the floor. "Lad, it's me. Are ye alright?"

"Fine. I am fine. Just another Cratillus dream." I answered my roommate. "Do you blame me for Raf's death? Or is it that I just blame myself?"

Brother Ironknuckle looked at me with sadness. "*Gobvoknya*; 'The sorrow of the living'. I've seen it happen ta many a warrior. When one survives in battle while his comrades fall, he wonders why he was spared; why he is not travelling to the Halls of Honor with his battle mates. Ye are not to blame for Raf's passing. In fact, we canna be sure he's well and truly dead, only that he and that monster fell through tha' portal together. But *he* chose ta act at that time and place in that manner. It's not on either of us."

"So, you feel it as well?"

"Aye." We sat in silence for a long time before he spoke again. "I miss him as much as ye do. He brought a lot of joy wherever he went." He let out a long sigh. "We should both get some sleep."

Too exhausted to answer, I merely nodded and began to lie back down on my bedroll, oblivion catching me before my head reached the pillow.

The next morning, I awoke to find Brother Ironknuckle doing his regular exercises, building strength in muscles I am fairly certain I do not even possess. While he squatted to the ground and slowly rose back to standing, all while holding the room's footlocker over his head, I grabbed my spell-book and began preparing runes, alarms, and other protective glyphs. My companion waited until I closed my book before speaking.

"Any plans fer th' day?"

"Glitter and I are going to return to Ormak's tower to secure it against invaders. I am certain there are still guardians within that we did not discover, but we thought it best to keep out any who might think to plunder it, seeing as we, actually, you and the others, destroyed all the undead wandering about on the grounds. Afterwards, we are going home to take care of our Mistresses' remains and secure our households. You are, of course, welcome to come if you wish. You were already asleep when I came in last night and had not been thinking about it after my nightmare. We should see if Vondro wishes to go also. He might wish to stay with Tsukatta, though the distraction might do him good."

"It might do me good too. Some open road might clear me head."

We gathered our traveling gear together and walked across the hall to Glitter's room, just as the Rose shook with thunder.

"Must it always rain when we head to Ormak's?" I sighed aloud.

Glitter opened her door as I was raising my hand to knock. "Another beautiful day for travelling, eh?" she said with a wry smile.

"I suppose we could wait it out. We are not pressed for time," I suggested.

"Lad makes sense. I wanted a large, hot breakfast anyway!" smiled Brother Ironknuckle. Whereas a hot breakfast to me is normally a bowl of porridge, the Rose's kitchen produced a stack of griddle breads and a trio of small sausages, with the addition of hot cider for a beverage.

Turning to Glitter, I smiled, "We should not get used to these accommodations, else we shall look like Blythad afore too long!"

She nearly choked on her cider with laughter.

We waited until nearly midday for the storm to pass, then went to Mamoel's temple to seek out Vondro. As expected, he was still sitting on one of the benches circling the main room.

"You should really get some rest in your own bed," Glitter suggested, frowning at Vondro's untidy and unclean appearance.

"I can't. Not yet," he responded, exhaustion evident in his words.

"Why?" I asked. "There is nothing you can do for her at this point."

"I must maintain my vigil. The priestesses say there is a chance they can bring her back, should I prove worthy. Also, they would require a tidy sum of gold for the rare ingredients for the spell."

"Ye stay the course lad. We're off to Ormak's anyway, an' we left a pile of coin. We'll bring back what ye need; she was our friend too."

Tears welled up in Vondro's eyes. "Thank you," was all he managed to choke out before openly weeping.

Glitter sat beside him and gave him a long, tight hug. With a kiss on his wet cheek, she got up and we left once again for Ormak's tower.

Although the storm had passed, the sky stayed overcast, and it rained periodically as we rode. There were no signs that anyone had trespassed, and we made our way easily to the hidden stairway before remembering that Tsukatta had sealed the wall with stone.

"Can we dispel it?" asked Glitter, as we wiped away our runes.

"Unfortunately, no. Once her spell was complete, the effects became permanent. There is no longer any magic to dispel."

"I can handle this," said Brother Ironknuckle gently pushing us aside. He ran his fingers along the wall until finding the exact spot where he wished to strike, closed his eyes in concentration, and punched the wall just above his eye level. At first, nothing appeared to happen, then cracks began to form in a spider-web pattern from where he struck, spreading out about two feet in all directions. A moment later, the wall crumbled, leaving a large hole that we had to climb through.

"That... was amazing!" exclaimed Glitter while I merely stood in awestruck fascination.

"Ancient family secret," he grinned, holding up his fist. "They don't call us the 'Ironknuckle' clan fer nothing!" He clambered through the hole with a greater ease than either of us and began to ascend the hidden staircase. The treasure room remained just as we left it; coins, many at least partially melted, lay scattered about, with a number of utilitarian items, some magical, mixed in. We gathered a few small sacks half-full of gold and silver; a full sack was both too heavy to carry and too much for the leather to hold without the stitches tearing. Four of them fit in my satchel before filling the extra-dimensional space within. More would have fit, but we had all we needed, and I was not going to leave any of my tomes behind. In fact, I returned to the library for more.

Glitter and I placed wards on the back of the bookcase hiding the stairs to the treasure room, closed it, and having learned from Raf, dusted the floor and, unfortunately, ourselves. We also warded the main staircase and the front door to prevent would-be thieves from ransacking Ormak's tower. A gentle rain traveled with us all the way back to Dureltown, which soaked us to the bone in short order. We rode straight to Mamoel's temple and gave the sacks over to Carmia and her fellow acolytes while Varli, the High Priestess, sat with us and explained the Ritual of Returning and its associated costs.

"You did well to preserve her body before bringing her here," she praised. "A fresher body helps the soul return with less distress."

I merely nodded in response, afraid of saying something awkward, such as how *drasevla* prevents odors and maggots, for I honestly had no idea that it helped with the *zuklawavriiwa* ritual. We waited in the large, round main chamber of the temple awaiting our fallen friend, nervous with anticipation.

"With magic like this," Glitter wondered aloud, "why should anyone have to stay dead?"

"I suppose the wealthy could forestall it for a time," I answered, "but I do not believe the spell makes one any younger; all bodies fall into decrepitude in time. In addition, I cannot imagine that the Dark Lady would open her gates to let just anyone return. It will not surprise me if the priestesses use those rare incenses and other materials to supplicate Her. But then, who am I to understand the desires of the gods?"

Hours passed before we received any sign from the Mamoel priestesses. Eventually, Varli came to us, the look on her face starting Vondro to tears.

"I am sorry, but we were unable to bring Tsukatta back," she said, her voice barely audible. It took all her effort to not avoid our gaze. "Honestly, I do not understand what went wrong, for we were unable to even contact her. One does not force a soul to return to the land of the living, and permission is always asked for before performing the full ritual. It seems as though our communications were blocked before ever reaching her. We tried multiple times. There is nothing else we can do. I'm sorry," she whispered, her voice cracking with pain.

"Ye've done all ye can. That's all we can ask. Thank ye," Brother Ironknuckle with a forced smile, his heart broken. "May we see her?"

"Of course. Follow me." Varli lead us to a side chamber, where Tsukatta was laid out upon a table; they were both covered with white linen. One by one, we all approached our friend's body to say goodbye.

"Ye were a great companion," began Brother Ironknuckle. "Ye traveled with me all the way from the Temple of Kimitsu, o'er the mountains and plains, seeking only to spread yer kindness to a cruel and harsh world. Here, ye found new friends, and love, and I couldn'a be happier fer ye. I only wish ye could have spent more time with us," he finished, tears streaming down his craggy cheeks.

Glitter hugged him, then spoke as she released her grip. "You came into my life when I most needed a friend, after I had lost my mentor and my home. Your joy, laughter, and kindheartedness helped me to heal the pain of loss, and I can never thank you enough for that. I will miss you," she choked, unable to say anything further.

I placed a hand on her shoulder, comforting her as best as I knew how.

Before I could speak, Vondro stepped forward. "I love you. We had only just found one another before you were cruelly taken from me, and I don't know what to do with myself now that you're gone. I never expected to fall so quickly, so easily, with someone I barely knew, but it happened, for both of us. Somehow, we will be together again, in this world or the next. No matter what it takes, I *will* find you again!"

"Tsukatta," I sniffed, "I will miss your comforting presence. Just as you helped heal Glitter's heart, you healed mine. Your gentle words, your wisdom, and your peaceful aura made everyone around you a better person." A strange darkness was beginning to take form over her body as the tears flowed from my eyes, one that I confirmed later that only I saw. "Thank you for being our friend." As I finished, the darkness coalesced into the sinister, smirking visage of Cratillus.

Appendix I

Book List

Absolute Darkness: A Treatise on the Negative Energy Plane – Dalen

Accentuating the Positive: A Study of Divine Channeling and Its Arcane Equivalent – Falleoraeli Zolthliam

Animating Principles Differentiating Constructs from Undead – Dalwren

Designs, Runes, and Symbols – Tahje

The Dirges of Calnerion

Earth's Toxins

Healing Herbs

The Immobile Caster: Directing Magic without Gesticulation by Geimoll Ovicht

In Between: On the Transition from Life to Death to Life

Insubstantial—Dealing with Spirits and Nearby Planes – Borthe

The Light of Life: Positive Energy and Magickal Healing – Cerinaj

Magivore: Nourishing the Body with Magick

Making Space: The Art of Expanding Volumes through Use of Extra-Dimensional Pockets – Forderoft Theralis

Nature's Eyes: Understanding the Ffolk of the Fey

A Philosophy of Magic – Revance

Quiet Focus – Nara-qi

Staddi's Book of Potions

Transconducing Magickal Energies – Copprin Flauginbood

Wholeness of Body: Understanding the Connections Between the Physical and Spiritual Selves

Willow, Ash, and Oak – Ormak

Winter Herbs: Useful Growth During the Cold Season – Therena Willowbark

Writing Magick: Proper Ingredients for Inks, Scrolls, and Tomes

Appendix II

Draconic

Although its influence is still strong in many modern languages, Draconic is generally lost as a spoken language, save for wizards, a few scholars, and of course, dragons themselves. All magical runes and words stem directly from Draconic, and it is theorized that both dragons and the Weave came into existence together, or that one led directly to the other. Even the eldest of dragons do not have the answer, or are unwilling to share this secret with lesser beings. As Draconic has been used extensively throughout this work, it seems prudent to give a short primer on the language.

Rules:
- The letters c, f, g, n, p, q, and x are not part of Draconic, as these sounds are either difficult for dragons to enunciate, or their sounds are represented by other letters or combinations of letters.
- 'y' is always pronounced as a hard consonant, as in 'you' and 'yet'.
- 'yt' at the end of a word denotes plurality.
- All letters are pronounced. There are no silent letters in Draconic, nor any dipthongs.
- A single vowel has the short sound (e.g. hat, bin); a double vowel is pronounced long (e.g. seen). The Draconic word for 'light' is *juut*, which is pronounced 'jute'.
- The only vowels to start a word are 'a' and 'u', except as follows:
  - 'i' begins a word to show possession.
  - 'em' at the beginning of a word indicates one who uses or does something. For example, *aji* is the word for magic, and *emaji* is the word for wizard.
  - 'oo' at the beginning of a word denotes femininity, where applicable and necessary, while 'o' denotes masculinity. Otherwise,

1

nouns are essentially neutral. For example, 'vrii' can be either a masculine or feminine god, 'oovrii' denotes a goddess, and 'ovriiyt' is a number of masculine gods.

Umani	Draconic
acid	skialosk
armor	avulhysayt
attack	tzi
aura	ubrel
bag/sack	dmalv
blood	aktwa
bone	dulaa
break	yuv
breath	tiimu
bundle/group	bokvi
burst	bolmos
cavern	avrim
charm/enchant	mlarliska
claw	aatok
comfort	roziit
compel/force	umslykt
conjure	buvli
crowd/group	bokwa
darkness	looskim
dead	zukla
death	zuklii
detect/perceive	trezel
dispel	yuvii
disrupt	yuvam
dragon	uldrak
dream	vlivriiwa
eat	vul
elsewhere	vli
explosion	bezyaamyuv
far/away	lial
feel	tre
fight	tzizi
fill	vrokt

fire	srukak
float	aaslska
fly	aasl
frost	klivev
globe/sphere	arih
god	vrii
great/major	bezyaam
heal	mak
hold/trap	liska
horse	uose
human	khuuma
injury/wound	raazt
invisible	mimzel
iron	avul
lance/spear	dovlek
large	bezyam
life	vriiwa
light	juut
lightning	vezivi
line	hilsk
little	uvaz
lock	sklid
magic	aji
message	kaaskiil
messenger	ikaaskiil
mind	mlur
minor	uvaaz
negative energy	zumul
non-/un-	mim-
quiet/silent	drase
ray	alsk
read	embul
reflect	koomba
repair	umak
resistance	bimzilt
rune/symbol	bul

scale	hysa
see	zel
servant	hruk
shadow	yuvjuut
shake/shiver	seedu
shard	lek
sleep	uvla
soul/spirit	wa
steal	mrayk
stop	ska
summon	hivli
sun	vriijuut
sword	avulaatok
tentacle	jejleem
thief	emmrayk
thunder	uuom
tooth	uzul
touch	vad
tree	dovwa
ward	bulhysa
warrior	emtzizi
water	akt
wizard	emaji
wood	dov
zyla	ulv

Author's Biography

 David F. Balog was born, raised, and still lives in the Greater Cleveland are with his wife and cat. He grew up in the libraries of Lakewood and Parma, and his babysitters were the creatures of the Cleveland Aquarium; he had a special fondness for the giant octopus. Ever inquisitive, he dove deeply into science, paranormal studies, mathematics, and mythology at an early age, and never let go of the idea that they, and other studies, were all tightly connected.

His fascination with fables and mythology led him first to Dungeons & Dragons, then other role-playing games. Here, he learned to hone his talent for character creation, world building, and storytelling, more so as individual games extended into long campaigns. Over time, basic concepts became fully realized, and months and years spent focused on a single character gave time for them to develop depth.

An avid reader, particularly, but certainly not limited to, science and science fiction, David always sought to learn more about the world. In his youth, he went to the Gifted Challenge Institute, essentially a summer camp for knowledge set on campus at local colleges, where he studied mathematics, biology, and physics far above his grade level. This had the unfortunate side-effect of putting him off traditional academia for a time, as regular classes were not available at his age to continue with his accelerated learning, causing his grades to slide from boredom.

Years later, he would attend Cuyahoga Community College, Ursuline College, and Cleveland State University, eventually earning a Bachelors' Degree in both History and Social Studies, and a Master's Degree in History. All through his studies, he continued to focus on the theology, mythology, and fables and how they connected societies throughout time and regions. Though the stories and characters change, the underlying truths always remain the same: primarily, the constant striving of individuals to become better people.

At long last, it fell on David to contribute his own stories and mythologies to the public consciousness. With the experience of developing characters and worlds combined with writing numerous research papers, David began work on his first novel: Necromancer's Lament, the first in a planned trilogy.

Visit https://www.davidfbalog.com for more information.

If you liked what you read, please leave a review on Amazon.

RockHill Publishing LLC

There are some lessons that only time can teach, but you do not learn talent, you only perfect it over time.

www.rockhillpublishing.com

CHECK OUT ALL OUR TITLES IN ADULT FICTION, FANTASY, ROMANCE, AND SCIENCE FICTION

https://bit.ly/RockHilleBooks